SAVING

GRACIE

By Nancy DeMarco

ISBN 13: 978-1492204381
ISBN 10: 1492204382

Library of Congress Control Number: 2014903322
CreateSpace Independent Publishing Platform
North Charleston, SC

Cover Image ©Vladimir Morozov, www.vladimirphotography.ie, with special thanks to model Megan O'Malley.

Author photo, featuring the real-life Scout, © Tammy McCracken.

All other images are the results of the author's silly doodling.

Book Design by Mosaic Book Works
www.mosaicbookworks.com

This book is dedicated to my husband, without whom I would never have had the chance to write.

CHAPTER ONE

Gracie Ouellette's dreams of family died the day she gave birth to a stillborn baby girl. She was sedated, of course, same as most days, her being incorrigible and all. And the psych nurses were under-staffed and cranky, so she wasn't permitted to hold the child and never knew if her daughter had all of her fingers and toes and red hair like her own.

That was fifty-two years ago today, and Gracie planned to com-memorate the date with a hike down the railroad bed followed by a swim in Echo Lake. Most days, this wouldn't be a problem. But Molly was at the store, which meant no one was in charge, and Jillian, who wasn't in charge, had nonetheless seized control. All two hundred pounds of her now blocked Gracie's bedroom door, and she wouldn't stop saying, "You can't go."

"And why is that?" Gracie knew the answer. Jillian, who watched far too many documentaries on alien abduction, was afraid to go out-side. Therefore, no one else should go, either.

"Everyone says that lake is disgusting. Foamy as dishwater."

"No it isn't." Gracie tucked her heels against the bed's pink dust ruffle and counted backwards from five. What did Jillian know? Echo Lake was spring fed with a good runoff, clean enough to drink. If Jil-lian were brave enough to venture through the front door, she might find this out for herself. "It's beautiful. Every kid in town swims there."

"Kids maybe, but you're seventy-five."

"Don't remind me." Seventy-five was just a number. With it came morning stiffness and creaky knees. But hiking and swimming loos-ened Gracie's joints, lifted her spirits, and took her places no one else cared to go. Haunted caves, abandoned quarries, deserted houses—they all had stories to tell, and Gracie listened.

1

When her feet were too sore for hiking, she rode the lawnmower. What better way to celebrate a summer morning than by drinking in the smell of newly mown grass while bumping over the knots and scars of this rugged New Hampshire land?

Problem was, if she wanted to do any of those things today, she had to find a way past Jillian.

There was the window, of course. Her bedroom was on the first floor, the windows oversized, easily opened, and close to the ground. Climbing through the wide opening and stepping down into Molly's hummingbird garden wasn't much harder than walking through the front door.

But Gracie's shoes were on the plastic mat in the entryway and, while she did enjoy walking barefoot, the hike to Echo Lake was long and rocky.

Back to Jillian, then. Convincing her to step aside could take all day. The woman wasn't smart, which made discussions one-sided and frustrating. She couldn't move quickly, either, thanks to bad hips. But she was strong and determined and, like the other boarders, Jillian was a bit delusional.

Gracie stole a glance at her window. Beyond the lace curtains, a drowsy sun slumped in a hazy sky. The day was hot as a griddle, but that was okay—soaring temperatures would make the water more inviting.

"If you go out your window again, I'll tell Molly, and she'll call Dr. Usef."

"Molly will do no such thing." Probably not, anyway. Molly was a sensible young woman, wise for her years. She wouldn't see a hike to Echo Lake as evidence of becoming a danger to oneself.

Jillian was tightly wedged, and she showed no sign of backing down. Gracie told herself to be patient, work on being kinder and more sensitive to the special needs of her fellow boarders. But this was a special day, and Gracie had no time to waste on Jillian's foolishness.

"If you don't get out of my way," she said to Jillian, "I'll tell the little green men to come and see you tonight."

"You can't." Jillian's confidence collapsed into something far twitchier. "It's ghosts you talk to, not aliens."

"Are you sure?" Gracie took a step toward her.

Following a brief hesitation and a drawn-out grumble, Jillian moved to one side. "Try not to drown," she said. "Molly worries about you."

"That's her problem." With a huff that sounded crankier than she'd intended, Gracie pushed through the door and hurried down the hall, stopping in the entryway long enough to squash her clean socks into dirty sneakers. Then she slipped through the front door while Jillian sputtered.

The midday heat was a hindrance, the air thick and wet and far too hot for July. Even so, Gracie's steps were bouncy. She'd been a resident of the Blue Horizons Boarding House for going on twenty-five years, and memories of the State Mental Hospital were hazy at best. Even so, time failed to diminish the high spirits that came with walking unescorted.

When she reached the butterfly bushes lining the verge, she paused and pretended to inhale the gooey scent. With a furtive glance at Blue Horizons's bay window, she eased her way into the brush, then ducked low. Half hidden, she peeked through a box-wire fence into the Thompsons' yard. She wasn't spying, exactly—just looking.

The lawn wasn't mowed, despite Eric Thompson calling himself a landscaper. And the junk cars were still there, despite snippy little Officer Pelletier coming in person and putting orange tags on each and every one. All was quiet, which meant the Thompsons must be at work.

Good.

Gracie whistled through her teeth, one sharp burst of sound.

A beagle leaped from the wrap-around porch and bounded across the yard. Like a projectile sausage, he hurled himself headfirst against a seam in the wire mesh. The crash reverberated along the length of the fence. Cicadas stopped thrumming. Squawking bantams flew to the trees. The beagle cartwheeled through the gap.

"Good boy, Scout," Gracie whispered, already walking away. The dog fell in behind her, a wandering shadow, nose to the ground.

As she walked down Sandpit Road to the railroad bed, Gracie realized even the trees were sweating. Bits of sap dripped to her cheeks and made her hair sticky. Her T-shirt clung like a fussy child while warm droplets dribbled down her forehead and tickled her cheeks. By the time she reached Echo Lake, her neck was slick as a pollywog.

The water, though, was perfect—warm and bright as sun tea. While Scout ground himself into a cool wallow, Gracie waded in with her socks and sneakers on, slowly at first, mindful of the lake's uneven bottom. The glassy surface crept past her socks and shorts, drenched her shirt, and made her belly quiver. The final step was a big one, a sudden neck-deep plunge that always left her gasping.

A smile eased its way across her lips while quiet stillness seeped through her skin, smoothing away the sharp bite of sadness that always came awake and squalled on this day. With arms thrown wide, she turned her face to the sky and let herself fall.

For a moment she relaxed, cradled in the water's embrace. Lost in a dream state, she drifted to a better place, a made-up world in which her daughter lived. She was tiny like her mother, smart and pretty with auburn hair. An actress. A singer. Sometimes a poet. She rode horses, skied Loon Mountain, went to college, and became a veterinarian. She married a man who loved her more than life, and they had three kids, all of them redheaded girls.

Her daughter lived a perfect life, and she was happy. Happy and very, very grateful to be alive. Even if it was only a dream.

The tip of Gracie's nose itched, but she ignored it. She had to focus, keep her daughter close, and not sneeze her away, not yet and especially not today. But no matter how hard she tried to ignore the intrusion, the itch became more of a bother. Ghostly fingertips wandered through her hair. A phantom touch tugged at her eyelids, brushed her cheek, and finally came to rest as a sharp pinch in the dimple of her chin.

"It's just a bug," she told herself, distracted for the briefest moment. Too late. Her daughter evaporated and the fantasy world dissolved, leaving Gracie alone and suffocating on this airless day with minnows nibbling her age spots and mosquitoes buzzing past her lips.

Darn insects ruined everything. She swatted at them harder than she meant to. Water bugs scattered, minnows darted away, and a voice so soft she almost missed it came from everywhere in a desperate *Help me.*

"What did you say?"

It was nothing, of course. But just to be certain, she counted backwards from ten, slowly, one number at a time with *Mississippi* between them. She must have imagined the voice.

Probably.

The weeds tightened their grip. The water seemed to boil, though the temperature hadn't changed. The voice continued its relentless whisper, more insistent with every breath. *Help me, help me, help me, please, please, please.*

Gracie lunged toward shore. "I haven't missed a dose," she told herself. "I can't be hearing things that aren't there." Water sprayed ahead of her when she flung herself to solid ground. Scout ran past her and plunged into the lake, floppy ears pricked in interest. Gracie spun toward him, hands balled into fists and feet ready to run.

She looked out over water calm and clear, realized her mind was playing its usual tricks, and felt like a silly old woman.

With an uneasy laugh, she squatted on the shore and dug algae from her shoelaces. Scout backed out of the water. His woof was more air than voice and ended in a worried little moan.

"Shush, Scout. There's nothing there." Even so, a wave of prickles swam over her, and she realized she was sweating again, sweating and shivering at the same time. Scout leaned into her calves and tipped back his head, then let out a mournful howl.

Gracie sank her fingers into the loose folds of the dog's neck and followed the tilt of his ears to something tangled in the weeds. A clump of flotsam bobbed toward her, and the voice seemed to come from within it, *I'm here, I'm here,* over and over, louder and louder.

"Oh, balls."

She ran. The beagle scrambled past her and blocked her escape with drawn-back lips and a menacing growl, but his tail wagged, and his eyes filled with apology.

"Not you too, Scout." Gracie ducked around the dog and skittered toward the road. Best to ignore the voice, go home and pretend this was a dream. She had no time for dead people and their demands, no desire to risk exposing this ghost to the pesky doctor and his endless pills. But when she tried to get away, something cold and unyielding pressed against her chest, wound into her hair, and drew her toward the water, back the way she'd come.

A woman's voice begged her, *Please don't leave me here alone.*

"Find someone else!" The words came out like gravel. Arguing was pointless, always had been. Already something searched for an opening, burrowed into the dark places. The ghost wouldn't back down. It needed something.

She looked wistfully at the path to Blue Horizons, but allowed the spirit to tow her back into the shallows. Gracie willed herself to remain calm and pliant. If she cooperated, perhaps this ghost would be reasonable, might even allow her to keep an outward appearance of sanity.

Stupid. The dead were selfish. And pushy. And they had a lot of free time in which to figure out how to affect things like water and wind. Even now, a breeze rippled the lake and set the clump of detritus bobbing toward her. A flash of crimson caught her eye as the object crossed the final inches and came to rest, nodding insistently against her knees.

Gracie looked down at Raggedy-Anne hair wrapped in green coontail. She reached out and poked it with stubby fingers, pulled back when it sank, then bounced to the surface. The thing turned beneath the water until finally it floated face-up. Pale blue eyes opened and looked straight at her.

"Great. Just great. Officer Trudeau is gonna lock me up for sure." With a growl, she slapped at her cheeks. Crying was pointless and weak and never helped anyway.

She gripped a fistful of hair and pulled the head from the water.

"Good boy, Scout," she said, stroking the beagle with her free hand. "But why do they always pick me? Everyone knows I'm batshit."

The dog pumped his tail and panted up at her with a satisfied beagle grin. Gracie frowned back. She wanted to bury the head and forget she'd seen it, pretend she didn't have this so-called gift or condition or whatever it was supposed to be. But escape was unlikely. Phantom hands gripped her shoulders and thrust her toward the road while someone else's purpose took hold of her feet. She pushed back, a matter of dignity, but she knew she couldn't last.

"I'm going, ya bully," she told the air. "It's not as if I have a choice."

The head was heavy, the road more uphill than down. By the time she and Scout reached the little police station at the center of Coyne Falls, Gracie was tired and sore. The door was open, so she trudged up the ramp and shuffled inside, resting the disembodied head against the small of her back. She looked up at the counter and wondered what it might be like to be taller than her piddling four feet, nine inches.

"Anyone here?"

A chair scraped the floor, and Officer Marcel Trudeau looked down at her through John Lennon glasses. Gracie had known him since he was a boy, the chubby kid who played with little Molly and Candy on Blue Horizons's lawn. Back then, she'd thought him average, from cowlicky brown hair to thickset frame to straight B's on his report cards.

He was thinner now, not bad looking, but still more bulk than height. Must be in his mid-twenties. Marcel had always been kind, never failed to listen to Gracie's stories, even when they seemed far-fetched. Even so, she was glad to have proof.

She held out the head.

"What have you brought me?" The patient look on Marcel's face didn't waver. Odd. She'd expected a gasp, maybe a few cuss words.

"Scout found this in Echo Lake." Gracie hefted the head above her shoulders and deposited it on the clean vinyl counter.

Marcel spoke in a tone he probably reserved for children and the mentally ill. "What do you think it is?"

Gracie watched the dead girl's eyes. They blinked.

"It's a head, Officer." She stared at the redhead. The redhead stared back. Gracie poked the girl's freckled cheek, looped a finger through her curls. "Isn't it?"

The forced evenness of Marcel's breath told her he'd swallowed a sigh. "It's a handbag."

"No it isn't."

The dead girl's mouth opened, and she said, *Help me.*

Marcel lifted the head by its hair. He raised the hinged counter, motioned Gracie through, and then carried the thing down a short hallway to a metal table butted up against a bare wall. Gracie followed with Scout at her heels. And . . . now Marcel was carrying a handbag, not a head at all.

After spreading a clean towel, Marcel upended the bag, and its contents spilled out. A sandwich landed in a splat, along with a hair brush, a cosmetic case, a phone, and a wallet.

Scout lunged for the sandwich. Gracie caught his collar and pulled him away. Fear settled over her, along with the familiar touch of something less ordinary.

Darn ghost. Now she whispered, told Gracie which words to use and insisted she say them out loud. The pushy little dead girl was just getting started.

"Grab that wallet," Gracie said. "It's a clue."

"Gracie." Marcel looked more worried than annoyed, which only made her feel worse. "It's really hot out. Let me get you something to drink."

She focused on the beagle and tried to ignore the pang of disappointment. Marcel was a practical sort, always had been. He might listen, but he'd obviously made up his mind. "I'm fine, Officer."

"Are you taking your meds?"

"Yes." Even though she hated them. Talking to ghosts didn't make a person crazy, did it? And the pills—all they did was make her nervous. Weren't they supposed to keep the ghosts away?

Not this ghost. The dead redhead had already made herself at home, settled into the empty places that always needed filling. With her came a sense of stubborn attachment along with the scent of cookies, warm from the oven. The ghost spoke, and Gracie realized she'd repeated the sentence aloud.

"Someone will die tonight." She tried not to say the rest, but the words pushed their way past her throat and jumped from her tongue. "A murder."

Marcel picked up the wallet and thumbed through the plastic sleeves. "Why do you think that?"

"Because the dead girl says so." Gracie stood as tall as she could and spoke more boldly than she felt. "She's right beside you." No point mentioning she wasn't wearing her head.

"Is this her?" Marcel held out a driver's license. A pretty woman with soft brown hair and clear blue eyes looked out from beneath the plastic laminate. Her name was Shay Cooper.

"Don't think so." The handbag was gone, and the head now lay supine in its place. Blue eyes stared at the ceiling while crimson ringlets swirled past the table's edge. "The eyes match, but the hair's the wrong color."

"Hair can be dyed." He turned the license over in his hand. "How old is your ghost?"

Gracie squinted at the china-doll face, its eyes now closed, lips slightly parted. "Eighteen? Maybe twenty?" Too young to be dead.

Marcel seemed to consider for a moment, and Gracie's heart hesitated along with her breath.

"Wait right here."

He left her alone and jogged to the rear of the building. This might be a good time to head for home; no good would come from being a bother. But Marcel returned before she'd taken a step, and he brought a ventilated box marked *Evidence*.

"It's just in case," he said.

He squatted down to Gracie's eye level, which was kind of him, and he took a moment to pat the beagle. Most likely, he needed time to choose his words, say them in his head before speaking aloud. His mother must have taught him how to talk to crazy folks, her being a sheriff's deputy and all.

Finally he said, "I know you believe in ghosts and stuff, and I know you think what this hallucination told you is real." He looked self-conscious and skeptical, but a part of him looked curious, too. "I'll track down Shay Cooper and make sure she's okay, but as for somebody dying tonight—" He shrugged, but the gesture didn't make his words come out any less sticky. "I hope this time you've got it wrong."

CHAPTER TWO

As usual, riding in the passenger seat of the police department's SUV had Gracie's stomach in fits. Marcel always had more than one reason for driving her home. He'd want to make sure she got back to Blue Horizons safely, of course, but he'd also want to talk to Molly and tell her about the handbag that wasn't a human head.

Scout sprawled across Gracie's lap, twitching in his sleep. She rested a hand on his head and tried not to think of everything that would happen next. Molly would feel compelled to call Dr. Useless. He'd probably want to swap the green pills for some other color, and he might want to do it in the hospital.

The dead redhead wouldn't stand for such foolishness. She'd want Gracie available for whatever scutwork needed doing.

Scout woke when Marcel drove up Blue Horizons's steep driveway. Gracie clamped down on the jitters and tried to sound calm. "You're going to hurry up and find Shay Cooper, right? Before somebody dies?" She frowned down at her hands and counted on her fingers. She'd only asked him five times. Definitely not nuts.

"Sure thing. Chief Farrell is already on it." Marcel parked near the handicap ramp and walked around to open Gracie's door. "Is Amanda home?"

"Amanda retired three months ago." He knew that, so he must be checking to see if she knew it, too. Being treated like a deranged old woman, especially by someone young enough to be her grandson, had Gracie bristling. "Amanda Gavin still owns the place, but little Molly McLoughlin runs it now." There. Succinct and to the point. That ought to convince him she was fine.

Marcel smiled. "Sorry. I meant to ask if Molly was home."

Gracie bit her lip, but the words came out anyway. "How would I know? I just got here." She wiggled out from under the beagle and pushed past Marcel, grumbling, "Just because sometimes I talk to dead people doesn't mean I can see through walls."

Scout yawned and stretched and smiled up at her. Gracie's, "Go home, Scout," came out gruff. She thought about apologizing, but the beagle didn't seem offended. He jumped to the driveway and trotted down the path that joined the two properties, threading his way between Molly's car and the gate that always stood open.

Molly's car. She must be home after all. Best get indoors quickly and hope Marcel drove away.

He didn't, even though Gracie called out, "Bye! Thanks for the ride!" before she turned away. Her feet seemed determined to make noise, so she stomped up the ramp and across the threshold with Marcel following close behind. The living room to the left was empty, and she couldn't see anyone in the hallway beyond. Molly must be in the basement, probably folding laundry. If she had her headphones on, she might not notice the visitor.

A quick turn to the right, five steps across the kitchen, and Gracie ducked into the pantry. Eyes closed, she leaned against the well-stocked shelves. If only the dang ghost hadn't caught her off guard and made her see things that weren't there. "A human head that wasn't," she muttered. "There will be consequences."

She grabbed a can of tamales and stuffed it into her pocket.

"Marcel! What are you doing here?" Molly, darn it—she never missed anything. Gracie listened to Marcel's footsteps, a dull squeak across the vinyl, sharper through the marble entry, and finally muffled by the living room carpet.

Not good. Gracie picked up a can of tuna and tucked it into her bra. Poking her head past the doorway, she focused on the back hallway—empty. Her bedroom was within spitting distance.

"I gave Gracie a ride home." Marcel's voice was bright as sunshine. Then it dropped to something less cheerful. "I thought I should tell you, she's hallucinating."

Halfway to her room, Gracie slowed her steps, took a sharp breath, and held it. The tuna can dug into her ribs.

"Are you sure?" The wistful quality of Molly's voice had Gracie's throat bunching up. "Maybe I should call her doctor. I think that's what Amanda would have done."

Gracie slipped into her room and eased the door shut. Molly's voice was muted and a little bit guilty when she said, "Dr. Usef wanted to admit her when he changed her meds last week, but Gracie refused. I'll talk to her after dinner, see if maybe now she's willing."

Molly wanted to have a conversation about psychiatric care? Interesting. Amanda Gavin's surprise chats had always started and ended with, "Gracie, get in the ambulance."

With an overlong sigh, Gracie dropped to her knees on the rug beside her bed and pulled the cans from her pocket and bra. Then she reached as far as she could beneath the dust ruffle—why this made her grunt like an old woman was a mystery. She wrapped her fingers around a sturdy strap and pulled. A pink backpack with a unicorn embroidered across the flap slid into view.

Once she'd unzipped the flap and placed the cans inside, Gracie clambered to her feet and hoisted the pack to her hip. Kid-sized or not, the backpack was heavy. Soon she'd need to bring it to her secret stash. Not now, though—afternoons were for napping.

Insomnia was a side effect of her new medication, and catnaps took the place of a good night's sleep. She dropped the backpack and shoved it beneath her bed, then pulled off her sneakers and set them near the window. Once she'd crawled under the covers, she lay still and stared at the ceiling.

Tomorrow, she'd have to deal with her doctor, but today wasn't over yet. Maybe the headless redhead would visit while she slept. With luck, the ghost might ask for something easy—a phone call to a loved one or a note to a friend. By morning, life could return to normal.

"Okay, ya carrot-topped twit," she said to the air. "If you have something to say, now would be a good time." She rolled onto her side, hugged her pillow, and closed her eyes. For a moment she wished, just this one time, she might be allowed to sleep without dreaming.

Marcel pulled up to the station and waded out into simmering heat. There'd be storms tonight for sure, probably boomers. Lightning made him jumpy, but he looked forward to the rain.

His shift was nearly over, but he wanted to find out whether the Chief had been able to locate Shay Cooper. Gracie was worried and, while she might not be entirely right in the head, once in a while she seemed to know things—things she shouldn't know along with things that hadn't happened yet.

Like when she'd found the body of a dead deer hunter way up in a tree stand, even though a full search and rescue had turned up nothing. Or the time she'd directed traffic around Cider Mill Road, claiming some sort of catastrophe was about to take place. The mudslide hadn't happened for another month, but when it did, it took out the very stretch of road she'd been trying to keep clear.

Coincidence, Chief Farrell claimed, and he was probably right.

Once inside, Marcel grabbed a diet soda from the fridge and rolled it against his forehead. There was a message from the Chief: *Re: Shay Cooper, vacationing alone, no contact with husband since today 0800— missed her usual lunchtime check-in.*

There'd be a search, then, probably a handful of volunteers along with a canine unit and maybe a diver. Marcel put on a pair of Nitrile gloves and retrieved the handbag from the evidence locker. He leaned over the computer station just as Dayna Pelletier, Coyne Falls's temporary patrol officer, burst through the door.

"It's only 4:59," she said, breathing hard. Her uniform was rumpled, and wisps of hair had escaped her otherwise neat gold braid. "I'm not late."

"Didn't say you were." Dayna was never late. Most days she was more than a minute early, though. He picked up the handbag and dangled it over her head. "Look what Gracie found in Echo Lake."

"Holy shit! Is that Prada?"

"Whu?"

She snatched the bag before Marcel could yank it higher. Dayna was barely five feet tall, but wiry as all get-out. She could jump like a gray squirrel to a bird feeder.

"It is! This one retails for just over a grand, but sometimes you can find it in the four hundred range. Too bad about it getting wet." She grinned up at him. "What?"

"It's just—" He should be used to Dayna by now. She knew everything about everything. "It may be evidence." Now he felt stupid. He knew darn well Gracie wasn't the most reliable of sources, and Dayna never missed an opportunity to make fun of him, not when they were kids, not when they'd lived together, and not now that they were "just friends."

"And you let me touch it?"

"You didn't exactly ask."

Dayna gingerly handed the bag back to him. "Evidence in what?"

"Might be stolen, and the owner is MIA." He focused on the handbag and tried not to mumble. "Gracie thinks it's connected to the dead girl."

"What dead girl? Did Gracie find another body? Why didn't you call me?"

"This dead girl is in her head." Marcel waited for the ribbing that would surely follow. He and Dayna had known Gracie since they were in highchairs. Dayna wasn't one to buy into Gracie's abilities, and Marcel's willingness to keep an open mind always earned him a verbal eye roll.

"Don't tell me. Another ghost?"

He nodded. "Looks like."

"Is it making her do things?" Coyne Falls got interesting when Gracie ran errands for the dead.

"Not yet. Just predicting a murder."

Dayna opened the fridge, picked up a stale pizza slice, and sniffed. "A murder? Who? Where? When?"

"Tonight." Marcel double-tapped the keyboard and waited for the screen to wake up. Dayna didn't say anything, but her breath was impatient, probably because he'd only answered one of her questions. "Gracie wasn't clear on the rest."

She snorted. "That's what makes it seem plausible. If somebody gets knifed in Manchester, you'll say Gracie's prediction came true."

"Will not." Probably not, anyway. The Falls PD page appeared. He entered his login and password, careful to hide the keyboard with his shoulder while he typed. "The handbag belongs to someone named Shay Cooper. Gracie thinks she's gonna be involved."

"Shay Cooper from Nashua?"

He stared. Sometimes Dayna was just plain spooky. "How'd you know?"

"Jeezus, Marcel, don't you check the log?" She pitched the pizza into the trash bin. "I tagged her for speeding yesterday. She said she's renting that little cabin behind Candy Thompson's."

"Seriously?" Candy lived less than a quarter mile from Echo Lake, and he'd been right next door not twenty minutes ago. Even had Candy's beagle on the front seat of his SUV.

Dayna grumbled her way to the computer station, leaned past him, and tapped through half a dozen screens, finally landing on one with a picture that matched Shay Cooper's driver's license.

"Is this the woman?"

"That's the one." Too bad he'd driven Gracie home before running that ID. Dayna would have been all over it, but she'd spent a year in narcotics with the State Police. She had a lot more investigative experience than he did, even if it was only a desk job.

Why she'd walked away from all that opportunity in order to fill a temporary position in Coyne Falls was a mystery. Her explanation, "The pressure was too much," didn't ring true. Dayna loved pressure. Thrived on it. Maybe even created it, just so she wouldn't be bored.

He knew he was being dumb, but a small and hopeful part of him couldn't help wondering if maybe she'd come back because she'd changed her mind about packing up, moving out, and throwing away the twelve years they'd spent loving each other.

Maybe he shouldn't count junior high, but he did.

Dayna was already punching information into her phone. "What's in the handbag?"

"A wallet, make-up, and a sandwich."

"Cash? Credit cards?" Dayna looked all kinds of huffy.

"Yup."

"So it wasn't stolen. Was there a phone?"

"A TracFone, and it's too soaked to save."

"A crappy phone doesn't go with a Prada handbag."

Marcel shrugged. "You think it was a burner?" Just like Dayna to see things that weren't there and look for excitement where there was none. "Could be she got herself a cheap phone for vacation, and then maybe she rented a boat and lost her handbag over the side."

"Probably. Or maybe she fell in with it." Dayna's phone chimed with an incoming message. She read it quickly, the same way she did everything. "Guess I'll head on over to Candy's and knock on the cabin door. If no one's there, maybe Candy or Eric can tell us where to find Shay."

"Hold up a minute." Dayna and Candy got along about as well as vinegar and baking soda. "Let me go to Candy's. She can't stand you, not since you cited Eric for having all those junk cars."

"You're right." Dayna ground to a stop, but she twitched like a hornet in a spider web. Must be tough, reining in all that initiative. "How 'bout I go to Echo Lake," she said. "I'll ask around and see if Shay rented a boat. You can go see Candy and Eric. Print out Shay's file. Take it with you. Ask them if it's okay to record the conversation. I wanna hear it."

"Will do." He appreciated the advice. Some people thought Dayna was bossy, but he knew better. She might be intense, but she was always helpful. This was real investigative work and, in Coyne Falls, that sort of thing was rare. The town hadn't had so much as a break-in in three years, and that was when Marty Frick got drunk and forgot where he lived. Aside from the occasional escaped livestock or missing hiker, life here was peaceful.

And Dayna might be right—sometimes it was a little bit boring. There was nothing bored about her now, though, the way she skipped to the parking lot. Seeing her happy always made a good day better, and Marcel couldn't help grinning as he dialed Candy Thompson's number.

He let the phone ring a dozen times. No one answered, so he got into his SUV and drove back to Sandpit Road, darn near scalding the backs of his thighs on the black vinyl seats. He passed Blue Horizons at 5:45, turned into the Thompsons' driveway, and paused a moment at the fork.

The left path would take him to the cabin, but politeness required he first knock on Candy's door. So he turned right, steered past the potholes, and wiggled the SUV into a patch of shade near Candy's front walk.

The day couldn't get hotter. The air was burnt; even the trees wilted beneath a murderous sun. Scout ambled toward him, lifting his paws high with every step on the hot walkway. Marcel ushered him into the shade before heading for the doorway. The beagle's happy mutterings followed him all the way up the stairs to the wraparound porch.

When Marcel knocked on the door, the sound carried in an empty sort of way. Odd how houses sounded lonesome when no one was there. His own place had the same sort of voice, sometimes even when he was home.

Dayna sure had left a hole. And now she'd come back to dig it deeper, maybe push him over the edge.

That was unfair, but something about her was different. Dayna was the most honest, direct person he knew, but these days, she couldn't seem to meet his eye. Probably just uncomfortable being around him, not sure how to act now that they'd been apart for eight long months.

"Nobody's here." No good reason to say it out loud, but Scout waved his tail in reply. "Are ya comin' with me to the cabin?" The tail wagged harder. "Maybe we'll luck out." Not likely, but he sure hoped they'd find Shay Cooper roasting marshmallows over the outdoor fireplace.

The rental cabin was about a tenth of a mile past the fork, down a dirt drive with a grassy crown between dusty tire ruts. He maybe should have driven, what with the heat and all. But he'd been sitting for the better part of the day, and all that forced inactivity made him twitchy.

That probably accounted for the way his stomach jerked as he walked toward all those memories. He hadn't been to the cabin since he was a teenager and naïve enough to still be friends with both Candy and Eric. Back then, there'd been a pool table in the center of the cabin's one room, along with a fold-out couch with a mattress that had more lumps than his mom's gravy.

Today there was a jeep tucked right up alongside the building, the same jeep Marcel parked beside most every day of the week. It belonged to Officer Todd Lyman. Old Lyman was due to retire in a month, and he never did more than he had to, especially on his day off. Chief Farrell must have begged, and that meant he was more concerned about Shay Cooper than he'd let on.

Lyman was cooling off with a cigarette in the shade of a mountain ash, and he looked as if he might be nodding off. Marcel called out, "Trudeau here!" and Lyman's head whipped in his direction.

The man had oversized ears and eyes that were nearly always squinting beneath bristly gray hair with faint remnants of brown. His height was well above average, despite his having shrunk a couple inches over the last year or two. Right now he looked surprised—must have thought no one else had been asked to check the cabin.

Marcel smiled and said, "Any luck?"

Lyman only grunted, so Marcel asked again. "Any sign of Shay Cooper?"

After a moment's hesitation, Lyman blew out a lungful of smoke and answered, "Not that I can see."

"Have you checked the cabin?"

"Locked."

"Mind if I take a look?"

Lyman shrugged. "Knock yourself out."

Marcel walked around to the back; Lyman might not have realized there was another door. The cabin itself was built high off the ground with room to store wood beneath it. Marcel climbed the old stairs and twisted the knob—it didn't budge, and no one answered his knock. So he stood there for a moment, looked out across the cluttered yard, and tried not to be distracted by the memories.

The outhouse was still there, twenty paces from the bottom step, next to a hand pump over a ceramic basin. Eric had built a pull shower, partially enclosed by knotty tongue & groove with an old bed sheet for a door. The water tank sat atop the outhouse, sun-warmed and almost certainly scalding on a day like today.

Marcel turned his back to the yard, squatted down, and peeked through a gap between the door's old boards. His heart gave a happy jump when he realized the place hadn't changed. The couch was still there, half hidden by a curtain on a metal rail, and beside it was a table where two people could share a pizza, maybe beer. Perishables in a cooler.

You could see all the way to Burnt Mountain from the window alongside that mattress. He and Dayna had shared their first kiss in front of that view. A couple other firsts, too.

He was still squinting when Lyman's breath hit his neck. He hadn't meant to jump like a teenager caught with his hand where it didn't belong.

"Chill out, Trudeau." Lyman's laugh was half chuckle, half snicker. "You sure are skittish."

"Sorry." Marcel's heart coasted back to its normal rhythm while he did his best to smile. His mom said he ought to be friendlier towards Lyman. The old guy didn't have a family and, for whatever reason, he'd sort of adopted theirs.

The man wasn't much of a cop, though. Ever since he'd made his retirement plans known, he'd spent fewer and fewer hours on the job. Chief Farrell said it was Lyman's way of relinquishing a big part of his life. He had to let go in stages.

"Shay's car isn't here." Lyman was already stumping back down the stairs. "Looks like she hasn't been around for a while."

"Guess not." Marcel jogged down the steps and came to a stop. Might as well come back later and talk to Candy. Eric, too, although that never went well. Meanwhile, maybe he'd head for Echo Lake and see if he could help with the foot search.

He sure hoped Shay hadn't drowned. Chances were she'd tucked herself into that Mercedes-Benz G-Class registered in her name, and now she was halfway home to Nashua. He tried to focus on that probability as he came up behind Lyman, now standing at the edge of Beaver Brook.

Marcel allowed himself one last memory: him and Dayna and Eric and Candy playing in that brook, floating homemade boats over miniature falls and betting sticks of gum on whose would sink last. Dayna always had the best boat, of course, along with the best grades, the biggest smile, and the most gum.

And Eric—Marcel could see him, knee-deep in clear water, gray eyes gleaming as he trapped a bullfrog in his hands and crept over to wherever the girls were standing. "This time they'll scream, Marcel. You'll see."

They'd just laughed, though. Candy and Dayna were like twins, right up until the eleventh grade when Candy shot up six inches and towered over little Dayna. Both of them were blond and brave—probably had no idea what it meant to have questions and doubts.

"Must be nice having Dayna back in town."

"Huh?" Marcel startled back to the present.

"I've seen the way you look at her." Lyman stomped out his cigarette, allowed a sideways glance. "You'd better make your move before somebody else does."

Marcel managed to say, "I suppose," but he didn't mean it. Dayna was the one who'd called things off, packed up and left town, stayed away for eight months without so much as a phone call.

Lyman grunted. "Get off your ass. Gals like Dayna don't stay single for long."

The old guy had a point, but Marcel knew better. There was no point in telling Dayna he still loved her, no reason to ask if she felt the same. Because that wasn't the way things worked with him and Dayna. She'd always been the one who asked, and he was the one who did the answering.

Except for the one time. He'd been fool enough to get down on one knee and ask the most important question of his life. And Dayna—she'd had no trouble saying no.

CHAPTER THREE

This was the kind of dream that delivered messages. Even though Gracie knew it wasn't real, her palms were slippery, her neck stippled with sweat.

She stood in a field with Scout at her side. All around her the grass was seething, whipped to a frenzy of heaving waves that sailed across the expanse and broke like surf at her feet. A Van Gogh sky, fat with stars, swirled overhead. Eric Thompson stood where grass and forest met amid mowed-down weeds that thwacked the earth in a thousand death rattles.

His voice was rigor-taught. "It's your fault, Gracie. You did this."

"Did what?" She clutched her T-shirt more tightly around her neck. "Where's the dead girl?"

"You ruined everything."

Well, if she'd ruined something, she was sorry, but that didn't give Eric the right to butt into her dream. Gracie closed her eyes and willed him gone, but the image of Candy's husband burned clearer, brighter.

"Fine," she said. "What is it you think I did?"

"You killed me."

Clouds swirled across the horizon. Stars spun and dipped amid unearthly shrieks and groans. Lightning sizzled. Thunder cracked like a gunshot in its wake.

"Did not." Ridiculous. "Why would I?"

"You couldn't help yourself."

Raindrops whirled downward. The vision of Eric dissolved like sidewalk chalk, blending until all that remained was russet ooze bleeding into Echo Lake's great maw. The wind screamed, the sky blurred, and the dead redhead's voice floated above the waves.

"Follow the beagle."

Gracie stared at Scout. He smiled up at her.

"Follow the what?"

"Gracie? Wake up." Molly stood over her in tight-lipped concern.

"I'm awake." The dream faded as disorientation gave way to frustration. If Molly hadn't interfered, the ghost might have said what she needed to say. Now the dream was over and, according to the clock on Gracie's nightstand, it was nearly 8:30. She'd never get back to sleep, not tonight.

She tried to keep the spit from her voice. "What do you want?"

"I was worried. You were shouting in your sleep." Molly glanced toward the window. "There's someone here to see you. Can you get up and dressed, please? We need to talk."

Molly never did have much of a poker face. Something was up. Gracie felt beneath the blankets and assured herself she was still fully dressed. "Can you give me a minute?"

"Of course." Molly moved into the hallway and closed the door. Gracie waited until the footsteps faded. Then she whipped off her covers and scrambled to her feet. Swearing softly, she reached for the door and slipped the lock.

A glance out her window told her everything she needed to know. An ambulance sat in the driveway, stealthy with its lack of lights and siren. Obviously Dr. Useless had been disturbed by the dead girl's arrival.

"Darn do-gooders are at it again."

Nose pressed to the glass, she considered her options. A trip to St. Fillan's wasn't the most unpleasant thing in the world, but it couldn't happen tonight. The dead redhead would demand her attention, so Gracie had no time to waste with a meddlesome psychiatrist and his new pills.

From her top drawer, she grabbed a headlamp and strapped it to her head. An afterthought, she took cotton underwear and two pairs of thick wool socks and stuffed them into her bra. Her mirror told her the stuffing was lopsided, but otherwise she deemed the effect rather fetching.

The stepstool in her closet was wobbly, but she kept one hand on the door jamb and clambered up. From a high shelf, she took two chocolate bars from a package of twelve and tucked them into the straps of her headlamp. They stood up like mule ears, and again she went to the mirror and grinned. Chocolate always made her feel better.

Pushing the stool aside, she riffled through hangers. A pair of fire-engine red long underwear, complete with a buttoned drop-seat, caught her eye. But these were overkill in July. Instead, she pulled a dry cleaner bag from atop a Sunday dress and held it to her shoulders. It hung nearly to the floor.

Perfect.

With a final glance at the hallway door, she pulled her backpack from beneath the bed and crammed the plastic inside. Reluctantly, she pulled the chocolate bars from her head and stuffed them into the pack; they'd never stay on her head, not if she planned to hike all the way to Bald Hill.

Once she'd popped the screen, she poked her face through the window, closed her eyes, and listened. Crickets chirped. Peepers sang in the water hole across the street. Coyotes yipped in the distance, and somebody's dog answered in determined high-pitched yelps.

Satisfied the yard was clear, Gracie ground her feet into her sneakers, not bothering to untie them. Then she pushed the window all the way up, shoved her backpack out ahead of her, and climbed through.

The sun had set, but there was enough light to make her way across the yard and into a winding path flanked by mountain laurel and pine. The trail brought her past Candy Thompson's rental cabin; must be occupied what with its lights bright and a white sedan idling alongside it. Keeping to the shadows, Gracie followed the shore of Black Brook until she reached Eric Thompson's field. For a moment, she wondered if Eric might be waiting, just like in her dream.

Of course he wasn't, though the thought had her jumpy. She crossed the freshly mown field with the headlamp turned off, allowing herself to blur into the gloaming.

By now, Molly would be tapping on her door. In a few minutes, the big nurse from the psych ward would walk around to the open window.

Then they'd come for her.

At the far end of the field, she picked up a deer trail and walked as quickly as she could into the trees. She thought perhaps she heard voices from the cabin, or maybe from the field, but when she paused and listened, there was nothing.

Already her back ached from the weight of her canned goods, so she set the backpack on a rock and then dropped down beside it and listened harder. Not a sound hinted at pursuit. She rolled her shoulders and stretched her neck, first left, then right.

CRACK!

The gunshot had Gracie diving behind the rock and burying her face in pine needles. She lay still and waited, but the shot wasn't followed by another. The woods returned to silence except for the distant yowls and high-pitched yips of the coyotes.

Silly, the way her knees shook when she pushed herself upright. No one would be shooting at *her*. It was probably Eric dispatching a woodchuck at the edge of his field.

Once she'd calmed herself and shouldered the pack, she continued at a slower pace. She had a head start, so there was no need to hurry. Besides, she was almost there.

A bloated sun crouched low in the sky when Marcel drove past Blue Horizons and pulled into Candy Thompson's driveway. Chief Farrell had relayed more information: Shay was still out of touch with family, and her husband David Cooper was on his way to Coyne Falls.

Marcel told himself there was no reason for the way his insides had flipped over at the news. The Falls had spotty cell service. Having vacationers out of touch with nervous family members was more normal than not. Besides, Shay's cellphone was ruined—death by drowning.

Candy and Eric ought to be home by now, although they still hadn't answered the phone. Could be they were having a quiet evening together, feet propped on the coffee table in front of the widescreen Eric had found for free on the side of the road.

Or so he'd said.

There was a lengthy pause when Marcel rang the bell, but then he heard Candy's whisper and giggle. A man shushed her; must be Eric.

When the door swung wide, three bantam hens exploded through the opening with Scout close behind. A tall blonde stood on the threshold. Her too-tight blouse was unbuttoned to her belly and knotted just north of a gold navel ring. Scout planted both paws on Marcel's thighs and shoved a sharp nose against his crotch.

"Is there anything I can help you with?" Candy's voice was sultrier than the evening. "Or is Scout takin' care of your needs?"

"Very funny." He nudged the beagle away from his privates. "Got a few minutes?"

"More than a few." When Candy bent to stroke Scout's head, Marcel caught a glimpse of a fresh bruise peeking out from beneath her makeup. Damn Eric. All grown up and still hittin' girls.

"You and Eric have a fight?"

"You know better, Officer." Candy looked as if she'd practiced in front of a mirror. "I walked into a door."

"You don't need to call me *Officer*." He felt silly when his friends did that. "It's just Marcel, same as when we were kids."

"That was a long time ago." Candy left the door open and headed for the kitchen. "I expect this isn't a social call. What's Eric done now?"

Marcel started to follow, but movement caught his eye. He turned to see a man sprinting from the rear corner of the house to a van parked alongside Eric's junk cars. He read the lettering across the vehicle's side: *Plumb Crazy, Professional Service for All Your Plumbing Needs.*

Abe Rafferty. He'd been panting after Candy since they were all in high school. But then, who didn't have a thing for Candy? If she hadn't latched onto Eric like a fish to chum, and if Dayna hadn't said, "You're my boyfriend, Marcel. Get used to it," then he might have asked Candy out himself. At least she wasn't frightened by a wedding band, not that she gave it the level of respect he might have hoped for.

"That you, Abe?"

The man skidded to a stop and leaned his forehead against the driver's door.

"Yep." Abe wore a ragged fedora, and he looked as if he hadn't shaved in a while.

"Why you runnin'?"

"Seemed like the thing to do." With his pants unzipped and his shirt draped over his arm, Abe's hat looked sillier than usual. But when he took it off and pitched it into the van, his hair stood straight up.

Candy must have been on top.

Marcel did his best not to laugh. Candy's husband was a bully, Abe an opportunist, but Candy, well, she always did land on her feet. "I have a few questions for Candy," he said. "You might as well come on over here, Abe, and for God's sake pull up your fly."

Abe zipped his cargo pants and shuffled back to Candy's front door, blotchy from his ruddy cheeks all the way to his zipper. Marcel followed him inside.

Candy pulled three tall glasses from a cabinet. She didn't have the decency to look embarrassed. Never did. "You on duty, Marcel?"

"Nope, but it's official business anyway."

"Iced coffee, then." She motioned to a white plastic table flanked by three mismatched lawn chairs and one blue milk crate. "I assume Eric's drunk and disorderly again. Has he been charged?"

Marcel shook his head. "It's not Eric. We found a handbag earlier today, and we're trying to locate its owner."

"Whose is it?" Candy knocked a Maine Coon cat off the table with a "Scat, Harold," then poured iced coffee while she stroked the cat with her toe. When she sat down, Abe took the seat next to hers and slipped his hand across the small of her back. Scout flopped at her feet.

Even though it seemed silly not to ask his questions straight out, Marcel withdrew a digital recorder from his pocket and placed it on the table. "Okay with you two if I turn this on?"

"That depends." Candy glanced at Abe. Probably preferred no one know he was there. "It's not gonna be public, is it?"

"Nope, just law enforcement."

They both nodded, but they looked ill at ease. Marcel recorded the necessary information—time and date and people in attendance. Then he set a manila file folder on the placemat and withdrew Shay's photograph. "Have you seen this woman?"

Abe pushed his chair back and shook his head, but Candy didn't take her eyes off the photo. "It's Shay Cooper. She's been stayin' out back in our rental unit fer about a week."

"When did you last see her?"

"Yesterday." Candy's face scrunched up the way it always did when her voice was about to turn squeaky. "The three of us went shooting at the sandpit, but then she and Eric . . . they were like strawberries and rhubarb, Marcel. I could just—"

"Take it easy," Abe said. "Calm down."

"I don't wanna calm down. Idiot Eric took off with her, and they didn't come back, not till this mornin'." Candy backhanded tears from her cheeks, slapped at her nose as if it were misbehaving. "He denied sleepin' with her, but I'm not stupid. I told him not to bother comin' home."

"Is that where you got the bruise?"

Candy thrust her lower lip out. "I told you already, I'm clumsy."

She wasn't. Never had been. And right now Marcel couldn't look at her without letting her see how disappointed he was. Instead he picked up the file and glanced at the freckles scattered across Shay's nose. She was a pretty thing, with blue eyes and full lips. Tall, too. Definitely Eric's type.

"This morning . . ." Maybe he hadn't heard right. "Did Shay come back with Eric?"

"She sure did." Candy sniffed into her iced coffee. "She swore up one side and down the other that it wasn't like that with Eric, but I saw the way he looked at her. Eric isn't subtle."

That was true. Not subtle, not kind, and not forgiving. "So the last time you saw Shay was this morning, not yesterday?" Candy was obviously too upset to think straight. She wouldn't lie on purpose.

"I guess so. Sorry, Marcel. I wasn't thinkin'."

"That's okay." An honest mistake. "Any idea where she is now?"

Candy nodded. "Eric's pickup is out back where he left it, so I have to assume they're together. They'd be drivin' Shay's car—a fancy Mercedes."

That was good news. Shay might not have ID or credit cards, but she had transportation, and she had a friend. "When do you expect Eric back?"

She hiccupped, swallowed it down. "Darned if I know. He's mad at me for accusin' him, and he's got himself a new girlfriend. So he'll likely be gone a day or two."

"Eric's a jerk," Abe added. "Always has been."

"Stop it, Abe." Candy glanced behind her. "Sometimes I feel like he's listening."

Marcel's neck prickled, even though he knew he was being silly. Eric wouldn't watch through the window when he could scare the sin out of Candy by bursting through the door. "Any idea where Shay and Eric might have gone? Her husband is worried."

"David?" Suddenly Candy looked more angry than hurt.

Marcel's interest piqued. "What can you tell me about him?"

"Oh, I could tell you plenty, but I doubt you'd believe any of it." Candy grabbed Abe's hand, and she must have squeezed awfully hard, because he winced. "Shay was a mess when she got here, Marcel, and I think maybe she was hidin' from him."

"From her husband?"

"Uh-huh."

"Did she say that?"

Candy shook her head. "Not in so many words, but she was messed up, and I'll lay odds it had something to do with that asshole. David Cooper makes Eric look like a damn Boy Scout."

"In what way?"

A little shudder rippled across Candy's frame, and she sank lower in her chair. "Shay and I met that year I went to college, so we go back a while." She glanced at Abe, dug fingernails into his hand. "I never could figure out what she saw in that man, but I suppose that's her business. As for me," she lifted her chin, but the fright in her eyes sent a quiver down Marcel's spine. "I'm not sayin' another word, not unless you turn that thing off."

CHAPTER FOUR

Gracie hiked at a reasonable pace, following a deer path that edged the gradual rise of a rock-strewn ridge. The trees were sparse here and wind-gnarled, roots twisting over the hill's granite scaffolding before plunging into great bowls of sandy turf. Far below her, the land spread out in a patchwork of mountain laurel and maple surrounding a field of highbush blueberries. The berries were netted against birds, secreted beneath great billowing clouds. The valley steamed as night air cooled over muggy ground.

She stopped when she reached a rim of exposed rock affording a clear view of the landscape below. An ancient white pine surrounded by a grove of stunted hemlocks provided cover against the weather. She shrugged the backpack over her left shoulder and ran her hands over the great trunk until her fingers closed around metal climbing sticks.

Halfway up the tree was a deer stand—a metal deck bolted both to the trunk and to a sturdy branch. A deer hunter had long ago dragged up fallen pine boughs and anchored them in place. These acted as a railing, allowing Gracie to nap without fear of falling. An added bonus, they hid the stand from curious eyes.

The climb was more awkward than difficult, what with the pack dangling from her shoulder and throwing her off balance. Once safely on the deck, she dropped to her knees. In the growing darkness, she groped along the tree's trunk until her fingers touched the smooth surface of a metal chest.

Gracie reached inside and retrieved a thin foam mattress, a wool blanket, a staple gun, and a bolt of mosquito netting. She stowed her canned goods among those already hidden there, and was disappointed to find many of her cans had gone missing.

Aw well, the stand wasn't hers. She'd be silly to think she was the only one using it.

Within minutes, she'd laid out the mattress and stapled mosquito netting tent-like around her. Then she sat cross-legged on the blanket, leaned against the tree's rough trunk, and giggled when she realized she still had socks and underwear stuffed into her bra. Might as well leave them there. At least this way she knew where they were.

Still laughing, she pulled a chocolate bar from the pack and stuffed it into the metal chest. Reverently, she tore the wrapper of the second bar, unpeeled delicate foil, and breathed in the rich scent. Some things deserved to be savored.

She took a bite.

With chocolate melting on her tongue, Gracie settled down for the night. "Okay, you pain in the ass dead girl," she called to the trees. "I don't know how soon they'll find me, so you'd best hurry up and let me know what you want."

A drawn-out rumble replied. The wind arrived slowly, starting as a distant rustle, creeping closer and closer until it ruffled pine needles and lifted Gracie's hair like electricity. Soft moaning sighs where trees rubbed branch-to-branch mixed with eerie creaks and moans.

"Oh, balls."

She pulled the plastic dry-cleaning bag from her backpack and, with a dozen bursts from the staple gun, tacked it to the tree.

Lightning flashed. She counted to six before thunder rumbled. Not bad. The storm was over a mile away. She bit off a chunk of chocolate. Another flash. The answering boom came in three seconds. The tree shivered. Wind gusted. Raindrops the size of marbles splatted around her.

She scrambled beneath the plastic, grabbed onto its snapping corners, and held on. Only then did she realize she was at the top of a ridge in the tallest tree, and she was sitting on a metal stand with steel climbing sticks that reached nearly to the ground. A lightning rod. Not the brightest choice for a thunderstorm.

But going home now amid heavy winds and falling branches wasn't an option. The tree had stood over a hundred years. How likely was a strike tonight?

The landscape lit up. Bird netting danced like ghosts in the valley below. A great bolt of lightning arced overhead. The air crackled like cellophane a moment before a shattering boom shook the platform. Gracie stuffed the rest of the chocolate into her mouth just as an angry gust ripped the plastic away.

For a moment, she was too astonished to think. Rain plunged from the sky and poured over her. Wind pierced the blanket and eddied beneath her wet clothing. A tremble began deep in her belly, building until her body convulsed with such force that she thought her bones might snap.

Shivering harder than she thought possible, Gracie thought of Molly's apple crisp, warm and sweet and fresh from the oven. She turned on the headlamp, curled herself into a ball, and pulled the blanket over her head.

Rain thrummed against Candy Thompson's tin roof and sheeted from overfull gutters. In the fifteen minutes Marcel had sat at her kitchen table, the thermometer outside the window had plunged from eighty-eight all the way to seventy-four.

Abe had put his shirt on—an improvement. Marcel handed a napkin to Candy. She'd spilled her coffee, but she didn't seem to notice.

"What's the deal with Shay's husband?" Marcel had turned off the recorder, but Candy still wasn't talking. Frightened or angry, she'd gone awfully quiet since her initial outburst over David Cooper.

Thunder shook the house and rattled plastic cups in Candy's glass-front cabinets. Through the kitchen window, trees bent against a roiling sky. Searchers must be packing it up, running for cover. A severe weather alert chirped across his mic. About time.

Candy was worrying her lip, and Marcel decided she did, in fact, look frightened.

"I'll tell you about David," she finally said. "But you didn't hear it from me."

Marcel nodded. If she was scared, he'd best pay attention. Their moms were best friends, so he'd known Candy since they were both in diapers. She was the little girl who tagged along on snake hunts, the ponytailed tomboy who dove from rock walls into the black water of the abandoned quarry. She didn't scare easily.

"Remember that year I went to college?" Candy dropped her eyes, probably still embarrassed she'd partied too much, studied too little, and quickly flunked out. "Shay and I shared an apartment. She was my best friend, and he . . ." Her lips vanished between teeth made perfect by four years of orthodonture.

"What did he do?" Even in the dim light, the bruise still darkened Candy's cheek. Marcel tried not to bristle at the sight of it.

"Shay was somethin' else, Marcel." Candy's eyes lit up the way they used to when they were both a lot younger and less disappointed. "When I was a freshman, she'd just graduated pre-med with all sorts of honors. She was scary smart, coulda' done anything she wanted. To be honest, she kinda made me jealous."

"You're smart." Abe wasn't convincing, but he'd probably say anything for another chance at Candy's bed. She was hot, with a dancer's body and a face that could be on a lipstick commercial. Half a foot taller than Dayna, most of it thigh.

Candy shot Abe an exasperated glare and socked him.

"Ow!" Abe cradled his arm as if it were a wounded child. "What's that for?"

"Lyin'." She huffed and turned back to Marcel. "Where was I?"

"Shay and David?"

"Oh yeah." She made an I-smell-skunk face. "Shay fell for him hard. I think it was 'cuz she was kind of a geek, ya know? Mousy brown hair, glasses, always with her nose stuck in a book. He was probably the first guy who'd ever paid attention to her." A low growl worked its way past her throat. For a moment she looked less fearful. "They got married way too soon. She hardly knew him. But David knew a sucker when he saw one."

"A sucker?"

"Shay dropped out so they could afford for him to finish his degree. Criminal Justice, if you could imagine."

Marcel waited, but Candy had gone silent. He kept his voice low and gentle, trying to coax the words out. "What aren't you tellin' me? What makes you think he'd hurt someone?"

"Because of what he did to me." Normally, Candy didn't have an indoor voice. But right now, Marcel had to strain to hear her.

"How could a sane person do stuff like that?" Her eyes told him she'd gone somewhere else, and she wasn't happy to be there.

"Like what?"

"You'll think I'm bein' stupid. Ya always do."

"No I don't." Candy wasn't stupid. Well, maybe when it came to Eric, but Marcel had been a cop long enough to know that love could make a person do things.

"Did I mention he asked me out? And that was after they were married."

"Oh." Marcel made a note on his pad. Shay probably got tired of her husband's fooling around. That's why she'd gone on vacation without him.

"Did you go out with him?"

"Fuck no. What do you take me for?"

He glanced at Abe and kept his mouth shut, but her cheeks colored anyway.

"You still haven't told me why you're scared of him."

"He's not right, Marcel. I ought to know."

True. Candy's mom had founded Blue Horizons, and Candy had grown up alongside people who gave most folks the heebie jeebies. But now she was scared and talking in circles and, if he had any hope of finding out why, he needed to steer her off the loop.

"Candy, can you please tell me one thing David Cooper has done that makes you think he's capable of anything worse than stepping out on his wife?"

She pulled Abe's hand onto her lap and pressed it between both palms. "He was into weird sex stuff, Marcel. He wanted me to do things." She stopped, swallowed hard. "He asked me to . . . I told him to go to hell, and . . . when I got home that night, my entire doll collection had been murdered."

"Your doll collection?" Marcel couldn't help gaping.

She jerked her chin up and down. "I opened the door to my room, and there were little naked Barbie dolls lying in a pool of pizza sauce, arranged in horrible, unnatural positions. And their heads were flushed down the toilet. Clogged it fer a week."

Marcel couldn't keep his jaw from hanging. "That's it? Beheaded Barbie dolls?"

Candy shook her head. "You don't get it. It was his way of tellin' me I couldn't refuse." She slid closer to Abe and rested her cheek against his shirt. He dropped an arm across her shoulder and glared at Marcel. Nice that Abe had a protective nature, but he'd best watch himself with Eric.

"Did David ever make good on his threat?"

"No, but that's because Eric scares him."

"How does he know Eric?"

"C'mon, Marcel." Candy executed a perfect eye roll. "Eric visited me at school."

Of course he did. Eric wouldn't risk Candy meeting someone who treated her right. He'd drive over to Durham every weekend just to piss all over his claim.

"David Cooper scares the hell out of me, Marcel. If somethin's happened to Shay, it's because he came here and found her."

"I'm sure she's okay." He wished his gut agreed. Shay had been missing less than a day. Chances were, she was still with Eric. She was fine.

Of course, David could easily have driven from Nashua to Coyne Falls and back in the twelve hours Shay had been out of touch. Or he could have been here right along, stalking her. There was nothing to keep him from checking his home answering machine remotely, calling the Falls PD on his cellphone, and claiming to be somewhere he wasn't.

"Just promise me you'll be really careful, Marcel."

"I will. Thanks for the heads-up." He gave Candy and Abe a half-smile. "Can I get Eric's number from you? I'll give him a call and see if he answers."

After jotting down the information in his notebook, Marcel collected his papers and blotted Candy's coffee from the corners. "Thank you for the coffee, Candy. Good to see you, Abe. And Candy, if you do see Eric, tell him I want to talk to him."

"What if he's gone for good?" Candy rested her elbows on the table top, dropped her gaze to the wet napkins. "What if he and Shay did run off together?"

"Well then, I guess you and Abe won't have to watch your backs." Marcel's attempt at humor fell flat as road kill. He gave himself a mental dope slap and tried again. "If Eric comes home drunk, call me, okay? I'll keep it unofficial."

Candy answered with a lift of her chin. As Marcel left through the door, he glanced back to see Abe plant a kiss on her forehead. They seemed good together. Too bad about her being married to someone else.

A wall of water poured off the roof and curtained Marcel's escape. He ducked low, tucked the file folder inside his shirt, and sprinted for the SUV. His cell phone rang just as he flung the door open and jumped through.

"Are you still with Candy?" It was Dayna. "I'm next door. Molly McLoughlin called to report one of her boarders is missing."

"Which one?" Only Gracie ever left the house on her own.

"Gracie Ouellette snuck out through her bedroom window around 8:30." Dayna's sigh punctuated her words. "Near as we can tell, she's only wearing shorts and a T-shirt, and the temperature's falling fast."

CHAPTER FIVE

Less than a minute after Dayna's call, Marcel knocked on Blue Horizons's front door. A young woman wearing a hunter green uniform rolled at the cuffs and ankles answered with a glum, "Hey, Marcel, looks like we lost one." She had milk chocolate eyes, a farmer's tan, and a mass of maple brown cowlicks corkscrewing past a ball cap with EMS printed across the front.

"Hey, Zoe." The two bumped knuckles as he crossed the threshold. He still wasn't used to seeing his little sister in uniform. She'd gone through a certification program right out of high school, and she'd already been on the job four months. But she was a kid, always would be. To him, she would always look fifteen, maybe sixteen on the rare occasion she wore makeup and heels.

Zoe leaned close and whispered, "Jack Broussard is with me—the nurse from St. Fillan's? You know what a prick he can be."

Marcel did know. How Zoe managed to work with that jackass was beyond him. "How's Molly holding up?"

"Not so good. She blames herself, and Jack blames her, too. So . . ."

Marcel squeezed his sister's shoulder and eased past her into the living room. Two of the Blue Horizons residents, Walter and Jillian, sat at opposite ends of a plastic-covered couch. Walter was in his mid-sixties, nearly bald, with a fringe of downy hair. Per usual, he looked nervous, vanishing into the cushions and talking to himself.

Jillian—she was big and bearded, and she always seemed happy when she thought somebody might be in trouble. She was grinning now, probably because Gracie had messed up again.

Face flushed and red hair swirling past a loose ponytail, Molly McLoughlin stood in the center of the room, face-to-face with a bear of a man in hospital scrubs.

Molly was tall and lanky, but Jack Broussard made her look like the runt of the litter. He must be well over six feet and maybe two fifty, most of it muscle. Beside Molly was Dayna Pelletier, lips mashed together the way they always were when she was locking down her temper. When Marcel walked in, Dayna's eyes lit up. He reminded himself she was glad for the assist, nothing more.

He hung back. As first responding officer, Dayna was in charge. If she needed something, she'd let him know.

Jack, face blotched with outrage, shoved his nose inches from Molly's. "You shouldn't have left that woman alone! You can't trust these people."

"What do you mean, *these people?*" Molly's voice ground past her throat. "If this is the sort of welcome Gracie gets from *you* people, it's no wonder she ran."

"She always runs," Jack said. "Why these windows aren't barred, I'll never understand."

"What if there were a fire? Did you think of that?" Molly never shouted, but spoke with a quiet intensity that cut through stupid like an ice pick through pudding. "This is a private boarding house, not a prison. My residents enjoy the same freedoms you do."

"Not today. Her doctor ordered an IEA."

"So you told me." Molly's tone got even softer. "I had no idea a hallucination would trigger an involuntary emergency admission. All I asked for was a callback so we could schedule an appointment."

Jack looked smug now, but no less furious. "Gracie has a history. Who knows what that hallucination told her to do? She might be out there right this minute holding up a convenience store or setting fire to someone's house."

"She would not—" Molly snapped her mouth shut. Marcel could feel her counting to ten, shutting down all the things she wanted to say. Finally, she jerked her chin toward the door. "Get out of my house. For all we know, Gracie's out there watching, waiting for you to leave. Maybe she'll come back on her own if you and that ambulance get the hell out of my driveway."

She turned to Zoe. "You too. And next time please do me the favor of calling ahead. I don't like surprises."

"I'm sorry, Molly." Zoe looked awfully apologetic, even though none of this was her fault. "Dr. Usef is leaving next week, and Dr. Wheeler is taking over. There are new procedures. Sounds like something fell through the cracks."

"So what?" Jack was shouting now. "It wouldn't have mattered if that woman had been properly managed."

Dayna, silent until now, moved between them. She wasn't tall, but she'd always had presence, especially in her Falls PD uniform. "I think you've made your point, Mr. Broussard. We'll take it from here."

"C'mon, Jack." Zoe tugged at the big man's sleeve and headed for the door. Jack slouched behind her, still muttering.

Zoe stopped for a moment and mouthed *Sorry* to Molly before shutting the door behind them. Marcel could hear her giving Jack an earful all the way from the door to the ambulance. Zoe always said what she meant and, while he respected his little sister's honesty, he did sometimes wish she'd learn to be more diplomatic.

The room was silent for a moment, but then Walter's moon face broke into a grin, and he began to clap.

"Not now, Walter," Molly said. But Jillian joined in, and more clapping could be heard from behind Charlotte's bedroom door. Molly looked embarrassed, but it was all Marcel could do to keep his hands at his sides.

"Jack can't help bein' a jerk, so let's try to be charitable," Molly said. Her voice was flat, lacking its usual conviction. She must be worried half to death.

"He's like us," Walter said. "Everyone calls him Cracked Jack."

"That's unkind, Walter." Molly's face pulled in at the edges, probably squashing back tears. She'd hold herself together, though. Molly was tough—had to be.

Charlotte poked her head through the living room door before creeping inside. She was a few years older than Gracie, tall and skinny and bent like a paper birch. Mildly autistic, she was bullheaded about adherence to her daily schedule. Charlotte had an amazing memory, too, and she wrote down everything in a moleskin notebook. Everything.

"Dessert is at 8:30, during *Dancing with the Stars*," she announced in a high-pitched voice that always made Marcel wince. "The current time is 9:07."

"It's okay, Charlotte, I DVR'd it." Molly headed for the kitchen with Marcel chasing after her. "I have pie, but it's cold now. Okay if I microwave it?"

Walter's head snapped up. "Not yet. Let me get my shield." He bolted for the hallway.

A peal of thunder rumbled from one end of the house to the other, and Molly spoke in undertones. "I can't stand the thought of Gracie out there all alone in this storm. Where could she have gone?"

Dayna caught up to Marcel and inserted herself between him and Molly. "Does she have friends who might put her up for the night? Family she might have called? Anyone?"

"Not really," Molly said. "Her best friend is Scout. She and Candy's beagle are like apples and cinnamon."

"She has chocolate," Jillian called from the living room, "and tuna."

"What do you mean?" Dayna asked. "I thought Gracie missed dinner."

"Gracie missed lunch and dinner," Molly said. "I don't think she's eaten since breakfast."

"She took tamales, too," Jillian said, "the ones in the yellow can."

"She keeps them in her escape pod," Walter added, returning from his bedroom holding a round metal shield with *Captain America* printed across the front. "Ready for the microwaves."

"Microwaves won't hurt you," Jillian said. "Aliens pose a far greater threat." She whispered to Marcel, "It was on PBS, twice."

Marcel knew Dayna would think he was silly, but . . . "Walter, what did you mean by an escape pod?"

Dayna snorted, but Walter tucked his chin into his collar and backed from the room. "Can't tell. Not allowed."

"Wait." Marcel followed, but Walter half-ran down the hallway and ducked into his bedroom, still muttering, "Can't tell, can't tell, can't tell."

Marcel paused outside Walter's door—must have pushed too hard. Walter tended to be sensitive, and he'd need time to calm down. Maybe he'd talk later.

Something brushed Marcel's shoulder. He turned quickly and came face-to-face with Jillian. He'd always seen her as a tattletale and a gossip—couldn't wait to pass on anything she knew. A character flaw, he supposed, but tonight, that flaw could be useful.

Jillian whispered loud enough for the whole house to hear. "Gracie steals food."

"It's not stealing, Jilly," Molly called from the kitchen. "Everyone here is welcome to eat anything they want, whenever they want to."

"She doesn't eat it. She takes it." Jillian looked like a cat with a chipmunk—self-satisfied and a little bit cruel. "She hides canned food in her backpack."

Marcel winced. "She has a backpack?" Damn. Gracie might be planning to hide for days. Maybe longer. "How much food?"

"Enough." Jillian headed back to the kitchen.

Marcel walked after her. "What else does she have with her?"

"Not enough, not for a storm like this," Jillian said, tsking, "but she never listens."

Gracie was resourceful; she'd be okay. There were lots of places she could have gone—abandoned buildings, the cave behind Ribbon Falls. Marcel caught Dayna's eye. "Did you check her bedroom before I got here?"

"Of course. She'd popped the screen out. The flowers below the window are crushed."

"Is anything missing?"

Molly answered, "Nothing I noticed." She placed apple pie in the microwave and set the timer. Once she pressed the start button, she stood staring while the pie turned in slow circles. "She does have her shoes, at least. They aren't in the front hall."

Marcel touched her elbow. Molly had been a part of his family ever since her folks were killed. Seeing her in pain darn near broke his heart.

"Call if you think of anything that might help," he told her. "Use my cell. You don't have to go through dispatch."

She turned toward him, still squinting back tears. For a moment, she rested her head against his shoulder. He patted her back. "It's gonna be okay, Mols. I'll find her. I promise."

"We should go now." Dayna's reminder had Molly backing away. "The temperature's already dropped twenty degrees, and there's a wicked wind."

"Take some pie." Molly was already slicing two wedges with steaming apples and flaky crust. She slid them onto paper plates and covered them in plastic. "Thank you both for your help." With the remaining pie in hand, she headed for the kitchen table with

Jillian and Charlotte in her wake. Marcel and Dayna let themselves out.

A full moon rose over the clearing horizon. Wisps of black clouds coiled around it like smoke. Marcel pulled up his collar against the chill.

"The Sheriff is expanding the Shay Cooper search to include Gracie," Dayna said, "but the Chief wants us to look for her on our own."

"Any idea where to start?" Gracie knew Coyne Falls better than anyone.

"She's not stupid," Dayna said. "She must have found shelter somewhere. I mean, it sounds as if she planned ahead."

"She could be in someone's barn. Or she may have let herself into the abandoned house on Starch Mill Road."

"How 'bout I take Starch Mill. You start on the barns." Dayna headed for the cruiser. "Let me know what you find."

"Will do."

"And, Marcel . . ."

"Yup."

"You shouldn't have promised. You know better."

"Yeah, I do." But he had promised, and now he needed to come through. And not just for Molly. He wouldn't admit it to Dayna, probably not to anyone else either, but he liked Gracie. The thought of her drenched and cold had him aching inside.

As he placed Molly's pie on the seat of his SUV, a black and tan blur brushed past him. In the dim light, he made out a white-tipped tail waving among Molly's squashed snapdragons.

"Scout? Is that you?"

The little dog snuffled and muttered while he crisscrossed the ground beneath Gracie's bedroom window. Then, with a sharp, "Roo! Roo!" he hurtled across the lawn, ran down the path toward Candy's house, and turned down the driveway that led to Eric's rental cabin. Marcel wavered for half a second before he slammed his door and broke to a run.

"He's heading for Candy's cabin!" he shouted to Dayna as he sprinted over the grass. "The barns will have to wait. I'm gonna follow that beagle."

CHAPTER SIX

Never had Gracie been so very cold. She'd huddled beneath her blanket long after the clouds scuttled away, leaving behind a thorough drenching and a screaming wind. Her shivering was so fierce that her mind must have shaken loose and drifted . . . to Blue Horizons, where Molly sat a lonely vigil . . . to Echo Lake, where the waves churned beneath a sullen sky, to Eric's field, where two figures shared a heavy burden. Then, just as her thoughts were stripped bare and the world dimmed, the chill faded.

A yellow glow brightened the pine railings, and she realized the night must be over. Exhaustion rooted her legs to the mattress, begged her to sleep. But dreams and dead girls would have to wait; the sensible choice was warmth.

Hugging her blanket to her shoulders, she made her way down the climbing sticks to the sodden earth below. Then, with a flip-top can tucked beneath each armpit, she trudged toward a rising dawn.

Fat droplets floated to the ground as hemlocks unburdened themselves. Tiny searchlights of sun slanted through the trees and followed her, forming a kaleidoscope pattern on the forest floor. Spider webs ghosted across the trail, and she glided through them, disconnected from her feet, wafting on currents of air.

Her medication was overdue—that must be why she felt as if she were floating. Maybe she ought to take a chance and sneak into Blue Horizons. Even Molly's pancakes, although too fluffy for her taste, were tempting.

Too risky, of course. She had to be free in case the dead girl tried to contact her.

The thought brought with it a gnawing fear. Caught between visitations and withdrawal, she couldn't trust anything she might see or hear. Who knew if she'd be able to sort figments and fantasy from useful illusions, or sightings, or whatever they were supposed to be?

And what if the redhead wasn't real? The thought was disconcerting. Perhaps a trip to the hospital would have been a more sensible course of action. Too late now—she'd made her choice, and there was nothing to be gained from fretting.

Her feet, when she looked down, appeared to soar high above the ground. Hemlocks tickled her cheeks and made her giggle. The path wound on, unfamiliar and rough, until finally she broke from the woods onto the eastern face of a granite outcropping.

Yellow lichen formed a thin coverlet over stone slabs, steaming in morning sun. Cocooned in her blanket, Gracie lowered herself to the ground. The lichen cushioned her bottom, softer and warmer than she'd expected. While the night's cold seeped from her bones, she let go of her misgivings and turned her face to a shimmering sun.

Better eat something.

The two cans gathering sun on the rock beside her were far from warm, but they weren't completely cold. She opened the sweetened condensed milk and drank it down, gagging against the syrupy feel. Then she started on the tamales. The sauce was gelatinous, and the expected spicy taste was bland—a disappointment. Molly's oatmeal had more flavor.

She missed Molly. Hell, right now she'd be glad to see just about anyone.

"Did you bring enough for two?"

Gracie startled at the sound of the dead girl's voice. But there she was, bare legs splayed on the rock beside her, face screwed up in concentration as she peeled waxed paper from a cold tamale.

Gracie realized she'd misjudged the girl's age. She looked to be in her early twenties—young, yes, but with a bit of the world rounding her shoulders. The ghost bit into the tamale and closed her eyes. Red sauce trickled from one corner of her mouth, and she wiped it with the back of her hand.

Maybe she was real. But how was a person supposed to know?

As if reading Gracie's thoughts, the redhead pointed to the can. Gracie had eaten two tamales, and there were six total. If the ghost had taken one, there should be three left.

Gracie peered into the can. Four tamales looked back. She rocked onto her haunches and laughed.

"You're not real."

"I'm real, but the tamale isn't." The dead girl smirked. "But then, neither are you."

"Am too." Gracie snorted to hide her doubts. She took another bite, touched the fabric of her shorts, poked at her thighs. Everything felt real. The ghost was playing games. Dead people did that sort of thing.

"So, you're pretending to eat?"

The redhead nodded. "I'm trying to be less off-putting. You weren't happy to see me in the lake."

"It was a handbag," Gracie muttered. "You nearly got me locked up."

The ghost smiled. "I knew you'd get away. You're clever."

The flattery was transparent—a ploy to gain willing cooperation. Gracie smiled anyway. She took a hard look at the ghost, a pretty woman with powder blue eyes and delicate features. Her soft garment, one piece with a flared skirt and a sailor collar, was the same shade as her eyes.

"What are you wearing?" Silly ghost must be roasting. "It looks like wool."

"It's a swim dress—an Elsa Schiaparelli design and very dear. Of course, mine was a hand-me-down." The dead girl smoothed the fine material over perfect breasts. Mounds of red curls fell across delicate shoulders and glowed like fire against the powder blue knit. "It may look old-fashioned now, but these bathing suits were all the rage."

"How old were you then?" Gracie took a third tamale, peeled back the wax paper, and nibbled. She wasn't hungry, but perfectly good food shouldn't be wasted, even if it did taste like clay.

The ghost licked sauce from her fingers. "These are good. You have no idea how fortunate you are to have such convenience."

"You're avoiding the question. Just when were you born?"

"It's not important."

"Or maybe you're in my head. Maybe you can't tell me because it's not something I already know."

"We're both in your head." The dead girl shrugged. "Does it matter?"

"Of course it matters." Why did ghosts have to be so darn cryptic?

"Don't over-think things, Grace. Just ask me something."

Wasn't the ghost supposed to do the asking? What a waste of time. There was only one question Gracie wanted answered. Too bad it was rude. "How do I make you go away?"

"We'll get to that." The ghost looked offended and maybe a little bit hurt, but she didn't disappear. "Ask me something else—something easy."

Easy? As if any of this was easy. "Do you have a name?"

"Of course I do." Now she was huffy. "It's Hannah."

"Convenient, using my middle name."

"Coincidence."

"I don't believe in coincidences." She did, but there was no point admitting that. Besides, the ghost was familiar. Gracie wanted to dislike her, but she couldn't, and that made no sense. "Why are you wearing your head?"

"I told you, I'm trying to appear normal."

"Why'd you take it off yesterday?" Gracie popped the rest of her tamale into her mouth, careful to act disinterested.

"I was trying to jog your memory." Hannah sighed, visibly deflating even though she couldn't be breathing air. Ghosts were funny like that, always pretending to be alive. "We used to talk all the time, Grace, before those doctors and their pills shut me out."

"Wait. You've visited me before?" No wonder she seemed familiar. "Were you the one haunting me when I was little?"

"Guilty." Now the dead girl grinned, as if delighted to finally be recognized. Her hair bounced like rubber bands when she nodded.

"Why would you do such a thing to a child?" Gracie kicked the redhead's foot. "Maybe if you'd go away, I could have a normal life, what's left of it, anyway. You've already screwed up my first seventy-five years."

"I did no such thing!"

"Liar!" Who did this ghost think she was, haunting a little girl, making everyone believe she was nuts? The redhead deserved a punch to the gut.

And a good hair pulling. Gracie lunged forward.

Darn ghosts never played fair, though. Hands wound tight around Gracie's middle, clutching and pulling and hauling her back, pinning her wrists and pushing her down. She let out a growl. "Quit that."

"I didn't do it." Of course she did. "And I think you mean I screwed up the last seventy-one years. You were perfectly fine until you were four."

"Whatever!" Invisible arms held Gracie so tightly that she could hardly breathe, but she refused to let the ghost see how nervous that made her. "You've ruined my last seventy-one years. Do you have to muck up the rest, too?"

"I'm not the one who messed up your life. I'm the one who's try-ing to set things right."

"Well, cut it out!" This was too much. "Why can't you go away? I've been Crazy Gracie for as long as I can remember, thanks to you and your kind popping in and out of my life."

"At least you got to live! A hell of a lot longer than I did."

The girl's anger landed like a slap to the face, sudden and sting-ing. Gracie answered automatically, "I'm sorry for your loss," and she was sorry, deeply sorry. But— "Why does it have to be my problem?"

"Think. There's a reason I'm haunting you."

A reason? Sure, the same reason as every other ghost who'd ever barged into her life. "Because I can see you, and you think that makes me your personal slave."

"That's part of it," the ghost admitted. "But there's more."

"What?"

"I'd prefer you figure it out on your own."

"Why?" Ghosts never told the whole truth. They were stingy and stubborn and loved their games. "If it's important, then why not tell me?"

"Because . . . there's an order to things."

"I doubt that. My life hasn't been any too ordered." Gracie tried to stand, but something still held her down. Why couldn't the ghost hurry up and say what she'd come to say? Get this over with so a poor old crazy woman could go home, take her pills, and maybe have waffles for breakfast. "Life isn't all that great," Gracie muttered, "especially not today."

"You only say that because you haven't died. Yet." The ghost was angry now; even her hair burned with fury. "Besides, you like a challenge. Always did." She snorted her disapproval and vanished.

"How would you know?" Gracie searched for a scrap of blue knit or a flash of red hair. "Why do you have to be so mysterious?" The ghost didn't answer, but now the silence was broken by a sharp, undulating wail. Sirens? Not possible, not here, deep in the woods on a hiking trail.

"What's happening?" Gracie cried out when the ground jerked sideways. If only her heart would beat more slowly. "Whatever you're doing, Hannah, cut it out!" Pain pricked at her while phantom fingers poked and prodded. She snarled at the air around her, shouted, "Stop it, you pushy bitch of a ghost!"

The dead girl's voice came from all around her. "Think harder, Grace. We're almost out of time."

The sun dissolved, and night sky looked down, a delirium of stars amid twisting shades of cinder. Ghostly shadows conveyed Gracie toward a medley of colors, flashing and blindingly bright. The dead girl's face rippled above her like a watery reflection.

Gracie strained against her bonds, tried to free her hands. If only she could grab the ghost by the throat. "Why is it night?"

"It always was."

"But the light." She'd seen it, felt its warmth.

"In your head."

"But—" This wasn't possible. The ghost was playing with her, swatting her around like a cat with a cricket. "What do you want me to do? Am I supposed to solve your murder?"

"The identity of my killer was never in question."

"Then why are you here?" Gracie gave in to fear and thrashed against her captors. She spit and kicked at the ghost, tried to shout, but couldn't squeeze out more than a whimper.

"I'm here because I need your help. Someone I love is going to die."

Gracie tried to squirm free, but something dug into her ankles and wrists. "That's awful, but no one listens to me. Why not pester someone who's not crazy?"

"Because it's your fault."

"What?" First Eric said she'd killed him, and now this ghost thought she was about to kill someone else? "What the blazes is it you want me to do?"

"Save her." The ghost bowed her head.

"How?"

"Follow the beagle."

"Enough with the damn beagle!" Gracie bit down hard enough to crack a tooth. "How can I help this person if I don't know who she is?"

The ghost's lips no longer moved, but Gracie heard the words in her head. "It starts with your daughter."

Deal breaker. Gracie would have chortled, had she the strength. "Now I know you're full of baloney. I don't have a daughter."

"Yes, you do."

"No, I don't." How could something hurt so much after so many years? "She's dead. Stillborn."

"That's what they told you."

This ghost was crueler than most, a cold-blooded, heartless shrew. She probably deserved to be dead. "That's crazy." Vomit rose in Gracie's throat, and something turned her head to one side, held it there. Hannah moved closer.

"The truth is crazy." Her eyes softened, the sharp gaze now tempered with compassion. For a moment, Gracie felt as if she looked into the face of an angel. "Don't be afraid to help me, Grace. You're the only one who can."

Gracie pulled one arm free and reached out. A hand caught hers, coarse but reassuring. The dead girl's face dissolved and reformed. Red hair was replaced by brown, framing a square jaw and trustworthy, tired eyes.

"Officer Trudeau?" Why was her voice so weak?

"She's awake," a woman said from just beyond Gracie's view.

"Hang in there, Gracie. You're gonna be okay." Marcel spoke above the steady beep of a heart monitor and a siren's wail. "I got ya."

CHAPTER SEVEN

Animal clouds loped through a cornflower sky scrubbed clean by the night's wind and rain. Marcel pulled up to the Coyne Cot Motel, whistling.

He hadn't whistled in a while, not since Dayna moved out. Eight months later, he still missed her—missed her girlie shampoo next to his anti-dandruff, missed the way she left her shoes all over the house and never could find the pair she wanted. Missed the way she'd held onto him at night as if he were worth having.

Maybe she'd held him so tightly because she'd always planned on letting go.

Aw well. He'd found a routine and stuck with it, told himself better things were around the corner. Last night, he'd rounded that corner.

Gracie's doctor was confident she'd be fine, and Marcel's notepad, previously reserved for police work, now held the phone number of a cute nurse named Kate who'd judged him a hero. Being hit on by a complete stranger stretched his usual smile to a grin and made his steps extra bouncy.

He knew his actions were far from heroic. Trying not to trip over the beagle had been his greatest challenge. Besides, he had a soft spot for Gracie, admired her pluck. And the relief on Molly's face, well, that was better than maple syrup on pancakes.

"I promised Molly I'd find Gracie, and I did," he told himself as he jotted down the license plate of the Ford dually outside Unit 7B. "And now we need to locate Shay Cooper."

Shay had been gone twenty-four hours now. Eric hadn't come home, either, and he still wasn't answering his cell. This could be a good thing—the two were probably together. That's what Marcel chose to believe because alternatives weren't something he wanted to consider.

Shay's husband seemed anxious to help. David Cooper had driven the hundred miles up from Nashua and booked himself a room at the Cot. Time to talk to the man, get a sense of who he was.

There was Candy's claim of coercion alongside David's deviant sexual appetite. Bullying and intimidation—that part didn't sit well. But the sex . . . while such things weren't Marcel's personal preference, they weren't damning, as long as the partners were like-minded. Weird to one person was normal to another. The way Candy dressed, along with cheating on her husband and flirting with every man she met, suggested she might have more kink in her than she was willing to let on.

He reminded himself that such thoughts were impolite and unbefitting an officer of the law. But damn, Candy was pretty. Tall and sleek, with the longest legs he'd ever seen, she was the perfect mix of athlete and beauty. He'd have to be gay not to notice her.

Even then.

He knocked once, called Dayna on his mic, and checked in. She replied with a terse "Ten-four," just as the door swung open.

David Cooper looked as if he'd just tumbled out of bed. He wore drop-seat PJs with the top unbuttoned to reveal thick, curly hair covering a chest that obviously frequented the inside of a gym. His pajama bottoms were tucked into white tube socks with L.L. Bean stitched into elastic tops. Furry slippers with bear claws rounded out the ensemble.

Marcel had to look up to meet the man's gaze. He judged David to stand just over six feet, fair skinned, with a head of dark hair nearly as curly as that on his chest. The pouches beneath his eyes said he was tired and ill at ease.

"You're early." David's gaze darted to the bathroom. "I didn't expect you until sometime this afternoon." When Marcel crossed the threshold, David strode to the bathroom and pulled the door shut. His bear-claw slippers lit up and growled with every step.

"Couldn't be helped." A lie. By showing up unannounced, Marcel hoped to see David less rehearsed and more forthcoming. "We have a small force here. We need to take advantage of free time when we have it." That part was true. Coyne Falls only had two full-time patrol officers—himself and Todd Lyman. Then there was the Chief, of course, and Dayna, but she was only part-time and temporary.

David gestured to a worn but plush armchair. "Have a seat. Can you give me a minute?"

"No problem." Marcel placed his file folder on a wobbly writing desk and sat beside it, back to the wall.

David riffled through a suitcase, pulled out a selection of clothing, and then opened the bathroom door just wide enough to squeeze through. He said, "I'm glad you stopped by," but his smile was tight and lipless. "I think this whole missing person thing may have been premature. How do I call it off?"

"Call it off?" Marcel's suspicion played tug-of-war with relief. "Have you spoken to Shay?"

David squashed through the bathroom door and pulled it shut behind him. A sharp thud shook the wall. David cursed like a high school senior caught with marijuana; he could string expletives with the best of them. Better than Candy.

"You okay in there?"

"Yup." David's voice was a few notes higher than it had been. "Tripped."

Marcel took another look at the bed. The blankets were twisted beneath the quilt, and both pillows had been used. Unless David was awfully restless, two people had slept there.

"Has Shay called you?"

Another thunk against the toilet, half drowned by the sound of the shower being turned on. What the—

"Nope. Shay hasn't called." The shower door scraped shut.

"Is there any reason she might not want to be found?" When David didn't answer, he tried again. "Does she have reason to run away?"

"You've been talking to Candy Gavin, haven't you?"

Her name was Candy Thompson now, but that wasn't David's business. Marcel opened his folder and touched a finger to the photo of Shay. She looked sweet, just the sort who might be taken in by a smooth-talking jerk.

"I've been told you can be a bully." Marcel got to his feet, kept his eyes on the bathroom door.

"Candy would think that." David's words burbled through wet lips. "But she'd be wrong."

"Did you vandalize her doll collection?" Probably a dumb thing to ask, but curiosity had him in a headlock. Every story had at least two sides.

"Is that what she told you?" David's voice carried over the squeak of water being shut off and the shower door sliding open.

"Did you?"

"Fuck, no. I never did anything to that girl. She's the one who poisoned me."

"What?"

"You heard me." Following the normal sounds of someone toweling and dressing, David cracked the bathroom door. His hair was slicked back, and he wore a crewneck tee and faded jeans. He met Marcel's gaze with a frustrated scowl. "Candy hates me, always has, and I have no idea why."

David shut the bathroom door behind him and stepped into a pair of black Hush Puppies. "Can we talk over breakfast? I'd like to get out of this damn room for a while."

"Sure." Marcel picked up his paperwork. A groan from the bathroom kicked his heart up a notch. "Who's in there?"

David headed for the exit. "Just a girl I picked up at a bar last night. She'll show herself out."

A thud followed the groan. Marcel took a step toward the bathroom. "Is she sick? She doesn't sound good."

"She's fine, just hung over," David insisted. "Look, I'll drive to The Maple Shack. Meet you there?"

Marcel hesitated. "Hold on a moment." He walked around the bed, eyes on David. When he reached the bathroom, he knocked on the door and waited, knuckles hovering an inch from the pine laminate. "Are you okay in there?"

Another thump answered, followed by a soft whimper. David hadn't waited; he was already outside. Marcel reached for the knob and turned it. The bathroom door creaked open, and steam fogged his glasses.

Surrounded in misty haze, a woman sat on the toilet. Her mouth was taped shut. Zip ties bound her wrists and ankles, and duct tape anchored her calves to the commode. She was liberally freckled. Everywhere. Beyond the bindings, she wore nothing at all.

"What the—" He spun around in time to see David Cooper pulling out of the parking lot, kicking up gravel with his diesel whining like a Boeing 747.

Marcel hit his mic. "Possible ten fifty-three. Suspect David Cooper leaving the Coyne Cot and heading west on Bass Road. Black Ford pickup with New Hampshire plates, sierra, alpha, foxtrot, echo, whiskey, romeo, delta."

He paused. The woman on the toilet was shaking her head. Vigorously. Bottle-red hair fell across furious blue eyes and clung to the duct tape across her mouth.

He pulled his Leatherman from his duty belt and cut the woman's wrists free. The mouth was going to hurt like hell. She could do that herself.

She didn't hesitate—reached up and ripped the tape from her face. Her lower lip bled. "Fer-the-love-of-cock! What the hell do you think you're doing?" she hollered the moment she was free. "David didn't abduct me. We were having fun, fer-dick's-sake."

She reached for the duct tape and yanked herself free, all the while glaring like a wet cat. "Is everyone in this town so, so . . . oh, never mind." Shaking her head, she got to her feet. She was tall. Even though she was barefoot, her eyes were level with his, and her naked breasts pointed straight at him.

"I'm Shay Cooper," she said, hands firm on her hips. "Who the fuck are you?"

CHAPTER EIGHT

Marcel opened the passenger door of his SUV, did his best to focus on Shay's face, and held out his hand. She swatted him aside and jumped past him, landing deftly in stiletto chap boots. Her leather micro-skirt flipped up just enough to confirm his suspicion she wasn't wearing underwear.

Chief Farrell, comb-over lifting in the breeze, walked out of The Maple Shack as Shay and Marcel crossed the dirt parking lot. Farrell, Marcel knew, had just apologized to David Cooper.

The day couldn't get worse. First he'd caused David Cooper to be subjected to a traffic stop and pat-down, and now Marcel was trotting after a woman who looked as if she'd cost him a month's salary. Probably more.

Back to normal. He held the door open. Shay's heels clicked from the restaurant's stone steps to its wide pine floor. She didn't say thank you.

David was seated, coffee in hand. When Shay slid into the chair across from him, he looked like a man who might just hit a woman.

"You bitch!" David flung a critical glance at Marcel before fixing Shay with a stony scowl. "For the first time ever you let *me* tie *you* up, and you not only cheat, you tell the cops I kidnapped you."

"It wasn't my fault." Shay gave Marcel a withering look. "Officer Genius here ruined it. But I didn't ask for his help, so I still win."

"Son of a—" David pulled out his wallet and withdrew a hundred-dollar bill. His glare smacked Marcel square in the face. "Thanks for nothing, Einstein."

"I didn't realize it was a game." Marcel pulled out a chair and sat with his back to the windows, giving him a clear view of the main entrance. "You weren't exactly forthcoming, and you took off in a hurry."

"I told you where I was going," David reminded him. He slapped the money on the table, red-faced and fuming.

"True, and now that we're all together, perhaps you can tell me what's going on."

Goth eyeliner clashed with a faint blush across Shay's cheeks—was she embarrassed? She didn't seem the type to second-guess herself or regret her actions.

"Our games are none of your business." Shay snatched up the hundred dollars and stuffed it into her sequined crop top. Her choice of clothes was beyond overkill, well into the bimbo zone. Even so, under the makeup and attitude, she was pretty. Prettier even than Dayna and, if Dayna were a few inches taller, she could probably be a *Sports Illustrated* model. For some reason the thought made Marcel's stomach ball up like a hedgehog.

"I wasn't asking about your bedroom activities. I want to know why your husband let us think you were still missing when you were right there in his motel room." He eyed David. "Or was it all part of this game you're playing?"

"No." Now David looked pleadingly at Shay. "She was out of touch all day. I had no idea where she was."

Vickie, the Maple Shack's waitress for going on forty-five years, set down a cup of coffee and a paper napkin in front of Marcel. "Your usual," she said. "Half coffee, half light cream, three sugars." Her face showed her age beneath hair dyed the color of plain donuts, and her cheeks dimpled in humor. "On the house, Officer."

"Thank you, Vickie." He'd pay for his coffee; wasn't right not to when everyone else did. "What's good today?"

"Same as always. We don't change the menu any too often."

When she turned to Shay, her friendliness vanished behind a schoolmarm persona. Marcel knew the look. Vickie used it on every child who dribbled soda on a straw-wrapper snake or lit the end of a wooden skewer in the tea candle at the center of the table.

"I brought you something for your lap, young woman. This here is a family restaurant, and your hoo ha is showing. The cook can't hardly keep from drooling into the pancake batter." Vickie held out a linen napkin with a turkey stenciled across the front. "As you can see, we only trot these out on special occasions."

Shay tapped blood red fingernails against the table. Marcel wondered if they'd leave a mark.

"I don't see how that's my problem." Spittle accompanied Shay's words. It clung to the very corner of her mouth, like a fleck of whipped cream over strawberries.

Vickie dangled the turkey print close to Shay's plate. "Maybe it's not, but do you really want to risk your pancakes?"

Shay ignored the napkin. She picked up David's coffee and took a sip. "Eggs," she said, "scrambled with a side of maple bacon. David will have the same. And it appears he needs coffee. Black." She took another sip and closed her eyes. The corners of her lips twitched upward. Like the *Mona Lisa*.

Marcel took the napkin and placed it on her lap, careful not to brush her thighs any more than necessary. She licked the edge of her mouth, pausing long enough that he got a good look at her gold tongue ring.

"I'll have the pancakes." Marcel was relieved when his voice sounded normal despite the reaction of other parts of his body. "Spit-free," he added, "if Earl can manage it."

Vickie was all smiles. "Comin' right up, Officer." With a curt nod to Shay and an eye roll at David, she collected menus and headed for the kitchen. "No spit in Marcel's pancakes, Earl," she called out when she reached the door. "Save it for the eggs."

Shay stiffened. Being duct taped to a toilet had probably put her in a bad mood. Marcel ignored her and addressed her husband. "How and when did you two end up together?"

"She found me last night." David reached across the table for Shay's hand. "She showed up at my door just past midnight wearing nothing but that red wig."

Shay dropped David's hand.

"And you didn't see fit to call law enforcement? A bunch of folks searched right through the night."

Now David looked affronted. "I did call the moment I knew she was okay. No one answers that non-emergency number of yours, and it wasn't exactly a 9-1-1."

That was true; the business number would have gone to voicemail after hours, and David might not have realized he ought to call the emergency line. Marcel made a note to check the missed call log.

Vickie returned, balancing a tray filled with scrambled eggs, bacon, a stack of pancakes, hash browns, a pitcher of orange juice, coffee for David, and a basket of muffin tops. "Spit free," she announced as she set down Marcel's pancakes alongside a mini pitcher of warm maple syrup. "Can't guarantee the eggs."

Anger sparked in Shay's eyes. David picked up a fork and pushed his eggs around. Marcel cut into his pancakes and tried not to think about Shay's breasts. Difficult, what with the sun slanting through the window and lighting them up like a double rainbow.

He'd never liked glitter. Dayna was a no-nonsense sort, and she'd never worn anything sparkly, not even back in high school when Candy bedazzled her entire wardrobe.

Shay, on the other hand—all that sparkle suited her. She was nothing like the mousy woman on her driver's license, and she sure as heck wasn't the geeky doormat Candy had described. Now he had to wonder if there was anything else his old friend might have misinterpreted.

Or misrepresented. He preferred not to think about that possibility. Candy Thompson was a lot of things, but she'd never been a liar.

David Cooper, though—he didn't look any more dangerous than Candy's beagle.

Marcel turned his attention back to Shay. "If you don't mind my asking, what brought you to Coyne Falls?"

"I do mind." She nibbled at her eggs, casting a suspicious glance at the kitchen door. "Can't a girl spend some time alone without it becoming a federal case?"

Marcel sighed. "Could ya help me out? Please?"

Just like that, the stubborn lines of her face softened. The woman's moods shifted fast.

"Fine. I needed a vacation, and David—he's a trucker—he had to drive that damn rig of his all the way to Florida and back. So I decided to visit Candy. Alone."

"I knew it." Now David looked angry. Maybe vindicated, too. "Why would you visit the psychotic bitch who poisoned me?"

Marcel hardly dared breathe. This had to be a misunderstanding. Candy wouldn't—"That's a serious accusation. Are you sure you want to keep making it?"

"Hell, yes. The twit invited me to dinner, said it was a peace offering since we'd got off on the wrong foot. And then she put periwinkle blossoms in my salad."

"Maybe it was a mistake?" Not likely. Even as a kid, Candy had known which flowers she could eat and which were best left alone. Amanda Gavin was an expert on wild edibles, and she'd taught her daughter well.

"She said she thought they were violets," David said. "I never did believe her."

"You're paranoid," Shay said, "but you're right about one thing. Candy can't stand the sight of you. I came here because I thought it was time I asked her why."

"What did she say? I'd sure as hell like to know." David looked as if he might be holding his breath.

"She said you murdered her Barbies."

Marcel couldn't get over the change in Shay's face. When she burst into laughter, she almost looked sweet.

"Poor Candy," she said. "Growing up with all those nut jobs didn't do her any favors." She reached for David's hand, clutched it tight. "You were right. I think she beheaded those dolls all by herself."

Marcel's mic chirped, and Dayna's voice caused the restaurant to quiet to an eavesdropping murmur.

"We have a ten-thirty-two at Echo Lake. Can you respond?"

Shay and David exchanged a glance. Marcel wished he hadn't let the shock get all the way to his face. The missing person case might be a big nothing, but a body right on the heels of Gracie's prediction . . . "Do you have an ID?"

"Affirmative. Chief Farrell and Officer Lyman are notifying the relevant party as we speak."

"On my way." Marcel took a final bite of his pancakes and immediately wished he hadn't. The thought of a floater in Echo Lake made the Maple Shack's pancakes taste like sawdust.

He wiped his mouth on a napkin and got to his feet. "Any idea how your handbag ended up in Echo Lake?"

Shay looked at the table, and Marcel could see her thoughts take a tumble. She recovered quickly, though, with an edge to her voice that suggested she might be trying too hard. "Candy's beagle took it while I was in that stupid pull shower. I couldn't very well chase after him naked."

Could be. Scout had a habit of stealing things. But with a body in the same lake where Gracie had found Shay's purse . . . "Could you two come down to the station once you're done here? The Chief will have questions."

"No problem." Shay answered too quickly, and that had Marcel wondering what she wasn't saying. He had no cause to detain them, but he was uncomfortable walking away.

He stopped at the counter and handed over a ten. While Vickie made change, he figured out the tip and dug another dollar from his pocket. From the side of his eye, he saw David heading into the men's room.

Shay didn't hesitate. The moment her husband was out of sight, she came straight over. Good. Maybe there were things she hadn't dared say in front of David.

Instead she handed him her turkey-print napkin with what looked like a phone number scrawled across it in red lipstick.

"What time do you wanna get off?" She leaned close and whispered against his ear. "I heard you can give me whatever I need. Weed? Maybe blow?"

"What?" He stared at her. She grinned back. "What are you talkin' about?" He backed up a step, relieved he hadn't tripped.

"What do you think I'm talking about?" She ran her tongue over her lips and clicked the stud against her teeth.

"I have no idea." Drugs? Sex? What the—

He steadied himself, leaned close enough to whisper. "I'm gonna pretend, just this once, you didn't say any of that."

"Another time, then." Her chuckle was deep and throaty, but her face had lost its softness. She could put out the welcome mat or squirrel it away faster than a deer outrunning black flies. He couldn't wait to get out the door, and it had nothing to do with a body in Echo Lake.

Once he'd climbed into his SUV and done up his seat belt, he looked back to see Shay framed in the doorway, eyes fixed and tight. He wasn't sure what to think, but one thing was clear: the woman was an actress, and he'd just been played.

CHAPTER NINE

Gracie refused to open her eyes. Instead, she shut them more tightly and pulled her covers all the way to her nose. Sleep remained just beyond her reach, though, thanks to the eternally pestering, pain-in-the-ass dead people.

If only she could close her ears as well as her eyes.

There were three spirits, maybe more, too garbled to understand, but all demanding her attention. Talk to one dead girl, and suddenly she was ghost central. So much for resting in peace.

She ignored the voices and let her mind drift back to the tree stand. The night had been miserable. Her wet tee and shorts, covered by a sodden blanket, had made the wind feel like November rather than July. Who would have thought such a hot day could turn so cold?

She'd hunched against the tree trunk, gripped her blanket, watched her hands turn blue in the headlamp's light. But then the sun had come out and the ghost appeared, and . . . after that, her memory blurred. She must have made it back to Blue Horizons, because now she was dry and hardly shivering at all. But her chest felt as if she'd been stomped on by a bull moose, and a quick investigation told her that her clothes had gone missing.

Strange. She didn't remember taking them off.

Still holding her eyes shut, she continued to feel her way around, not sure she was ready for the face slap of dawn. Snug sheets and a blanket bound her to a soft mattress and, as she inched her right hand over the back of her left, she found a little tube secured with tape. Cringing, she half opened her eyes.

"Oh, balls," she whispered, peeking at the IV. "I'm in the hospital."

She lifted her head an inch from the pillow and scanned the room. It was bright and clean, white, of course, and there were no bars on the window. The bed wasn't fitted with restraints—a good sign—and a curtain on metal sliders separated her from the hallway and the people walking by her door.

She wasn't in the locked ward, and she was hearing people, not ghosts.

So far, so good.

Fragments of the night came back in bits and flashes. Was Scout there? The dead redhead . . . Hannah . . . had eaten her tamales, held her to the ground, and made her dizzy. But then the ghost had turned into Officer Trudeau.

Was there an ambulance?

If so, then she must have messed up. Badly. and Marcel had braved the storm to rescue her. An apology was in order, but the only word that came to mind was *oops*. She'd have to think of something better, but what could she say? Her obligation to help the dead girl wasn't something she could admit, not unless she wanted to be transferred to the fourth floor.

Been there, done that, and no one ever listened when she told them what Cracked Jack did to people when no one was watching.

Besides, doctors were no help. They all shared the opinion that assisting the dead was an unreasonable thing to do with one's time, especially when it involved directing traffic or breaking into houses or making phone calls to people she didn't know. They'd made their views clear on countless occasions and, in return, Gracie had mostly learned to keep quiet about her paranormal dealings.

Better not mention Hannah, not again, not even to Officer Trudeau. And she wouldn't tell anyone about Eric Thompson. He was alive, of course, so if she told people his ghost had barged into her dream and accused her of killing him, she'd be locked up for sure.

The question now was where to go from here. How was she supposed to save the life of this unidentified person—someone the ghost cared for? And the rest . . . her own daughter? Pfffft. That child was not only dead, she'd never really lived, not beyond a made-up world in an old woman's dream.

That's what they told you.

Gracie shut her eyes against the possibility. Even if her daughter was alive, how could she hope to find her? And how would finding her stop someone else from dying?

Follow the beagle.

Seriously? She might be bonkers, but she wasn't gonna chase after Candy Thompson's dog just because a hallucination told her to.

Defeated, she turned to the window. The sun was blazing, probably ten o'clock already, and where was breakfast? She took a good look at the table beside her bed. Empty. Nothing had been left for her. Even worse, she'd been awake several minutes, and no one had checked on her.

Beyond the table was a chair, oversized and lightly padded. She'd assumed it was empty, but now auburn hair spilled in weary ripples across a woman's shoulders. The sun's rays gave the vision an unearthly glow.

"Dead girl?" She only managed a whisper. "Hannah, are you still following me?"

Nothing. Gracie rubbed the blur from her eyes and looked more closely. The woman wore jeans and a simple camp shirt, faded green, not the powder blue swim dress of the dead redhead. Her face was turned toward the window, but Gracie realized who she was. There'd be a tongue-lashing, for sure.

"Molly," she said, much louder. "Is that you?"

"Gracie!" Molly turned. Her forehead had new worry lines, and her nose was swollen and red.

"You don't look so good." Gracie shrank back into the covers and pulled the blanket tight against her chin. "I suppose that's my fault."

"Maybe just a little." Molly looked as if she were snagged somewhere between sobbing and celebration. "Don't worry about that right now, okay? Just get better."

"They always tell you not to worry when you're in the most trouble."

"You're not in trouble." Molly dragged her chair closer to the bed. "And I need to talk to you, when you feel up to it."

Uh-oh. The locked ward might still be in the offing. Gracie tried to get a look at the exit, but the darn curtain blocked her view. Besides, if she tried to escape, she wouldn't get far. She couldn't outrun folks half her age, not when they outnumbered her and not when they knew the hiding places better than she did.

She sighed in acquiescence. "Okay."

Molly spoke earnestly, same as she always did. "I had a conversation with an attorney here, and she suggested I take a more active role in your healthcare." She held up a sheaf of papers and shook them. "So in the future, if you don't like what's happening, tell me. I can help."

"You can?"

"Yes, I can." Molly sat straighter, seeming to regain her usual fire. "I don't know what happened when Amanda Gavin ran Blue Horizons, but just because you have a disability doesn't mean they can lock you up without your consent, not unless you pose a threat. So don't go running away again. You could have died."

She choked on the last word. "I don't know what I would have done, Grace. You're my family."

The words landed like a fist to the belly while a warm glow spread upwards from the bruise. Molly liked her. Who knew?

"I thought I had it all figured out," Gracie said, feeling even more guilty. "I was cold at first, but then I warmed up, so I thought I was okay."

"That happens when people get hypothermia." Molly pulled a tissue from a box in her lap. "You're lucky Marcel found you when he did. He carried you all the way to the road, over a mile."

"Sorry."

"At least the lightning missed you." Molly blew her nose, then scrunched her tissue and added it to an already full waste basket. "And now I know why you went through my canned goods like a teenager with a tapeworm."

"Sorry about that."

"No, you're not." Molly stifled a laugh. "I swear, Grace, you're quicker than the rest of us combined."

Apparently, Molly saw thievery as a sign of cleverness. Either that, or she was being kind. Molly was tenderhearted to a fault, but even she must have her limits.

"How long am I in for?"

Molly went from anxious to stern. "They want to keep an eye on you for a day or two, maybe longer, so please don't run away again. You were delirious. Marcel says you called him Hannah, and you tried to slug the EMTs. He had to hold you down—he even rode in the ambulance." She dropped her gaze. "I'm sorry. That must have been terrifying."

"It does explain a lot." There was only one thing that made no sense. She'd been deep in the woods, over a mile from Blue Horizons and well hidden. "How in the world did anyone find me?"

"It was Scout. Marcel followed Scout."

"He followed the beagle?" Gracie wished her mouth wouldn't open quite so wide before she'd had a chance to brush her teeth.

"He sure did. And when Marcel got close enough, he spotted your headlamp."

"My . . ." Gracie reached for her head. "I turned it on when the wind took my plastic away."

"Good thing you did." Molly grabbed another tissue. "There's no way Marcel would have found you twenty feet up a tree without that light, and no way he would have tracked you to Bald Hill without Scout." She wiped her nose again, but she couldn't seem to stop snuffling. "You're lucky Candy's dog is so taken with you. That beagle probably saved your life."

Gracie tried to listen, but her mind was frantically adjusting everything she knew to be true. Was it possible Hannah's *Follow the beagle* message had been meant for Marcel?

If that were the case, the ghost had been right. And if she was right about that, could she be right about Gracie's daughter?

Gracie wrapped her arms around herself and closed her eyes. That baby couldn't be alive, and it was foolish to wish for something that could never be. Even so, an unreasonable hope took root in her belly and spread like bittersweet all the way to her fingers and toes. It made her want to laugh out loud and jump up and down. And that wasn't all.

For the first time since the thunder, she was warm.

CHAPTER TEN

When Marcel arrived at Echo Lake, he found Dayna facing off against two ten-year-old boys. Both wore swim trunks, and each had an ATV parked alongside the railroad bed. The skinny one wore a fedora several sizes too large.

How could Dayna be so cool? The body sprawled near the water's edge seemed not to bother her as she dealt with the arguing youngsters. Jared Morris folded his arms across his chest while Kevin Bergeron held the hat tight to his head. Marcel's legs were wobbly, and the Maple Shack's pancakes had set off a rumpus in his stomach. So he swallowed hard, leaned against his SUV, and pretended he was just fine.

"But I found it." Kevin's voice was reed thin. His nose ran, and straggly hair dripped beneath the sopping hat. "It was all caught up in muck, and I pulled it out. It's mine."

Jared hiked up his shorts past a flop-over belly. "He was screaming like a girl. Not me, though, 'cause I've seen a dead body before. Been to a funeral and everything."

"But this is different," Kevin said, scrubbing his nose against his forearm. "Something killed this guy."

Jared puffed his chest out. "I'll bet it was that mountain lion everyone's talkin' about. Can I go look? I've seen pictures of the claw marks."

"No, you can't go look. This is a crime scene." Dayna snapped a Nitrile glove over her hand and, in one smooth motion, snatched the hat from Kevin's head.

"Hey! Give that back!" Kevin tried to grab the fedora, but Dayna held it out of reach.

"You can't have it. You took it from a dead body, for goodness' sake. What were you thinking?" She placed the hat in an evidence bag and pitched it to Marcel. He caught it one-handed.

"I didn't take it off the dead guy." Snot bubbled from Kevin's nose though he managed not to cry. "It was floating over there, stuck in goo." He pointed to a deep stretch of water just beyond a granite outcropping where teenage girls often sunbathed while the braver boys dived. Marcel remembered how Candy dove with the best of them, fearless, staying under the water until they all thought she'd drowned, then breaking the surface laughing with cow lilies spiraled in her hair. Could she have done the things David accused her of? Poisoned a man?

Not the Candy he knew.

"And it never occurred to you the hat might have started out on the body?" Dayna bent low so her eyes were level with Kevin's.

"How could it?" He gestured to the corpse. "There's no head."

"I imagine that wasn't always the case." Somehow Dayna managed to roll her shoulders instead of her eyes. "Yank out a couple hairs for me, will ya? That way we can rule out the ones in the hat that match your head."

Jared grabbed Kevin's shoulder. "She can't make you. You got rights."

"True, but if Kevin here cooperates, maybe I won't tell your folks you had your ATVs on the rail trail."

Jared backed away. Kevin made goldfish eyes and grumbled about police brutality, but he did as he was asked. Marcel winced along with him when he pulled hard on a fistful of hair.

"Is this enough?" Kevin's lip quivered.

"Five strands, three with roots intact. Thank you, Kevin, that'll be fine." Dayna dropped the hairs into an envelope. "I have your information so, for God's sake, get out of here. And no coming back with your friends."

The boys punched and shoved one another all the way back to their ATVs. "Whiney baby," and "Quit it," floated back to Marcel as he watched them go.

"Stay off the railroad bed!" he shouted after them. "Keep to the side trails." He boosted himself away from the SUV and tested his legs—steady. "You said you have an ID." He hated to ask, but—"Is it Abe?"

"Abe? Why Abe?"

"The fedora." Marcel couldn't help cringing. "Isn't it his?"

"Hell if I know." Dayna barely glanced at the shapeless lump at the water's edge. "We're pretty sure the body is Eric Thompson."

"Our Eric? Candy's husband?"

"Looks like." Dayna was all business, cool as a spring-fed pond.

"Aw, shit. Hoo boy."

"What?" Dayna busied herself labeling the evidence.

"Can I tell you something? Can you keep it between us, just for now?" Candy's relationship with Abe wouldn't look good, and Marcel hated the thought of breaking her confidence. Besides, he'd been interviewing her on an unrelated matter—Shay Cooper's disappearance—so it hardly seemed fair to use the information against her now.

But Abe had tried to hide from him—ran for his van rather than risking discovery. Was he protecting Candy's reputation? Or protecting himself?

Dayna gave him what was probably her best patient look. "Depends. Is it about the case?"

"Might be."

"You'll have to tell me what it is before I can promise." She headed for the cruiser. Marcel followed.

"It's just that Abe and Candy were, well, seeing each other."

Dayna kept walking.

"Havin' sex," he added for clarity. He held up the bag with the fedora. "And that does look like Abe's hat."

"Abe's not the only guy with a fedora, Marcel. Don't go jumping to conclusions for the second time today."

"Ouch."

She tossed the envelope with Kevin's hair into a milk crate and then reached for the hat. "Kidnapping. What the hell, Marcel?"

"She was duct taped to the toilet." He handed over the fedora, then reached past Dayna and hauled out an orange duffel—heavier than it looked. He unzipped the flap and dug inside. "It wasn't exactly farfetched, and Candy already told me David was trouble."

"Did he seem like trouble?" Dayna raised one eyebrow. It was the left one, same as always.

"I dunno. If anything, David seems sort of geeky." Poor guy probably couldn't think straight, must have been happy as a frog in a bog to find Shay alive and unharmed. And then she'd taken advantage, hooked him into a sex game and out-maneuvered him. "Even tied up and naked, I'd say Shay was the one calling the shots."

"Is she pretty?"

No matter how he answered, he'd be wrong. Marcel delayed a moment by pulling out a roll of yellow tape. "You mean Shay?"

Dayna nodded without looking up.

"I guess, but in a scary sort of way." He tore the seal on the tape and unrolled a couple feet while he sorted through his breakfast conversation. Shay's lack of underwear and abundance of glitter had made it hard to focus. There was something off about that woman. He'd instinctively distrusted her, even before she'd asked him for drugs.

Might as well give Dayna an honest answer, no matter the consequences. "Shay might be pretty, but she's manipulative. Can't say she's anyone I'd like to spend time with." He cracked a smile. "Not even for a booty call."

Dayna smiled back. "That's good to hear. Chief Farrell said she looked good on you."

"She's married." No point admitting he hadn't been with a woman in eight months, not since Dayna moved out. She probably already knew.

"Marriages end all the time." She picked up a stack of metal stakes and walked toward the trailhead. He followed, still waiting for an answer, even though he knew what she was going to say. Trouble was, he agreed with her.

"We have to tell the Chief about Abe and Candy," she finally said. "He's asked the Staties to take over, and they're sending some hotshot detective to head up the investigation. We can't be withholding information."

Yup, exactly what he'd expected. Besides, he'd already told Dayna. If the time of death matched up, and if that hat turned out to be Abe's, she wouldn't hesitate to build a case against old friends. She had ambition, and she never let her emotions get in her way. Even when they were kids, she'd made it clear she wasn't staying in Coyne Falls. First chance she got, she was moving to Boston or New York and making something of herself.

Yet here she was, right back where she'd started, working for the Falls PD.

"Any idea who the Staties are sending?" He drove a stake into the ground and tied off the tape, then walked a dozen paces unrolling the words *Crime Scene Do Not Cross*.

"Doesn't matter. Whoever it is will coordinate with the Chief, not us." She didn't look at him. She'd been avoiding eye contact ever since she'd come back. Today, that was starting to bug him.

He watched the side of her face. "Shay Cooper's handbag was found right where the body was dumped, and Candy says Shay was with Eric yesterday. For all we know, she might have been the last person to see him alive."

"Let the Staties talk to her." Dayna held the roll of tape while he forced another stake into the ground. "Stay out of it."

"Fine by me." Better to let someone else handle Shay. Maybe they wouldn't be distracted by the walking peep show. He glanced back at the water. "How do you know that's Eric?"

"Chief Farrell found a wallet in the pants pocket, and once we get the okay, we'll do fingerprints. Eric's prints are on file, of course."

"That they are." Marcel made himself take a better look. Whoever dumped the body hadn't bothered to sink it. There it was, not two feet from shore, probably sitting right about where Gracie had found what she thought was a woman's head.

He tried to sound nonchalant. "It's odd though, isn't it?"

"What's odd?"

"Gracie thought she found a head in this lake. Next thing ya know, we have a headless body." He knew he shouldn't have said anything. Out loud, the words sounded all kinds of stupid.

Dayna wrapped tape around the stake he'd just driven. Her hip brushed his. "Gracie thought she saw a girl's head. Eric isn't a girl."

"True." He paced out twenty feet and sank another stake. Dayna moved with him. She stood closer than he thought she needed to, and the scent of her body wash had him remembering stuff he was supposed to forget. Maybe now was a good time to ask her what went wrong . . . probably a bad idea to bring up personal stuff. He ought to focus on driving stakes—never easy. There was more rock than dirt in the Granite State.

He wiggled the last stake into the ground. Dayna tied off the tape and ripped it from the roll. He backed up a step, put a professional distance between them. It might be best if he left before he said something he'd regret.

He cleared his throat. "Are you okay waiting for the Staties? I'd like to visit Gracie before I go back on duty."

Dayna groaned. "Shit, Marcel, I'm an idiot! I forgot you're off this morning." She did look contrite. Marcel hurried to put her at ease.

"That's okay." He glanced back at Eric's body. Not easy, not yet. "It's my first murder, and it's not as if I have a life."

"You could have, if you wanted one."

"What?" For a moment he wavered between renewed hope and firm resolve. He landed somewhere in the middle with sweaty palms. "We tried that. It didn't work."

"I wasn't talking about you and me." She nearly met his eye, bit her lip instead. "You're a great guy, Marcel, and I'd be lying if I said I don't still have feelings for you."

"But?" He'd never been sure why she left. Just did.

"We were together for most of a dozen years, more than half of it while we were teenagers. I think if we were going anywhere, we would have by now."

"You're the one who said no." Funny how that still rankled. Dayna was more than willing to share his bed, even his home, but not so keen on rings and promises.

She tossed the unused tape into the duffel, leaned against the cruiser and, for a moment, looked straight at him. "Guess I didn't want to get married before I had a chance to grow up."

"Like your mom?"

"Nice one, Marcel."

He should have kept his mouth shut. Dayna's mom hated living in Coyne Falls, blamed her husband for saddling her with a baby before she managed to finish high school. Marcel folded his arms to stop them from reaching out. He ought to say something helpful, but all that came out was, "I still think about you way more than I should."

She tossed the duffel onto the back seat. "You need to stop that."

"Sorry." He wasn't. If anything, he was proud he'd finally told her.

When she turned and faced him, something in her eyes said she still cared. But all she said was, "You should ask Molly out. She has a thing for you."

"Molly?" Now he felt stupid. Dayna had no interest in him. If she did, she wouldn't be pushing him toward someone else. But Molly? "She's like a sister. Always has been."

Dayna's little huff told him she was trying hard not to say how clueless he was. "We all grew up together, but she doesn't look at you like a brother. Why do you think I kept getting between you two yesterday?"

"You did what?" Women sure were tough to understand.

Sorting through the mixed signals would have to wait, though, because now the ground pulsed with pounding hooves. A flaxen gelding galloped down the railroad bed, feet flying. Marcel recognized Barbara O'Neil aboard her Missouri Foxtrotter, Tank.

Barbara pulled the horse to a halt and jumped to the ground, panting and flushed. "Officer Trudeau! Oh my good God, am I glad to see you!" She clutched at Marcel's shirt, eyes wild and words in a jumble. "Oh my Dear Lord, Sweet Mother McCree, Blessed Virgin with a Tupperware seal, there's a human head on top of Coyote Rock!"

Dayna hit her mic. "Possible ten-thirty-two at Coyote Rock. Could be the missing piece of the one we already have." She spoke in a professional drawl, chilly as November. "Marcel's off-duty, but he's happy to respond anyway."

She glared. He wasn't sure what he'd done wrong, but it must have something to do with Molly. On the other hand, it might be that his armpits had started to smell, or maybe he had lettuce in his teeth. One thing he'd learned from living with Dayna: there were lots of things he ought to know and didn't.

Barbara's horse dragged her to the edge of the trail and buried his face in orchard grass. She tugged ineffectively on his reins and kept on talking. "It's right up on the top of the rock, jammed onto the flag holder. And there's a dog there, a beagle, howling his fool head off."

"Could be Scout."

Dayna whispered, "Good. Let's hope that head belongs to Eric."

A snarl of irritation caught fire in Marcel's belly. "That's an awful thing to say."

"You'd rather it be somebody else?" Dayna pulled him aside, turned her back to Barbara, and spoke in an intense whisper. "I don't like the idea of Eric being dead any more than you do, but I sure hope Scout isn't howling at a girl with red hair."

"I thought you didn't believe Gracie."

"I don't, but her memory is crap. Who knows what she might have stumbled into?"

Damn Dayna, anyway. She had a point. "I'll go over to Coyote Rock and secure the area. You get a statement from Barbara."

"What about visiting Gracie?" For a moment, Dayna looked as if she might apologize for volunteering his services.

"First things first. Gracie will have to wait."

He was more pissed off than he probably ought to be. Sometimes Dayna's pushiness was annoying, and Eric's death had hit too close to home, but that wasn't it. The ice pick in his belly was attached to something worse. If he were honest, he'd have to admit he was mad as hell for agreeing with her, for hoping the head turned out to be Eric's.

Three minutes later, Marcel left the SUV idling while he unlocked the metal gate to Coyne Falls's rail trail. The tracks had been pulled up years ago, and now the railroad bed was used for recreation: horseback riding and hiking in the summer, snowshoeing and snowmobiling in the winter.

He shifted into 4-wheel drive and eased his way over fifty yards of loose shale into a short stretch of mud. Clouds of mosquitoes hurled themselves against the windows when the running boards swished through needle grass and ferns.

Once through the muck, he sped down a stretch of smooth cinder, siren wailing. He pushed the thirty-mph speed limit and nearly outran the deer flies in his wake. When he reached Cider Mill Road, he pulled into a stand of knotweed and shut off the engine.

Cider Mill had washed out three years ago, and the town had voted to let it revert to trail status, rocky, steep, and mostly impassable without an ATV or decent hiking shoes.

He decided to walk the half mile from the trail to Coyote Rock, carrying a compact crime scene kit. That way he could keep an eye out for tire tracks rather than risk obliterating them with his SUV. He grabbed a water bottle, two dog biscuits, and a collapsible drinking cup. Then he opened a roll of crime scene tape and strung it across the trailhead.

The woods were quiet except for muffled howling coming from farther up the trail. The little dog sounded lonelier than a just-weaned lamb. Much as Marcel wanted to hurry and reach the beagle, he took his time, watched the ground, and made sure he didn't step in mud and ruin evidence when there was a dry option.

There were ATV tracks, but then, there were always ATV tracks on Cider Mill Road. The dually tracks—those were unusual. With Cider Mill blocked at both ends by fallen trees, the only access was by way of the rail trail. That required a key. The truck had to be either road crew or law enforcement.

He marked and photographed each and every track, hoping the Staties wouldn't run them over in their haste to reach the crime scene before some local know-nothing contaminated it. When he rounded the last bend and stepped from washout to sweet grass, he got his first look at Coyote Rock. He told himself he was just out of shape, not shocked, and certainly not scared.

Eric's eyes were open.

Marcel raised the camera and snapped a picture, even though doing so felt like an invasion. He took a few more from different angles, just to be thorough.

Thanks to Google, he knew a severed head could remain conscious for half a minute after it was separated from its body. The experience must be surreal. He wondered if Eric had looked down over Cider Mill Road, thought back to the days when they'd climbed Coyote Rock on a dare, and realized he was already dead.

Then he wondered if it hurt.

"C'mere, Scout." He sank to the grass, pulled the drinking cup from his belt, and poured water. Scout wobbled over like a dumped stray, his normally jovial expression hidden behind folds of skin and hair standing on end. Marcel had assisted in enough livestock rescues to recognize the signs.

"Looks like you've dehydrated yourself, buddy." He held out the water, felt better about everything once the dog began to drink. There was something soothing about the steady slup, slup, slup as Scout licked the cup dry. Marcel poured more water, set a biscuit beside it, and got to his feet.

While Scout crunched his biscuit, Marcel strung yellow tape between the trees, careful to include a large area and to check the ground before each step. Once he'd finished, he sat down on the outside of the newly established crime scene and waited. Scout flopped beside him, rested his head on Marcel's lap, and closed his eyes. A moment later, he snored.

"You miss Eric?" Scout grumbled in his sleep. "I'll bet he fed you cookies, rubbed your ears." Marcel stroked the dog's head, listened to the contented sigh, and tried to pretend he was somewhere else.

"Wouldn't surprise me if he kicked you a few times, though." He snuck a look at Eric's face. A trick of the light made the eyes turn downward, and his cheeks sagged, low and regretful.

"Sometimes ya just gotta take the bad with the good."

Sirens sounded in the distance, blending with the *krek ek* of tree frogs and the tireless hum of a white-faced hornet. The Staties would be there in a few minutes, and they'd likely prefer to use their own people—he'd be in their way.

"Time for you and me to pack it up, Scout." He stood and brushed off leaves, checked his pants legs for deer ticks. Then he walked a few steps patting his thigh and smiled when the beagle got to his feet and followed.

"Soon as we're done here, I'll take you home, little buddy. I expect Candy could use the company."

He kept his back to Coyote Rock; didn't want to see the disembodied head, didn't want his mind comparing it to Candy's Barbie dolls and didn't want Shay's words poking at him and urging him to pay attention.

Growing up with all those nut jobs didn't do Candy any favors. I think she beheaded those dolls all by herself.

Shay couldn't be trusted, of course. Bad enough she'd allowed herself to be stripped naked and bound to a toilet; that showed poor judgment. But she'd also tried to unbalance him, come on to him, even asked him for drugs.

Despite all of that, she'd planted a seed. Candy probably had more motive than anybody. Opportunity, too. And if she'd done what David claimed—

But that was silly. No way did Candy Thompson poison Shay's husband, and she certainly couldn't have killed Eric, cut his head off, and stuck it on top of a town landmark like a goddamn trophy. Sure, she was a hellion, but she had a compassionate nature; couldn't even run over a salamander without stopping to give it a proper burial.

He tried to hold on to his conviction, but the questions kept on coming. What were Candy and Abe doing together, besides the obvious, on the night Candy's husband had probably died? No doubt Eric would have done some damage if he'd caught those two together. They'd taken an awful risk.

Unless, of course, they were damn sure Eric wasn't coming home.

CHAPTER ELEVEN

Gracie was bored.

Through the hospital window, the sky was clear blue. July sun glistened over a caterpillar-green forest dotted with furry splotches of pine. Someone had mowed the lawns, creating patterns that eddied and swirled like a sidewalk painting. Gracie wondered what it might be like to jump into the practically perfect world beyond the chalk.

With a grunt, she turned her attention back to her lunch tray. A cup of lime gelatin stared up at her. It was plain green, lacking the sliced grapes and strawberries Molly would have added. Artificial whipped cream drooped like a truce flag over the rolled plastic edge.

Someone had once told her to always eat the best part first, in case she died before she finished. She couldn't remember where she'd heard the words, but she'd always thought them sound advice for meals and for life.

"I'm glad you remember."

"Dead girl?" Gracie scanned the room. "Where the balls have you been?"

Hannah hovered at the foot of the bed, a vague shimmer slowly brightening over gauzy haze. Her hair was pulled up in a loose ponytail that bounced against the sailor collar of her powder blue swim dress. She pressed a finger to her lips and pointed to the door. "Not another word. Come with me."

Gracie looked through the ghost to the hallway beyond. To her relief, it was empty. So far, no one had heard her talking to someone who wasn't there.

"I'm not supposed to leave my room. I might even get to go home today if I don't do anything nuts."

"It's important. We have to go now."

"No. It's not my fault you waited till the last minute." Darn ghost could have come during the night when no one would have noticed.

"I've been here all morning with nothing to do. Now I have dessert, and you want me to go walk-about."

The dead girl's growl had Gracie wishing for ghost-proof blankets. "Remember what happened at the lake, Grace. I don't have to ask."

"You're a bully."

"Only if I have to be." Hannah pointed once again to the door. "I said now."

"Why?"

"Come with me, and I'll show you."

Gracie wedged herself between the bed rail and mattress. "If you could make me move, you would have done it by now."

"Must you always be so—" Hannah bit off the last word, probably a good thing, since her voice had risen to a pitch Gracie was certain could only be heard by herself and a subset of yappy dogs.

With outstretched hand, the ghost extended her fingers toward Gracie's chest and said, "You always were too stubborn for your own good."

Something like electricity scalded its way down the bumps of Gracie's spine. She tried to ignore the burn, but it gained power with every breath, intense cold melting into fiery heat, building until she thought the mattress must be ablaze.

A jittery compulsion took hold of her. Invisible arms lifted her from the sheets and stood her on the floor. One foot flung forward in a stilted arc, and she walked forward, wooden as a marionette. She wound her fingers into the blankets and hung on tight, but they slid from the bed and trailed behind her, useless.

"Do I have to drag you the whole way?" Hannah's voice shook. "Or are you going to walk on your own?"

"Drag me." Gracie dug in her heels but, despite the hospital socks' rubber soles, her feet slid along the polished floor and down the deserted hallway. Hannah pushed and Gracie fought back until she stood, red-faced and panting, in a carpeted alcove facing an elevator.

"Get in."

"Make me."

"Fine."

The doors sprang open. Gracie braced against the increasing force, dug her toes into the commercial carpeting, and leaned back toward her room. For a moment, she thought she might win. But one of her feet slid from its sock, and she was dragged, sputtering, through the doors. The ghost's control became stronger by the moment, and Gracie glared at her, too incensed to be scared.

"I'm about mad enough to spit, young woman. You'd better have a darn good reason for kidnapping me."

"I do."

Gracie's knees buckled when the elevator jerked upward. She lunged for the metal railing and hung on tight, still fuming at the back of the dead girl's head. A moment later, the doors slid open, and she gaped at the wall plaque across from her. *Mental Health Unit.*

"The fourth floor? Why?" She tried to scramble to the back of the elevator, but the ghost forced her out.

"You know I don't want to be here, no matter how badly Dr. Useless wants to mess with me."

"If you'd walk under your own power, you'd stand a much better chance of getting through this without being caught."

"Where are we going?"

"This way." Hannah glided down the hallway, pausing to read room numbers.

Some of the dread left Gracie's shoulders. The ghost was heading toward the long-term care facility, not the psychiatric wing. With luck, this outing might go unnoticed.

Gracie's remaining sock caught in the carpeting, and even curling her toes couldn't keep it on. The sensation of bare feet chafing against coarse carpeting and then squeaking across linoleum was far from pleasant. Stubbornness was getting her nowhere.

"Fine. I'll walk on my own." Gracie stopped resisting and allowed herself to be towed down the hallway. Hannah didn't look back and didn't let go. She must be waiting for an apology, a verbal acknowledgement of surrender.

Gracie did her best to sound gracious. "You win. I lose."

The sensation of release, of becoming a lump of flesh bound by gravity, sent Gracie tumbling against the wall. When she finally found her balance, she took a few careful steps before trusting her legs to a longer stride.

"Good luck keeping up," she said, already passing the ghost.

Hannah smiled and, despite her temper, Gracie flushed at the hint of approval. Maybe if she softened her tone, tried to be less rebellious . . . cooperation might speed things up, get her back to her room before anyone noticed she'd gone missing.

"Where to?"

The ghost vanished and reappeared farther down the hallway. She glided to a stop in front of a private room. "Here."

Gracie caught up as quickly as she could and poked her head inside the door. An elderly patient lay beneath starched sheets, white hair drifting atop a withered face. Her mouth moved, but the sounds that rattled about her throat were impossible to understand.

She wasn't alone. A man in hospital scrubs wrapped big hands around her arm. His thumb bore into the nerve at the back of her elbow. The woman squirmed and groaned, but the man only chuckled and dug deeper. Too late, Gracie backed away, looked behind her, beside her, up and down the hallway. There was no one. Even the ghost was gone.

Typical.

When Jack Broussard turned toward her, his face transformed into the one she knew well. There was something perverse in his tone, like syrup over skunk.

"Grace Hannah Ouellette. What are you doing here?"

Gracie tried not to be frightened by the old woman's tears. "I guess I took a wrong turn."

The big man moved across the room with surprising agility. His voice dropped to the forced sweetness he always used for the left wing of the fourth floor. "Can't fool me, Grace. Let's get you back where you belong."

Relief whooshed through her. "I'm on the third floor, not this one."

"Unlikely." Fingers dug into the back of her neck and, for the second time that day, she was propelled somewhere she didn't want to go. Jack pushed her down the hallway, through double metal doors, and into the psychiatric wing. He paused before the entrance to the locked ward and swiped a card key. The door swung open, and Gracie flinched at the familiar smell of too many patients and not enough bleach.

"I'll put you in an observation room and go find out where you belong," Jack said. "Drop your johnnie at the door."

"Why?" She already knew the answer.

"I need to make sure you haven't brought in anything that might be harmful, or that might help you to escape."

Gracie knew better. Jack liked to humiliate the patients, play on their fears. The ward was a lot crazier when he was on duty.

Resistance would do no good. She'd be here until someone figured out where she'd gone, longer if Dr. Useless decided to exercise his authority. "This will all be straightened out by tomorrow," she said, as much to herself as to Jack. "I have no reason to run away."

"You always run." Jack pulled the door closed behind him and double-checked the lock. "And that's not happening on my watch."

CHAPTER TWELVE

Marcel bounded across the parking lot and through the hospital doors, cradling a vase stuffed with daisies and black-eyed Susans. He'd even crammed in blue pickerel weed from Echo Lake. Tucked amid the foliage was an iron spike he'd picked up on the railroad bed when he was eight years old. If Gracie couldn't hike the rail trail, he'd bring it to her.

He stopped at the information desk and asked for Gracie's room number. The sleek brunette behind the counter glanced at his floral arrangement and snorted. While Marcel rode the elevator to the third floor, he wondered if his bouquet might not be as attractive as he'd thought.

When the door opened, he noticed a blue hospital sock surrounded by drag marks on the carpet. He would have picked it up, but his hands were full. So he made his way from the alcove to the main corridor. Once he'd studied the map on the wall in front of him, he turned right, scanning room numbers as he went.

Gracie's room was empty. He backed into the hallway and rechecked the number. Then he walked inside, set the vase on a table beside the bed, and bent to retrieve a sheet and blanket from the floor. A shudder nudged at his skittish places, but he shook it off. This was odd, but not alarming. An orderly was sloppy. That was all.

He walked back to the nurses' station and tried to catch someone's eye. "Anyone know where Grace Ouellette is?" Two women sat behind computer monitors. Neither looked up. "She's not in her room. Was she released?"

The woman nearest the counter glanced up at him, eyes overly wide behind prescription lenses. "Wait just a moment, Officer. I need to call my supervisor."

"Why?" The only answer he could think of kicked off another shudder. "Did something happen to her? Is she—" He couldn't say the word, not so soon after Eric.

"Officer Trudeau!" Marcel turned to see Kate, the nurse he'd met when Gracie was admitted. Even though he was close to hyperventilating, he couldn't help but notice she was cute as a bug.

"Gracie's missing." Kate clutched at her side, face flushed, breathing hard. "I've run from one end of this floor to the other. No one's seen her."

Marcel's relief came out in a gust. "Oh, thank goodness."

"What?"

"I thought maybe she'd croaked." Lord, that was a stupid thing to say. He inwardly kicked himself before mumbling, "I apologize for my choice of words."

"I get it," Kate said. "You really care about Gracie, don't you?"

"Guess so." He hadn't realized how far the old girl had dug beneath his skin until he thought she might have passed on. And why couldn't he have thought to say *passed on* instead of *croaked*?

"You don't think she'd leave on her own, do you?" Kate looked past him toward the side hallway that led to the elevators.

"It's not entirely out of the question." Marcel reached for his cellphone and scrolled to the Lebanon Police Department. He jotted the number down on his notepad, tore off the page, and passed it to Kate. "You'd better let the local PD know you have a patient missing and ask them to keep an eye out for her. Is she still in a hospital gown?"

"Let's find out." Kate trotted back to Gracie's room. Marcel kept up easily at a walk. She pulled a bag from the bathroom door and dumped the contents onto Gracie's bed. "Shorts, shirt, socks, a bra, and two pairs of underwear," she said. "As far as I know, Gracie's wearing an open-backed johnny, pink flowered undies, and blue hospital socks."

"Blue socks? Like the one by the elevator?" In response to Kate's blank stare, Marcel led her down the corridor and turned left.

"Exactly like that," Kate said. "Gracie insisted on sky blue, and I had to scrounge all over the place for them." She picked up the sock and made a fist around it. "I should have looked here. I ran right past this hallway more than once."

"Didn't her psychiatrist want to admit her? Could she have decided to go see him on her own?"

"From what I've seen, Gracie's pretty independent," Kate said. "She's spry for her age, too, still out hiking and swimming. That's impressive."

"Not in Coyne Falls." Marcel punched the *Up* elevator button. "She's only in her seventies. We have quite a few seniors who walk those woods."

"But still." She took a step toward him.

Cute or not, Kate was standing awfully close, and Marcel started to fidget. The elevator doors parted, and he nearly ran over Molly when she tried to step out.

"Marcel! What are you doing here?"

"Visiting Gracie. You?"

"Uh-huh." Molly glanced at Kate and back to Marcel.

"She's missing."

"She's what?" Molly pushed past them and ran toward Gracie's room.

"She's not there, Mols. I'm heading upstairs to see if she went up to the psych ward." Marcel jogged after Molly and caught up to her at Gracie's bedside.

"She can't be gone. They're not supposed to make non-emergency changes in her care without my say-so, and that includes transfers." Molly's eyes had already puffed up. Marcel wasn't sure whether she was about to start hollering or crying. He grabbed a preemptive tissue from the box beside his bouquet and stuffed it into her hand.

"I'm gonna find her," he said. "Maybe she's just gone visiting."

"How long has she been missing?"

"Ten, maybe fifteen minutes," Kate said from the doorway. "We hoped she'd turn up in another patient's room or even in the lounge." Her voice got softer. "I called Security, but they hadn't seen her."

Marcel headed back toward the elevators with Kate and Molly in pursuit. "Can you please let the psych ward know we're on our way?" He pushed the *Up* button again, relieved when the doors opened immediately. "And don't forget to call the Lebanon PD."

Kate turned away as Marcel and Molly got into the elevator. Molly stared straight ahead, every part of her rigid. Marcel thought about reaching for her, maybe offering a bit of comfort. But he decided she'd probably hold herself together better if he kept his mouth shut and reassurances to himself.

When the doors squeaked open, he spotted another blue sock on the floor. He squatted and ran his fingers over more drag marks in the carpet. They went left, toward the long-term care wing.

"Son of a—"

"C'mon, Marcel. Let's hurry up and see if she's here." Molly took off toward the nurse's station. She sure could run when she wanted to. He had to stretch a bit to keep up.

Marcel figured the nurses on this floor must already know Molly pretty well, because when she asked, "Is Gracie here?" the woman behind the counter didn't ask questions—just reached for a keyboard and tapped the monitor awake. Her floor badge identified her as Bonnie Dixon, LPN.

"I just got here a few minutes ago," Bonnie said to Molly with a nod to Marcel. "Before that, Jack Broussard was covering. He's in psych now."

"Jack?" Marcel tried to ignore the queasy feeling. Jack was a jerk, someone who might lock Gracie up and ask questions later if he found her wandering alone.

"If Gracie's in the psych ward, it's a mistake," Molly said. "I know she doesn't want to be up here."

Bonnie flicked through screens on her monitor, stopped and ran a fingernail down a roster. "Here she is. She was just admitted. Looks to be voluntary."

Marcel let out a breath he hadn't realized he'd been holding. "I'm not convinced it was her idea. May we talk to her?"

Bonnie shook her head. "No, I'm sorry, Officer. According to my information, Gracie isn't accepting visitors today. It's Doctor Usef's orders, but . . ." Her forehead crinkled. "That doesn't make sense. He left here an hour ago."

The queasiness came back. "Molly hasn't been informed of any changes to her treatment. There must have been a mistake."

"Let me check." Bonnie picked up a phone and turned her back. She inched to the far end of the counter, hand cupped over her mouth. When she glanced toward them, she looked worried.

"Dr. Wheeler is our new department head, and he's just come on duty. He says Molly can come back. Does that work for you?"

"I guess it'll have to." The sick feeling landed like a Pop Rock in Marcel's stomach. "I'll wait here."

Bonnie swiped her card and let Molly through. Marcel barely managed a smile.

"I'm sure everything's fine," Bonnie said, not quite meeting his eye. "Jack was here when Grace was admitted, so he can update Dr. Wheeler."

"Is that the same Jack who does transfers with EMS?" Marcel knew it was, but he hoped to get Bonnie's impression of the man.

She snorted. "Only when he can't get out of it. He hates that ambulance, says the EMTs treat him like a leper."

"My sister's an EMT." Marcel did his best to keep his tone reasonable, but when it came to defending Zoe . . . "She treats folks pretty much the way they deserve."

Before Bonnie could answer, footsteps slammed down the hallway, and Molly burst through the door muttering a chain of expletives that would make Candy Thompson blush.

"I don't want to hear a word out of you, Bonnie," she said, her face red as a cardinal. "Marcel and I are going back in there, and you don't get to try and stop us." She grabbed Marcel's hand and pulled him through the door.

"What's going on?" Molly wasn't the volatile sort, but something had lit her fuse.

"I don't know what the blazes these people think they're doing, but I need an officer of the law."

"Why?"

"You're my witness." Molly broke to a jog. "And I sure hope that gun's loaded, because if you don't shoot whoever the hell is in charge, I will."

CHAPTER THIRTEEN

Immediately following the incident, Marcel drove Molly and Gracie back to Blue Horizons. Molly said little, just sighed a lot. He figured he probably shouldn't speak either, and Gracie was too busy snoring to carry on a conversation. As he took a left onto River Road, he kept his thoughts to himself and did his best to put together the exact sequence of events.

The moment he and Molly entered the locked ward, a lot of things had happened at once. They'd run down a bare hallway, turned a corner, and then come up against a scene that, even in retrospect, seemed surreal. A young doctor named Gary Wheeler yelled at Jack, and Jack yelled back. Molly hollered at both of them. Gracie twirled round and round in her birthday suit singing "Like a Virgin." Marcel couldn't help thinking of vintage photos from his grandfather's *National Geographic* collection. Old breasts really did hang like tube socks, even on white people. That was one boyhood question he wished had remained unanswered.

One moment stood out like a stop-action photo. Molly, he now knew, didn't hit like a girl. When she slugged Jack Broussard, she put her whole body into the punch. The power rose from the balls of her feet right on through her hips before it slammed out through her fist. Jack was on the ground with blood pouring from his nose like a rat shot through the heart, and he never saw it coming.

Marcel glanced at Molly, curled up on the passenger seat with her face buried between her knees. He'd never seen her come apart before, not in the twenty-three years since she'd been born, three houses down in a household a couple pay scales above his.

He'd envied her when they were kids. She had a new dirt bike while he rode his cousin's hand-me-down—the one that stalled every time they hit anything steeper than a gentle rise. She'd always waited, though, no matter how long it took him to push the old clunker to the top and get it started again.

"Is there anything I can do to help?" He knew he should keep his mouth shut and give her time to process all that had happened. But Molly was the silent one, always had been, while he suffered from a verbal case of the trots.

"You've done plenty, Marcel. I really couldn't ask for more." She let go of her knees, and her feet slid to the floor. She had a big red mark on her thigh where one leg had rested against the other. "I want to thank you for calming everyone down the way you did. I thought I might end up in a holding cell."

"I still can't believe you laid him out so easily. Jack's twice your size, at least."

"He's a coward, bullying old people and mental patients. I hope he loses his job over this, even if it means being charged myself."

The thought of Molly behind bars wasn't something Marcel wanted to consider. "Jack agreed not to file a report as long as you let the matter drop. Let Dr. Wheeler handle it, him and the Ethics Committee."

"What if Jack talks his way out of it?" Molly let out a groan and scrubbed at her eyes. "I shouldn't have hit him. If I'd kept my temper, we wouldn't have had to make a deal."

"Well, it didn't help havin' me along as a witness. I do wish you'd slugged him when my back was turned."

"I suppose that would have been better." Molly's breath fogged the glass in a hazy rainbow. "But he was yellin' about how Gracie was a menace and had to be locked up so she couldn't spread her disease. And he'd obviously drugged her."

"I know." Marcel had wanted to punch Jack, too. If he hadn't been busy holding his own temper, maybe he could have stopped Molly before she'd lost hers. "Gracie will be okay, Mols. The doctor says the effects will wear off in a few hours."

"That doesn't make it right." She sucked air between pursed lips, held it a moment, and then let it out all at once. Marcel wondered if any of her anger had left with the sigh.

"Dr. Wheeler didn't come out and say it," she said, "but it was obvious he's not the one who authorized that medication."

"You think Jack acted on his own?"

"I do."

Marcel stopped at the red light by the feed store, thought about how he never seemed to catch it green. "How well do you know Dr. Wheeler?"

Molly pulled her feet back onto the cushions and rested her forehead on her knees. "Charlotte and Jillian have been seeing him for a couple months. I think he's helped them quite a bit."

"So he's a good doctor."

"Seems like." A little shudder went through her, and her voice came out in a hiccup. "You must think I'm an idiot."

"No, of course not."

The light changed, and he headed straight across, listened to the unevenness of Molly's breath, and wished he could smooth it out for her. He hadn't seen her this upset since she was eleven years old and her folks were killed. That was when she'd gone to live with her Uncle Victor in a trailer on Black Bear Road, and everything changed.

At least three times a week, she'd arrive on his doorstep with her face all puffed up, saying everything was fine, but could she stay the night, anyway. He'd let her in, and she'd head for Zoe's room. His mom always brought her a plate of supper and told Marcel not to bother her with questions. There were some things a young lady didn't talk about with boys, not even one who loved her like a sister.

"You're just overtired, Mols. You've been worrying yourself sick ever since Gracie ran away, and I'll bet you haven't talked to a living soul about any of it."

Molly made a sound like one of those squashed-faced dogs. She turned to look into the back seat where Gracie lay sleeping. "Who would I talk to?"

"I dunno. A friend."

"You're as close to me as anyone."

That made him feel worse. He and Molly were friends, maybe even good friends. But it wasn't the kind of close that made a person feel part of something. He dropped his hand over hers.

"You're family. Always have been."

"No, Marcel, my family's gone. Your mom was kind, is all."

"You have your uncle."

"Uncle Vic?" She laughed, but there wasn't a bit of humor behind it. "Even if he were anything but a thorn in my shoe, he's long gone anyways. Haven't heard from him in years." She glanced at Gracie. "It's just me now, me and my boarders. And I'll take them over Uncle Vic any day."

"All those times you showed up at my house when we were kids . . ." He'd wanted to ask so many times before, never had the guts. "What happened with your uncle?" In the silence that followed, he wondered if Molly could hear his heart ricocheting behind his ribs.

"Uncle Vic was fine when he was just stoned." Molly's voice got softer. Even in the dim light he could see her pale. "But when he was drunk, sometimes he didn't know what he was doing."

"Geeze, Molly, you could have moved in with us."

"I sort of did." She went back to breathing against the window. "Staying with your family a few times a week reminded me of everything I'd lost. That part hurt. But it also showed me what I wanted to build for myself someday. You and your folks kept me sane."

"Molly . . ." Marcel clamped down on all the things he wanted to say. Stuff like how he'd been stunned to silence when she'd punched Jack, not because she did it, but because, in that moment, she was the most passionate thing he'd ever seen. He tried to keep his voice from turning husky. "If you ever need anything, just ask. I mean it."

"Thank you, Marcel, but I've been on my own ever since Uncle Vic moved away."

"When was that?"

"I was fifteen." She still had her back turned, and there was something uneasy in her voice. "I kept it secret, but Candy's mom knew."

"You were living alone as a minor? And Amanda Gavin knew about it?"

"Uh-huh." She was quiet for a moment, her breath unnaturally even, as if it took all her concentration to make it so. "I was doing volunteer work at Blue Horizons. Amanda knew Uncle Vic had been hittin' me, and she went over and told him he'd best disappear, else she'd have him arrested."

"Amanda did that?"

"Sure did. And she didn't tell anyone I was on my own, so I got to stay in his trailer without Social Services gettin' involved." She glanced at Marcel, lifted her chin. "Amanda checked in on me and made sure I had what I needed—food and propane. She even took care of the property taxes, not that they were much. I was just fine."

"But you were alone? All that time?" Marcel couldn't help thinking about his own family, his dad coming home from work at six o'clock every evening, his mom throwing her arms around him as if they'd been apart for a month. All four of them sitting around the table, his folks talking about work while he and Zoe discussed friends and school. He'd been warm and safe, and Molly had been all alone.

"Cracked Jack, Cracked Jack, Cracked Jack," Gracie chanted from the back seat, the words slurred with sleep. "He hurts people for fun, and then he laughs and laughs." She pulled herself upright and sat listing toward the door. Her eyes were overly bright, and she seemed mesmerized by the console lights.

"Hurts who?" Molly's voice throbbed with concern.

Gracie's nose started to run. "That poor old woman . . . couldn't stop crying," she blubbered. "She was so afraid."

"Gracie, take it easy." Marcel tried to use a soothing tone, even though he wanted to go back and punch Jack a few times himself. "Everything's okay. I'll have you both home soon."

"Cracked Jack, Cracked Jack, Cracked Jack . . . he hates us all, takes away our clothes, searches in places we don't need searched at our age."

"I'm so sorry, Gracie." Molly whispered to Marcel, "That's why he sedated her, isn't it? So she wouldn't remember well enough to accuse him. I'll bet he does that to all the patients."

"Aw, shit. Really?" It was obvious Jack had no compassion, but did he— "Dr. Wheeler will handle it. We need to butt out for now, give him a chance to hold up his end."

"My poor baby," Gracie moaned. "They told me she died, but Hannah says they lied to me."

"Who's Hannah?" Molly's voice had picked up a shudder. "Was she one of the nurses at the hospital?"

Gracie reached between the seats and tugged at Molly's elbow. "She's dead, just like Eric Thompson."

"What did you say?" Marcel nearly forgot to watch the road. Framed in the rearview mirror, Gracie looked guilty as a kid caught with her fingers in her mom's wallet.

"Eric's not dead," Molly soothed. "He and Candy were hollerin' at each other as usual yesterday morning."

"I probably shouldn't tell you until the official statement, but we found Eric's body in Echo Lake today." Marcel watched Gracie's face and crossed his fingers over the steering wheel. "Looks like someone killed him."

"Eric Thompson is dead? For real?" Molly went pale again. "Oh, my Lord, Marcel, that's awful."

"Told you so." Gracie's voice quavered from behind them. She reached up with both hands, grabbed Molly's headrest, and pulled herself forward. "Eric is dead, dead, dead, dead," she chanted, her eyes blurry as hummingbird wings.

"Yes, Gracie," Molly said. "Eric Thompson is dead."

Gracie slumped against the cushions and muttered, "Darn redhead will have to wait." Marcel watched through the rearview mirror as she slid farther and farther down the seat until all he could see was a drift of silver hair.

"I killed Eric," she said in a carrying whisper. "I guess you're gonna have to arrest me."

CHAPTER FOURTEEN

"Damn it, Marcel, you're late." Dayna Pelletier's high heels clicked across the Falls PD's floor while her index finger stabbed the air between them. Her duckling-yellow sundress showed more skin than seemed appropriate for a patrol officer, but then, she should have been off duty half an hour ago.

"You're never late! For once in my life, there's someplace I need to be. What took you?"

"It's a long story." Marcel flopped onto the stool behind the counter, squeezed the lever beneath the seat, and lifted it to his height.

"It better be good. I planned ahead, brought a change of clothes to work, used the public shower. Where have you been?"

"The short version is, Gracie got put in the psychiatric wing by mistake, and Molly and I had to get her out."

"And the long version?" Wherever Dayna had to be, it wasn't as important as satisfying her curiosity. She never could let anything go.

"Molly lost her temper and slugged Jack Broussard right in the nose."

"She did not!"

"I know, right?" Marcel chuckled even though Dayna looked shocked. "Zoe's been wanting to slug that idiot since the day she met him."

"She shouldn't do that, Marcel. Jack isn't someone she wants to mess with."

"What do you mean?"

Her face said she thought he was dumber than a flock of guinea fowl. "He's not right. He gives me the willies."

"Well, he went down like a whore on a Senator," Marcel said, grinning. "He doesn't seem all that tough."

"I didn't say he was tough." Dayna's voice dropped to a whisper. "Tough and creepy are two different things. Tough looks you in the eye when he kills you. Creepy poisons your oatmeal."

Marcel's throat got sticky. He tried to swallow without looking like he was swallowing. "I'll keep that in mind."

Dayna looked as if there might be more she wanted to say, but she turned her back and messed with a stack of papers on her desk. When finally she spoke, there was a bit of sharpness in her voice. "The bullet that killed Eric was a 9 mm. One shot to the heart at maybe twenty feet. He bled out fast."

"So he was dead before someone cut his head off?"

"Well, duh."

Dayna logged out of the Falls PD site, but there was another page behind it—official-looking. Even though he wanted to sneak a peek, Marcel managed not to go butting into her business.

"How's Gracie?"

"Pretty much back to normal, whatever that is." He answered succinctly. Dayna was asking out of politeness. She obviously wanted to leave, and he couldn't help wondering where she was going all dressed up. Not his business, not anymore. But still . . . "Gracie confessed to Eric's murder," he said by way of distraction.

"Seriously?" Dayna moved away from the computer, almost as if she wanted him to look. "Now someone has to follow up. What a waste of time."

"I suppose, but it shouldn't take long to rule her out." Marcel studied Dayna out the side of his eye. Damn, she was pretty. That dress was smooth as lemon ganache, and her hair poured past her shoulders and sparkled like Ribbon Falls. She was finally logging out of her computer and . . . he tried not to look, but he couldn't help catching a glimpse of the New Hampshire DEA logo and what looked like employment opportunities.

So that was it. Even though Officer Lyman was retiring and the Falls PD would have a permanent opening, she was moving on. This must be her way of letting him know. He'd been stupid to hope she might stay, and doubly dumb to feel quite so disappointed. "Do we have a time of death yet?"

"He was pretty fresh. The M.E. thinks between 8:00 p.m. and midnight. It's a tough call what with the body being submerged, so he compared the condition of the body against that of the head."

"Great." Marcel swallowed a gag and headed for the coffee pot—empty, of course, so he reached for a package of filters and a can of dark roast. "Gracie was missing from a couple minutes after 8:30 to just before ten. I was hoping the times wouldn't match up."

"But Gracie was a mile away."

"I know." Marcel poured water into the coffee maker and flipped the switch. "I don't see how she could have been involved, but we can't just ignore her confession."

"Can too." Dayna pulled a stool out from under the counter and boosted herself up. "Gracie's always confessing to something. She gets confused."

"I guess." Hopefully the detective in charge of the investigation would agree. Gracie didn't own a gun. Even if she did, there was no way she could cut off a man's head and drag it up onto Coyote Rock. "Did anyone talk to Shay Cooper?" He still couldn't say her name without thinking of duct tape and zip ties.

"I did."

"And?"

"And I don't think she knows more than she told me." Dayna's sigh brought her shoulders right up to her ear lobes. Two mosquitoes buzzed around her head. They probably liked her shampoo. She smelled like Juicy Fruit gum.

Dayna looked at her watch and frowned. "Might as well stay and have this conversation. I can be a little later than I already am."

She walked to the back of the building with her cellphone mashed against her ear. "Marcel was late" and "I'll get there as soon as I can" drifted back. The coffee maker gurgled and hissed, drowning the rest of Dayna's half of the exchange.

"Shay seemed nice, actually." Dayna wobbled in her heels when she climbed back onto her stool. She hooked her ankles over the rungs and propped her elbows on the counter. "She came here in an old polo shirt with faded jeans and sneakers, and her hair was plain brown. Not a bit of makeup, either, and not a cuss word to be heard."

"Really." Marcel tried to picture Shay without the trappings, but that made him think of freckles in places he shouldn't have seen. "What did she say?"

"She said the weird sex stuff is all David's fetish, and she plays along to keep him happy."

Marcel poured a cup of coffee, added one and a half sugars and a splotch of cream, just the way Dayna liked it.

She smiled when she took it from his hand. "She didn't come right out and say it, but I don't think she's happy with the arrangement."

"I meant, what did she say about the case?"

"Oh, that!" Dayna's cheeks flushed, but she cleared her throat and rushed on. "She says she has Candy's cabin rented through the end of the month, but she and Candy weren't getting along, so she got a room at the Coyne Cot. That's when she saw David's truck and realized he was there."

"Wait—I thought Eric left with Shay."

"Nuh-uh."

"That's not what Candy said."

"Then one of them is mistaken." She cuffed his shoulder. "I met that detective fellow—Reggie Clark. He's in charge of Eric's case."

"And?"

"He's okay, I guess." She shrugged, but her lips curved up at the edges. "He says he'll be here first thing tomorrow, and he'd like to use both of us in the investigation. The Chief said that was fine, so long as we stay available for dispatch."

"Really?"

"Yes, really." She grinned with more enthusiasm than he'd seen since high school. "Reggie sat in while I interviewed Shay, and he followed up with a few questions I hadn't thought of." She blew out a breath. "He's good."

"That's great." He was glad to see her happy, but a needy little part of him wished her eyes still lit up like that when she looked at him. "What about Candy?"

"Reggie and the Chief questioned both her and Abe. Reggie said you can have a shot at her tomorrow. Abe too, since you know them both so well."

"Will do." However necessary, questioning Candy felt heartless—she'd just lost her husband. "Anything from forensics yet? What about the fedora?"

"There's some hair that could be Abe's, going by texture and color. And they did find a few strands with matrix intact, so we might get some DNA."

"Let's hope we can rule him out."

"Gee, Marcel, I was hoping we'd catch the guilty party." Dayna poked him in the belly and made him double over, wondering if he was supposed to laugh and not sure what to do with the mixed signals. "You're a softie, Marcel. You need to toughen up."

"I'll do what needs doing, but I don't have to gloat about it."

"I'm not gloating." Dayna's playfulness vanished. She set her coffee down and slid off her stool. "Sheesh, Marcel, I'm just doing my job."

"I know." But she didn't have to be so happy about it.

"Make sure you have Candy and Abe come in separately."

"I will. And I'll look for inconsistencies in their stories."

"They've had plenty of time to rehearse, so I'd be more interested in the parts that match too closely."

"Uh-huh." Truth was, he hadn't considered that.

"You planning a patrol run tonight?" She hovered by the door.

"Of course. As soon as you leave." He smiled because she didn't seem in a hurry to go. He had no business asking, but—"Dinner with your mom?"

"Mm-hm." She ducked outside.

Dayna never used whole words when she lied, and she only lied when she was trying not to hurt someone. He was still watching her drive away when the phone rang. The caller ID said it was Julia Pelletier, Dayna's mother. An ice-cream-sundae grin split his face. Maybe Dayna was heading to her folks' house after all.

He answered with a cheerful, "Hi, Mrs. Pelletier. Dayna just left."

Julia's voice was brittle, same as always, but that didn't blunt his enthusiasm. Her words, on the other hand, hurt like bee stings.

"I couldn't reach her cell, and I was hoping to catch her before she left for her date. Guess I'm too late."

"Yup." Marcel was proud of the nonchalant quality of his voice. "Who's it with?" Damn, why the hell did he ask?

"Her new young man." Her daughter may not have been gloating, but Julia sure was. "Gary Wheeler. You know, the doctor she dumped you for."

CHAPTER FIFTEEN

The night passed more quickly than Marcel had anticipated. He did a patrol run, ending with a trip down Sandpit Road. Blue Horizons was dark. Next door, the lights were on, and Abe's van was parked in the driveway. Could be he and Candy were up late comparing stories. Or maybe they were all talked out and tangled up in each other.

He went home, had a bowl of cereal, and catnapped on top of the covers with his uniform still on. Dispatch let him sleep until 5:15 when three horses galloped down the middle of Meetinghouse Road. The local equestrian club's telephone tree turned up the owner, and volunteers arrived to assist with capture. The sudden influx of helpers, combined with flashing blue lights, sent the horses into a dead run through Jimmy Latham's giant pumpkins. They did three frantic laps of the field dragging the remnants of Jimmy's electric fence before they ran out of yeehaw.

At 5:44, Marcel waved to Dr. Benjamin when they met at the intersection of Old County and Pole Hill. "Foaling at Donovan's!" the vet called out the window.

"Late in the year, isn't it?" Marcel called back.

They shrugged and went on their way. Marcel always felt a kinship with the veterinarian. Neither of them slept on a regular schedule, but they had to perform as if they did.

At 6:08, Martha Henniker's guinea hens planted themselves in the center of Valley Road, all eighteen of them hollering at their reflections in the grille of an eighteen-wheeler. Traffic was tied up a full twenty yards in both directions. Marcel took out the stash of millet he kept in the way-back and tossed a handful in the drainage ditch. The guineas scrabbled after it, and the road returned to its usual state of emptiness.

At 6:24, he got a noise complaint—some idiot was mowing the lawn at the crazy house while normal people were trying to sleep. He turned off Starch Mill onto Sandpit and drove past Candy's house. The plumbing van was gone, and he wondered if it was too early to drop in. Then he thought about Candy and David Cooper and periwinkle blossoms and beheaded Barbie dolls.

What if David Cooper was right about Candy? And who was lying, Candy or Shay? They'd either gone shooting together, and Eric had left with Shay, or they'd had an argument right in Candy's backyard, and Shay had left alone.

Dayna didn't think Shay was lying, and Dayna could see through fiction better than anyone. And hadn't Molly said she'd heard Eric and Candy fighting on the morning of the day he'd died?

Marcel pulled up to Blue Horizons and sat a moment, listening to the sound of Gracie's lawnmower and breathing the smell of pancakes over freshly cut grass. He wondered if Molly still spooned the batter into animal shapes like she did when they were kids. She'd made the best coyote pancakes he'd ever seen, and she was the only one skilled enough to flip a giraffe without breaking its neck.

Thoughts of Dayna niggled at him as he walked to Molly's door. He hadn't gone out with anyone since she and her half of the closet had piled into her Subaru Forester and driven away. Now it seemed he'd spent those months being stupid. Dayna had been honest with him. Her white lie last night was meant to spare his feelings. He was the dope who kept hoping she might change her mind.

That brought him to Molly, pretty as pink mountain laurel and already like part of the family. But the more he thought about asking her out, the more he figured she didn't need a cop on the rebound complicating her life.

Maybe he ought to call that cute nurse. Kate. She was interested. But he doubted she could land a decent punch or flip a giraffe.

Molly met him at the door with plastic gloves on and pancake batter in her hair. "Don't ask," she said. "Walter saw a mosquito on my forehead, and he was worried about Triple E. Come on in."

"It's not a social visit." The smell of melted butter and hot maple syrup reminded him he'd only had cereal for dinner. He hoped Molly couldn't hear his stomach objecting to the oversight. "I've had a noise complaint."

"Chuck Perkins again?" Molly stomped on the corner of carpet that always curled up and tried to trip her. "He's half a mile away. The whippoorwill in his back field is louder."

"I know, but if Gracie could start up her lawnmower a little later, it would go a long way towards keeping the neighborhood happy." He followed Molly into the kitchen. "And you do want happy neighbors. Every couple years everyone gets up in arms about having crazy people live here. It's best to head folks off before they get started."

"Don't say crazy, Marcel. It's not polite." Molly turned on the blender, probably to drown him out while she thought things through. Pancake batter swirled to the top and almost spilled over. He never could figure out how she managed to fill it so close to the brim without splattering the cabinets.

Her fingers slipped when she hit the *off* switch, and a fat blob of batter sailed into the air and ended up on her face. Marcel bit back a chuckle.

"Okay, fine, it wasn't Walter," she admitted as she wiped herself clean on a paper towel. "Go ahead and laugh at me."

That was the great thing about Molly—she meant what she said. He laughed so hard, he nearly doubled over. "You look cute with pancake mix in your hair," he said, gasping a little. "Don't be in a hurry to wash it out."

She dipped her fingers into the blender and flicked a glob in his direction.

"Hey! That's assaulting an officer." He grabbed the sink sprayer and put on his best police face. "Stop, or I'll be forced to shoot."

Molly giggled and bent to wipe up the floor. "Okay, I give up. Take me into custody."

He hadn't planned it, but the next thing he knew he was hugging her, and she was clinging to him like a scared kitten. He was pretty sure the way her shoulders were shaking had nothing to do with laughing.

"Hey, what's the matter?" He slipped his thumb under her chin and tipped her face up. "Are you okay?"

She nodded, but the tears in her eyes said otherwise. "I just need a hug." She burrowed into his shirt. "I'll be fine in a minute."

"Is it Gracie?"

She sighed into his chest. "When she got up this morning, she started right out confessing to Eric's murder again. I think you're gonna have to talk to her."

99

"No problem." He patted the swale between her shoulder blades, stopped when he realized he was treating her like a baby in need of burping. "It's not as if Gracie owns a gun, and she was delirious when Eric was killed."

"I know that, but she's convinced she did it. You know how she gets." Molly hugged him harder for an instant before she stepped back. Funny how he missed her when she pulled away.

She rinsed her gloves beneath the tap and flicked water onto the griddle. Droplets skittered across the hot surface, hissing like baby snappers.

"You still check the temperature with water, even with a fancy griddle and a built-in thermostat?"

"Of course." She poured out six perfect pancakes before spooning extra batter into the space at the griddle's edge. Marcel leaned over her shoulder and let out a whistle. She'd made a giraffe with an impossibly long neck.

"You'll never flip it."

"Will too."

The sound of Gracie's lawnmower got louder. A moment later, she and her pink ball cap raced past the window.

"Where was she mowing?" Marcel squinted through the glass. Gracie had come from well beyond the yard. "The lawns were done when I drove in, but I could hear the tractor."

"She's been working on that field out back. Eric used to raise nursery stock there, but Gracie says it's nothing but weeds now." Molly flipped all six pancakes, one at a time. They were golden brown and fluffing up fast, but a couple had landed on top of one another. She maneuvered the spatula under the giraffe and flicked her wrist. Only half of the giraffe turned over.

"You sure you're okay?" Marcel took the spatula from her. With an awkward flip, he turned over the second half of the broken giraffe. Once he'd managed to butt the two pieces up against one another, he glued them together with extra batter.

"I'm not entirely okay, but it's nothing I don't deserve." Molly peeled off her right glove and held up her hand. The color of her knuckles reminded him of Concord grapes.

"Ouch! Is that from hittin' Jack?"

"Uh-huh."

"Did you put ice on it?" Marcel cupped her hand and gently flexed her fingers. "Got a bandage?"

"Of course. In the first aid kit by the sink."

He grabbed frozen peas from the freezer and took the dish cloth from the sink. Once he'd wrapped the fabric loosely around her knuckles, he tucked the bag of peas on top. Finally, he wrapped the whole thing with an elastic bandage and pinned it in place.

"If you'd done this last night, it wouldn't be so swollen this morning."

"I suppose. It's not as if I have a lot of experience hittin' people."

"True." He picked up the spatula from the counter and gave it an appraising flick. "Let me make the rest of the pancakes, will ya? I still remember how."

"But you only make round ones." She looked as if she was trying not to laugh. Her nose wiggled like a rabbit.

He slipped the pancakes Molly had made onto a plate, then added them to a platter of twelve already keeping warm in the oven. The dozen she'd made earlier looked better than the six she'd made while he was watching. Most of them were shaped like animals.

"Here goes." He poured another batch onto the griddle. They weren't spaced perfectly, and a couple ran together and made something that looked like a snowman, but they smelled as good as he remembered. "I guess that'll have to do," he said. "Go get the boarders. Tell 'em breakfast is served."

A moment later Jillian and Walter filed into the kitchen and took their places at the wide wooden table. Marcel placed the platter of pancakes in the center, feeling more useful than he had in months. Walter ran back to the dining room and dragged a spare chair to the head of the table. When he took his seat, he placed his Captain America shield between himself and Marcel.

Charlotte came in walking toe-to-heel and grabbed the glued-together giraffe from the countertop along with a pancake that looked a lot like a cat. Gracie arrived last. Molly hushed her as they walked in together, but Gracie wasn't easily silenced.

"I already told you. He's dead. I did it. What's for breakfast?"

"Pancakes," Molly answered, "with buttered maple syrup and blueberry compote. And we have a fruit salad on the side."

Gracie stopped beside her chair and stared at Marcel. "Has he come to arrest me?"

"Of course not." Molly smiled encouragement. "He just wants to hear what you have to say."

Jillian searched the platter until she found three identical round pancakes. She placed them equidistant from one another on her plate. "What happened to Eric?" she asked. "Did they come for him?"

"Did who come for him?" Marcel asked.

"Them!" Jillian pointed to the ceiling.

"Dead," Gracie said. "I killed him."

"Stop and think about it, Gracie," Marcel tried to explain. "There's no reason to think you killed Eric. You were a mile away in a tree stand when he died."

"Then I must have killed him before that." Gracie filled her plate with fresh fruit and spooned blueberry compote over it. "And I'm not wild about butter in the syrup."

"I thought you were making bacon today," Walter complained. He'd taken an elephant pancake, but he pushed it to the edge of his plate and cut into a plain round one. "Too pretty to eat," he said, pointing to the elephant.

"Not everyone has strong teeth," Molly said. "Bacon is too tough."

"Mine are fine, and I'm the oldest." Charlotte bit the giraffe's head off. "Why did Gracie kill Eric? Was he angry that she mowed his field?"

"Dead bodies are a breeding ground for disease," Walter said. "Eric ought to be embalmed, and soon."

"You know I don't like pancakes. I like waffles," Gracie said. "And I have no idea why I killed him. Just did."

"Well that doesn't make a bit of sense," Walter cut in.

"I agree." Jillian had placed a teaspoon of ketchup in the center of each pancake. "Gracie always ate pancakes before."

"I thought you liked my pancakes," Molly said. "I have plain syrup in the fridge. Would you rather have that?"

"Is it real maple or Mrs. Butterworth's?" Charlotte asked.

"Oh, I do hope it's real," Gracie said. "And of course I killed him. He said I did."

"Can we all just settle down?" Marcel pleaded. "Gracie, what makes you think you killed Eric?"

"He said so."

"When did you talk to him?"

Gracie stuffed cantaloupe into her mouth and struggled to talk around it. "The night he died," she said, smacking her lips, "he looked right at me, and he said, 'I'm dead, Gracie. You've killed me.'"

Marcel relaxed. This was nothing more than Gracie's usual confusion. "You couldn't have spoken to Eric if he was already dead. Dead people don't have a lot to say."

Gracie snorted. "There are some things you just don't understand, Officer." She took another bite of melon and chewed with her mouth open. "And I can so eat bacon. Try me."

CHAPTER SIXTEEN

Marcel left Blue Horizons at 8:30, drove fifty feet, and turned into Candy Thompson's driveway. Scout met him on the steps and stood with his paws against Marcel's thighs, waving his tail so hard, his hind end nearly collapsed. Marcel rubbed the beagle's ears with a "Hey, buddy, buddy, buddy," before straightening up and ringing the bell.

Candy answered the door dressed in a robe that fit like a sack of whole oats. Her hair was down and obviously hadn't seen a brush. It hung limp and tangled to an inch beyond her shoulder blades, and its usual pale yellow was faded as parchment. Her ankle socks spelled out No Nonsense.

"Hi, Marcel, I expect you want to talk about Eric. Everybody else does." Her face was puffy, and she had yesterday's mascara smudged beneath her eyes. "Come on in. I've got coffee."

"I'm very sorry for your loss." He knew the words didn't mean much, but they did cause her shoulders to stiffen when he followed her to the kitchen for the second time in three days. "I need to ask you to come down to the station to answer some more questions, but I thought maybe we could talk here first."

"Won't that get you in trouble?" Candy rummaged through her cupboard and pulled out a Holstein-patterned coffee cup. She set it on the counter next to a mug that said Pass the Bong.

"Maybe a little." Marcel sat on a plastic chair and rested his feet on the floor. Harold the cat climbed into his lap.

"I appreciate the kindness, Marcel, but don't do anything dumb on my account." Candy carried the Holstein cup to the table along with a napkin and plastic spoon. "Extra cream and sugar, right?"

Marcel shook his head. "No thanks. If I have any more caffeine I'm not sure I'll be able to pay attention."

"Have two cups, then." She didn't smile. Instead her lips trembled. "Abe left right after you did that night you questioned us both, so I was here alone from around 9:00 on. I assume you want to know where I was when Eric died."

"Alone?"

"Yes, alone." Candy's hands shook when she set the mug on the table. She splattered coffee on the clean placemat and stared at it as if it were mocking her. "Abe offered to lie for me."

"He what?"

"He's such a doof." She picked up her napkin and laid it carefully over the spill. "We were up past two a.m. last night with him trying to convince me it would be better to say he was here, but if you're gonna find the person who did this, I figure you need the truth."

"Can anyone verify your whereabouts?"

Her eyes welled up, but she managed not to cry. "Scout and Harold, I guess. I doubt the word of a dog and a cat will carry a whole lot of weight." She looked out the window toward Blue Horizons. "I even called Molly to ask if she remembered seein' me, or if she noticed whether I had my lights on. But they had other things on their minds."

Gracie, of course. Molly would have been too worried about her missing boarder to notice what her next-door neighbor was doing. And now Candy had lost her husband, and she'd be investigated. Normal procedure, but it still seemed wrong. "Thank you for your honesty, Candy. You always were brave."

"Not as brave as you think." She reached for a box at the center of the table, pulled off the lid, and withdrew a Glock 17. When she handed it to Marcel, she kept the muzzle pointed toward the floor and her finger well away from the trigger. "I figure you'll want to check my gun."

Candy always looked straight into a person's right eye, and Marcel had never been able to hide anything from her. She was the one who'd said, "Hallelujah! You and Dayna did the deed!" the morning after Senior Prom. He still couldn't figure out how she'd known.

He pulled out a pen and used it to hook the gun from her hands. Probably ought to thank her again, but the words seemed wanting.

"Do you have any idea where Eric might have gone that night?" He tried to watch Candy's eyes as closely as she watched his, but he knew he'd never have her talent for sifting through fodder for needles of truth. Must be a woman thing.

When Candy went pale, the spots of mascara looked even blacker. Her next sip of coffee made her gulp. "I don't know what Eric was up to, Marcel, but I can tell you it paid a whole lot better than anything else he's ever done."

She pushed her chair back and got to her feet, faltered a bit and gripped the table's edge. Marcel reached out to steady her, but she straightened before he managed to be helpful.

"You okay?" Of course she wasn't. How could she be? But she nodded anyway.

"Come with me, Marcel. There's somethin' I probably ought to show you." She headed toward the hallway, resolute as an old house in a wind storm.

Marcel set the cat on the floor. Harold growled up at him before trotting off after Candy, down the crooked hallway and into the master bedroom. There was something creepy about crossing the threshold of a dead man's private space.

Not all that private, though, was it? The blankets were rumpled, and clothing was strewn across the floor, but Candy didn't seem to care. She squatted, reached into the closet, and pushed aside four shoe boxes. Then she sank down onto the bare wood and dragged out a small trunk. It was heavy enough to scratch the pine flooring as it ground over the surface, and Marcel ducked down to help her.

She closed her eyes. Her chest lifted with an overlong breath before she raised the lid.

"You're not gonna believe this, Marcel. Abe found it last night and damn, I think it might be real."

When she opened the trunk, Marcel's mouth fell open, and he couldn't close it. He reached out and picked up one roll, just to be sure his eyes weren't playing tricks on him. There had to be hundreds more, a whole trunk full of what looked like American Eagles, twenty-two-carat gold coins. He'd bought one himself and watched with excitement as his investment grew, but he only had the one.

"Crap, Candy, with the price of gold these days, you probably have half a million dollars there."

"I know, right?" She tipped her face up, and the tears in her eyes finally leaked out. "I can't imagine what Eric's been involved in. He's done some stupid things, but they never amounted to anything. This looks like—"

"Like enough to change your life."

"No, Marcel. It looks like enough to get killed over." Her face scrunched up, and she sort of crumpled toward the gold. "I know you think I'm awful, cheatin' on Eric the way I did. But at least I never gave up on him, not like some people."

Marcel winced. He was one of those people. "Candy, I—"

"Maybe all Eric needed was some direction; did ya ever think of that? Maybe if his best friend had stood by him, he'd still be alive."

Candy always said what she meant, and there was no escaping her meaning. Marcel's "I'm sorry for the way things turned out," didn't begin to describe the way his insides toppled in on one another.

"Too late now." Candy turned away. "You people don't seem to understand how much I loved Eric. He just hurt me so bad so many times, I guess I wanted to hurt him back."

He wished she hadn't said that—motive spelled out and offered voluntarily. Marcel squatted beside her and put a hand on her shoulder. It was warm as sunburn. "Look, Candy, up until now we've just been having a conversation. But next time we talk, it'll be official, just like yesterday when Chief Farrell and that detective fellow questioned you. You probably shouldn't say anything without a lawyer."

"Are ya gonna arrest me?" She sounded so beaten, Marcel hated to say what had to be said.

"I doubt we have enough to charge you, but the way Eric treated you, together with the money, gives you a hell of a motive."

She looked up at him through wet eyes. "Thanks for tellin' me the truth. Like I already said, I want everything out in the open. I'll get a lawyer, but I'll still tell you anything, anything at all."

"I know you will, but you need to listen to your counsel and look after yourself, too." He gestured to the gold. "I'm gonna have to turn this over to Detective Clark. You might not be safe keeping it here, anyway."

"If someone comes looking for it, and it's not here, do you think I'll be any safer, then?"

"Good point." Set a tenth of a mile back from a dirt road with porch sliders and woods all around, Candy's house was easily broken into and tough to secure. "Can you stay with your mom for a few days?" Amanda's house was brand new, even had a fancy alarm system.

"I suppose." Candy got to her feet. She took a tissue from a box on her dresser and blew her nose. "If you'll excuse me, I'm gonna splash some water on my face. Then I'll pack a few things." She walked into the bathroom, not waiting for a reply. "Tell Chief Farrell he's welcome to search the place. I've already written him a note and signed it all nice and legal. And you can take a house key if ya want."

Candy was being cooperative. Maybe too cooperative. But she'd always had courage, along with more strength and optimism than anybody he knew. "Thanks, Candy. That's a big help."

"Give me a minute, and I'll grab one end of that trunk," she called through the door. "It's too heavy for one person."

"Maybe for a skinny girl." Marcel hefted the trunk. It felt like maybe thirty pounds.

He waited while Candy packed an overnight bag and then shoved a hissing Harold into a cat carrier. Scout followed close at her heels, making little muttering sounds and doing a hopeful dance. She bent low to stroke his chin.

"I know it's a lot to ask," she said when they reached the driveway, "but can you look after Scout for me? You know how my mom is with dogs."

"I remember she never liked you keeping pets when you lived at Blue Horizons." Amanda had kept the place pristine, ran it like the business it was. Seemed Molly thought of it more as a home.

"Her new house is way nicer, and Scout's always stealin' her stuff and droppin' it in the pool." Her gaze slid sideways. "Scout's good company, Marcel. Seems maybe you could use some."

Candy always knew how to cut to the heart of things. He reached down and gave the dog a pat. "Shouldn't be a problem."

"Thanks, Marcel."

The cat yowled when Candy loaded him into her car. Marcel could still hear him complaining when she turned onto Sandpit Road. With a bit of coaxing, Scout hopped onto the passenger seat and stood with his paws on the dash, eyes fixed on the spot where Candy had vanished from view.

Marcel peeked into the trunk one last time, just to be sure the gold was real and not some sort of brain stutter caused by too much work and too little sleep. He thought of the Eric he used to know, tow-headed and scrawny, the most accident-prone kid in his class.

That was before Eric had started smoking pot with Molly's uncle, and before he'd been caught dealing. Almost went down for it, too, and would have if Officer Lyman hadn't lost the evidence.

Aw well. Aside from the occasional drunk and disorderly, Eric had cleaned up his act. At least that's what he'd told people, and Marcel had believed him. Until now.

CHAPTER SEVENTEEN

Gracie slipped out Blue Horizons's back door just as Marcel left Candy Thompson's house. She watched him turn left onto Sandpit Road, and she caught a glimpse of Scout's face pressed against the side window of his SUV. Where was Marcel going with Candy's beagle?

None of her business, of course, but she did hold her breath, just for a moment. She reminded herself that Scout wasn't hers. Most likely, he'd be back before she had a chance to miss him.

All that nonsense about following the beagle was a bunch of hooey, anyway. And her daughter being alive . . . doubtful, no matter how much the ghost insisted and no matter how badly Gracie wanted to believe it might be true. Ghosts lied. Hannah would say anything in order to trick an old woman into doing her bidding.

With a sigh that was two parts frustration to one part wishful thinking, Gracie ducked into the garage. She'd nearly finished mowing Eric's field before breakfast, but there was a patch of weeds that refused to surrender, and she wanted to pulverize the woody stems that had sprung up in her wake.

The moment she climbed aboard the mower, a cold vapor brushed her cheek. Darn ghost. Why did the dead always butt in when there was something interesting to do?

"I have a job for you." Hannah appeared beside her, translucent in a simple white frock and calf-high work boots. "It won't take long, and you shouldn't be mowing today, anyway."

"Why not?"

"You just got out of the hospital. You almost died."

"Almost doesn't count."

"Once you're dead, you're dead." The ghost gave her a look that was probably meant to be intimidating. "Don't rush it. There's no going back."

"The last time I listened to you, I ended up drugged and violated. I think I'll take my chances with the lawnmower." Gracie stomped the clutch and turned the key. The mower rumbled, coughed, and gradually evened to a steady roar.

Hannah planted herself in the mower's path, hands up and palms facing outward. "Perhaps I've not made myself clear. I said no."

Gracie hit the gas. Her head snapped back as she tore through the ghost, shivering at the sensation of ice water and electricity. She blew a raspberry in Hannah's direction, roared across the lawn, and then veered into the woods. The deer path she followed was barely wide enough to allow the mower to pass. Mountain laurel reached out and snagged her clothing and hair. Head down, she bulled her way through.

Moments later, she burst from the woods into a two-acre field. The dead girl stood atop a hillock at the center of the expanse. Mounds of cherry-red ringlets corkscrewed around her face, haloed by morning sun. She looked sweet, worried, and determined.

Gracie jammed the clutch to the floor. The mower jerked to a stop. She squinted up at Hannah and tried to say something polite. "What, exactly, do you want me to do for you?"

"Finally." The redhead smiled down at her, once again looking more angelic than annoying. "We need Molly's help finding your daughter. You have to talk to her."

"I can't tell Molly about you." Couldn't tell anyone, not unless she wanted to be locked up. "She'll think I'm nuts."

"You are nuts."

"Says who?" Gracie blasted the mower across the field, kicking up a spray of mangled weeds. She shouted, "You wanna see nuts? I'll show you nuts." Darn ghost needed to learn manners, ought to try asking people rather than insulting and threatening them.

Hannah vanished from the hill and reappeared, floating backwards ahead of the lawnmower and waving her arms. Uppity little thing. She wasn't easy to ignore, but Gracie did her best to look past her and focus on mowing; easy, even with a dead redhead in her way. All she had to do was keep the outside tires in the inside track made by her previous pass. And rocks—she had to drive around rocks.

Hannah continued to glide ahead of her, arms now folded across her chest. "If you don't talk to Molly right now, I'll make you."

Interesting. It might be fun to go limp and make Hannah do all the work. On the other hand, being dragged around by a ghost was uncomfortable at best, and what if someone saw? Molly would assume there was some sort of delusion involved, and she might call Dr. Useless.

Gracie sighed. "You don't give up, do you?"

"Not when someone's life is at stake." Hannah's face flickered in worry. As far as Gracie could tell, the dead girl wasn't faking her concern.

Nor was she saying everything she knew, though, and that was unacceptable. Hannah could, at the very least, identify this person who was going to die.

"Who is it I'm supposed to save?"

"I told you. It's someone I love. Very much."

"Not good enough."

Hannah folded her arms and scowled. "It's all you're getting."

"Then I guess we're done."

"What?" The dead girl could shriek when she wanted to. "You have no choice!"

Gracie managed to ignore the way her heart jackrabbited against her ribs. "So what if you get me locked up again? I'm done helping unless you tell me who it is I'm supposed to save." It had better be somebody worthwhile. Not a politician or a lawyer or a psychiatrist.

"She's . . ." The ghost was wavering. She seemed less belligerent and a tiny bit more vulnerable. Good.

"Who?"

Hannah clasped her arms around her chest. "It's my great-granddaughter."

Family, then—no wonder the ghost was so concerned. She was lucky, though, to have a great-granddaughter. Some folks had no family at all.

"I'll talk to Molly as soon as I'm done with this field." No point getting locked up before she had a chance to finish mowing.

"No!" The ghost probably would have spit if she were flesh and blood. "Now!"

"In an hour." Gracie gunned the motor and blew through the ghost, gritting her teeth against the cold. "Darn ghosts and their portable freezers. I should have brought beer."

"Ninety-nine bottles of beer on the wall, ninety nine bottles of beer. Take one down, pass it around, ninety-eight bottles of beer on the wall. Ninety-eight bottles . . ."

"You can't be serious."

"of beer on the wall . . ."

"Stop singing!

"Ninety-eight bottles of beer . . ."

"You're not gonna stop until I give in, right?"

"Ya take one down . . ."

"Fine!" Gracie stuck her tongue out even though she knew it would do no good. "Same old games," she said. "You hardly tell me anything, and I'm supposed to take all the risks." She up-shifted to third. "One more lap, and I'll call it quits."

"And you pass it around, ninety-seven bottles . . ."

"Fine!" Gracie spun the wheel and sped back toward the deer path, shouting, "If I get sent to St. Fillan's over this, I'm gonna make you pay."

"Oooh, I'm scared." Hannah shook herself in mock dread. "You could always lop off my head again."

"What do you mean *again?*"

"Nothing." Hannah turned away and drifted toward Blue Horizons. Her hair seemed duller now, as if part of her fire had been doused. "Let's go see Molly," she muttered. "There's a lot to do, and we're running out of time."

With Scout leading the way, Marcel walked across the parking lot to the Falls Police Station. Carrying Candy's trunk had his back complaining, and the beagle's leash had already burned the tender skin between his fingers.

Chief Farrell was in his office, and he wasn't alone. A man sat across from him, back to the door, profile to the fishbowl window. Must be that detective fellow Dayna was so hot on.

And why not? He certainly was good-looking in a hunky, athletic way, with a broad chest and shoulders crowned by a face that could have belonged to a Sears underwear model. The thought had Marcel standing straighter and sucking in those extra ten pounds he'd never been able to lose. No wonder Dayna had that all-you-can-eat-at-the-Maple-Shack look on her face.

He set Candy's trunk on the counter, let Scout off his leash, and then tapped on the fishbowl glass. Farrell looked tired and strained, but the detective waved and smiled like the Grand Marshall at the Greenville Pots and Pans parade. His eyes were green. Emerald green. Like the goddamn storybook character who always gets the girl.

Great. Marcel returned the detective's smile, pointed to the chest of gold, and made a hand gesture meant to invite the two of them into the hallway. Chief Farrell countered by waving Marcel inside. So he hefted the trunk for what he hoped would be the last time, balanced Candy's gun atop the lid, and headed for the Chief's door.

This ought to earn him a few brownie points. He couldn't wait to see what the fancy State Police Detective had to say about half a million in American gold.

"You must be Marcel Trudeau." The man held out a hand. Marcel set the trunk on a metal table before accepting the gesture. The handshake was firm, and the detective made no effort to crush his fingers in a show of superiority. A good thing.

"Detective Clark, I presume." Why did things sound so good when James Bond said them and so corny coming out of his own mouth?

"Call me Reggie. Everyone else does." Reggie smirked at Scout. "Yours?"

Marcel supposed beagles weren't the most masculine dog a guy could have, but he felt a little bit insulted, anyway. "Looking after him for a friend." No point mentioning that friend was Candy Thompson.

Reggie's attention had already shifted to the trunk. "What have you brought us?"

Marcel stepped back so he could address them both. "I stopped in to see Candy this morning." Chief Farrell started to interrupt, but Marcel kept talking. "I was next door anyway, discussing a noise complaint, and I figured I could ask Candy in person if she wouldn't mind stopping by here today."

"And?" Normally Chief Farrell was easy-going. Right now, though, he didn't look any too flexible.

"She's happy to come down at a time convenient to the detective here. She'll be staying with her mom, so I have her cellphone number." Marcel tore a sheet from his notepad and placed it on the Chief's desk.

"She gave me her house key," Marcel continued. "We have permission to search the place without a warrant. I have it in writing." He pulled Candy's letter from his vest pocket. The key made a dull clunk when he set the envelope down. "And she volunteered her firearm." He took the evidence bag from atop the trunk and set the gun beside the phone number and key.

"What's in the trunk?" Farrell looked a little less rigid.

"You're not gonna believe it." Marcel reached into his pocket for the pair of gloves he'd stashed there in preparation, put them on, and took hold of the trunk's lid. "Here goes."

Reggie did a drum roll on the edge of the desk. Chief Farrell looked as if he might be holding back an eye roll, but Marcel cracked a smile as he lifted the cover and took out the roll he'd picked up earlier. "I did touch this one, and I'm real sorry about that. But the rest haven't been handled by me."

"Is that—" Farrell raked fingers through his comb-over and back down through a neatly trimmed calico beard. Reggie seemed at a loss for words.

"Looks to be about thirty pounds of American Gold Eagles. Abe found them in Eric's closet, and Candy thinks they're real."

"Why did you bring it here?" Reggie was tough to read. His question might be some sort of a test.

"I thought maybe Eric got shot over the money, and somebody ought to at least look for prints, fibers, that sort of thing. And I thought if someone came looking for it, Candy might be in trouble." He hoped he didn't sound like the rookie he undoubtedly was. "So I suggested she stay with her mom until we know what's goin' on."

"Good plan." Reggie returned the grin that darn near split Marcel's face in two. "There's a good chance Candy won't be getting this gold back, you know, not if Eric obtained it illegally."

"Ill-gotten gain," the Chief said, nodding. "The Falls PD might even get a piece of it."

Marcel had forgotten about that. New Hampshire had what he believed to be reasonable laws when it came to seizing a criminal's assets. But Candy—while her husband had occasionally scuffled with the law, she'd never been anything but honest.

Didn't seem fair that finding the gold and turning it in had made her a more interesting person of interest.

Reggie was still smiling. "How 'bout you set up another interview with Candy for me. She seems to trust you."

"I trust her, too."

"You sure?" This time it was the Chief asking. His tone was sympathetic, but firm. "Just because you grew up together doesn't mean you know a person."

Marcel hated that he'd had a moment of doubt. "I think I know Candy pretty well, but you're right, I guess. We still have to follow the evidence and go where it leads."

Reggie looked impressed. Marcel wished he'd meant what he said. He *knew* Candy, and no way in hell did she kill anyone.

"What do you think of Grace Ouellette's confession?" Chief Farrell wasn't one to let him stand around contemplating. "Dayna told me you planned to check it out."

"Near as I can tell, Gracie had a dream. I don't think it's worth pursuing."

Farrell shook his head. "You know her brain works differently than yours and mine. We have no way of knowing what she might have witnessed, or even done."

"Gracie?"

"Yes, Gracie. You have to follow up. Check out that tree stand where you found her. Treat it as a crime scene. If you find anything worth the detective's attention, secure the area and wait for someone who knows what they're doing."

"Will do." Gracie's involvement was unlikely. Even if she'd been delusional enough to shoot somebody, she couldn't have hiked to Echo Lake in that storm, and then dragged Eric's head up onto coyote rock.

On the other hand, she wasn't opposed to handling what she thought was a human head. Checking the tree stand made a certain amount of sense, and Marcel didn't mind taking a walk with Scout on a perfect summer day.

He didn't waste time—drove straight to the trailhead and hiked to the top of Bald Hill. When he reached the stand, it looked pretty much the way he'd left it, except now the sun was shining, and Gracie wasn't there with skin like ice, rambling on about somebody named Hannah. He put on gloves before heading up the metal climbing sticks. Once on the platform, he sat for a moment and enjoyed the view.

Scout nosed through mountain laurel, invisible but for his white-tipped tail. The valley stretched below them, a gathering of pine, oak, maple, and ash, surrounding what looked like a field of clouds. Probably raspberries, or maybe high-bush blueberries, double-wrapped in reflective netting to save them from hungry birds.

This would be a great place to sit and watch over that crop. From atop the tree stand, with a decent rifle, he could pick off starlings one by one before they ate a single berry.

If he had the stomach for killing.

With a sigh, he rolled Gracie's blanket and foam mattress and then tied them with twine. He removed the snap from the clasp of the wooden chest and opened the lid, then absently shined his flashlight over the neat rows of canned goods.

The familiar shape made his breath catch. Illuminated in a narrow beam were seven cans of beef stew, two cans of tamales, and one nine mm Baby Eagle.

He sat for a long time, wishing the ache in his chest would give up and go numb. This could be the murder weapon. Dayna would be dancing a jig. But all he could think about was Molly's face and, worse than that, the plucky old woman whose life he'd saved.

He wondered if she remembered she had a gun.

CHAPTER EIGHTEEN

"She'll think I've unspooled." Gracie slowed to a shuffle as she and Hannah headed down the hallway toward the sound of singing. Molly was belting out a happy melody. That gal was in high spirits today, had been ever since Officer Trudeau's breakfast visit.

Hannah pushed Gracie toward Walter's bedroom, whispering even though no one was likely to overhear. "Hurry up. Talk to her."

"What am I supposed to say?" Gracie dug her heels into the carpet. Hannah pushed harder.

"Just tell her the truth."

"No." The word was more mime than speech; what if Molly heard her talking to ghosts? That wouldn't go well. Gracie balanced on Walter's threshold now, careful not to cross his invisible line. He was in the living room, but if she allowed a toe past his doorway, he'd know. Then Molly would be all day bleaching the furniture and steam-cleaning the rug.

With her palms braced against the door jamb, Gracie cleared her throat. The singing stopped, and Molly turned to face her.

Molly wore clean slippers with baggies over them. Her clothes were white and smelled of bleach, and an accordion surgical mask covered her nose and mouth. Gloved hands and a hair net completed the picture. Molly's adherence to Walter's rules made her the only person allowed in his room.

"Can you spare a minute?" Gracie looked past Molly at the perfect hospital corners on Walter's Captain America sheets.

"Sure. What's up?"

"Can we talk?" Asking for help wasn't something Gracie did often. She supposed she and Molly had that in common.

"I was just thinking I ought to take a break and have some apple pie." Most of Molly's face was hidden by the mask, but her forehead smiled. "Want to join me?"

"Depends. Got ice cream?"

"Vanilla bean." Molly's eyes sparkled while Gracie's heart pounded. What if Molly thought she'd gone around the bend? What if she called Dr. Useless again? Head down, Gracie walked toward the kitchen on rubber legs. Molly and her baggies crinkled behind her.

Gracie sat in silence while Molly pulled off her mask and gloves, and prepared two plates of pie and ice cream. She slid a serving in front of Gracie and then sat across from her.

As always, the pie was very good. Rivulets of ice cream melted over the crust and formed creamy curlicues in the baked apples, soft and caramel sweet. Perfection was meant to be savored. Conversation could wait.

The dead redhead fidgeted like a little girl on a Sunday pew, obviously unhappy with Gracie's delaying tactics. She hissed between her teeth, "Get on with it," all air and no bite.

Gracie ignored the ghost and nibbled her pie, determined to enjoy what might be her last slice for a long time. No telling what would happen once she told Molly about Hannah and her demands.

"I have an idea." Hannah sat taller, and a grin spread across her face. "You don't need to mention me. Just tell her you remembered something you'd forgotten. That way, you'll sound less crazy."

"Why didn't I think of that?"

"Think of what?" Molly wiped ice cream from the side of her mouth. "Are you finally gonna ask me something? Or are you holding out for another slice?"

Another slice sounded good. Gracie tried to look at Molly, but her gaze skittered to Hannah. The ghost's smug expression was irritating. And what if she was lying?

My daughter can't be alive.

Hannah rolled her eyes. "Yes she is."

"It's impossible."

"What's impossible?" The lines of Molly's forehead deepened. Gracie looked at the tablecloth and counted the blue and white checks.

"Just say it." The dead girl leaned closer. "Now."

Gracie's spine tingled. "No."

Hannah opened her mouth wide enough to swallow her fist. "Ninety-nine bottles of beer on the wall . . ."

"Shut up!" Gracie clapped her hand over her own mouth.

"I didn't say anything." Molly leaned across the table. "Are you okay, Gracie? Do I need to call Dr. Useless for you?"

"Ninety-nine bottles of beer . . ."

"I had a baby. I was told she died at birth." Gracie said the words as quickly as she could, but they still hurt. A lot.

"Oh, Gracie!" Molly reached across the table and grabbed her hand. "I can't imagine what that must be like."

The checks on the tablecloth blurred, *like it happened yesterday.* Gracie held Molly's hand tighter than she meant to. "The thing is, I swear I heard that baby cry."

"You think you were lied to?"

Molly sounded angry and, for reasons she couldn't explain, Gracie began to shiver. "They said I was crazy."

"They took your baby because you were mentally ill?"

"Maybe, maybe not. How would I know?"

"How could you not know?"

Gracie shrugged. "I forget everything, and I make stuff up, too. So I'm never sure what's real."

"But you want to find out."

"I don't know. Would you?"

"Of course I would." Molly leaned closer. "How can I help?"

"I don't know where to start."

"Neither do I." Molly's hand was steady and comforting, and her touch made Gracie feel a little less hopeless. "But I'll find out."

"How?"

"Well . . ." Molly smiled, and the sparkle returned to her eyes. "Let's ask Marcel. Maybe he'll know what to do."

An hour after he'd found the gun in Gracie's tree stand, Marcel pulled up in front of Blue Horizons. Reggie Clark had been far more accommodating than expected. Marcel was to question Gracie and, as long as she remained cooperative, she wouldn't have to appear at the station. Not yet.

The Chief, though, had called to clarify: "You know Gracie better than anyone on the force. Feel her out. Use your discretion."

The meaning was clear. If anything Gracie said caused Marcel to think she might be involved in murder, he'd have to place her under arrest. The thought didn't sit well. Molly would flip. He might have to call for backup.

Scout had his paws on the door a moment before Marcel's knock. Molly answered the door with a grin that shone like sunshine. Marcel wished he didn't have to say the six words he had in mind.

"I'm here to talk to Gracie."

The smile went into hiding. "What's this about?"

He looked past her toward the kitchen. Gracie might already be stuffing cans into her pockets. "Can I come in?"

"I don't know, Of-fi-cer." Molly said each syllable separately, making it clear she'd switched from his friend to Gracie's advocate. "Do you have a warrant?"

"C'mon, Mols. I just need to talk to her."

"About?"

Marcel turned a little to the side so his words would land more softly. "I found a gun in her tree stand. The caliber matches the murder weapon."

"You can't possibly have it processed yet." Molly knew the ropes. As a kid, she'd hung out with Officer Lyman while her uncle slept off a Jack Daniels dinner in a holding cell. Old Lyman always bought pizza with extra anchovies, and little Molly had eavesdropped on enough conversations to have a basic understanding of the inner workings of the Falls PD.

"The Staties have it." He lowered his voice. "One of their detectives is heading up the investigation. He's letting me talk to Gracie, since I already have a relationship with her, but if that gun comes back with her prints, he'll have her brought in."

"He'd do that?" Molly looked a whole lot more surprised than she ought to.

"He sorta has to, Mols."

"Gracie doesn't own a gun." Doubt flickered across Molly's face, but it vanished behind her usual determination. "Someone else must have put it there."

"Who?" Marcel had thought the same thing, but it seemed like wishful thinking. "Who even knew she was there?"

"Well, I guess that's where your detective ought to focus his attention. If you figure out who knows about Gracie and her tree stand, maybe that'll give you an idea who put the gun there."

"I've been trying to work it out in my head," he said, feeling useless. "Those woods are deserted this time of year. Hikers don't want to deal with mosquitoes. The few horseback riders willing to brave the ticks and deer flies stick to the rail trail and run like hell, and the hunters won't be back until fall. There's maybe five people who know about that stand."

"There's more than you think, Marcel, so you have your work cut out for you tracking them all down." Molly joined him outside and pulled the door shut behind her. Scout trotted down the steps and turned toward the backyard.

"I even heard nurses talking about it at the hospital," Molly said. "They all thought it was a hoot and a half, an old woman hiding in a tree."

"But they didn't know *where* it was, did they?"

"Gracie told everyone it was the tallest tree on the highest ridge in Coyne Falls. That means Bald Hill. I think most people could figure it out."

"You may be right." Marcel wanted to rule out Gracie as much as anyone. His gut told him she couldn't have shot Eric. But even he had to acknowledge she was, for lack of a better word, nuts.

"Look, Mols, I don't think Gracie had anything to do with Eric's death. But she might know something, and I need to talk to her."

"Talk to who?" Gracie came up behind them. Her knees were black with garden soil, and her hands looked even worse. Scout leaned against her shins, tail waving.

"I thought you were in your room," Molly said. "What have you been doing?"

"Weeding." Gracie glanced at Marcel. "I figure since Eric's Landscaping Service is pushing up daisies, somebody had better take over for him." She shoved her way past Marcel and Molly and let herself into the house. Scout followed. Molly moved to one side and gave Marcel a quick nod.

He jumped through the door. "Are you up for answering a few questions, Gracie?"

"Of course I am." She climbed onto a stool in front of the kitchen sink and turned on the water. Black dirt ran from her hands over the clean dishes in the drainer. "What do you want to know?"

"Gracie!" Molly scolded. "Can you please do that in the bathroom?"

"It's clean dirt." Gracie held up her hands, touched the tip of her tongue to her palm. "I'd eat off it."

"You told us you saw Eric the night you ran away," Marcel said.

"Yes." Gracie added soap and rubbed her palms together. Gobs of black suds plopped onto a flowered dinner plate.

"Can you tell me more about that?" She'd already claimed that Eric had spoken to her and insisted she'd killed him. But sometimes her memories got all twisted up. Marcel hoped maybe this time she'd manage to get her thoughts a little less tangled. She might even remember when and where that conversation had taken place.

"Gracie, just because you don't have a problem with mud on your dishes, doesn't mean no one else minds." Molly reached past her for a sponge. Gracie gave her hands a final rinse and climbed down from her stool.

"I was standing in a field." Gracie wiped her hands on Molly's white dish towel, leaving behind brown fingerprints. "There was a storm coming. Eric was near the edge of the trees, and all around him were dead weeds. He told me I'd killed him."

"But, Gracie," Marcel explained, "if he were dead, he couldn't have been talking to you."

Gracie clicked her tongue against the roof of her mouth. "Of course he could."

"Okay, then." Might as well do this her way, try to get into the old gal's head. "Can you tell me when you killed him?"

"Must have been sometime before that." Gracie knelt down to rub Scout's head, shrugging as if the answer was obvious.

"And when, exactly, did you talk to him?"

"Right before Molly woke me up."

Relief swept over him like spring runoff. "You were asleep in bed when he talked to you?"

Gracie lifted the beagle's ear and spoke in a carrying whisper. "Isn't that what I've been saying?"

"Yes or no." Just as he'd assumed, she must have dreamed the conversation with Eric.

"Yes." She turned down the hallway and shook her fist at nothing. "And not another word out of you, Hannah."

Molly grabbed Marcel's shoulder, but he shrugged her away and followed.

"Who's Hannah?"

"The darn dead redhead who thinks I'm her personal slave." Gracie stuck out her tongue at an empty corner.

"The one from Echo Lake? The one with no head?"

Gracie looked unsure whether he might be making fun of her. Then she looked worried. "I was just kidding around. I know ghosts aren't real."

She was lying. Marcel could see it in the way her eyes cut off to the side. "Do you own a gun, Gracie?"

"Yes. Would you like to see it?" She swatted at something imaginary, then seemed to catch herself. The *uh-oh* on her face would have been comical if the stakes weren't so high.

"I sure would." Marcel's belly twitched like a horse shaking off a fly.

Gracie shuffled to her bedroom, dragged a ladder-back chair to the closet, and then clambered up. Matted grass fell from her sneaker treads, and she kicked it to the rug. Molly sputtered and headed down the hall. A moment later, she returned with a hand-held vacuum cleaner.

Gracie pulled a chocolate bar from the top shelf along with a shoe box tied up with green baling twine. "I bought this for Candy when she and Amanda lived with us," she said, handing the box to Marcel. "I told her it would keep Harold off the kitchen counters, but she thought it was mean."

Marcel opened the box and took out a bright green plastic squirt gun. He turned it over in his hand. "Thanks, Gracie. Is this your only gun?"

"Yes, Officer." She climbed down from the stool and then plopped onto her bed. She seemed unconcerned, already unpeeling the wrapper from her chocolate bar.

"Do you have any idea how a real gun might have found its way onto your tree stand?"

"No, Officer." Gracie cracked off a piece of chocolate and offered it to Marcel in a dirt-stained hand. He shook his head. With a shrug, she popped it into her mouth.

"You don't seem surprised, though, about a gun being there."

Gracie closed her eyes, and a smile spread across her face. "Well, that stand doesn't belong to me. I was just using it." She licked a smudge of chocolate from the corner of her mouth. "And isn't that what a tree stand is for? Sitting and waiting for something to walk by so you can shoot it?"

"I guess so." Sometimes Gracie was more logical than he expected.

She broke off another square of chocolate and held it to her nose. Her forehead creased. "It's not just me using that stand, you know."

"What makes you think that?" Good old Gracie—she didn't miss much.

"Every time I go up there, some of my cans are missing." She placed the chocolate on her tongue, closed her mouth. Marcel waited until she'd rolled the chocolate around, sighed in bliss, and swallowed.

"Someone was helping himself to my supplies, especially the tamales." She peeled back the foil and took another bite. This time she managed to talk and chew at the same time.

"I'm no policeman, but . . ." Gracie pulled dirty feet onto her bed. "I do love those canned tamales, and it looks to me as if I'm not the only one."

CHAPTER NINETEEN

When Molly hugged Marcel goodbye, she didn't let go right away. The scent of her lilac shampoo and the feel of her body against his, avoiding the parts below the waist, of course, was more pleasant than he'd imagined.

Dayna was a rush of excitement, while Molly was a refuge of calm. Dayna stirred him up in ways he'd never discuss with anyone but himself. But Molly was the sort of person a guy could nod off with and not have to apologize afterwards, even if he drooled. He could picture her head resting on his shoulder while they watched *Iron Man* for the fifteenth time, her 3-D glasses lopsided on her face, one hand holding his, the other—

"How long until you're off duty?"

His heart jumped. "In about an hour." Maybe they could grab a pizza, head into Lebanon and see a movie, talk about something other than Gracie.

Molly's face twisted up, and Marcel jerked himself from romance to reality. "Uh-oh, what's up? How can I help?"

Tears came out of nowhere. He brushed them away, of course—seemed rude not to. Her skin was soft, her freckles darker where they were wet.

"You know how you said I could ask if I needed something?"

"Uh-huh." Definitely not romantic. He felt a little bit shorter and a whole lot less good-looking.

"Could you give me a . . . lift to the hospital? My car's still there, and . . ." She sniffed and looked at the floor.

Molly could stand up to someone twice her size, had endured years of abuse, and had lived on her own at a point in her life when she ought to have had a mother. Why was she coming apart over asking for a ride?

Sometimes women made no sense at all.

"I thought you'd already done it, or I would have offered."

"Your mom was gonna . . . drive me, but she . . . pulled extra duty . . . and I know she'll be . . . tired when she gets home."

He probably ought to hug her again, an A-frame hug like the first. That way he wouldn't have to look at the worry in her eyes. "My mom loves you like a daughter, Mols. She's happy to help you whenever she can."

"I know. I don't want to take advantage."

"So why the cryin'?"

Molly hugged him harder, mumbling into his chest so he could hardly make out the words. "I feel like a . . . failure when I can't take care of things on my own . . . and if I hadn't lost my temper . . . and slugged a man . . . and got myself too worked up to drive home . . . I wouldn't have to inconvenience anybody."

Did all girls know how impossible it was to say no to a woman with salt on her cheeks? Probably. "Take it easy, Mols. Of course I'll give you a ride."

She planted a kiss on his cheek. Her lips were even softer than her freckles. "Thank you, Marcel. You're the best."

"Do you have any questions for me?" Jillian stood in the hallway. She sure did have a way of sneakin' up on folks.

He managed not to growl. "Not that I can think of, but thank you for the offer, Jillian."

Molly jumped like a teenager caught necking on her father's couch. "Jilly! I didn't know you were listening."

"Everybody listens." Jillian looked friendlier than usual, less like someone who'd tattletale for fun. "Charlotte's the one who keeps notes, but we all notice things." She winked.

"That's useful to know." Embarrassing, almost making a move on Molly while the whole household cupped ears to doors. To Molly, he said, "We could pick up your car right now. I've been working since yesterday, what with Eric's murder and all. I'll just give dispatch a call."

"You work too hard, Marcel."

"Well, it appears I don't have a life." The words came out bitter, so he draped a smile over them and offered his hand. "Shall we?"

Molly dried her face on a paper towel and then looped her arm through his. Her eyes sparkled the way Dayna's used to and, for some reason, the thought made him grouchy. Having Molly in his arms had felt good, even with the tears. Darn Jillian's timing anyway.

"Can we stop at the mailbox?" Molly climbed easily into the SUV—she didn't have to jump up onto the running boards the way Dayna did. "I'm expectin' something."

"A donation?" Not many people knew about the anonymous cash donation Blue Horizons received every month. It varied from about five hundred right up to ten grand.

Molly nodded. "Amanda always said she couldn't make ends meet without it. I think I could, but it's a big help."

Marcel pulled up alongside the mailbox and spoke more to himself than to Molly. "I wonder who leaves it." Everyone at the Falls PD had tried to catch a glimpse of the Blue Horizons benefactor. Officer Lyman had camped out on Sandpit Road for nearly a month. He never saw anyone, even joked that the secret backer must be one of Gracie's ghosts.

"I don't care who it is, although I sure would like to say thank you." Molly reached into the mailbox and pulled out an envelope. A fat one. She lifted the flap and flipped through the bills. "About three grand, I think. It'll pay off the medical bills not covered by insurance. Those visits to that new Dr. Wheeler have been a big help to Charlotte and Jillian. I'd hate to have to cut back."

Marcel couldn't help the resentment that came with the mention of *Dayna's new young man* Dr. Wheeler. But he was glad to see Molly smile.

Once he'd dropped off the department's SUV at the Falls PD, he and Molly climbed into his car—an older model Honda Pilot. He did his best to keep from talking about anything that might bring her back down.

That meant he spent the ride boring her with stories of catching speeders at the bend in Devil's Elbow, and using the bumper of his SUV to nudge the black bear out of the middle of Darling Hill Road. "Darn thing suns itself on that blind curve every morning. One of these days he's gonna tip over the school bus." She didn't seem bored and, when he dropped her off at the hospital, she gave him a smile that made the day a whole lot brighter.

Whistling, he made a loop past the front entrance and turned back toward the street. A quick check in his side-view mirror had him hitting the brakes.

Dayna was walking toward the hospital doors, and she wasn't in uniform. She wore a violet scoop-neck blouse and white jersey skirt slit to mid-thigh. Her hair was loose and wild, tumbling over her shoulders and shining like double-struck gold.

Beside her was Shay Cooper, looking far less slutty without the red wig and glitter. She wore jeans and sneakers, and she had plain brown hair pulled up in a ponytail. Probably even had her underwear on.

Dayna was undoubtedly there to meet Dr. Wheeler. Bad enough the thought had Marcel's insides churning with a force that reached up past his throat and fogged his brain. But now here she was with Shay, the missing person who'd never been missing, the woman who changed her skin like a damn chameleon and never did answer a question full on.

The two shared an easy sort of camaraderie, their body language and laughter conveying a casualness that suggested familiarity, maybe even friendship.

What the hell? Dayna had been hiding things since the day she'd come back to the Falls, and now she was consorting with a person of interest in a murder investigation. For all he knew, Shay Cooper might end up a suspect, could even be the killer. She certainly was an actress, and he hadn't figured out which of the parts she played was real.

He took back the allowances he'd made for his ex-girlfriend's behavior—what if Dayna was hiding something worse than a new boyfriend? Maybe her lies weren't all that white, and maybe she wasn't keeping secrets in order to spare his feelings. One thing was certain: there was something going on that she didn't want him to know.

A night of wrestling Scout for the blankets did nothing to improve Marcel's disposition. He wasn't on duty until noon, but Dayna started at eight, and he had no intention of postponing a long-overdue conversation. He wanted answers, and he wanted to look right at her when she gave them.

The parking lot was empty save Dayna's Subaru Forester and Todd Lyman's Jeep. Good. He and Dayna could have a discussion without being overheard by Reggie or the Chief.

He did his best to walk through the door same as he would any other day. Dayna looked up same as she always did, with the same conscientious gaze radiating from the same trustworthy face. Not fair that a lying sneak could look so damned innocent.

"What the hell, Dayna?" It probably wasn't the best way to open a conversation, and he realized he maybe should have practiced in front of a mirror.

"What the hell *what*, Marcel?" Dayna sat up as tall as she probably could. Her feet didn't reach the floor, so she had them resting on a footstool. She had a copy of *Modern Gun* in her lap, and she was looking at the new Baby Eagles. Researching. Dayna was always beyond thorough.

"What were you doing at the hospital yesterday afternoon?"

Her forehead puckered. "I thought that was you. I called, but you kept going."

"You're avoiding the question."

"Am not." When she crossed her legs at the knee and lounged against the counter, her shoulders fell so her boobs popped up and looked at him. Had she always done that? Did she use her gender the same way Shay did? Maybe they compared notes in the parking lot, made a list of tactics for unhinging a guy who hadn't been with a woman for eight months going on forever.

"I'm choosing not to answer, Marcel, not until you calm down."

His voice would have risen to a roar if it hadn't cracked like a pre-adolescent. "You're choosing to keep lying to me."

Dayna's chin dropped halfway to her chest. How could she be surprised? Didn't she and her mother talk to each other? She seemed to consider for a moment before she lowered her eyes. "Okay. I met someone for lunch."

"Gary Wheeler, *M.D.*?"

She folded over the corner of her page and set the magazine on the counter. Then she pointed down the hall and whispered. "We're not alone."

"I know. I saw Old Man Lyman's car when I drove in, and I don't care if he hears me."

Dayna's eyes got wide. "Well, I do care. This is our personal business, and as such none of his."

She slid off her chair and stalked to the exit, motioning him to follow. Once outside and down the ramp, she flung open the passenger door to her Subaru and pointed. When he got in, she slammed the door behind him, let herself in the driver's side, and slammed that door, too. The silence was a shock after all the banging. Dayna's breath was quick, and her words came out in rapid fire.

"I should have told you the truth, Marcel, and I'm very sorry I didn't."

He had to swallow several times before he could trust himself not to shout again. "Me too, and I appreciate the apology."

Dayna started the engine and flicked on the AC. The cool air felt good against the heat in his face.

"I never cheated on you. I only met Wheeler a couple weeks ago."

Now Marcel felt worse. She broke up with him *just because*, which meant she hadn't left him for the rich doctor. Even with no one in her sights, he hadn't been good enough.

"Let's drop this subject and move on. What the devil were you doing associating with Shay Cooper?"

She turned to him with eyes guiltless as a child's. "Jesus, Marcel, you're jumping to conclusions again. Shay and I met in the parking lot."

"Coincidence?"

"I guess."

He snorted. "You're the one who says there are no coincidences."

"I'm not always right." She still didn't look him in the eye. Instead she stared out the windshield. There was nothing there but the station's front door with Todd Lyman's craggy face pressed against the glass. "I just do the best I can like everyone else," she muttered. "I'm not perfect."

Certainly not as perfect as he'd once thought she was, but he'd never expected perfection. "Did you and Shay talk to each other?"

"A little." Dayna adjusted the vent so the air blew her hair back. She looked like a model on a photo shoot. "I didn't ask Shay what she was doing there, but she told me anyway."

"And?"

"She had a bee sting on her baby toe, swelled halfway to her knee. She went to Urgent Care to get something for it." Dayna reclined the seat and lay against it, one hand draped near his thigh. Eight months ago it would have been an invitation. *Hold my hand, Marcel.*

"You and Dr. Wheeler——" It was none of his business, but he asked anyway. "Is it serious?"

"Too soon to tell." She shrugged, as if meeting Gary Wheeler for lunch meant nothing. "We're getting to know each other. So far, he seems nice."

"That's good." It didn't feel good, but Dayna deserved someone who treated her right.

"You'll be happy to know Cracked Jack got the boot."

"Jack's gone?" For the first time since dropping Molly off, Marcel felt something akin to satisfaction. "Gracie will be happy to hear that."

"Molly, too?" Dayna poked him in the shoulder, but it was a gentle little nudge, nothing like her usual karate jabs. "You can tell 'em both Dr. Wheeler got rid of Jack. Seems he's been abusing the patients. It's probably not actionable what with such unreliable witnesses, but Wheeler's doing his best to make things right."

The news was like a balm, soothing the angry places. Marcel regretted taking such an accusatory tone. Dayna sure did bring out the idiot in him.

"I'm sorry," he said. "I shouldn't have gone off on you that way. I was upset."

"Ya think?" She was smiling out of one side of her mouth. The other side still turned down. His fault, he supposed, but she wasn't blameless.

"If you lie about the personal stuff, it's hard for me to trust you when I need to, on the job." He stopped and tried to ease the whine out of his voice. "Would you help me out here, and please tell me the truth from now on? I know you're gonna date other guys, and I can handle it."

"Even if I date a good-looking doctor? Even if he commutes with a helicopter?"

Marcel winced. Dayna's mom was probably picking out china. "Even then." He swallowed a couple times to make sure his voice came out steady. "Do we have a deal?"

Dayna looked straight into his right eye, steady as a laser sight, and said, "Of course we do." But the moment the words left her mouth, her gaze shifted to somewhere alongside his nose. His heart slipped, too.

He wanted to ignore the warning in his head, but it was no use. He'd known Dayna since the first grade, and he could look through those wide eyes of hers and see straight through to her core. Her sincerity was thin as spider silk, and that made her chance encounter with Shay all the more suspect.

For whatever reason, Dayna was still lying. She wasn't about to let him in on her secrets, though, and he could only think of two reasons for her deception: either she didn't trust him, or she had something to hide.

CHAPTER TWENTY

With several hours to himself and nowhere he had to be, Marcel left Dayna at the station and wondered where to go. He couldn't show up at Blue Horizons again, not without making a lame excuse and letting Molly see how pathetic he was.

His house was no better. Scout danced on his hind legs and worked himself into a sneezing fit when Marcel walked through the door. The dog had licked his bowl clean, and Marcel took him for a walk so he could do his business. Afterwards, too preoccupied to cook breakfast despite his stomach growling, he kicked off his boots and sat on the couch where he and Dayna used to snuggle. Scout dove onto his lap, all wiggles and kisses and thumping tail.

Marcel rubbed the beagle's ears and tried to relax but, even with Scout for company, reminders of Dayna filled the room. He couldn't be with those memories, not when he didn't know how much was real and how far back she'd started to lie. Feeling baffled and irritable, he left Scout snoring on the couch and went for a drive.

He wasn't surprised when his SUV parked itself in front of the house he'd grown up in. His mother was in the backyard bent over the garden. It was her day off, so she was dressed in plainclothes rather than her usual summer-weight deputy uniform. The tomatoes were ripe, and zucchini had choked out the cucumbers and melons, same as it did every year.

"Hey, Mom."

Suzanne Trudeau straightened up and shook dirt from her gardening gloves. The older he got, the more Marcel wished he looked a little less like his mother. Medium height with wavy brown hair and love-handled bodies, they shared an ability to gain weight on a water fast. Marcel figured he must have been fathered by the mailman, since he shared none of his dad's lean athleticism.

"Marcel! What are you doing here?"

"Can't a guy drop in on his mom without a reason?"

"Sure, but you hardly ever do." She draped an arm around his middle and walked with him to the house. "What is it this time? Dayna trouble?"

Trust his mother to cut to the heart of the matter. "I decided to grow the heck up and move on."

"Oh." She reached up and ruffled his hair as if he were ten years old. "That's probably the sensible choice."

She didn't say the word that dangled at the end of her sentence, so Marcel held the door open and said it for her. "But?"

"Sensible doesn't always make you happy. You know that, or you should." She dropped her shoes on the welcome mat and headed for the refrigerator. "Too early for a beer?"

"Thanks, but I'm on duty in a couple hours, and it'll make me sleepy." Marcel bit his lip to keep from hollering for the second time in one day. What was it about mothers? Near as he could tell, they all seemed to know where the buttons were and how hard to press. "Dayna's the one who dumped me, Ma. I can't always go trotting after her like a dog that doesn't mind gettin' kicked."

"Of course you can't." Suzanne set out celery sticks and low-fat dip. Marcel carried them to the table.

"And she's dating someone else. It's time I did the same."

"Sure thing, Marcel." She took two glasses from the cupboard and poured diet soda.

"And I was thinking about maybe asking Molly out."

The soda foamed over the edge of the glass. "Molly?"

"Yes, Molly. Dayna says she has a thing for me." He sat in the chair he'd always used—the one with the caned seat that drooped in the middle.

"Dayna said that?" His mother mopped up the soda without looking at him.

"What's wrong?" Not the reaction he'd expected. His mom loved Molly.

Suzanne's back rounded like a teen embarrassed by her boobs. "Molly's wonderful, sweetie, but—"

"But what?"

"But she's an awful lot like you." His mother shrugged back to her normal posture while Marcel prepared for a lecture on his shortcomings. She walked to the table and set the sodas down hard. "Molly is steady and sweet and kind and—"

"And?"

"Well, you have to admit she's maybe a little bit boring."

Great. His mom thought he was boring, too. She'd never been much of a diplomat. That was probably why she worked at the prison where she didn't have to interact much with the public. He forced a chuckle. "Thanks a lot, Ma."

"Well, I'm just saying, she's like family." Suzanne picked up a celery stick and crunched down on it, chewing with her mouth open. "There's nothin' to discover with Molly because you already know everything there is to know."

"Not everything." Not by a long shot. "I didn't know her Uncle Victor treated her as badly as he did."

"Well then, you were blind." Suzanne opened the refrigerator and dug through the crisper, pulled out a head of broccoli, and dropped it onto the chopping board without washing it. "And that's another thing. I know it's not her fault, but Molly's kind of a downer."

"What do you mean?" He knew exactly what she meant. It seemed every time he saw Molly she was either crying or trying not to.

"Well, the poor girl's had so much tragedy in her life, I doubt she even knows how to have fun."

"She has fun." He and his mom never did see eye-to-eye. "We have fun together. Just yesterday, we made pancakes and had breakfast with the boarders."

"I dunno, Marcel." His mother sliced broccoli with more vehemence than the job demanded. "Molly turns on the tears a lot quicker than she turns on laughter. You need someone who knows how to laugh."

"She does laugh."

"But, Marcel." Suzanne's voice took on a pleading quality. "You never could walk away from somebody in need. It clouds your judgment."

"Molly isn't needy. She's doing just fine for herself."

"Molly's too easygoing. You need a little excitement."

"What's wrong with easy?" He got to his feet, tried not to shout. "I could use a little easy."

Suzanne motioned for him to sit. He did so, feeling as if he'd done something stupid, or was about to. "Well okay, then." She picked up the platter of broccoli and set it next to the celery, then plopped down onto the chair across from him. "Dayna left you eight months ago. Why haven't you made your move?"

He chewed a celery stick, hoping to buy himself time. "I don't know." Probably because he still loved Dayna and, no matter how hard she pushed him away or what she might have done, he still hoped maybe she'd change her mind.

Stupid. He had to face facts. Dayna didn't want him. But Molly . . .

The thought of pancake batter stuck in Molly's hair made him smile, that and the way her mouth curved up when he laughed at her. Molly was . . . "Molly's pretty, and we have a good time together. But up until yesterday I never thought of her as . . ."

"As what?"

"Well . . ."

"As someone you want to screw?"

Marcel's stomach curdled. "Jesus, Ma, that's private."

"Well? Does she turn you on?"

"Cut it out, Ma."

"Any wet dreams?"

"Mom! That's enough!"

"Is that a no?"

He kept his mouth shut, just fumed down at the table top, but he figured his mom already had her answer.

"That's what I thought. She's a good friend. Keep it that way."

"But what if there could be more?" What about the way Molly's eyes lit up when she saw him, how she protected Gracie with a ferocity he doubted he could match? Being loved with that sort of passion would be a wonder. And even broken, her pancakes were the best he'd ever had.

"Doesn't love sneak up on you sometimes, Ma? Don't best friends realize they've been in love right along?"

Suzanne pushed the celery away. "Well, Marcel, you always do the opposite of what I say. Problem is, this time you're risking an awful lot."

"I know. I could lose a friend. A good one."

"More than that." The concern in Suzanne's voice went from pleading to husky. "Molly's part of this family, and she needs that. What if you two end badly, and she loses all of us?"

He hadn't thought of that, and he sure didn't want to be the one to yank the foundation out from under Molly's life. "You're not much help, Ma."

"Nope." This time she smiled. "It's up to you, sweetie. But if you do still have feelings for Dayna, leave Molly alone. She deserves better."

"So I should date someone besides Molly? Maybe Kate—that nurse from the hospital?"

"A palate cleanser?" Suzanne chuckled. "You could." She got up and walked around the table. Before he knew it, she'd squashed him in a hug. "You know my vote's with Dayna." Her breath was so close it moistened his ear. "Give her some time. See if she comes around."

"She isn't coming back." The words still hurt worse than they ought to. "It doesn't matter what I want. Dayna's is the only vote that counts. Near as I can tell, it cancels out yours."

Suzanne's arms slackened. "There's stuff you don't know about, hon. Don't give up on her just yet." The way her voice turned hoarse told him he ought to listen to what she had to say.

"What don't I know?"

"Just girl stuff." His mother headed for the sink, grabbing the celery dish on her way. "Forget I said anything."

"What aren't you tellin' me?" Did everyone keep secrets? Even his mom?

"Nothing."

He knew by her tone the subject was closed. No point pushing, not today.

"Fine."

"The M.E. is releasing Eric's body tomorrow." Just like his mother to change the subject. "Are ya goin' to the funeral?"

"'Course I am. It's gonna be a home burial, and Candy asked me to help her dig the grave."

"I'll see you there, then." Suzanne dumped the uneaten celery into a baggie and tossed it into the refrigerator. Then she grabbed a sponge, loaded it with soap. "You'd best be gettin' home. Take that beagle for a walk. Clear your head." She picked up the dish and scrubbed hard, even though the celery hadn't left anything worth that sort of effort. Marcel couldn't help wondering what in the world she was trying to wash away.

CHAPTER TWENTY-ONE

A dozen feet beyond the edge of Candy's lawn, Marcel lowered the business end of Eric's backhoe into a hole about four feet deep. Something snapped like driftwood, and *not again, not again, not again* shouted in his head. Cringing, he raised the bucket high and dumped its contents. A skull with an elongated nose and slanted, blunt teeth tumbled down the little hill he'd made and came to rest upside-down. A collection of neck bones rolled past it.

He opened the cab door and shouted, "Damn it, Candy! It's a horse." Using cuss words in front of a woman wasn't something he normally did, but he'd abandoned politeness three holes ago. "That's five holes and five skeletons! How many animals do you have buried back here?"

Candy fiddled with the drawstring at the base of her black V-neck crop top. "I don't know," she shouted, peeking past monster tires into the hole. "Before Eric and me bought this piece of land, my mom buried everything here."

"Like mother, like daughter." Marcel raised the bucket and pulled the skull back into the hole. "We'll have to try somewhere else. I mean, we can't bury Eric in the same hole as your mom's horse."

"I dunno why not, Marcel. Eric liked horses."

She couldn't be serious. "It's disrespectful." He twisted around so Candy wouldn't notice he'd gagged. "I know Eric was a dick and all, but can't you just call the funeral parlor like a normal person?"

"Don't you dare call Eric a dick, Marcel. He's dead and can't defend himself." Candy stomped her foot and thrust her lower lip out. "And why should I spend thousands of dollars when I don't have to? The state of New Hampshire allows home burials. For once, the law's on my side. Eric is gonna rest in peace right next to King the German shepherd, Sophie the goat, Alice the Percheron, and those three cows I don't know the names of."

"But, Candy—"

"Don't you *But Candy* me." Candy jammed her hands atop hips clad in black leather short shorts. "Eric will be happier than a nuthatch eatin' a hornet's nest, because I'll have to walk over the top of him every damn day, and I'll always wonder whether he's lookin' up my dress."

Marcel threw the tractor into reverse, grinding the gears and wishing he hadn't agreed to help. *I just need a hole dug*, she'd said. *I don't know how to run Eric's backhoe*, she'd said. She hadn't mentioned her entire property was an unmarked grave.

And that wasn't all—she had no idea where the septic system might be, and she'd neglected to contact Dig Safe. Coyne Falls didn't have town water or gas, so he wasn't worried about causing a flood or exploding the house. The number of graves, though, was disturbing.

"Where's Eric now?" He knew he wasn't gonna like the answer.

Candy had the decency to look at the toes of her high-heeled sandals. "The coroner dropped him off a few hours ago, and we left him in the garage with about a hundred fifty pounds of ice from the Coyne Toss."

"The package store?" They sold ammo, too. And bait.

"He stunk real bad, Marcel." She fanned her nose, probably for emphasis. "It's not my fault the coroner kept him so long. I wanted to get him in the ground before he started to turn."

Remnants of breakfast bubbled into Marcel's throat. "Is Eric just sittin' in there with no head?" He hated that his voice wobbled like the trestle bridge over Jackson Road.

"They stitched it back on for me, but it didn't hold. So they stuffed him into the hangin' part of my grandmother's wardrobe and put his head into one of the drawers." Candy sniffed. "It was the only thing I had that was big enough, and it's made of good, solid maple. It's way better than a pine casket."

"He's in a closet and a drawer?" Good thing it was July. If this were the end of October, high school seniors wouldn't hesitate to steal that corpse for the Town Hall Haunting. Eric's remains would be the cherry on the top of that particular sundae.

Marcel scanned the backyard. "How 'bout if we move a little closer to the woods? There's a sheltered spot at the edge of the trees, and you won't even have to walk over him if you don't want to."

Candy shaded her eyes and looked across the lawn, past her poppy garden to a line of hemlocks standing like sentries on a gentle rise. Some of the tension left her shoulders. "I think that might be where my mom buried my dad. Thank you, Marcel, that'll be fine."

She tromped behind him while he drove over the hummocks and rocks to where the meadow ended and woods began. His gaze wandered beyond a thick screen of maple and oak to a stretch of open land. Must be a couple acres, and it looked to be freshly mown.

"Is that the field Gracie's been mowing?" he shouted to Candy over the whine of the hydraulics. "The one we used to play ball in when we were kids?"

"Sure is," Candy shouted back. "Eric used it for growin' nursery stock, but this year he let it go to weeds." She pointed to Blue Horizons. "Gracie took it upon herself to start mowing it—just went and did it without asking. Fine by me, but Eric was pissed."

"Was he?" Interesting. Maybe Gracie's dream was connected to a memory. Better sit down with her again, see if she might be able to remember more than she already had.

"You know Gracie. She's out on that mower by six a.m. most days. Eric always said we didn't need an alarm clock. Just Gracie and her ride-on." Candy scrubbed at her face with the back of her hand. Marcel felt a whole lot worse for calling Eric a dick, even though he was one.

He guided the bucket past the edge of what looked like ledge. Once again, it crunched into something too soft for rock and too hard for wood. "Son of a bitch." He couldn't look, not again. So he glanced back toward the lawn, stared at the mourners gathering near the house, and tried to focus on *anything but that hole*. Another cow? A goat? Please not a dog.

"Who is it this time?"

Candy leaned on the bucket and stared into the hole. She froze for a moment, but her voice betrayed nothing beyond her usual bossiness. "Doesn't look like bones. Just move maybe a couple feet to the left, Marcel. And keep on diggin'."

"Ya sure?" He half stood and strained his eyes, but the bucket blocked his view.

"Uh-huh. It's just roots off 'n those hemlocks."

It had better be. Marcel dug in. *Please* let this be the last grave he had to excavate today. Three scoops went without a hitch, and he started to relax into the rhythm. Dig, lift, swing the bucket, dump the load, reposition. Dig, lift, swing the bucket, dump the load, reposition. Pebbled dirt accumulated in a neat pile, along with a few boulders half the size of a washing machine. Before long, the top of the hole was even with the six-foot mark on the backhoe's arms. He watched the final scoop pour from the bucket and dribble down the sides of the ever-growing mound.

Something rolled past, bounced higher than a rock ought to, and then tumbled back into the hole. It couldn't be.

"What the hell, Candy?"

"What?"

"Was that a—"

"Nope."

He rubbed his eyes. Maybe he'd imagined eye sockets and teeth, the shape of the skull impossibly human. "I'm gonna take a look."

"You stay right where you are." Candy gazelle-jumped onto the platform and held the door shut. "I'm as sick of digging holes as you are. The guests are all here, and Eric will only stink worse if he and his head have to sit in that hot garage much longer."

"But, Candy!"

"Don't even think about it, Marcel. You're gonna carry that wardrobe out here and dump it in this hole. Then you're gonna cover it up nice. Understand?"

"But—"

"But nothin'." Candy's nose started running, and her voice got a whole lot higher. "This here is Eric's funeral. You don't get to ruin it, no matter what you thought you saw in that hole."

Marcel pushed the door open and elbowed his way past Candy while she waved her arms as if locked in a game of keep-away. At the bottom of the hole was—damn it—a human skull alongside what looked like part of an arm.

"Candy, I can't."

"Yes, you can." She stood her ground. Candy never did back down. "Looks like we found my daddy. Where better to bury Eric than alongside someone who'll keep him in line?"

"You have to be kidding." The sight of human bones had Marcel thinking of conspiracies and murders. He had to climb down the backhoe's arms and scramble into the hole. With dirt filling his shoes, he squatted low and took a closer look. The skull did look old, picked clean, probably been there for a decade or more. Strangely, it didn't look all that creepy.

Maybe he was being an idiot.

He grabbed the backhoe bucket and hauled himself up to ground level. "Are you sure that's your father?"

"Mostly."

"*Mostly?*"

Candy looked close to tears. Small wonder, what with all the graves and skeletons and Eric being dead. She was still loud enough to hear over the backhoe, though. "Look, Marcel, come back later and dig it up again if you must, but right now, could ya give a girl a break? Please?"

Maybe she was right. With guests already assembled on the lawn, this wasn't the time to be thinking like a cop. This was the time to be Candy's friend. He could check out the gravesite on another day, at a time that didn't cause Candy quite so much heartache.

"You win," he said, even though he already regretted his choice. "I'll check the deed later and make sure this is where your father's grave is recorded."

Marcel drove back to the garage with Candy leading the way and occasionally glancing back to mouth *Thank you.* Chief Farrell and Todd Lyman, looking extra spiffy in dress uniforms, helped to position the wardrobe containing one stinky Eric body and one stinky Eric head into the loader bucket.

Marcel drove back across the yard in first gear low, trying to take the least bumpy path so he didn't jostle the corpse any more than he needed to. Visions of Eric skimmed through his head—an Eric zombie walking through the field, his head tucked under his arm. Gracie bringing Eric's head to the station, saying Scout dug it up. Headless Eric mowing the field, Gracie complaining he'd borrowed her lawn tractor without asking.

Finally he reached the hole, centered the bucket over it, and lowered the wardrobe. He let Eric's remains slide into the grave, a muffled thump marking the end of a brief and ill-spent life. Once Marcel had covered the grave beneath sand and pebbles, Candy visibly relaxed, and the air smelled a whole lot cleaner.

She took a last look at the grave, shouted, "I owe you one," and gestured Marcel towards her.

He climbed down from the cab, brushing dirt from his clothes. The other mourners were dressed up, but it was too late to go home and shower now. If only he'd realized digging a hole could take so long. "Sorry, Candy. I'm a mess."

She brushed tears from her cheeks. "I doubt Eric will mind, and he's the only one who matters." The look on her face, sad and worried and a little bit guilty, had him second-guessing his decision to ignore that skeleton. And now, just like Dayna, she couldn't seem to look at him.

That, and there was a funny little hiccup in her voice. "Eric always said if there was anything anyone needed, anything at all, you were the one to ask."

"What?" He and Eric had barely spoken since high school, not since Eric got himself involved with drugs, and not since Marcel had realized he was the one leaving bruises on Candy. "Eric said that? I thought he hated me."

"He did." Her words got stuck for a moment before they found their way out. "And I need to talk to you about that. I was sure you two stopped bein' friends a long time ago, and I resented you for it." She turned toward the mourners on her lawn and walked a little way in silence.

"We did." And no matter what anyone said, he'd always felt guilty about cutting Eric off the way he had, like his old friend wasn't worth the effort. Even though his dad said it wasn't Marcel's job to save Eric, and it wouldn't have worked anyhow—people had to find their own way.

Then there was guilt by association, a phenomenon both parents had explained. Eric was trouble. If Marcel wanted to work for the Falls PD, he'd have to avoid being friends with people who might land him in a holding cell. Eric was one of those people.

Aw well—that was a long time ago.

When Candy reached the edge of the crowd, she still didn't meet his eye. For once, she spoke softly enough that only he could hear. "I got a call this mornin' on Eric's business line. When I told 'em Eric was dead, they asked how to reach you."

"Me? Why?" He didn't know anything about landscaping.

"Eric told this guy you could get him whatever he needed."

"What?" Wasn't that what Shay Cooper had said to him? It sure didn't sound like someone who wanted a lawn mowed or flowerbeds weeded.

Candy's whole demeanor got a whole lot more intense. "Remember when Eric got caught dealin', and he got off because the Falls PD lost the evidence?"

"Uh-huh." Eric had been caught holding well over a kilo of pot, and it appeared he'd be facing felony charges. But Lyman, transporting the evidence from Coyne Falls to Concord, had been rear-ended and wound up in a ditch. When EMS arrived on the scene, the pot was gone.

A few hours later, Eric was free, and Candy was over the moon.

Candy spoke quickly, as if there was a lot she had to say in a tiny space of time. "After that, Eric swore to me he'd learned his lesson and quit the business, but I never was sure he did. And I'm real sorry, but I have to ask you somethin' important." She turned to face Marcel dead-on. "Marcel Trudeau, tell me the truth. Were you part of it?"

"What?" His jaw darn near hit his collarbone. "How can you even ask?"

"Yes or no?" Candy looked like she did back when they were kids, demanding he tell the truth or get socked where it hurt.

"NO!" He hadn't meant to shout.

She stared at him for several seconds; must be sorting through every line on his face, every muscle twitch, every rumble of his ever-hungry gut. Finally, she put a hand on his shoulder.

"Well, okay then." Her fingers squeezed convulsively. "I'm sorry, Marcel, but it sounds to me like Eric told people you're dirty."

"Eric told—" Realization landed like a blow to the gut. *What the hell?* How many people did Eric lie to? Who else had believed him? Was that why Shay had asked him for drugs? Because Eric told her he was dealing? "Why would he do that?"

Candy shrugged. "I dunno. Could be he wanted to get back at you."

"For what?" They both knew the answer. Friends ought to stick by their friends. "Can't say I blame him."

"Not your fault, Marcel." Candy turned away and headed for the lawn and the gathering mourners. "I know I yelled at ya, but I was upset. You have nothin' to feel bad about."

"But still."

"If you'd kept on bein' Eric's friend, he would have tried to use you. And you would have been torn between friendship and duty every damn day."

"I know." But hearing it from Candy helped. A lot.

"I can't imagine why he'd bother makin' up stories about you, though. I mean, I know he held a grudge, but why now?"

"No idea."

"Me neither." Candy paused long enough to wave to her mother. Amanda waved back as she parked her white Camry beside Dayna's bright blue Subaru.

"I gotta go talk to my mom," Candy said, "but think about what I told you." She leaned in and hugged him hard, probably so she could whisper. "You need to watch your back, Marcel. Be careful. Somethin's not right, and I'm bettin' there's a whole lot more goin' on than either of us knows."

As usual, Gracie's feet didn't touch the ground. Even in a lawn chair, she had to cross one leg while the other dangled. She glanced at Molly, who sat relaxed and comfortable with both feet on the grass and her knees level with her lap. Must be nice to be tall.

The other boarders sat beyond Molly, and Gracie still marveled that they'd agreed to leave the house. "Only if we all go together," Walter and Jillian had proclaimed, "and only if we don't have to take the car." Charlotte had come along, too, brought three notebooks and hadn't stopped writing.

Marcel had just returned from digging Eric's grave, and now he stood apart from the other mourners with Candy Thompson at his side. He looked upset, maybe even angry, but mostly shocked. His face settled into its usual smile when Scout sidled up to him, tail whacking both him and Candy in the shins.

Marcel's sister Zoe sat in the front row, half on and half off her chair, as if she hadn't decided whether to stay or go. She looked uncomfortable in a simple linen dress and flats rather than her usual EMS uniform. Beside her was a hunk of a man in a tailored black suit with dress shoes that looked as if he'd used both polish and spit. On his far side was Officer Dayna Pelletier. She was so short that her toes barely touched the ground even though she'd scooted to the edge of her chair, and Gracie decided that she looked very much like a poodle dancing on its hind legs.

She giggled at the thought. Molly turned to her with a gentle shush. "It's a funeral, Gracie. Candy just lost her husband."

"And that's supposed to make us sad?" Gracie snorted. "It's about time someone shot that walking carbuncle."

Jillian scowled and said, "It's not right to speak ill of the dead." She'd shaved that morning, curled her hair, and put on a flowered sundress. She clutched a beaded purse close to her belly, flattened by a magic corset from Frederick's of Hollywood.

"Why ever not?" Gracie folded her arms across her chest. "He didn't suddenly become worth a damn when he died, did he?"

"Was he a bad man?" Walter hunched in his Tyvec suit. A dribble of sweat made its way past the two hospital masks he wore.

"In some ways," Molly whispered. "Even so, Candy has suffered a loss, and we need to be polite for her sake."

"Eric said I killed him." Gracie let herself slide to the chair's edge, touched her toes to the grass. "But Officer Trudeau doesn't seem to think I did."

"Please don't talk about that here." Molly gave Gracie a nudge. "Someone might hear you."

"Am I on the lam?"

"It's not possible to be on the lam if you've already confessed to the police," Walter said, his voice muffled behind the masks. "Ask Charlotte."

"On the lam," Charlotte said, "meaning on the run, as in a criminal hiding from the law."

"You see?" Molly whispered. "As long as you're not hiding, you're not on the lam."

"Oh." Gracie's attention had already skipped to Amanda Gavin. She'd parked near the mailbox, and now she made her way to Marcel and Candy as quickly as her heels would allow. A moment later, mother and daughter hugged at the edge of the grass.

When Amanda grabbed Marcel's hand, he put an arm over her shoulder, but he seemed more intent on scanning the crowd than in offering comfort to Candy's mom. A frown had returned to his normally mild face.

Gracie ducked behind Molly. "Is he looking for someone?"

"He already found the body," Charlotte said. "About time somebody did."

"What body?" Walter ducked.

"In the hole," Charlotte squeaked.

"Yes, Charlotte," Molly said. "They put Eric in the hole."

"I meant Marcel," Gracie said, "the nice policeman who likes Molly's pancakes."

"Gracie, stop." Molly's cheeks flushed.

"He fixed my giraffe," Charlotte added, "but then I bit its head off."

"Well, what's he doing?" Gracie turned in her chair and tried to see where Marcel was looking. "He's staring at everyone as if they've done something wrong."

"That's what police do at funerals of murder victims, Gracie. They watch to see if anyone looks like a killer." Molly pointed to the row opposite them. "See the man between Zoe and Dayna? That's the new detective who interviewed me. Reggie Clark. He's been asking everyone lots of questions."

"Flushing out the murderer," Jillian said, squeezing her purse more tightly.

"And there's Suzanne Trudeau—you remember Marcel's mother—she's a sheriff's deputy." Molly pointed through the crowd to her right. "She and Dayna Pelletier were off by themselves, probably making plans and comparing notes on who looks guilty."

"Do I?" Gracie hid behind Jillian.

"Do you what?" Molly hadn't taken her eyes off Marcel.

"Do I look guilty?"

Molly sighed. "Always."

Gracie ducked lower. "Have you asked him if he'll help us?"

"With that thing we discussed?" Molly dropped her voice to a whisper. "Not yet."

"When?" Gracie searched the crowd for the dead girl. Hannah hadn't shown up since Molly had agreed to help, but she'd be back if they delayed too long.

"He'll be at the station tomorrow. How 'bout we go down there and ask him together?"

"Okay." Today would be better, but Gracie supposed tomorrow would do just fine.

Molly shushed everyone when Pastor Baker stood and walked to the little podium set up next to Candy's goldfish pond. Careful not to kick the chair in front of her, Gracie pushed herself upright and let her legs swing, hoping she wasn't expected to sit completely still.

The pastor's voice boomed across Candy's lawn. "We gather today to mourn the death and celebrate the life of Eric Thompson. Remember in your sadness that as long as Eric's memory endures, he is with us."

"But I thought we were rid of him." Gracie's foot brushed against a flat stone, poking up from the grass beneath her chair. She bent down and took a closer look. It was a plaque, so shiny it looked wet. She nudged Molly and pointed.

"Is that a grave?"

Molly just pursed her lips in a silent *shhhhh*, but Charlotte whispered, "It's Candy's father. Peter Gavin." Charlotte had a memory that would shame an elephant. If she said this grave belonged to Candy's dad, then it did.

Gracie hooked her heels into the chair rungs, careful not to disturb the stone beneath her. She'd never known Amanda's husband. He'd died before Blue Horizons came to be. But Charlotte—she'd lived right across the street back then, probably even walked to Peter Gavin's funeral.

Gracie nearly jumped from her chair when an idea came to her. Why hadn't anyone else thought of it? Charlotte didn't miss much. She rarely volunteered information, but if someone were to ask the right questions . . .

Careful to whisper, Gracie leaned past Molly and whispered to Charlotte, "Do you know who killed Eric?"

Charlotte said nothing, but she bore down hard on her pencil, wrote the words *LOVE KILLS* in capital letters, and snapped the lead.

CHAPTER TWENTY-TWO

Walking up the ramp to the Falls PD, Marcel tried to shake off the apprehension that clung like cat hair on a clean uniform. Why would Eric spread stories about him dealing drugs? How many people might have believed him? Did the Chief know? Dayna? His mom?

He'd best tell the Chief what Candy had told him, even though his heart did hiccups at the thought of revealing a piece of information that some might consider motive.

Chief Farrell was on the phone, so Marcel walked past the fishbowl window and headed for the coffee pot. Todd Lyman roosted on the stool beside the counter like an old crow contemplating road kill. Having three officers in the station at the same time was unusual, especially at twenty to nine on a Monday morning.

Lyman looked up from his coffee and jerked his chin toward Farrell's office. "Chief wants to see you ASAP. Where the hell you been?"

"I'm twenty minutes early." Marcel knew better than to take the older man's bait, but he couldn't help the shudder. "What's up?" He hoped it wasn't about him and Eric.

"Heard from the forensics boys. Ballistics, too. We got a busy day."

Damn. Marcel knew he should be excited, but what if the evidence pointed to Candy or Abe, or even Gracie? He hoped no one he cared about had been upgraded from person of interest to suspect.

"Aren't the Staties handling it?"

"We get to pick up the suspects. They'll take it from there." Lyman took a swig of coffee. "Don't keep Farrell waiting. Not today."

Chief Farrell sounded frustrated, so Marcel let himself into the office and sat stiff-backed against the wall. He only half listened to the Chief's suggestion that Ed Garmin on Pole Hill might consider putting away his bird feeder by tax day if he didn't want bears in his yard.

He checked his watch. Barely 8:45, and here he was, already sweating through a fresh duty shirt. And if Lyman were to be believed, the day was gonna get a whole lot worse.

Farrell put the phone down and rounded on Marcel. "Just how close are you to Candy Thompson?"

"Why?" The sinking feeling in his chest got a whole lot deeper. "We've known each other since we were kids, and our moms are best friends. You know that." Farrell didn't say anything, but he looked more sympathetic than Marcel thought he ought to. "Candy's been nothin' but cooperative."

"Of course she has." Farrell's tone shifted from sympathy to impatience. "You, Officer Trudeau, are too naïve for your own good." The Chief slapped a printout on the desk and tapped it with his index finger. "Your friend Abe Rafferty seems to have left his hat at the crime scene. We lucked out with DNA, and we have a better than sixty percent chance of a match."

Not good. Abe was a peaceable sort, though, not the type to give in to temper and unlikely to break the law. He didn't have so much as a speeding ticket to his name. And DNA wasn't as reliable as television cop shows liked to suggest.

On the other hand, Abe cared for Candy. A lot. And Eric was horrible to her. Love could make a person do dumb things.

"And I know you think Candy is too sweet and pretty to be a killer, but her prints are all over that Eagle."

Marcel startled to attention. "The Baby Eagle? The one from the tree stand?"

"I'm afraid so." Farrell pushed another page across the desk. Marcel picked it up, hoping for good news. Candy's prints were there, all right, all over the ammo. But there was another print on the gun's grip, as yet unidentified.

"The Staties got lucky with a clean history of transfers," Farrell continued, "and that gun belongs to Eric Thompson."

"Seriously?" Marcel fingered the pages, read the remarks.

"Look at the prints, Trudeau. The widow's fingers were all over those casings, both the chambered round and every last one in the magazine." Farrell stabbed his finger against the report, probably trying to convince himself of the findings. "That magazine contained thirteen of a possible fifteen rounds—one chambered, one probably fired. She loaded that gun, and chances are she used it."

Damn it. Not Candy. Not the girl who taught every last one of them how to be brave. "Ballistics?"

"A match to the slug the coroner pulled out of Eric. Dumbass was shot with his own gun." Farrell paced to the hallway and motioned Lyman to join them. "We have to proceed as if she did the deed, regardless of our personal feelings on the matter. No way she dumped the body alone. She's too skinny. Abe must have helped her. Probably lost his hat when they dropped the remains in the lake."

"Maybe." But—"What about the tree stand? How did the gun end up there?"

"The beagle took you there. He's Candy's dog. Do the math." Farrell opened a pack of gum and stuffed two sticks in his mouth. He was probably trying to quit smoking again. "And forensics found marijuana on Eric's clothing."

At the mention of Eric and drugs, Marcel's stomach pitched. He reached for the back of his neck and dug fingertips into the tight ropes alongside his spine. "That's not exactly news. Eric gave up dealin', but we all knew he was usin'."

Lyman shuffled down the hall, a sneer deepening the furrows of his cheeks. "But the lab boys think he landed in weed when he got shot. Young plants, alive."

"You think Eric was growing pot?" That wouldn't be a surprise. "Where?"

"No idea." Farrell snapped his gum. "You knew him better than I did. Any thoughts?"

There was the field behind Eric's house. Plants might be concealed along the edge. And then there was—"What about his greenhouses out on Depot Road? Has anyone checked them?"

"Not yet." Farrell's cheek popped in and out when he chewed. "Officer Lyman and I are heading over there now. Meanwhile, I want you to pick up Candy and Abe."

"Me?"

"You got a problem arresting someone you know?"

Arrest Candy? Marcel supposed the news might be easier coming from him. Candy knew he'd do his damndest to get to the truth. The thought should have quieted the dread, but all he felt was sick. "I'll take care of it."

"I know you will." Farrell rested his hand on Marcel's shoulder. "Go get Candace Thompson. Read the woman her rights and lock her up. Then bring in that boyfriend of hers. I'm calling Officer Pelletier for backup."

"Backup? For Abe and Candy?" Dayna Pelletier was the last person Marcel wanted to see. "I don't think—"

"No, you don't, and that's becoming a problem." Farrell looked disappointed now, and there was nothing to do but wait for a long-overdue tongue lashing. Marcel hadn't exactly gone by the book where Candy was concerned.

The Chief didn't raise his voice, though. Somehow his quiet concern was harder to take. "Abe and Candy are both suspects and should have been handled as such from day one. Instead, you told Candy she ought to lawyer up."

Lyman's face mirrored the Chief's—a level of disapproval that Marcel might have expected from his own father. "Watch what you say to that gal," Lyman said. "She never could keep a secret."

The Chief went for his mic. "Officer Pelletier. We need you. Now."

Dayna wasn't due until evening. Her sleepy "Ten-four" was barely audible.

"Don't drop the ball, Trudeau." Farrell and Lyman headed for the door. "You need to toughen up and realize there are moments when you can't be everybody's friend." The two older men paused in the doorway, lighting Marlboro Reds just beyond the threshold.

"Do your job and quit getting distracted by that ex-girlfriend of yours." The Chief spit the gum into a lilac bush and took a long drag off his cigarette. "Don't think I haven't noticed the way you follow that woman around like a moose in rut. It's a wonder either one of you gets anything done."

Lyman nodded agreement. Marcel's ears heated up.

"Make it up to me by following procedure with the arrests." The Chief blew a perfect smoke ring before striding off in Lyman's wake.

"I'm hoping Dayna might want to stick around. That means you two need to sort out your differences and figure out how to work together."

Marcel didn't answer. Not much he could say about Dayna without making unfounded accusations.

"If you two can't get along," Farrell said, "I'll have to make a choice. And you might not like what I decide."

Marcel didn't say a word beyond those needed when Dayna arrived at the station. He filled her in as they took a left on Meetinghouse Hill, his voice flat as the dead possum they drove over at the crook in Devil's Elbow.

Dayna sat against the opposite door, staring straight through the windshield. She hadn't wasted time getting there. Her hair was a frizzy mess, and he doubted she'd so much as brushed her teeth. Even her uniform looked slept in.

Probably spent the night with her doctor. The thought lit a slow burn at the base of his ribs.

"Do you think we can ever be friends again?" Dayna's voice was wistful. The plaintive tone caught him by surprise.

"We are friends," he said, marginally less irritated. "We always have been."

"No, we're not." Now she sounded accusatory, like everyone else who'd spoken to him today. "We haven't been friends since Senior Prom."

"What do you mean?"

"Once we started sleeping together, we stopped talking. We stopped having fun. We just took each other for granted."

How could two people live separate lives pressed up against one another, skin to skin? "I never took you for granted." At least, he hadn't meant to. "I thought you were the most special person I'd ever met. I thought fate brought us together. I thought someone up there must like me an awful lot to give me a chance to be with you."

"Stop it, Marcel."

"It's the truth."

Dayna turned and faced the side window. "Where are we going? Candy's house is half a mile back."

"She's staying with her mom."

"Oh." A pause. Then, "I always liked Amanda."

"Me, too." He put aside the thought of Candy's mother. She'd spent her life looking after folks who had nothing, and soon he'd be cuffing her only daughter and taking her away.

Maybe he could skip the cuffs. This was Candy, not some criminal.

"Amanda was ahead of her time," Dayna said. "Not many women would have opened their home to mental patients, not a quarter century ago."

"Being a single mom and all, she had to come up with some way to earn money." He'd never thought about why Amanda had founded Blue Horizons, but she must have had good reasons. "Coyne Falls is too remote for a boarding house for normal people. The commute's too long. Blue Horizons gave her an income and a place to raise her daughter."

"Can't believe we're gonna arrest Candy."

Neither could he. "We're just gonna question her. Candy didn't shoot Eric."

"You sure?"

"The gold, Dayna." He tightened his grip on the steering wheel. "Eric's murder had something to do with the gold. I can't believe the Staties are spending so little time on that angle."

"Well, Reggie says there doesn't seem to be a trail to follow." Dayna hung her hand out the window, let it ride the air currents. "There were some prints, but they don't match anyone in the system. Funny thing, though."

"What?"

"They match that print on Eric's gun." She spoke dismissively, but Marcel could see her mind sifting through the information, determined to make sense of it. "Reggie thinks it might belong to Abe. I guess we'll know once he's been processed."

"Abe might have touched those coins when he first found them," Marcel reasoned. "But I can't see him shooting anyone. He's not the violent sort."

"Most people aren't violent until they have reason." Dayna was way too calm. "Abe and Candy could have killed Eric for the money."

"You don't believe that, do you? Candy loved Eric." Even though she cheated on him. Even though she told him not to come home.

"I dunno." Dayna put her feet on the dash, brought her hand inside and flung her arms up over her head. All stretched out with a sort of careless abandon, she looked like a kid, but she didn't sound like one. "I trust procedure, Marcel. I believe we'll find the information we need, and everything will turn out the way it's supposed to."

Marcel darted a glance. She looked confident, even serene. "Ya know, that's almost comforting."

She quirked a smile and folded her arms behind her head. Marcel tried not to notice what the posture did for her figure.

"You should try it sometime. Put a little faith in the system." She let out a peaceful sigh. "Maybe then you wouldn't worry so much."

"I don't worry."

"Sure thing, Marcel. And Candy Thompson's never had a murderous thought in her life."

"Thinkin' isn't the same as doin'."

"True." Dayna went back to staring out the window. "But she's our best suspect right now, like it or not. And ya gotta admit she had a hell of a motive."

CHAPTER TWENTY-THREE

The arrest warrant felt sticky in Marcel's hand. No one answered the doorbell, so he and Dayna followed a brick walkway to the backyard. Behind a nose-high lattice fence, they spotted Amanda Gavin, hose in hand, watering a mass of yellow sunflowers beside a kidney-shaped pool.

Candy's mom still looked good in a swimsuit, and her hair was more golden than gray. Unlike his own mom, she hadn't thickened around the middle. Her two-piece showed off the even tan of someone who had time to sunbathe properly and, even though she'd always worked bent over cooking and scrubbing, she stood up straight and tall.

Her daughter floated on an inflatable lounger in the deep end, head thrown back and face tipped to the sky. Not a care in this world. Candy always could put the nasty bits of her life into compartments, hide them away, and focus on being happy. She looked over the top of her sunglasses when Marcel waved.

"Oh, shoot! This doesn't look good." Candy spoke in her normal voice—the one that carried farther than it ought to. She rolled off the lounger in a fluid motion and swam like an otter to the ladder, already shouting, "Do you have a lead on who killed Eric?" Water streamed from her black bikini as she jogged toward them across travertine pavers.

Amanda Gavin set the hose down, plucked a towel from a nearby chair, and wiped her hands. Her worry was evident in sudden stiffness overlying her usual grace. Mothers always knew when something bad was about to happen to one of their own.

"I'm afraid we do." Dayna snatched the warrant from Marcel's hand. "We're gonna have to ask you to come down to the station."

"Seriously?" Candy's big eyes got even bigger. "You're gonna arrest me?"

"What?" Amanda Gavin's shriek had Marcel wincing. "You can't be serious, Marcel! What the hell, Dayna?"

Dayna stood her ground while Marcel felt as if he was ten years old, hoping Amanda wouldn't tell on him to his mother. Candy stared for a moment before she opened the gate. "Don't worry about it, Mom; they're just doin' their jobs. Let's get this over with so they can go back to finding the killer." She headed toward the sliders at the back of the house. "Can ya give me a couple minutes to put some clothes on?"

"No problem." The words were out before Marcel managed to engage his brain. Dayna shook her head. She was probably right.

"Mind if Dayna escorts you? We're not supposed to leave you alone."

"Not supposed to—" Amanda was working her way up to a holler. "She can't even change out of a wet swimsuit?"

"Of course she can," Marcel said, trying to sound reassuring. "We just have to send Dayna along."

Candy flung her arms over her head and kept walking. "Fine by me. It's not as if Dayna and I have never seen each other naked."

Marcel's tongue glued itself to the roof of his mouth. "Excuse me?"

"High school locker room." Dayna nudged him in the ribs as she walked by. "Don't be getting ideas."

Too late for that. Amanda caught up to him and clutched his elbow. "You know Candy didn't kill Eric, right? I mean, this is some sort of formality, isn't it?"

"I sure hope so." It was hard to look his mom's best friend in the eye. "The Staties wouldn't have us arrest her unless they had compelling evidence. But don't worry. They'll keep on investigating."

"They'll change the focus of that investigation to building a case against her. I'm not stupid, Marcel." Amanda's voice dropped to a tone he'd never heard from her before, dark and menacing as the growl of a mama bear. "I won't stand for this. I'm calling my lawyer, and he'll come after the lot of you." She headed for the house, feet slamming the ground with every step. Marcel followed at a safe distance, up onto the deck, through the sliders, and across the kitchen to the base of the stairs. Candy and Dayna had already vanished down the upstairs hallway, visible thanks to a vaulted ceiling and exposed second story. He hoped he wouldn't have to prevent Amanda from following.

"You know I'll do whatever I can," he said, even though he wasn't sure Amanda would listen to him. "I know Candy, and I can't imagine she'd—" He couldn't say the rest. For all he knew, Candy could have killed Eric. In self-defense. Everyone knew he wasn't opposed to hitting her.

"You can't imagine it because Candy doesn't have it in her to kill anything," Amanda said. "She got a D in ninth grade Biology because she wouldn't dissect that frog. Remember?" Amanda already had her phone in hand, probably had Attorney Doug Marley on speed dial. "She just couldn't, Marcel. You know that."

He didn't have anything comforting to say, so he fixed his gaze on the hallway. Candy and Dayna had shut the door to Candy's bedroom, so he couldn't hear them. They must be discussing which clothing would be best for incarceration. Layers, probably. Would Candy pick up a crop top from the floor of her bedroom and sniff the pits to see if it was clean enough to put back on?

Women probably didn't sniff their things. That would be gross.

He backed into the kitchen and leaned against the granite countertop. For Coyne Falls, Amanda's place was a palace. But then, she'd worked hard running Blue Horizons for just shy of twenty-five years and, during all that time, she'd been a second mother to every kid who needed one. She had a comfortable early retirement. Near as he could tell, she'd earned it.

Candy, it seemed, wasn't following in her mom's footsteps. With her husband gone and a job that paid minimum wage plus tips, she might have to give up the little house she and Eric had built from scratch on the chunk of land they'd bought from Amanda. If Candy got to keep the gold, maybe things would be different, but the State wouldn't let that happen.

Marcel tried not to eavesdrop while Amanda left a message for Doug Marley. She sounded as if she might come apart at any moment, but she wasn't the type to give in to helplessness. Amanda would organize and plan and come after them with facts that would set those Staties on their collective asses.

At least, he kinda hoped she would.

"Doug's not up yet, so I'm gonna go over there and wake him," she said, wrapping a towel over her bathing suit and stomping into a pair of flip flops. "I'll catch up with you later, Candy!" she called up the stairs. "Don't worry about a thing. I'm gettin' Doug."

With a final glare, she was out the door. It swung shut with a crash that rattled the china cabinet.

Candy appeared at the top of the stairs wearing yoga pants and a scoopneck tee, with wet hair slicked back in a ponytail and bobby socks under white sneakers. Sewn to her hip was Dayna. Marcel took the opposite elbow, and the two of them led Candy to the SUV. She got into the back seat without a fuss but, once there, she looked as if she might just crumble.

"Can I keep my phone?" she asked. Her face was puckered in a little-girl pout. "I'd like to call my mom and see if I can't calm her down before she does somethin' she'll regret."

Marcel tried to console her with a smile. "No problem, Candy. Go right ahead."

Dayna shot him a glare, and he whispered back, "It's just Candy."

The look on her face told him she thought he was being stupid again. "Bad enough we didn't cuff her. She's a suspect. Start treating her like one."

They needn't have whispered. Candy was already on the phone with her mom, talking loud enough to drown out a THX sound system. "I'm sure this will all be cleared up in a couple hours," she said as Marcel started the engine and headed for Darling Hill Road. "I'm plannin' to be outta there in plenty of time to get to work, and I'll make that zucchini cheeseburger thing you like for supper."

Once she'd finished her call, Candy curled her fingers into the barrier that separated her from Marcel and Dayna and gave them both what was probably her best attempt at an evil eye. "So, are either of ya gonna tell me what you know? You didn't come and get me, with backup no less, without darn good cause."

Marcel cringed. Dayna let out a sigh and answered for him. "We have some new evidence that led to a warrant."

"Abe, too?"

Marcel caught Candy's eye in the rearview mirror. "We're not at liberty to discuss the case. Sorry, Candy."

She chomped on her lower lip and quit talking, but Marcel thought there was more she'd almost said. No matter. Candy couldn't keep quiet for long.

"It's not like I own him," she said before they'd driven fifty yards. She held her hair off her neck and fanned herself with her free hand. "But he's been kinda distant ever since Eric turned up dead, like maybe he's reconsidering being with me, or like there's somethin' he's keeping from me." She sighed. "Can't say I blame him, but I wish he'd tell me straight out."

Marcel reminded himself that Dayna was keeping secrets, too. He knew exactly how Candy felt, shut out and frustrated as hell. He wanted to ask if she'd talked to Abe, given him a chance to explain himself. Much as he hoped Abe hadn't been involved, if he had to choose between him and Candy—

Candy pushed herself away from the barrier and flopped against the seat. "Maybe he found himself a new girlfriend. He was awful mad at me for not lettin' him give me an alibi."

"Maybe he wanted one for himself." Why did words always jump out of his mouth before he had a chance to think them through?

"Not Abe." Candy gave Marcel's seat a kick. "He faints when he gets a pinkie cut. No way could he lop a person's head off."

"Could you?" Dayna's voice had a quiet intensity that had Marcel's neck prickling.

"If anyone here could do somethin' like that, it would be you, Dayna." Candy spoke more softly than Marcel thought she knew how. "And aren't you supposed to read me my rights before you go askin' me questions?"

Dayna didn't answer, but Marcel thought maybe her cheeks flushed. The last mile passed in silence. When he parked near the handicap ramp and reached for the door, Dayna grabbed his arm. "The Chief's not back yet, so why don't you stay here and babysit Candy. I'll pair up with a deputy from the Sheriff's office and go get the other party."

She twisted around and spoke to Candy. "I know you don't much care for me, so I figure you'll be more comfortable if I'm not around."

The statement was delivered in Dayna's usual matter-of-fact tone, no judgment, no apology, just calling things as she saw them. Why had she stopped being honest about other things?

Once Dayna drove away, Marcel brought Candy inside and made her as comfortable as he could with a cup of coffee and a seat cushion from Chief Farrell's desk chair. "We have a couple hours before the State Police detective gets here and this place gets crowded," he said, "so if there's anything you want to tell me, now would be a good time." He was glad Dayna had offered to pick up Abe. The Chief wouldn't mind if she handled the arrest, and he was thankful for some time alone with Candy.

"Can I ask you something? Off the record?" He already felt stupid. Candy didn't do anything.

"Sure, Marcel. Ask me anything you want." She sipped her coffee, black, same as Shay.

"How did David Cooper get poisoned?"

Candy's voice went up an octave. "You can tell that asshole the same thing I told him. I didn't even make that salad. It showed up in my refrigerator, so I went ahead and served it."

"Showed up?"

"It was college, Marcel. Lots of things landed in my fridge."

He wouldn't know, of course, since he'd only gone to the community college. Lived at home the whole time.

"So, you gave David the salad, but you didn't eat any?"

"Couldn't." She set her coffee down, spilled some, same as always. "It was full of hard boiled eggs."

"You're allergic?"

"Why the hell do you think I never ate a cookie when we were kids?" He'd always assumed she was watching her weight, not that she needed to worry.

"Shay lived with you, right? Could she have made it?"

"No idea, Marcel. Lots of folks were in and out studying and partying and shit." Candy shrugged. "My mom tried to keep tabs on who was there, since she was the one payin' rent and all, but it could have been anyone."

He settled back in his chair and let her statement roll around in his head. It all made sense and, even though he was probably being every bit as naïve as Chief Farrell thought he was, he believed her. "Thanks, Candy. I had to ask."

"No problem." But she was lip-quivering mad.

"I apologize for all of this." He placed a digital recorder between them. "From here on in, it's official, and I'm gonna have to record this conversation. Are you ready?"

Candy looked determined, even though her voice was shaky. "You know what I told you before. I haven't changed my mind."

He set a Miranda card in front of her and turned on the recorder, tried to sound professional while he rattled off her rights and recorded the necessary information. Candy trembled a little bit, and he offered a smile, not a very good one. "Please answer yes or no. Have you been apprised of your rights?"

"Yes I have. Signed the card and everything."

"And do you understand your rights as they've been explained to you?"

"Yes, Marcel. I heard 'em explained often enough to Eric."

"Do you have any questions before we get started?"

"Do you have a ladies' room?"

Marcel clicked off the recorder. "Right this way, Candy. C'mon."

He walked past the dingy bathroom next to the holding cells, the one with the barred window and a urinal, and showed Candy to the larger, brighter restroom they'd built for the public to use during power outages. He waited in the hallway for what seemed like a long time until he heard the toilet flush, then running water followed by the hum of the electric hand drier. Then nothing.

"Candy? Everything okay?"

There was no reply. He twisted the knob. Locked.

She wouldn't.

He charged out the front door, jumped the marigold garden, and ran over the grass to the bathroom window. It was wide open, the screen gone, the chicken-print curtains Dayna had insisted on hanging now streaming halfway to the lawn. He spun around just in time to see Candy hop into a plumbing van and speed down Meetinghouse Hill.

"Shit!" He hit his mic. "Suspects Candace Thompson and Abraham Rafferty heading north on Meetinghouse Hill toward County Road. White Chevy van with plumbing adverts on the sides."

He knew how it must feel to be a Thoroughbred straining against the starting gate, but he fought the urge to join the chase. Abe's van was distinctive. It wouldn't get far. He and Candy would be stopped the moment they reached County Road.

Abe's best alternative was to take a right through the Breezy Hill Orchard where he could pick up the dirt end of Black Bear Road and circle back. He and Candy would drive past Victor LeBlanc's abandoned mobile home, up Meetinghouse Hill and, in five minutes, they'd have to pass the Falls PD in order to get back onto a paved road. Then they'd hightail it down Devil's Elbow toward Vermont.

Or they'd try to.

He moved his SUV from the station lot and parked it crosswise in the road. Five minutes was a long time, but he recognized what he hoped was the sound of Abe's van—please don't let it be the school bus—bumping over holes and ledge on its way toward him. He called for backup. Then he turned on his blue lights, drew his weapon, and positioned himself behind the engine block.

When the van rounded the corner, he took aim.

Abe wasn't one to play hero. He pulled to the side and shut off the engine before Marcel could holler for him to stop. Candy looked as if she wanted to cry but forgot how.

Marcel's "Stay in the vehicle, hands where I can see them," was ignored. Abe and Candy jumped out their respective doors and headed straight toward him, each trying to out-talk the other.

Marcel hollered, "Stop where you are! Now!" Abe bumped into Candy when she skidded to a standstill, looking a whole lot more surprised than she ought to.

"Hands over your heads! Do it now!"

Abe and Candy complied, and they followed his commands when he asked them, one at a time, to lift their shirts and turn in a circle. Once Marcel was sure neither had a gun stuffed into a waistband, he made use of his cuffs. "You can walk on ahead of us, Candy," he said, keeping a hand on Abe's elbow. "Nice and slow, please, right up to the station."

Candy spoke in a small voice. "I'm sorry, Marcel."

"That's okay." Marcel gulped a lungful and let it out slowly. He managed to keep his voice calm, but his heart was running a sprint. "I'm sorry, too. But at least now we all know which side we're on."

Two minutes later, Abe was locked in a holding cell, and Candy sat in a hard chair, wrists cuffed to a metal ring. Marcel had canceled the call for backup, and he already felt less guilty doing what had to be done.

He placed a photo of Eric's Baby Eagle on the table between them. "Do you recognize this gun, Candy?"

"Maybe." When she leaned close, her hair fell over her eyes. She reached to brush it back, but the cuffs stopped her. Her little gasp sounded a lot like a sob, but she blinked and found her voice.

"That's a Baby Eagle. Eric has one, but he has so many guns, I can't keep 'em all straight."

"Can you tell me the last time you handled Eric's gun, the one that looks like this one?"

"Christ, Marcel. That would have been the day before he died."

"Did you fire it?"

When she nodded, her hair stuck to her forehead. "I sure did. I went through two boxes of ammo shootin' balloons at the sandpit with Eric and Shay."

"Shay was there?"

"Uh-huh. Just like I told you when you came to my house." She shouted toward the cells. "Remember, Abe?"

"I remember that's what you said," Abe called back. "But I wasn't there."

"I'll talk to you later, Abe," Marcel said. "Try not to eavesdrop."

"Ya want me to cover my ears and hum?"

"If that's what it takes." Marcel turned back to Candy. "Then what happened?"

"Once we finished shootin' stuff, Eric left with Shay, like I said before."

"Did you load the gun yourself?"

"'Course I did. I'm not an idiot."

"How many rounds were in there when you put it away?"

"Fifteen in the magazine, none in the chamber." She smiled a little bit. "Eric would have had my head if I didn't fill it up when I was done. It's like gas in the car—he wanted everything topped off and ready to go."

"Why did you run?"

She bit down on her lip. Marcel was surprised it hadn't started to bleed. "It's gonna sound stupid."

"It was stupid."

"I know." Candy looked embarrassed more than scared. "This is gonna sound crazy, Marcel, but I got a text message from Eric. And he said you were dirty, and I had to run."

"From Eric?"

She jerked her chin up and down. "I told you it was stupid."

"How did Abe know to pick you up?"

"No idea."

"Just a minute." Marcel walked back to the counter where he'd left the two trays of personal effects. Candy's phone was right on top of her handbag alongside the lucky pebble she always kept in her pocket.

He picked up the phone, scrolled to her inbox, and read the message. *Marcl killd me. Run.*

His throat bunched up. "Candy, I—"

"I know, Marcel. For God's sake, we've known each other since we were kids." Her voice cracked, and she made a hiccupping sound. "But I was scared, and it all happened so fast—the text from Eric, Abe pulling up outside and wavin' me over. I didn't stop to think—I just ran." She wiped her face on her shoulder. "And we'd already decided to come back. You didn't have to go all policeman on us."

Marcel crossed the room in three steps, grabbed a tissue, and patted it beneath Candy's eyes. Then he held it against her nose. "Blow if you need to."

"I'm okay, Marcel. Just put the tissue in my hand, if you wouldn't mind. If I can't bring my hands to my face, I'll bring my face to my hands."

He pulled two fresh tissues from the box and pressed them into her palm. "Do you have any idea who would have Eric's phone?"

"The killer, I expect." She bent over far enough to wipe the wet from her cheeks. "Either that, or someone who knows a hell of a lot more than I do."

CHAPTER TWENTY-FOUR

Dayna steamrolled through the door just as Marcel cuffed Abe to the table. She looked as if she had a lot to say, but all that came out was, "What the hell, Marcel?"

"What the hell *what*, Dayna?" It was the same greeting they'd used all through high school and beyond. Good times, at least for him.

She stopped short with a wisp of a smile. He tried not to read anything into it.

"Reggie won't be here for a couple hours," he said, "so I decided to get started without him."

"Think he'll mind?" Dayna vibrated like a setter on point. She must be torn between not stepping on the detective's toes and getting a crack at making sense of Eric's murder. She wasn't alone.

"I dunno. Maybe." He grinned. "But no one said not to question the suspects. So I figure we're in the clear either way."

She only hesitated a moment. "I just talked to the Chief. Eric's greenhouses were clean. Nothing but bedding plants and a few dozen rolls of bird netting." Marcel flinched when she dug her fingers into his elbow and towed him toward Chief Farrell's office. She called over her shoulder. "Will you excuse us, Abe?"

"I'm not going anywhere." Abe lifted his hand as far as the cuffs allowed.

Marcel closed the door and positioned himself behind the Chief's desk so he could watch Abe through the fishbowl window. Dayna pulled a chair across the braided rug, climbed onto it, and sat cross-legged. "What's this I hear about Abe and Candy making a run for it?"

"I was stupid." Understatement. Marcel pulled Candy's phone from his vest pocket and handed it over. "But you're not gonna believe this."

Dayna's eyes got wide. "A text from Eric?"

"From his phone, anyway."

"Shit, Marcel." She jumped from her chair and shielded the phone in the crook of her elbow. "You're not gonna show this to the Chief or Reggie, are you?"

Something about the protective way she cradled the phone made Marcel's heart do a happy dance. He had to remind himself she wasn't interested, not anymore. "Of course I am. It's evidence."

"But—"

"But nothin'."

"Are you nuts?" Dayna clutched Marcel's arm. "The Chief will hand it over to Reggie. You'll be investigated."

"Not likely."

"You sure about that?"

Marcel tried to swallow, but his throat had turned gummy. He hadn't considered the possibility of anyone taking the message seriously. Even Candy had only panicked for a moment. But if someone looked at the text alongside Eric's stories, somebody farther up the food chain might decide to look deeper. There wasn't anything to find, but . . . "How come you're so up on internal affairs procedure, anyway?"

"I'm up on everything, Marcel. You should try it." Dayna slipped Candy's phone into the pocket of her duty shirt. "Let me look into this myself, just until morning."

"No." Marcel stretched out his hand. "I'm not gonna withhold information. Give it back."

"Make me."

He knew it was a mistake, but he wrapped her in a bear hug and wiggled his fingers toward her pocket. Pain shot up his ankle when she stomped on his instep with a whole lot more force than someone the size of a child ought to be able to generate. Then she threw herself against him and smacked him into the wall.

"Give it up, Marcel. You never could beat me."

"Only 'cause I won't risk hurting you."

"Because you want everyone to like you." She cuffed his shoulder and pulled away. He realized he had hold of her hand and let go.

"Hell, Marcel, you can't stand it if anyone has an unkind thought about you. You even feel bad when the mailbox vandals flip you the bird."

He took a tentative step, weighted his foot slowly. "What's wrong with bein' nice?"

"Because you can't do your job and always be everyone's friend." Dayna headed for the door. "And because it means I have to be the bad guy."

He knew he was making a mistake, but a surge of fury had his mouth engaged ahead of his brain. "Maybe you are the bad guy. You only say what you mean when you don't have a personal stake."

She spun around and yelled into his face. "I always tell the truth, and I always do the right thing, even when it sucks."

"Then what aren't you tellin' me?" Marcel nearly spit. "Why the goddamn lies, Dayna? What the hell are you keepin' from me?"

"I'm not lying."

"The hell you aren't."

She bolted through the door and stormed down the hallway. Abe cringed in his chair while she blasted through shelves, withdrew a digital recorder, and slapped it onto the table.

The next thing Marcel knew, he'd stopped watching from the doorway and stomped after her. He knew his actions were far from professional, but he didn't care. "Damn it, Dayna, what's goin' on with you? Why can't you just tell me?"

Abe ducked behind the table. "Whatever you two have goin' on, could you maybe not put me in the middle?"

Dayna and Marcel shouted in unison. "Shut up, Abe."

"Anyone here?" The front door opened, and Molly MacLaughlin poked her head inside. Marcel backed away from Dayna, feeling all kinds of embarrassed.

"Do either of you officers have a few minutes to spare?" All the warmth had fled Molly's voice, replaced with something far less friendly. "Gracie and I need to ask some advice."

Dayna balled her hands into fists, shut her eyes, and made a noise that sounded a lot like a screech. The room went quiet. Marcel was pretty sure none of them dared breathe.

Three seconds passed. Four. When Dayna opened her eyes, she was right back to her usual professional self. Whatever she was hiding, it must be taking a hell of a toll. She never went over the edge. Never.

"Okay, Marcel, how 'bout I talk to Abe. You take Molly and Gracie on down to the Chief's office and see what they need."

"Whatever, Dayna." Marcel turned to Molly. Gracie was half-hidden behind her, staring at her sneakers. He'd better get hold of himself before he scared the old woman right out the door. "What can I do for you two today?"

Molly's eyes darted from Marcel to Dayna to Abe and then landed on Candy. She looked ready to start hollering herself.

"What's going on here, Marcel?"

"Nothin' I'm at liberty to discuss." He did his best to use his indoor voice, though a louder one butted against his throat. "Come on down to the office where we can talk in private."

"Private, my ass." Candy's voice echoed through the building. "If you talk above a whisper, we can hear every word out here." She pushed back from the bars and plopped down onto the narrow cot tucked up against the wall. "Hi, Molly. Good to see you, Gracie. Got that field mowed yet?"

"Twice. Put down some seed, too." Gracie shifted from one foot to the other and glanced at the door.

"What's this all about, Candy? Is there anything I can do to help?" Molly tried to push past Marcel, but he blocked her path. She backed away, still hollering to Candy, "Can I get you lunch, at least?"

"I'm fine, Molly, but thanks fer asking. I'm sure the Falls PD will spring for subs." She raised her voice, not that she needed to. "And I agree, Marcel. Don't tell anyone about Eric's text message."

"Eric texted you?" Abe jumped up so quickly, the cuffs jerked him back down. "Me too. Once back at my house, and again right when I pulled up outside."

Marcel knew he shouldn't be shocked, but—"Why didn't you say anything when Candy told me about hers?"

"I covered my ears and hummed, like you said." Abe shook his head. "There's just no pleasing you."

Dayna dove for Abe's phone like a hawk after pullets. She looked angry enough to start screeching again. "Oh, Marcel, you have to see this."

He took the phone, feeling more resigned than nervous. The first message said *Pick up Cndy @ Falls PD now.* The second made his heart flop like a beached trout. *Marcl kild me. Gnna kil Cndy too.*

"Really?" He ought to be angry, but he just felt bewildered. Somebody was messing with him, but why?

"Maybe someone tried to make Abe and Candy look guilty by getting them to run." Dayna had the same look on her face she used for crossword puzzles—forehead puckered in concentration. "Could be someone wants you out of action, Marcel. Maybe you were getting too close."

"To what?" He caught Molly's gaze, clear and steady, not slipping sideways the way Dayna's did. "Maybe it's just a prank, or—" It wasn't a prank. Of that, he was sure.

"Or?" Dayna again, but he hardly noticed she was there.

He turned back toward Chief Farrell's office, motioning Molly and Gracie to follow. His heart raced, and he couldn't help growling.

"Looks like someone out there thinks I killed a man."

CHAPTER TWENTY-FIVE

With her feet hooked into the rungs of Chief Farrell's chair, Gracie sat as tall as she could. Marcel and Molly searched the Internet while the dang ghost watched from a corner near the window. Gracie hoped a well-placed scowl would be enough to deliver her message: dead carrot-tops had better not interrupt the living.

"No singing." Gracie's whisper carried farther than she'd planned.

Molly twisted around. "I'm not singing."

Marcel's patient smile suggested he might think Gracie was two twists short of a cruller. Not that she blamed him, but the look on his face made her wish she weren't so short.

"Sorry, Molly. You can sing if you want. You too, Officer."

"Call me Marcel. Everyone else does." Marcel beamed at her, and she almost believed him.

"Marcel, then." Funny how being on a first-name basis made him less intimidating. To Gracie's relief, he and Molly turned back to the computer. Heads together, bright auburn beside mud brown, they discussed strategies for looking into Gracie's past.

Marcel, they decided, would see about accessing old records from the now defunct State Hospital, hoping to confirm the birth and possible death of a baby girl. Molly would get started joining websites that reunited adopted children with birth parents.

"Here's one, and it's free." Marcel pointed to the upper left corner of the screen. "All you need to get started is the child's date of birth and an email address."

"Let's use my Gmail account." Molly was already typing, moving from one screen to the next faster than Gracie could follow.

Marcel seemed a lot less fretful than he'd been when they'd arrived. Whatever was going on between him and Officer Pelletier, the level of agitation suggested it had nothing to do with police work.

Marcel and Dayna had always been a couple, Dayna with her aspirations and Marcel happy to live a simple life. If opposites attracted, they ought to be a good fit. Not that any of it mattered. They were too young to be getting serious.

Gracie scrambled down from her chair and squinted past Molly's head. "What are you looking at?"

"It's a registry. Birth parents can search for children given up for adoption, and adopted kids search for birth parents."

Marcel turned the screen to give Gracie a better view. "If you do have a living daughter, she may already be looking for you."

"Is it that easy?" Now Gracie's heart was pounding, and it wasn't with excitement. What if her daughter thought she didn't care enough to look? Who'd blame her?

Marcel touched Gracie's shoulder. His hand was warmer than she'd expected, softer too. "It might not be that easy, but it's a beginning. C'mon. Let's get you started." He pulled Gracie's chair closer to the screen and guided her into it. "Want coffee?"

"Sure." Molly answered before Gracie had time to get her mouth moving. "Cream and sugar, please, and decaf for Gracie if you have it."

"With lots of sugar," Gracie added, "and extra cream?"

"I'll check." Whistling, he ducked out the door. Gracie couldn't help but notice the flush in Molly's cheeks.

"So it's like that, is it?" Gracie tried to pinch off a smirk before it reached her face, but her lips got ahead of her.

"Like what?"

"You know." Gracie cut her eyes toward the hallway. "You *like* him."

"Of course I like him. We've been friends forever."

"Uh-huh."

"What?"

"Friends don't make you blush, young woman."

"It's sunburn."

"And I'm Mary Poppins."

The dead girl buried her face in her hands. "Must you irritate the people trying to help us? Apologize, please."

"Sorry." Gracie would have preferred to give Hannah a piece of her mind. Instead she settled back into her chair and turned her attention to the computer screen. "None of my business if Officer Trudeau gives you sunburn."

"Let's get this done, shall we?" If Molly was angry, she'd hidden it well, although her tone did carry more bite than usual. "Was Grace Hannah Ouellette your full name at the time of your daughter's birth?"

"Near as I can remember."

"Well, were you married?"

"Nope."

"I see." Molly typed Gracie's name, then double-tapped a flat spot below the keyboard. "Baby's date of birth?"

"July eighteenth, 1961. It was raining." Gracie's hand went to her chest even before she felt the pain. She made herself swallow several times while Molly filled in the information and clicked *Continue*. By the time Gracie caught her breath, another screen had replaced the first.

"I know someone with that birthday." Molly spoke in a wistful tone.

"You do?" Gracie's excitement bubbled into her voice. "Whose is it?"

"Don't get excited." Molly was using her soothing voice. "I know three people with my birthday, too. It's just coincidence."

Marcel pushed through the door with two cups of coffee, a plastic container full of cream, and a Styrofoam bowl filled with sugar. Molly thanked him and took a sip, then scooted her chair sideways so Marcel could sit in front of the computer. Gracie spooned sugar into her coffee while Marcel picked up where Molly had left off, asking questions and filling in the blanks.

Gracie answered as best she could. Parts of her memory were clear as Molly's picture window. Others were convoluted and seemed to make no sense. Then came the question she dreaded most.

"Can you tell me the name of the baby's father?" Marcel had the same patient look he'd worn since they'd started. He didn't look as if he were disgusted or judgmental. Not yet.

"No."

"You don't remember, or you don't want to tell me?"

"I never knew." Gracie felt as cold as when Cracked Jack stripped her naked and made her sit on the plastic chair next to the air conditioning.

"Is this something you'd be more comfortable explaining to Molly?" Marcel must be irritated by now. Anyone would be. Gracie barely heard him say, "I can leave the room."

"I already know the folks out in the hallway can hear me just fine," Gracie said, "so I expect it won't make a bit of difference if you stay here or join them."

"Just whisper," Molly said. "Whisper it to me. It could be important."

"I was pretty then." Where did that come from? The dead girl must have hijacked her voice, and now Gracie was saying things she would never have said on her own. "I lived in the State Mental Hospital, a giant brick building with hundreds of beds, all lined up in big rooms."

"What happened?" There was a little shudder in Molly's voice. Gracie felt guilty for putting it there.

"I don't remember much. They kept us sedated, of course." When no one said anything, Gracie realized they didn't understand. "Not enough orderlies," she explained. "The drugs kept us from being a bother."

Marcel's voice was surprisingly gentle. "You think you may have been assaulted."

"Most likely."

"I'm so sorry." Molly sounded as if she might cry. Molly cried too easily, but Gracie felt responsible for these particular tears.

"Near as I can tell, you didn't do it."

"I just mean I feel bad," Molly said. "I hate that you've been through so much."

Hannah whispered, "You can't change the past, Grace. It made you who you are."

"I guess. But it took away who I might have been."

"That, too."

Marcel caught Gracie's eye. "Is your ghost here? Is she talking to you?"

If she lied now, Marcel would know. Police officers were good at spotting that sort of thing. "Might be."

"This sudden interest in finding your daughter . . ." Marcel hesitated, and Gracie thought she heard a hint of accusation. "Is it Hannah's idea?"

"Marcel!" Molly's tone started out a reprimand, but ended as a question.

"Busted." Gracie glared in the dead girl's direction. "The dead redhead is pushy as all get-out, and she won't stop singing."

"She put you up to this?" Molly always squeaked when she was worried.

"She sings?" Marcel looked a good deal less enthusiastic about the search. Maybe she should go back to calling him Officer.

"Yes, her idea, and yes, she sings. Badly. Wouldn't let me finish mowing until after I talked to Molly."

"Badly?" The ghost took on a fiery glow. "I do not sing *badly*."

"I talked to that new Dr. Wheeler about your ghost," Molly said. "He thought it may be your way of accessing memories, things you've blocked or forgotten."

Hannah burned even brighter. "Or I could be real."

"I suppose." All this ghost talk was making Gracie nervous. "Whatever she is, she's a pain in the patooka."

"Lots of people believe in ghosts, not just the crazy ones," Hannah insisted.

"But I am crazy, so I have an excuse."

"I don't think you're crazy." Molly leaned close. "Never did."

Molly always seemed to know what to say, but she was probably just being kind. Dead girls with removable heads—how crazy was that? What if this whole thing was real as a snipe hunt?

"Maybe the dead girl is all in my head," Gracie said. "Maybe this business about a daughter is a bunch of hooey."

"And maybe it really is a memory," Molly said. "It can't hurt to check."

Gracie stared down at her hands. When had they begun to look so old? And what if this baby stuff was nothing more than a delusion— the dream of a crazy old woman? "We all know I'm not quite right."

"You could say that about a lot of folks," Molly said. "You're just more honest than they are."

Hannah moved to Gracie's elbow, pushing a wave of shivers ahead of her. "I should have said this sooner, but if you don't find your daughter on time, lots of people are going to die. Not just my—"

"Seriously?" Just like a ghost to keep on upping the ante. Next Hannah would claim she had to save the bees, cure cancer, put an end to genetically modified corn. "Marcel would have to be crazy to listen." No point pretending the ghost wasn't here. "Besides, what if he locks me up? What if nobody's in danger and you're in my head?"

"You think someone's in danger?" Marcel looked curious. Maybe he hadn't completely made up his mind. He spoke to Molly. "Do you think Gracie and I can have a moment alone?"

"I need to hit the ladies' room, anyway." Molly got to her feet slowly. "Gracie? You okay by yourself with Marcel for a bit?"

Gracie nodded without meaning to. She wasn't at all sure she agreed with her chin.

"Don't forget to whisper." Molly's shoes squeaked when she turned to go. "Be nice, Marcel. Don't go all policeman on her."

"Of course not."

Marcel closed and latched the door. "Do you want more decaf? I made a whole pot, and nobody else will want it." The kindness in his eyes slowed her heart rate, but he must be near the point where he no longer heard what she said.

"No. Thank you, Officer. I'm fine."

"It's Marcel." That smile again.

Through the fishbowl window, Gracie followed Molly's backside until she vanished into the bathroom. Candy sat in the holding cell with her knees pulled up to her chest. Abe was still cuffed to the table with Officer Pelletier firing questions. This place had too many bars. Head down, Gracie climbed from her chair and scrambled for the door.

"Wait." Marcel stepped in front of the exit. "Take a deep breath." He placed a hand on her shoulder, but this time it made her feel more trapped than comforted.

"I'll be honest with you, Gracie. I don't know what to think of your ghost." He let go of her and stepped back—a relief. "But sometimes you know things that don't seem to make sense until later. So I would be most appreciative if you could tell me exactly what your ghost told you."

"Okay." What choice did she have? Might as well blurt it out all at once, get it over with, and wait for the ambulance. St. Fillan's wasn't all that bad. They had apple pie, sometimes even cheesecake.

"I'm supposed to find my daughter, and she's supposed to help me save Hannah's great-granddaughter. And if I don't do it, a bunch of people are going to die." She felt light in the head and beyond credible. "I even sound bonkers to me. Everything the dang ghost says is crazy."

"Not so much crazy as incomplete." Marcel squatted low. He still looked attentive, but he might be pretending. "Anything else?"

"I'm supposed to follow the beagle. She loves that one." Gracie clasped her hands together and worked on a convincing glare. "It's all games with her. She never says what she means."

"This is not a game!" Hannah raised her fist, eyes blazing. With a shriek, she vanished.

"And then she disappears! She never sticks around once she gets me into trouble."

"You're not in trouble." Marcel's hand landed on her shoulder again, probably the only place he felt comfortable touching her. "Who is this granddaughter? Do you have any idea?"

"How should I know?" Gracie managed not to shout. "The darn dead girl likes to play with my head."

Marcel exhaled slowly, sounding almost like someone who wasn't frustrated. "So we have nothing."

"She won't tell me anything more, or maybe she can't. But Eric told me he was dead, and he is, so maybe I should pay attention."

Chief Farrell tapped on the door a moment before he cracked it open. The State Police detective was with him, the one who'd already been to Blue Horizons. Reggie Clark? Was that his name? Molly bobbed in their wake, peering past one shoulder, then the other.

Farrell smiled, but there was a sense of urgency in his manner. He didn't hide his impatience well. "Is this police business?"

"No." Gracie answered before Marcel had a chance to disagree.

"Well then, I apologize," Farrell said, "but I need to ask you to take your conversation elsewhere." He and the detective let themselves in. The surge of activity and resulting lack of privacy had Gracie near gasping. She headed for the exit with Molly in tow.

"I'll see what more I can find out," Marcel said, following them all the way through the door to the handicap ramp outside. "I'll call you."

Molly paused, one hand balanced on the railing. "You know Candy didn't do anything, right?" Her voice had a pleading note, and

Gracie slowed down in order to better eavesdrop. "I mean, my lord, Marcel, we went skinny-dipping together. We *know* each other."

"We were eight," Marcel said, "and I kept my underwear on."

"You always were modest." Molly positioned herself so her shoulder blocked Gracie's view. "Skinny-dipping was Candy's idea. She was the hellion in the group." Her voice caught. "But in a good way."

"I know." Marcel leaned close to Molly's ear. Gracie pretended to watch a gypsy moth caterpillar, alternately walking along the railing and then reaching toward the sky.

Marcel's whisper carried. "I care about Candy as much as you do."

Molly pulled away. She headed for her car with Marcel trailing behind and Gracie hurrying to keep up. Even after Molly was settled behind the wheel with Gracie seat-belted beside her, Marcel still didn't leave. Molly had the key in the ignition but, for some reason, she seemed incapable of starting the car.

"I ought to get back inside." But Marcel stayed where he was, and Gracie could think of only one logical explanation.

She leaned across the seat. "Oh, for the love of biscuits, just ask her out already."

"Gracie!" Molly looked as if she'd spilled maple syrup on the kitchen floor, a big sticky mess beneath her feet and way more cleaning than ought to be necessary.

Marcel chuckled. "You do say whatever's on your mind, don't you?"

"It's obvious you want to ask. Get on with it." Gracie folded her arms and tried to look wise.

Molly's face went from pink to red as a rooster's comb. Even her freckles gave way to blotches of sunburn.

"Molly, would you like to grab a pizza with me tonight? I get off work at seven."

Molly squashed palms to her eyes and shook her head. "You don't need to ask me just 'cause Gracie told you to."

He rested his arms on the window ledge. "Gracie had it right. I wanted to ask, and I was trying to figure out how."

"I knew it." Gracie tried not to gloat.

"Really?" Molly sounded doubtful and hopeful at the same time. "Won't Dayna mind?"

"Dayna broke up with me months ago."

"And you're not back together yet?" Molly looked unsure of herself. "How many months have ya been apart, if you don't mind my asking?"

"Eight."

"That long." A little smile inched across her face. Gracie crossed her fingers and toes.

"Well," Molly said, "in that case, I would love to have pizza with you this evening."

"It's a date." The moment he said the word *date*, Marcel looked as if he'd farted in public. But Molly flashed a smile, and he relaxed to his usual state of calm.

"It's a date, then." She grinned, dialed it back to a smile. "I'll look forward to it."

The door of the police station cracked open, and Dayna poked her head through. She looked more nervous than peeved, definitely on edge. "You about done, Marcel?"

"Be right there." He backed up and shoved his hands into his pockets. "Pick ya up at eight? Unless I get fired. Then I could be a whole lot earlier and less fun to be with."

"Then I guess I'll have to do something to make you feel better." Molly was blushing again. So was Marcel. Gracie pretended not to notice.

CHAPTER TWENTY-SIX

Dayna was waiting at the door when Marcel walked inside. She looked as spooked as he'd ever seen her, twitchier than the day she'd moved out. He'd forgotten the way she'd tiptoed around him then, words stuck in her mouth like peanut butter. Why hadn't she just spit them out?

"The Chief's been in there with Reggie for way too long." She pushed Marcel outside and pulled the door shut behind them. "They're talking about what happened with Abe and Candy. You need to figure out what you're gonna say."

"What are you talking about?" There was only one thing to say, and she ought to know that. "I thought I'll tell 'em the truth. I don't have anything to hide."

"The hell you say." She wrapped bony fingers around his elbow and dug in. "It's not just those text messages. There's a lot more to it."

"Like what?"

Dayna was worrying the inside of her cheek, and she still couldn't look at him. "We both messed up today. We should have cuffed Candy and relieved her of her cellphone. But you messed up worse. You left her unattended, almost like you wanted her to run."

He managed not to bristle, but damn. "How can you think that?"

"I don't think you let her go on purpose. I'm just saying how it looks."

He glanced at his watch. The Chief was gonna have his head if he didn't hurry up and get inside. But Dayna needed a moment. He supposed it wouldn't kill him to give her one.

"Look," he said, "I know I screwed up, but I didn't think Candy would let me down like that. I brought her back, though, and Abe, too. That has to count for something."

"But—"

"I'm not excusing myself, but I'm not all that worried." A white lie. He'd worked himself into an emotional lather, and his head ached right behind his eyes. "It's not as if people are lining up for my job. You of all people should know that."

Dayna's face pinched. For a moment she looked an awful lot like her mother. "What do you mean, me *of all people?*"

"I saw that website you were looking at." Marcel was proud his voice stayed steady. "Remember the day I got back late and you were all dressed up? You had the DEA site up, and it sure looked like job opportunities."

The life drained from Dayna's face and left her looking like a sun-faded photograph of herself. "You knew this was temporary."

"Of course it is." Marcel shouldered his way past her and opened the door.

Dayna trotted behind him, taking two steps to his one. "It's not as if I've been offered a job here. In a few weeks, I'll be unemployed."

"The Chief wants to make it permanent, but Coyne Falls isn't good enough for you, is it? Never was."

Her little gasp was a surprise. Marcel felt guilty digging into her sore places, but he still wanted to grab her and shake her and make her tell him what it was she'd been unwilling to say.

"Marcel, you don't know me at all."

"Whose fault is that?"

He stopped outside the Chief's office feeling a dozen kinds of sheepish. His outbursts were getting tiresome, even for him. And his mother was right. If he still had Dayna under his skin, he had no business asking Molly out.

"Look," he said, "all I'm saying is, if he fires me, he'll want to hire you. And since you're not interested, he'll likely have to replace me with some new recruit with no experience at all. I don't think he wants to do that, not with Lyman retiring next month."

"I guess." Dayna still looked hurt. She deserved an apology. Maybe this was a good time to be honest with her, say the things that were hard to say, and hope she'd respond in kind.

"I'm real sorry for what I said." He waited a moment, but when she remained silent, he figured he'd best try harder. "I know it's none of my business what you do with your life. The problem is, I care about you, and I'm worried about you, even if we are just friends. And I still think there's a whole lot you're not tellin' me."

She shoved her hands into her pockets. The way her jaw quivered suggested she might be starting to crack. Whatever she was holding inside, it was gonna hurt worse than *I'm moving out*, or *I'm dating someone new*.

"So what are you planning to say to the Chief?" Why did she still seem so uncertain?

"The truth." What else? "I'll tell him I messed up, and I learned from it. And now if Reggie will allow it, I'd like to talk to Shay Cooper and see if this time she'll corroborate Candy's story."

"She will, Marcel," Candy called from her cell. "Can ya hurry up and talk to her? I'm already late to work."

"I'm gonna ask the Chief right now," Marcel answered. "Sit tight."

"Can I get outta here, too?" Abe sounded whinier than a ten-year-old. "I don't even know why I'm here."

"Aiding and abetting, for starters," Dayna replied. "So keep your shirt on and let us sort this out." She went back to whispering. "Reggie won't want us interviewing Shay, not after this morning."

"Probably not, but we can ask."

Chief Farrell poked his head into the hallway, and Marcel's insides squirmed. Farrell had every right to be angry. Add Reggie to the mix, and they might decide a know-nothing with a clean slate was a better option.

"Ah," Farrell said. "The fuck-ups have arrived." The Chief let the door swing open before heading back to his desk. Reggie lounged in a chair by the wall, his face slack.

"That would be us." Marcel supposed he might as well agree. The brunt of criticism would be aimed at him. Dayna was a better cop than he was, and it didn't bother him, not much. He moved over so she could enter first, unsure whether being polite might demean her in some way. Once they were both inside, Marcel pulled the door shut behind him, an illusion of privacy.

"The text messages are obviously bogus," Farrell said, "and we have no way of knowing their intent. Could be somebody wants to make Abe and Candy look culpable. Or someone might be trying to convince us the killer is still out there, and these two are innocent." He stood behind his desk and drummed his fingers against the blotter.

"And I already know you're gonna say you messed up, and I'm gonna say you need to follow procedure, even if it's someone you grew up with." He sighed, a drawn-out gust of acceptance. "Then I'm gonna yell at you both and remind you that officers get killed when they ignore the rules, and you're gonna apologize and promise to do better." Farrell tossed an empty candy bar wrapper into the trash. It was dark chocolate. Marcel wondered if he thought that made it healthier.

"So how about we save ourselves some time and skip it." The Chief settled into his chair and motioned to Reggie.

Reggie took over. "You did manage to salvage the situation, and you did a decent job interviewing the suspects." He paused a moment, caught Marcel's eye. "I'd like you to take a shot at Shay Cooper, see what you can find out. I spoke with her earlier today. In my opinion, there's something she's keeping close to the vest, and it might turn out to be important."

"Did she corroborate Candy's story?" Dayna beat Marcel to the question. She beat him to a lot of things.

"No, she did not," Reggie said. "See if you can do better. Right now, I have a couple officers on their way to transfer the suspects to overnight lockup. Can't keep them here, tying up a quarter of your force."

"Damn." Marcel glanced through the fishbowl window. Candy had a beaten look about her, and it wasn't just the bruise.

Chief Farrell waved them out the door. "Shay's at the Coyne Cot. I want you two to work together for the rest of the day. Maybe if you keep an eye on each other, we can get the equivalent of one police officer."

Dayna looked as if she wanted to say something more, to make amends. She never could settle for being less than perfect. On the rare occasions she messed up, she always had to make things right.

Sometimes it made more sense to move forward. Marcel gave her a nudge. "C'mon, Officer Pelletier. We got work to do." He headed for the parking lot, certain she'd follow.

Much as he wanted to keep pushing Dayna for the truth, he decided to wait until after they'd questioned Shay Cooper. For the five minutes it took to drive to the Cot, he'd let Dayna hang on to her secrets, and he'd try to trust her. Working as a team was only possible if he respected her silence and made up his mind to believe she was the same person he'd grown up with.

Worth a try.

It was the plain version of Shay that met them outside the Cot. She'd staked out a picnic table where they could talk without eaves-droppers, and now she sat on one bench while Marcel and Dayna shared the one across from her.

She might be dressed down, but she was still Shay. Marcel couldn't figure out how she managed to angle herself to give him an unobstructed view of her crotch while Dayna would see one leg crossed over the other, demure as a 50's sitcom mom.

"Can you tell us what you did the day Eric disappeared?" Dayna's expectant look bordered on indulgent. "How did you spend the afternoon?"

Shay shrugged. "Like I told that detective, I hiked up to Rib-bon Falls, had myself a picnic lunch, and then hiked back." Marcel watched her body language. She sat up tall and smiled with the con-fidence of a politician on Primary Tuesday. "Then I went back to the cabin around dinner time. Candy was a bitch to me, said I was trying to steal Eric or some such nonsense. So I took off and got a room here at the Cot. The last time I saw Candy and Eric, they were together."

"So you didn't spend the afternoon with them?" Marcel ignored Dayna's glare. Sometimes it made sense to get right to the point.

"Nope. I was only there ten minutes."

When Dayna bent forward to write in her notepad, Shay winked and ran her tongue around her lips. Marcel focused on her eyes. There was something calculating behind them.

"Did the three of you ever go shooting together? Maybe another day?" Could be Shay had her dates mixed up. Or maybe Candy did.

Shay looked as if someone had set her hoo-ha on fire. "Shooting? You mean with a *gun*?" The way she emphasized the last word, Marcel was sure she'd had some stage training. "Of course not. I've never shot anything in my whole life."

She had to be lying. Or Candy was. But an old friend wouldn't use him like that, would she?

Then again, maybe everyone lied. Shay, certainly Eric, and Dayna, of course. Maybe lying was normal, and he was the one who'd veered away from the norm.

And then . . .

The moment was fleeting as October snow, but Marcel was certain he'd seen it. Dayna and Shay exchanged a look—a covert glance that told him they were co-conspirators, sharing a secret they didn't want exposed to daylight, to an old friend, or to an honest cop.

"Anything either of you feel the need to say?"

Dayna was silent, but Shay glanced at her watch and said, "Are we done?"

Near as Marcel could tell, they were. Dayna wasn't talking. If Shay knew more, she wasn't saying. Candy and Abe would remain guests of the state. Hell, for all he knew, they might be guilty.

Dayna followed him back to his SUV, and he tried to catch her eye, wished he could tell her how much he needed to know she was still on his side. He spoke as gently as he could, hope underscoring his words. "I know there's somethin' you're keeping from me. So is there anything you'd like to say?"

She shook her head. "I can't, Marcel. Wish I could."

"Shay's lying," he said. "I'm sure of it."

Dayna quickened her pace.

His heart felt too sore to beat. He dreaded the ride back to the station. Now his voice was husky, and he couldn't help but imagine the worst. It seemed Shay and Eric must have been involved in some way, either romantically or otherwise. Probably Eric had been Shay's supplier. That made sense.

But now it seemed there was also a connection between Dayna and Shay, and that meant Dayna might be linked to Eric and drugs and a trunk full of gold.

Dayna couldn't be dirty, but—

Even though he knew he still loved her, would welcome her back no matter what she'd done, that didn't matter. He'd lost her. And the pain of that realization hurt more than he could put into words.

The only thing he could think to say to her was, "Don't say I didn't try."

CHAPTER TWENTY-SEVEN

Marcel limited his side of the conversation to "Uh-huh" and "Okay" most the way back to the station. Dayna didn't say much more than that. After two minutes of being ignored, she lapsed into silence, anger radiating from the shoulder she'd turned toward him. Her breathing was louder than usual, her hair throwing sparks in the sun's slanted rays.

She had no call to be angry with him. She was the one who wasn't being honest. But the more he contemplated that fact, the more he felt like a hypocrite. Dayna wasn't the only one with secrets—he was hiding something, too. Maybe if he told Dayna about Eric's accusations, treated her as a confidante and showed her a little trust, she might answer in kind.

He had to try.

"Can I tell you something?"

She shrugged.

"Eric Thompson told people I was dealing."

"What?" There was a cascade of emotion tied to that word, a slew of feelings she was working hard to hide.

"It's not a big deal, I guess," he said, glancing at her rapt expression and trying not to read anything into it, "but if you add Eric's story together with those text messages, I don't come off lookin' too good."

"Did you tell the Chief?" She was breathless, and he could think of no reason why.

He shook his head. "I planned to this morning, but with everything goin' on and so many people in attendance, there didn't seem to be a good time."

"You need to tell him. It has to come from you before he hears about it from somebody else."

"I guess." Telling Dayna already had him feeling better. Funny how a problem always seemed less worrisome once it was shared. "I'll talk to him first thing in the morning."

"Call him now."

"What's the rush?" Eric's lies hardly seemed like an emergency.

"The longer you wait, the guiltier you'll look if he finds out."

"Huh." She was right. Dayna was always right. Marcel pulled over to the wide gravel shoulder and shut off the engine, took out his cell and scrolled to the Chief's number. There was no reason he should feel so jumpy, so he clamped down on the jitters and dialed.

"Here goes." He waited through an eternity of ring tones. When the Chief's voicemail kicked in, he considered ending the call. Instead he left a message—concise and to the point.

"I need to let you know that Eric Thompson told some people I was dealing drugs. I'm not sure why, but I suspect it was to settle an old grudge."

Dayna's eyes didn't leave his and, for the first time in all the years he'd known her, he thought she might cry.

She didn't, though. Instead she said, "Can I come over later? We need to talk."

"Can't we talk now?" He'd come clean. Seemed as if she ought to do the same. He started the engine and pulled onto Merriam Hill Road. The station was less than a mile away—not much time for talking unless she got started now.

"I can't, Marcel. There's a call I need to make before I say another word." She smiled, and it sure looked real, but he knew better than to hope. Claiming she wanted to talk wasn't the same as talking. For all he knew, she was delaying, changing the game, keeping him off balance.

She turned back to the window and clamped her mouth shut.

He knew he should ask again, try to get her to say whatever it was she'd been hiding. But he didn't want to know, not really. Because then he'd have to decide whether to believe the next bit of fiction so he could go on pretending she was the same Dayna he'd once asked to marry him.

Maybe it was best she'd said no.

He picked Molly up at eight, just after her boarders finished dinner. Amanda Gavin had agreed to spend the night, so Molly could stay out as late as she wanted. That probably accounted for the birthday-cake grin.

"Where to?" Molly wore a pair of jeans that fit snugly enough to hint at a dynamite derriere. Her usual peasant blouse had given way to a plunging V-neck showcasing a set of hooters that could gain her free access to any club in Lebanon, probably Concord, too. Marcel had to work to keep his eyes from opening wider than was polite.

"You clean up nice." Damn nice. Being here with Molly made Dayna's deception seem less pressing, more like something he'd seen in a movie. Gracie would probably understand how it no longer felt real.

"Well, you did say casual. Otherwise I might have gone all out and put on lipstick." Molly reached up and smoothed her hair. It rebounded to a mass of disorganized ripples that she probably wished would behave. Marcel liked the wildness. Dayna's hair was smooth and slick as her lies.

"You don't need makeup. You look perfect with nothing at all."

Molly blushed a dozen shades of crimson.

"I didn't mean . . ." Marcel's ears got warm. "I meant you don't need makeup. On your face."

"I know what you meant." She grinned down at her sneakers for a moment before lifting her chin higher than he'd ever seen it. "But just for the record, I do look damn fine with nothin' on."

"Jeez, Molly." Lingering shards of Dayna crumbled to dust. He'd never wondered what Molly looked like naked, her being like a sister and all, but now there wasn't room in his head for anything else. She slid across the seat until her bare shoulder rested against his. Her touch had him embarrassingly aware he hadn't been with a woman for eight months and a dozen days. "You're not playin' fair, you know."

She leaned closer. "It's not as if we need fifty dates to make sure we get along and trust each other. We're like family."

Family. There it was. Marcel's shoulders drooped along with the swell in his pants. "About that family thing."

"You are kinda like a big brother." She'd obviously been thinking along the same lines as his mother. "But I've always thought of you as a man, too, ever since I stopped thinking of you as a cute boy."

All of a sudden Marcel felt taller, better looking, and smarter. A scene from *Rudolph* played in his head, a misfit deer leaping through the air shouting, *She thinks I'm cuuuuuute!*

The smell of pizza pervaded the SUV, but Molly didn't comment. Marcel pulled into the little cleared area next to Echo Lake and hurried to open her door. "Remember when we were kids, and we said when we grew up we'd get pizza every day, and we'd sit at the edge of Echo Lake and—"

"And we'd be best friends for always," Molly finished for him. They stood in the dimming light, and Marcel wondered if he was the only one mentally undressing the other. He hoped so. Clothing was his friend.

He took her hand. Hers was cool and dry in his warm, sweaty one. "C'mon. I've got something to show you."

The sun was setting, and Marcel had to admit his little folding table looked awfully romantic. He'd set out a bottle of wine in an ice bucket, brought two beanbag chairs, a blanket, and best of all . . .

"Let me get the pizza." He jogged back to the SUV and pulled out two pizzas in hot boxes. When he opened them, he was pleased to find they were still warm.

Molly stood by the table, fingering cloth napkins and sniffing the scented candles. "Oh, my word, Marcel. I can't believe you did all this."

"A boy makes a promise to a girl, he keeps it, even if it takes fifteen years."

"You sure are corny." Molly flopped onto a beanbag and pulled the blanket over her lap. The sunset formed a waxy nimbus around her hair and lit her face in a tangerine glow. She pulled the second beanbag closer. "Have a seat, and I hope one of those pizzas has everything."

"Except anchovies."

"But I like anchovies." She stuck out her lower lip, but it didn't tremble the way it used to when she sat with him at recess with her stomach rumbling, and he gave her half the apple his mom had sliced for him.

"Good thing the other one has extra, then." He enjoyed the way her lips turned up when he teased her. Talking to Molly was easy. "Wine?"

"Please."

He filled a glass, and his fingers brushed hers when he passed it. Her touch made his hand tingle right up past his elbow. "Let me get you a slice."

He handed her a wedge with extra anchovies and drippy cheese, and they sat side-by-side looking out over the water. The diving rock hadn't changed. It made him think of Molly as a kid, skinny and pale, flat on her belly at the very top of that rock. Her hair licked her forehead like flames, and she flinched with every shout of, "Jump! Jump! Jump!"

She never had.

"Remember when we used to play here?" He couldn't help sounding wistful.

"Of course I do. Darn Candy always made me feel like such a chicken the way she'd dive off that ledge and swim like a fish." Molly was more matter-of-fact, and Marcel realized her memories would never hold a sense of longing. Her childhood was to be overcome, not to be remembered with fairytale fondness.

"Candy scared the hell out of me," Marcel admitted. His stomach got cold when he realized he'd repeated Candy's assessment of David Cooper, and that led him to David's accusation. Could Candy have tried to poison the man? The idea wasn't as impossible as he wanted to believe.

He shook it off. This was no time to be dwelling on where Candy was spending the night. Molly pillowed her head against his chest. He wrapped an arm around her, careful to rest his hand on her shoulder. She snuggled closer, laced his fingers in her own, and guided his palm down until it rested on the swell of her breast. "They don't bite, Marcel."

He choked. She turned her face up and licked a dribble of pizza sauce from her lip.

The next thing he knew, he was kissing her. Her fingers dug into his back as she twisted in his arms. He supposed he should have moved more slowly, but it was too late now because he had his mouth locked with hers, and he was pretty sure she was kissing him back.

Okay, make that damn sure. Molly kissed him with an intensity that said she wasn't just taking their relationship up a notch. She was staking a claim. The thought made him dizzy, and he came up for air.

"Holy crap."

She giggled. "I know."

Molly pulled her shirt over her head and unzipped her jeans while Marcel thanked the gods for the growing darkness. The sight of her naked made him forget all about the few extra pounds he'd never been able to shed and the problems he had yet to face. There was nothing but Molly, bathed in moonlight with waves at her back.

"Don't sit there teasing me, Marcel. I want you so bad I might die."

"Just let me look at you." He ran fingers across her cheek, cupped her chin, and stared into her eyes. She pressed herself against him, her hands roving across his chest, teasing, sliding, inching down.

"Ouch!"

Marcel nearly dropped her. "What? Did I hurt you?"

"No. It's not you." She laughed so hard she snorted. "Shit! Ow!"

Marcel felt it too—a pinch just below his right shoulder blade. "Mosquitoes! Damn it."

Molly leapt to her feet, grabbed his hands, and pulled. "Get up! Come with me."

"Um, we're kinda naked here."

"Well, duh, Marcel. Come on." She turned and ran, her footsteps splashing along the shore until she belly-flopped into the weeds. He chased after her, his stride less graceful, the splashes clumsy behind hers.

"Get out here, Marcel. It's warm as a bath." She stopped to tread water at the weed line. Then, with a daring glance, she paddled to the giant rock, took hold, and began to climb. A cascade rained from her hair, and he thought of mythic creatures of moonlight and lakes.

By the time he reached her, she was sitting at the top of the rock, her chest heaving, the last rays of sunlight dancing in her eyes. She pulled herself to her feet and stared off the sheer drop. "You comin'?"

Shit. "You're not serious."

"I'm completely serious. Come on."

Marcel stood next to her and took her hand. She doubled over in giggles before straightening up and sucking in a breath. He wondered how much of her newfound courage came from the wine.

"Pretend you're Candy!" She gulped another lungful and leapt, pulling him with her. The image of her falling was seared into his mind, her hair lifting on the breeze, framing a grin of pure joy. She was more beautiful than the moon, more perfect than Amanda Gavin's cherry popovers, the prettiest girl he'd ever seen.

They hit the water and plunged into black, hands clasped tight. Together they power-kicked until they broke the surface, laughing and choking amid cow lilies. Molly hugged him so hard, he nearly sank.

"I did it!" She kissed him with a passion he'd never dreamed of, and he crushed her against him, wanting her so badly he thought he might die, too.

She was shivering, though; her teeth chattered like Uncle Victor's wind-up chompers.

"You're cold."

"I'm fine."

He held her close and pulled toward shore. His feet found purchase, and he stood with her still in his arms. "No, you're not fine. I need to warm you up."

"But the mosquitoes."

"My house is a mile away. Come with me?"

She nodded once and buried her face against his chest. He carried her to the bean bags and wrapped the blanket around her, collected her things. Then he lifted her up and kissed her all the way to the SUV. Mosquitoes bit him in places he hoped he might need later, but he made sure Molly was comfortable and safe in the passenger seat before he stopped to dress himself. He took a moment to clean up the mess he'd made on the shore. By the time he joined her, she was fully clothed, but she still had the blanket wrapped around her shoulders.

"You sure you want to come to my place? I can take you home if you prefer."

"If you take me home, I may never speak to you again."

"Will you still kiss me?"

"Probably."

He drove with one hand. The other held hers. His house was set back nearly a mile from the road, the yard thick with trees. His driveway wrapped around to a parking area in the backyard, but he stopped by the front walk and carried her up the steps. She kissed his neck and nibbled his ear. He dropped his keys twice and finally set her down to unlock the door.

Molly walked in first, giggling like a middle schooler. Marcel reached around her waist, but her hands met his and flung them away.

"What's wrong?" The words were hardly out when he saw her. "Dayna? What are you doing here?"

Dayna stood by his bedroom door wearing nothing but shock. Scout dashed across the floor and leaned against Molly, haunches swinging with his tail.

Marcel stood in stunned silence. Molly turned to him, all smiles. "Thanks for takin' pity on me and cheering me up, Marcel." There was a catch to her voice, but he doubted Dayna would notice. "I've taken up too much of your time already, so I'll head on back to Blue Horizons now."

"How? You don't have a car." What a dumbass thing to say.

"I'll drive her." Dayna already had her shirt on, grabbed for her pants. "I'll drop her off and be back in ten. We gotta talk."

"NO!" Marcel surprised himself with his vehemence. "You're the one who showed up uninvited. Molly and I have plans."

"And we can get together another night," Molly insisted. "Really, Marcel, I don't want to be a bother. Stop by for pancakes next time you're free."

He reached for Molly's hand, but she snatched it up and tucked it in her armpit. Dayna repeated, "Ten minutes," and both women bolted out the door.

Marcel watched them go, knowing he ought to say something or do something. But holding onto the beagle was about all he could manage. Long after the tail lights vanished in the trees, he stared after them, frozen on the spot. Finally, a barred owl hooted overhead and startled him to action.

"Damn! Shit! Damn, damn, damn, damn!" Who did Dayna think she was, showing up naked? What the hell was she up to, and what the devil did she want?

He stormed to the SUV with Scout at his heels, let the dog into the passenger seat, and slammed the door. While the beagle turned circles, Marcel climbed behind the wheel and stared into blackness. Maybe he ought to wait, see what Dayna had to say for herself.

It wouldn't matter.

He shifted into gear and hit the gas. Dayna could come back if she wanted to, but he wouldn't be there. He took the long way to Blue Horizons—didn't want to risk passing Dayna on her way back. When he parked in the moonlight and crept to Molly's door, all the lights were off, and no one answered his quiet knock.

Molly couldn't possibly be asleep yet, so she must be ignoring him, hoping he'd go away without making a scene. He supposed he owed her that. Explanations and apologies could wait until morning.

He took a left on Sandpit Road and drove past Candy's place. Thick trees veiled the empty house from view, but a spark of light caught his eye, the briefest glimmer. He braked hard and jerked to a stop, rolled down his window, and searched for the source.

There was nothing, just an anxious moan from the beagle beside him.

Must be seein' things.

He turned back to the road, wondered where to go, and decided to drive until he came up with a plan. As he rolled away from Candy's house, the moon lit the windows of the rental cabin behind it, and it winked like an informant in the night.

CHAPTER TWENTY-EIGHT

Gracie couldn't sleep more than a couple hours at a time, hadn't had a good night's rest since Dr. Useless changed her meds. Tonight she woke with a start to the sounds of someone using the shower while somebody else knocked on the front door. But she must have been dreaming, because now the house was quiet and dark. Even the ghost was nowhere to be seen.

She went back to dozing, but it was no use. When the moon cast a steely glow through her window, she found herself wide awake. In these slack hours between midnight and dawn, she often longed for someone to talk to, even a damn nuisance, pushy as all get-out dead girl.

The darkness seemed to stretch like a rubber band, building more and more tension as dawn approached. Snacks helped to pass the time and quiet the jitters, but the chocolate in her closet was gone, and the canned goods beneath her bed, cold. So she crept past the bedrooms, careful not to wake anyone, and made her way to the kitchen pantry.

There were no crackers, not even those bone-hard multigrain things Molly was so fond of. Grunting her disappointment, Gracie felt her way hand-over-hand along the wall until her fingers came up against the fridge. The bulb flickered to life when she swung the door wide, illuminating a wedge of flowered linoleum and ghosting the table beyond.

The last slice of Molly's cheesecake, plated and plastic wrapped, sat among lesser offerings of banana pudding and rhubarb pie. Gracie cupped her hands around the cheesecake with a reverence reserved for special things. When she cradled it up to her nose, the sweet scent, heavy with sour cream and blueberries, made her mouth soggy. She grabbed napkins from the dispenser next to the paper towel roll, snatched a plastic spork from the Old Man in the Mountain mug below it, and turned to face the kitchen table.

"Hi, Gracie."

"Dead girl?" Gracie nearly dropped her spork. A figure sat at the kitchen table, hugging herself like a little girl. It wasn't the ghost.

"Molly? I thought you had a date."

"I did." Molly ran a hand across her face and sniffed. "It didn't turn out as well as I'd hoped."

Gracie's feet scuffed against moist tissues scattered like daisy petals on the floor. That, combined with an excess of sniffling, told her the date had gone even worse than Molly was willing to say. With a sigh, one part disappointment to two parts commiseration, Gracie set her plate on the table and pulled out a chair. She sat quietly and got to work removing Molly's plastic wrap—three layers of loving overkill. "What happened?"

"What didn't?" Molly reached behind her and turned on a reading lamp. It cast a thin glow across her tangled hair and terry robe, and threw crouching shadows over the littered floor. "Don't worry," she said. "I'll clean up my mess before Walter gets up."

"Why would I care?" Gracie took a bite with just a little cream cheese and a lot of graham cracker crust, a splotch of blueberries and a dab of sour cream. She closed her eyes. Molly's cheesecake was the best she'd ever had. Pity the woman couldn't make a decent pancake.

All the snuffling from across the table made the cheesecake less enjoyable, a shame, it being the last slice and all. Gracie swallowed and opened her eyes. "Wanna talk about it?"

"No." Molly blew her nose again and tossed the tissue over her shoulder. "I'm so stupid, I could spit. I ruined everything."

Doubtful. "I saw what you were wearing. The poor man couldn't have had much blood left in his brain."

"I took it off." Molly's sniffles turned to blubbering.

"Good for you. Men like that sort of thing." Gracie stuffed another bite of cheesecake into her mouth. This one had more filling and less crust. She still couldn't guess what the problem was. Molly had a hell of a figure. She probably even looked good on the toilet.

"Everything was perfect," Molly said over a whimper, "but then Dayna Pelletier showed up."

"The tiny police officer?"

Molly nodded.

Gracie licked the spork and went in for another bite. "She looks like a poodle."

Molly went back to sniffling. "Marcel and Dayna have been a couple since high school. They break up and get back together, over and over and on and on." Her voice got harder to understand when her nose started running. "Every damn time they split up, I think maybe this time he'll notice me. And he finally did." She wiped her face before blowing her nose and then tossing the tissue with the others. "I don't get it. Why do people keep getting back together when it never seems to work?"

Gracie wished she had an answer, but relationships made about as much sense as new math. She took another bite of cheesecake. Molly seemed to be waiting, so she rubbed her mouth on a napkin and tried to think of something to say. "What did you do?"

Molly's sigh sent Gracie's napkin fluttering to the table's edge. "I did what I always do. I pretended it didn't matter."

"Why?"

"Because I don't want to lose him."

"How can you lose him? He's not yours."

"I know." Molly made a little squeaking noise. "I'm not gonna be the cause of them breakin' up, so this has to be enough. We're friends."

"Friends?" Gracie snorted. "He sniffs your hair."

"He what?"

"Got milk?"

In the space of a drawn-out groan, Molly got up, grabbed a glass from the cupboard, filled it with milk, and placed it on the table. Then she wandered to the sink and looked out the window, even though there was nothing to see but black.

Gracie figured she ought to say something encouraging, but Molly was supposed to be the helpful one. Giving advice was hard.

"At least now he knows you're interested."

"I am, but he's not. Now he'll be mortified to be near me." Molly cupped her hands and splashed water on her face. Once. Twice.

"Of course he's interested." Gracie finished off the cheesecake and pushed her plate away.

Molly rushed over to pick up the plate and spork, walked back to the sink and reached for a sponge. "What makes you think that?"

"Why would he come here if not for you?"

"That's easy." Molly worked up a lather on Gracie's dirty plate. "I like to cook, and he likes to eat."

Normally, Gracie figured if she couldn't say something nice, she ought to keep her mouth shut. But there were exceptions to every rule, and perhaps this was one.

"There's your proof. He likes you so much, he even pretends to like your pancakes."

Molly still frowned, but she did look less miserable. Maybe this was a good time to change the subject.

"Have you heard back from anyone yet?" Funny how her throat tightened, even though all she'd done was ask a question. "You know, that thing we talked about."

Molly's answering nod had Gracie's heart skipping. "I spoke to the secretary at the church in Keene where you were born. She's going to look through her records and see if you might have family in the area."

"Why?" Gracie gulped her milk, licked off her moustache.

"Well, if you do have a daughter, she may have ended up with relatives." Molly dried the plate and put it in the cupboard.

"I never thought of that." Where her daughter was concerned, she'd never thought much beyond make-believe. But now—"What if I do have relatives? What if my daughter knows who I am and doesn't want me to find her?"

"I can't imagine that would be the case. Besides, I had a reply from the adoption site, too, from someone born the same day as your daughter."

"You did?" Gracie's heart took off in a sprint, and her mouth ran after it. "What did she say? When can I meet her? What does she look like? Is she short like me?"

"Whoa, slow down." As if that were possible. "She wouldn't give me her contact information, but she did ask for my cellphone number. She says she'll try to text me sometime tomorrow."

"Tomorrow?" Gracie felt light-headed. "Tomorrow? And she wants to be found?"

Now Molly looked worried. "Look, Gracie, this may be nothing. I probably shouldn't have said anything until I had more information."

"Tomorrow." Gracie knew she should stop repeating herself, but she couldn't help it. The clock on the wall said one o'clock. "Today." The word was smooth as chocolate on her tongue. She had to say it a second time. "*Today*."

"Well, the sooner you get to bed, the sooner the sun will rise," Molly said with a hint of a smile. "Maybe it will be a better day for both of us."

Gracie caught her foot in the chair rung and nearly fell in her haste to get back to her bedroom. She threw a hurried "Good night!" over her shoulder as she darted down the hallway, not caring who she woke up.

Sleep would be impossible, but that didn't matter. Even with her eyes stuck open, she could dream.

CHAPTER TWENTY-NINE

Marcel woke to the drawn-out glug of a bull frog and the steady slurp of water against a thirsty shore. He slid his hands beneath Scout's head and shifted the dog from his chest to his lap, then grabbed the seatbelt and hoisted himself upright. His neck kinked, and he stretched it straight back while rubbing grit from his eyes.

Echo Lake was still as a puddle, its surface reflecting a dawn turned upside-down. He hadn't meant to spend the night there, but when he'd started to drive home, he'd realized Dayna might still be waiting. And that made his chest feel as if someone had stomped all over it with tiny feet in high heeled shoes.

Blue Horizons was a quarter mile up the road, but he decided a proper apology required he brush his teeth and maybe take a shower. He couldn't help thinking of Molly's kiss, and he wondered if he'd ever have another chance to hold her. Hell, he wondered whether he'd be able to talk to her as a friend again, and if she'd be comfortable coming to his folks' house for Thanksgiving and Christmas. But mostly he wanted to smooth away the disappointment from her eyes.

What she must think of him. The possibilities had kept him awake most of the night. She probably assumed he'd lied about Dayna leaving him, and she had to think he'd been ready to cheat on his girlfriend. Either possibility was bad enough, but what if she thought of something worse?

Just please don't let her think I was looking for a threesome.

Feeling about as useful as long division, he drove home. Dayna wasn't there, thank the Lord, but she'd left a note. *I'm sorry for everything, but we need to talk. Please call.*

He scrunched the paper and stuffed it in the trash under the sink, feeling guilty since she'd had the decency to apologize and say please. But he needed to take a stand. She had to know he was through with her, and if he came running like a hound to bacon, she'd only get the wrong idea. Besides, he wanted to apologize to Molly before he did anything else. Then he could figure out which side Dayna was on and what he might have to do about it.

Once the beagle was fed and walked, Marcel drove straight to Blue Horizons. Scout's hackles went up when he jumped from the passenger seat to the driveway. The dog stared at the path to his own backyard, and a growl rumbled through his chest.

Marcel ran a hand over Scout's head. "What's up, buddy? Does it look different with no one there?"

Scout tucked his tail between his legs. Straining against the leash, he hauled Marcel toward Blue Horizons's front door.

No one answered his knock. The vacuum cleaner was on, so Molly might not have heard. Even though he knew he might appear desperate and maybe a little bit creepy, he walked to the back of the house—maybe he could catch her attention through a window.

He couldn't. But as he turned away, he heard a lawn tractor, and he caught a glimpse of Gracie's pink ball cap winking through the trees. He hesitated, still hoping Molly might notice he was there. But he also wanted to ask Gracie if there might have been anything more she'd wanted to tell him when the Chief had walked in and put an end to their conversation.

Gracie vanished, but he and Scout struck out in her direction, following a dirt path that wound past the vegetable garden and entered a stretch of woods. The trail was longer than he'd expected, and it opened to a field surrounded by forest. Eric's field—the one they'd all played in as kids. It sure did seem smaller now that he was grown.

Scout waved his tail when a ride-on lawnmower barreled across the grass. Gracie drove with one hand, the other clutching her cap to her head. Silver hair flowed behind her, and she whooped and laughed as she roared up to him and hit the brake.

"Scout!" Gracie shut off the engine and climbed to the ground. Scout threw himself at her knees, and she squatted down to hug him. Marcel made a mental note to bring the dog over for another visit, if Molly agreed.

Gracie had a grass catcher attached to the back of the mower, and it swelled to near bursting. She pointed to the field. "What do you think of my handiwork?"

Every inch was neatly mowed, and Marcel had to admit it did look nice. But the odor, like skunk cabbage mixed with ripe grapes, tripped a memory. If he added burnt popcorn and Jack Daniels, it would match the scent he remembered from Uncle Victor's trailer.

"Holy crap."

"Nice, isn't it?" Gracie was all grins. "I thought I'd catch the weed clippings today so they don't smother the new grass. See how nice it's coming in?" She pointed to pale green fuzz forming a cloudy haze between the fat, woody stems her mower had chopped two inches from the ground.

Marcel's mouth refused to close. A whole lot of things started to make sense. "When did you first mow this field? Was it right before Eric passed away?"

Gracie nodded. "How'd you know?"

"And he was upset with you?"

"Fit to be tied. I've never seen a man so angry over weeds." Gracie rolled her eyes. "I was almost done—just had a little patch left to mow, way over near his house. He wouldn't let me finish."

Marcel could have kissed her. "Damn, Gracie, I think I know what happened." He turned slowly in a circle and eyeballed the property. It must be nearly two acres total times maybe ten thousand plants per acre. The gold must have been payment, but from whom?

"He said I killed him." Gracie looked worried again.

"When?" She must be talking about that dream she'd had, but sometimes her memories got twisted around and came out sideways.

Not this time.

Gracie's mouth dropped open, and her eyes were wide as half dollars. "It was the day I mowed the field! Eric said I'd ruined everything. He said he was dead, and I'd killed him!"

Marcel's inner cop danced a jig. "That's probably why you had that dream. It wasn't some sort of visitation. It was a memory." He grinned down at her, hoping she understood. Instead, her face crumpled.

"What did I ruin?"

Marcel bent down, squashed a lonely sprig between his fingers, and held it to his nose. "Do you know what this is?"

"It's weeds."

"It's weed, all right. It smells like purple haze."

"Grace Hannah Ouellette!" Molly stomped up the path, a vacuum cleaner bag in her hand. She looked as if she'd just discovered mouse turds in her flour.

Red-faced and breathing hard, she shouted at Gracie. "You know darn well we have a zero tolerance policy." She flapped the bag under Marcel's nose. "Thanks to the heat from my vacuum cleaner, Gracie's room smells like one of Uncle Victor's chill houses." Back to Gracie. "Care to explain to me what I just vacuumed off your floor?"

Gracie looked from Molly to Marcel and back to Molly. "Grass?"

"Yes, grass! Where did you get it?" Molly's voice was shrill as a wood frog. Marcel figured he'd better reel her in before she said something she'd regret.

"She got it right here," he said gently. "She mowed a whole field of weed and probably tracked it in on her shoes."

"What?" Molly stared across the barren meadow. "How did it get here?" Her eyes got wide. "Eric?"

"What's wrong with mowing weeds?" Gracie was obviously confused and probably more than a little worried.

"It's a different kind of weed," Marcel explained. "It's marijuana."

"Are you sure?" Gracie stared at the field, a mixture of shock and eagerness on her face. "That catcher bag must be worth a fortune. Can I have it?"

Marcel coughed to keep from laughing and said, "I'm gonna pretend you didn't say that." He touched the bag, compared it to the size of the field. She must have filled at least three more bags before this one. "Where's the rest?"

"What's it worth to ya?" Gracie sure was a spitfire. Too bad she was nuts.

"It might be worth Candy's freedom."

A pause, while her face went through a dozen contortions. Then, "Oh, all right. Follow me." Gracie walked a hundred yards with Scout at her side, threading her way through blueberry bushes, until she reached a mound of fresh green chop. Scout dug his shoulder into the pile and rolled onto his back, feet kicking the air.

"It's all here," Gracie said, "everything I mowed today."

"Thank you, Gracie." Marcel turned to Molly. "I'll call the Chief so he can get in touch with the Staties. Meanwhile, could you not tell anyone about this?"

She nodded without looking up.

"And do you think we could talk about what happened last night? Please?"

She shook her head. "There's nothin' to say. I know how it is with you and Dayna."

"And how's that?"

"You break up, and then you get back together, same as always."

Marcel tried to push the hair from her eyes, but she pulled away. "Is that what you think?"

"That's the way it's always been, and I'm okay with it." She turned her back to him, her voice flatter than pancakes.

"I'm not." He rested his hands on her shoulders and gently turned her around. Tears brimmed in her eyes, and she looked as if she could use a hug. Instead he kissed her, a slow, gentle caress, his chapped lips against her smooth ones. When she didn't push him away, he drew her close.

"What about Dayna?" The question was so soft, Marcel considered pretending he hadn't heard.

He wasn't sure why the words came out husky, or why they started that cold place throbbing behind his heart. He said them anyway, needing to hear them out loud so he could judge them in the light. "I'm not with Dayna. I want to be with you."

Something inside him rose up and shook its head, but he hugged Molly tighter and told himself he'd made his choice. "It's been over between Dayna and me for a long time," he said, because saying the words out loud had to make them true. "I let her go."

CHAPTER THIRTY

Marcel held on to Molly for a long time. Her arms draped over his shoulders, head resting just south of his chin, cheek nestled where the bulk of his chest rose to the dip of his throat. A perfect fit, like puzzle pieces linked, swell to void.

"It's about time." Gracie poked at the weed pile. "So what happened with Officer Pelletier? Did you send her packing?"

That should be none of Gracie's business, but obviously she and Molly had talked. Gracie was like a nosy grandmother, bent on knowing things Marcel wouldn't even tell his mom. Given the chance, his mother would peck apart that date like a crow on carrion, all the while insisting he should have stayed and listened to whatever it was Dayna had wanted to say.

He let out a sigh, irritation mixed with regret. "Nothing happened." Molly's hair stuck to his lips, and he managed not to spit when he puffed it away. "Until last night, she hadn't been to my house in over eight months, not since she moved out."

He didn't mean to think about the last time he'd held Dayna, but now he weighed her smallness against the measure of Molly. Dayna was tiny. His arms naturally rested on the juts of her shoulders while her head pillowed beside his heart.

"What did she want?" Molly sounded uncertain whether it was her place to ask.

"Women want what they can't have," Gracie said. "She heard he got a new girlfriend, so she wanted him back." She muttered in Scout's ear, "Not that I'm eavesdropping."

Molly laughed, but it was a tight little sound, more like a yelp.

"I don't know what she wanted." But he had his suspicions. Dayna was trying to unbalance him, make him forget all about whatever it was she was hiding. Why else would she show up like that—naked—hoping his brain might disengage long enough for her to sink her hooks in?

He should have waited, though, should have heard her out.

Molly tensed. "What did she say when she came back?"

"I don't know." He squeezed her hand, hoping she'd understand he didn't want to know what Dayna had to say. "I didn't wait for her. I came here."

Molly stepped back, eyes wide. "Why in the world did you do that?"

"He didn't want to talk to her." Gracie folded her arms across her chest. "Right?"

"Because," he said, trying not to growl, "it was more important to come over here and apologize to you. Besides, she can't just show up like that. She can't expect to pick up where we left off, like I'm so desperate I'll . . ." He turned his back to Gracie and lowered his voice. "Like I'm so desperate I'll climb into bed with her no matter what she's done."

"I heard that," Gracie said, still petting the beagle.

"What has she done?"

"Nothing." Nothing he was sure of. "But I know she's lying about why she came back to the Falls."

Molly let go of Marcel's hand. "Dayna seemed really upset. I think you need to give her a chance to explain."

"It was probably an act."

"No, it wasn't." Molly wrapped her arms around herself like a shield. "She was trying not to cry when she drove me home. I felt like a home wrecker."

"What did she say?"

"She said she was really sorry for ruining our evening, and she never realized I liked you that way."

"What?" Another lie. What the devil was Dayna playing at? "She's the one who told me I should ask you out."

"Dayna did that?" Molly stared at him as if he were a puppy piddling on her best rug. "For the love of pancakes, Marcel, you have to know why."

He didn't. "Pretend I'm stupid."

"She wants you back, you ninny. Don't you see? She figured you wouldn't get anywhere asking out someone who thought of you as a brother. She was buying time."

"That makes no sense. If she wanted me back, she could have had me." He stopped himself too late. Of all the stupid things he'd ever said to a woman.

Molly looked resigned now. All of her hopefulness had hardened. How many times had she listened while he'd whined about Dayna? What if she'd had feelings for him, even then? She'd never said anything, never once given the slightest indication she might think of him as anything more than a friend.

"She wouldn't have come back to Coyne Falls without a darn good reason," Molly said, "and it sure looks like it has something to do with you." Her feet were rooted in place, but something in her posture widened the gap between them. "You need to go and see her, get things sorted out before you think about getting close to someone else."

Now she did step back. Gracie retreated along with her.

Marcel wished he could tell Molly everything he was holding inside—about Eric naming him as a dealer, about Dayna's secrets and all they implied. Dayna wasn't talking, and he doubted she would have come clean last night. She was just playing games, keeping him guessing, leading him in circles.

No way had Dayna come back to Coyne Falls because of him. She'd made that clear. And this was a good thing, because he didn't want her back, not now—not since he'd started to think of Molly as more than a friend.

Because Candy had been right; there had to be more going on than any of them suspected, and this field of marijuana—it was a hell of a clue.

And Dayna. What was she hiding? *Please don't let her be involved in Eric's murder.*

She wasn't. He knew her better than that. Even so, somebody out there had answers, and whoever it was didn't shy away from sending innocent people to jail. If the gold in Eric's closet was any indication, there was a lot of money in play.

Someone wanted that money badly enough to kill.

CHAPTER THIRTY-ONE

"Pot? Seriously? Eric Thompson was growing two whole acres of pot?" Reggie pushed through the station door, grinning like a market hog with a mouthful of corn. "I gotta say, this widens the net, makes me wonder whether someone else might have shot him."

Marcel's heart kicked up a notch. "I never did think Candy was involved."

"She's not out of the woods yet." The detective dropped file folders on the hinged counter and burst out laughing. "How the heck did Eric expect to get away with growing a whole field of pot?"

"I guess he was playing the odds."

"Those are long odds." Reggie pantomimed a golf swing, paused with his hands in the air. "Even a commercial flight could have spotted two acres."

Marcel tried not to laugh but, for the first time, he realized there were some things he knew that the fancy State Police detective didn't. "Lemme show you something," he said. "Come back outside."

Reggie followed him down the handicap ramp into the parking lot. Marcel looked out over the lawn behind the library, past the Meeting House, all the way down to the swampland and woods beyond. "Just focus on that dead tree at the bottom of the hill," he said, "and listen."

Reggie stopped breathing. Marcel was pretty sure he could hear the man's heartbeat. Beyond that there were other small sounds: the whine of mosquitoes, chipmunks rustling the leaves at the edge of the lawn, and a speckled flicker worrying the dead tree.

"Hear that?" Marcel hid a grin. He waited for nearly a minute before the detective took a breath.

"No, I don't hear anything."

"That's what I wanted to show you." Marcel spread his arms wide and turned in a circle. "The quiet. We hardly ever get a commercial flight overhead, just the occasional helicopter."

Reggie perked up. "A helicopter?" He pulled out his phone. "Good thought, Trudeau."

Marcel figured he ought to agree, but as he followed Reggie across the parking lot, he realized he didn't know what the detective was talking about. Probably ought to ask, even if doing so made him look dumb. "So, which thought was the good one?"

"Helicopters." Reggie looked all kinds of smug. "We use National Guardsmen for pot spotting. I wonder if Eric wasn't as stupid as we think. Maybe he had someone in his pocket."

"That is a good thought." Might as well mention another idea, see if his luck held. "I've been thinkin' about the pot found on Eric's body. What if he was shot in the field behind his house, and then dumped at the lake?"

"Another good thought." Reggie got a whole lot more serious. "But the head being cut off—that still doesn't make a lot of sense."

"Some sort of ritual? Or a warning?"

"Or someone's just batshit crazy." Reggie's tone told Marcel he wasn't gonna like what came next. "And that means we can't ignore Eric's next-door neighbors. I spoke to the woman who runs Blue Horizons, but I couldn't get any of the boarders to talk to me."

"They do get spooked by strangers." Marcel led the way up the ramp, opened the door, and waited while Reggie walked in past him. "You kinda have to sit down to breakfast with them. Just listen to whatever comes."

"Ah." Reggie gave the briefest nod. "That caretaker—she seemed nervous having me there. How well do you know her?"

"Molly?" Marcel's hackles went up. "Real well."

"Farrell tells me her uncle is into drugs and alcohol. Molly, too?"

"Hell, no. Molly hates drugs."

"How long has she been running that boarding house?"

"About three months now." Marcel's fists clenched of their own accord. Where was Reggie going with this?

"So what you're telling me is, Molly moved in about a month before that weed was planted."

A kick to the gut would have been less of a shock. Marcel had to admit Reggie was good at connecting the dots, but he had the wrong dots.

"Molly's Uncle Victor moved away a long time ago, and she has nothing to do with him."

"Tell me about Victor."

"Well . . ." Marcel formed the words in his head, careful to leave Molly out of them. "He was a pothead and a drunk. When I was growing up, he spent a lot of time in a holding cell, and there was talk he was dealing. But he packed up and moved away years ago."

"And you're sure he's not in contact with Molly?"

"She had to go and live with him after her folks were *killed* in a car accident." Marcel stressed the part about Molly's mom and dad being dead so Reggie would realize how much she'd had to overcome. "But once she was old enough, she severed ties and never looked back." He left out the part where Amanda Gavin had chased Victor out of town when Molly was fifteen. She'd only done what was best for Molly. No point painting either of them in a bad light.

"Any idea how to reach Victor?"

"No."

"Are you and Molly involved?"

And there went his credibility. Marcel wasn't sure whether it was embarrassment or anger that had his face heating up. "We've been friends since we were kids, and we had our first date last night."

"First date, huh?" Reggie's chuckle had layers, probably none of them humor. "Isn't the timing a little bit suspicious? How'd she maneuver you into asking her out right after Eric's body dropped?"

"She didn't . . . Gracie was the one who suggested it . . . but I was gonna anyway, just hadn't decided on how to go about—"

"Gracie, she's the one who confessed to the murder?"

Marcel swallowed to smooth the piss from his voice. "She'll be retracting that confession. Seems it was just a dream she had after Eric yelled at her for mowing the field."

"I'll bet Eric never saw that coming."

Marcel wasn't sure whether to laugh, so he kept his expression neutral. "Gracie did say he was fit to be tied. Ya gotta feel a little bit sorry for the guy."

"And this Molly, she never did drugs? Not even once?"

"God, no. Molly was like a drug-sniffing dog when we were kids. If she even thought someone had pot, she'd kick them right in the—"

"So she tends toward violence."

"No, it isn't like that." Now he was whining. Marcel wished he could back up a few sentences and tell the arrogant son of a bitch how hard Molly worked, how much the boarders loved her, what she looked like with moonlight on her face. "It's just that she hated drugs. She didn't want us ending up like her uncle, or like Eric."

"And now? Does she still feel the same?"

"Hell, yes." On this Marcel could be certain. "You should have seen the way she lit into Gracie when she found marijuana in her carpet."

"And you see her as a stable person, even though it sounds as if she has one hell of a temper?"

Marcel's throat went dry. If only he could punch something. "With everything she has to deal with, she's more than stable. She's amazing. And it's not like she blows up every day."

"Only takes once. Where was she when Eric was killed?"

So this was what it was like to be interrogated. Worse than Marcel had imagined. "She was at Blue Horizons, worried sick. Gracie was missing."

"And there was no time she could have slipped out the back? For all we know, Molly and the old bat worked together. Molly shot Eric and Gracie disposed of the gun."

"You're dead wrong."

"Maybe." But Reggie didn't sound uncertain. "You and I need to go there together, Trudeau. And you need to ask Molly straight out."

"She couldn't do something like that."

"Not even if it meant taking one more drug dealer out of the world?"

"No. Never."

Reggie sighed, leaned against the counter, and somehow managed to modulate his voice to something that radiated concern, maybe even regret. "If Molly was raised by this creep, and she lives adjacent to the property, you have to look at her more closely. It's your job."

Bad enough Candy was under arrest, but if Molly were taken into custody— "If you knew her like I do, you'd be looking somewhere else." An image of Molly flashed through Marcel's mind, righteous anger exploding through her fist, knocking a two hundred-pound asshole to the floor.

"You see, Trudeau, that's where you're wrong. You said it yourself. We have to follow the evidence and go wherever it leads." Reggie shrugged, a gesture of acceptance that said it didn't matter what Marcel knew in his heart. All that mattered was the damn evidence that kept on piling up and pointing fingers at everyone he cared about.

"You don't get it. These folks are my friends, my family. I *know* them."

"And you could be right." Reggie's tone still said he had doubts. "But if you look at the situation without all that emotion you're carrying around, I think you'll have to agree. The evidence is leading us straight to Blue Horizons."

"There's a difference between evidence and supposition. There's no evidence pointing to Molly."

"Not yet." And right there, Marcel knew Reggie was building a case in his head. "She did have motive and opportunity, and that makes her a person of interest." He already had his phone in hand, scrolling through contacts. "I'm gonna see if we can pull financials on this Victor person. Molly, too. Let's see if they've been spending more than they earn."

"Victor, maybe, but you won't find a thing on Molly." Marcel headed for the door, his feet landing harder than he'd planned. "I'll help you talk to the boarders, and I'll ask Molly where she was when Eric died. You'll see."

"No time like the present." Reggie dialed as he walked. "Then I need to head over to St. Fillan's to talk to a Dr. Wheeler."

"Gary Wheeler? The psychiatrist?"

"That's the one." Reggie was grinning again. "Seems Wheeler commutes in a chopper, and I'm told he reported a field of marijuana to the DEA a couple weeks ago." He chuckled as he jogged down the ramp. "I'm gonna see if he'll take me up. I'd like to get a visual of the layout—Gracie's tree stand, Echo Lake, and that path from Eric's field to Blue Horizons."

CHAPTER THIRTY-TWO

With the lawns already mowed, the field off-limits pending some sort of police investigation, and doctor's orders to stay out of Echo Lake, Gracie was running out of options. Weeding wasn't her favorite activity, but it needed doing, and she had time. The only problem was hard bricks against old knees.

She dropped her bedroom pillow onto the front walk, straddled it, and then lowered herself as far as she could before collapsing onto her bottom. Scraggy legs splayed in front of her, wrinkled and stubby, looking almost as old as her hands. Half a dozen cat hairs sprouted from her shins. She glanced behind her. "I suppose if I'm going to wear shorts, I might have to take up shaving."

No one answered. The dead redhead hadn't spoken to her in days.

She wiggled her way into a rollover and came to rest on all fours, knobby knees buried in soft down. The pillow was a tremendous improvement, and the expected dull ache didn't materialize.

Molly wouldn't approve, of course. Pillows were meant for bedrooms, and clean pillowcases belonged under one's head rather than on the ground. But Molly was young and elastic, able to bend in ways Gracie hadn't attempted in decades.

As she worked, Gracie listened to the sounds of Molly making butternut-apple soup in the kitchen. The smell of fresh squash and cinnamon coaxed her stomach into a series of high-pitched squeaks and low gurgles that might have embarrassed her as a younger woman, but she'd long ago learned to accept her plumbing. As with her mind, she was grateful it worked at all.

The chunks of Gala apples, Molly said, added sweetness that outshone sugar or honey. Amanda Gavin must have told her that. Doubtful Molly had learned to cook from Suzanne Trudeau. Marcel's mother was a wonderful woman, treating Molly like family and all. But on those occasions when she'd covered for Amanda at Blue Horizons, she'd always burned the rolls. Her salads were filled with grit, and she never put enough sugar in the lemonade.

An hour passed. Gracie pulled weeds and piled them alongside the bricks while her mind went swimming at Echo Lake, climbed Bald Hill, and explored the cave behind Ribbon Falls. By the time the mound of roots and leaves stretched the length of the walk, her hands had begun to blister. Tired, she pushed herself to her knees and stretched the stiffness from her back.

The sound of an engine drew her attention, and when Officer Trudeau's SUV crested the hill, she felt a whole lot lighter. Molly would be thrilled to see the young man, even if she didn't put those feelings on her face where he might see them. Gracie looked forward to his visits, too. He seemed to like her, although she couldn't imagine why.

"Marcel!" she called out. "We have a hit!" That was what Molly had called it. A *hit*. The woman who'd responded to Gracie's Internet posting had texted Molly. She wanted to meet, maybe as soon as tomorrow.

"I have to stop thinking of my daughter as a baby," Gracie reminded herself. "Must have kids of her own. Maybe grandkids."

And she probably hadn't survived at all.

Gracie picked up her pillow and shook off the worst of the dirt. Marcel climbed out of the SUV, and she waved to him. His answering smile was as tight as Candy Thompson's jeans, and the reason was right behind him. The passenger door opened, and Reggie Clark got out.

"Oh, balls. Dick Tracy is here." Head down, Gracie headed for the door. Once inside, she slipped the lock, hollered, "Molly! We got visitors," dropped her pillow by the door, and then headed for the kitchen.

"What?" Molly had steaming butternut and apple whirling in the blender, and she was pouring cream and melted butter through the hole in the cover. Gracie's mouth watered, and she forgot what she'd been about to say.

"Is it ready yet?" She reached up and rested her hand on the warm glass of the blender. "I could test it for ya, let you know what it needs."

Molly shook cinnamon over the top and laughed like she always did. "Sure thing. I'd appreciate the help." She poured a generous helping into a mug. The soup was thick and sweet, the scent spicy as pumpkin pie. Already Gracie wondered how soon a second cup might follow the first. The doorbell rang, and Molly jumped.

"That detective fellow is here," Gracie said, "the one who gives me the creeps."

Molly covered the blender and wiped her hands on a dish towel. "Reggie Clark? Why in the world would he come back?"

"For lunch?"

"Not likely. Is anyone with him?"

Gracie's mouth was full, so she squished her lips together and nodded before attempting to swallow.

"Marcel?"

"Mmmm." Gracie grinned at the combination of confusion and hopefulness on Molly's face.

Then Molly did a lot of things quickly—rinsed her hands under the faucet and splashed her cheeks, ran fingers through her curls, and smoothed her shirt over her jeans.

"He's seen you naked," Gracie said between sips. "He won't notice if you're rumpled."

"I'm rumpled?"

"A good rumpled. Men like women to be casual."

"Nice try." Molly headed for the entryway. "What happened to this pillow? And why is the door locked?"

"Darned if I know." Gracie helped herself to more soup. Balancing an overfull cup, she took a seat at the table and listened to the conversation revolving around the front hall. Both officers were inside now, which couldn't be a good thing.

She heard Molly's soft "Interview the boarders?" and "A little warning would have been nice," as she drained her cup and got up to pour another. But then, "I was right here! The whole night!" came out in a gasp.

"We have to ask, Mols." Marcel's apology came out in a jumble as Molly stormed into the kitchen. Both men followed her through the doorway. Gracie skittered from her usual chair to the one way back against the wall.

"Next you'll be askin' where the extra money comes from, even though you know darn well it's an anonymous donation!"

"I know, Mols." Marcel glanced at Gracie and gave her a weak smile.

"Why do you want to talk to the boarders? Do you think they did it, too?" Molly slammed a roasting pan into the sink, sending a wave over the splashguard.

"Of course not." Poor Marcel looked as if he'd broken Molly's best china. "We're just trying to piece together what happened, and you were right next door."

"Charlotte would remember," Gracie said.

"I'm not sure she'll talk to them." Molly grabbed steel wool and scrubbed hard.

"We're just trying to get a sense of what was happening in the neighborhood when Eric died." Marcel hovered near the table. Probably didn't dare get too close to the sink sprayer.

"I wasn't in the neighborhood." Gracie looked up at Molly, now standing with her hands wound up in a dish towel. "Besides, Charlotte's the one who remembers everything. I'm the one who forgets."

Walter appeared in the doorway and U-turned back to the hallway.

"Idiots," Molly said. "If you'd given me a chance to prepare him . . ." She bolted out the door, her voice dropping to soothing tones. "It's okay, Walter. Can I get you some soup?"

"I'm sorry, Walter. You too, Molly."

It was kind of Marcel to apologize for something the detective had obviously made him do. Gracie picked up her cup and tried to take another sip. But the soup had cooled and thickened, and now it clung like mayonnaise to the bottom.

"As long as you're up, can you get me a spoon?" Gracie directed the question at Reggie, but Marcel jumped to attention.

"Sure thing, Gracie. Spoon or spork?"

"Spoon, like I said."

Marcel brought Gracie a spoon and a napkin while Reggie grabbed an empty chair and moved it close to Gracie's knees. He relaxed into the cushioned seat just as Molly slammed back into the room and took a cup from the counter. "If you want to talk to Walter, you'll have to speak through his door. Right now, he's going to have soup in his room. Jillian won't come out either. I'll see what I can do with Charlotte."

"Sorry to mess up your routine, Molly."

Marcel did look sorry, but Reggie's face was blank as the notepad in his hand. His voice, though—that wasn't calm. It was clipped and intense and not at all friendly.

"Can you tell me if you saw or heard anything unusual the night you ran away?"

"Who? Me?" Gracie looked behind her to see if he might be speaking to someone else. There was no one there, not even a dead redhead. She tried to slide her chair farther away, but it came up against the wall. Reggie was waiting. She tried to remember his question.

"Reggie, would you consider sitting here?" Marcel took a seat halfway down the table and gestured to the chair on his left. "I think Gracie might be feeling crowded."

"Oh." The detective scooted back a few inches before getting to his feet. "Sorry. I should have noticed."

"Liar." Gracie hadn't meant to say it out loud, but Reggie stared at her with something like shock before he let out a one-syllable chuckle.

"You're right." He walked around Marcel and took the seat beside him. "I crowded you on purpose."

"Why?" The man's retreat gave Gracie a chance to let out her breath. She picked up her spoon.

"I wanted you to answer without thinking."

"Well, the joke's on you, then. I always do." Gracie folded her arms across her chest. Reggie Clark played more games than the dead girl. Thanks to all the ghosts in her life, Gracie knew how to play.

Marcel shot her a wink and, for whatever reason, the gesture slowed her heart.

Molly returned with Charlotte in tow. The older woman shuffled to the center of the kitchen, moleskin notebook clutched to her chest. She didn't look at anyone, just fixed her eyes on the floor.

"Charlotte has something she wants to tell you," Molly said. "Go ahead, Charlotte. We'll all listen."

Charlotte's memory was always fun—not as perfect as that redhead on TV but, with the journal backing her up, it was close.

"Ask her what she had for breakfast twenty years ago today," Gracie said. "She'll tell you it was eighty-two degrees out and misting while she ate eggs, and they were runny."

"It's true." Molly guided Charlotte to the counter, where she stood with her back to the police officers. "Charlotte has something approaching total recall, and she writes everything down. You can't hardly walk through her room but for the stacks and stacks of notebooks. I'm gonna have to rent her a storage unit."

"But all of that information is still filtered through her experience," Reggie said to Marcel. "Don't forget that."

"Same as anyone else," Gracie muttered.

"I know." Marcel was hiding a smile.

The detective turned a tolerant gaze on Charlotte. Well, she'd make a believer of him. She always did.

"Do you remember anything unusual that happened last Thursday evening?" He glanced at his watch. "Aside from Gracie's disappearance?"

"Unusual, no." Charlotte's high-pitched tone had Reggie visibly cringing. "Not unusual. Not unusual. Not unusual."

"So there was nothing out of the ordinary? Just a normal evening?" The detective's voice was fast becoming annoying. Too forceful, like gunshots.

"Dessert was late because of Gracie. Because of Gracie. That was unusual."

"What else happened?" Marcel spoke in the relaxed drawl he used for everyone. "How 'bout earlier in the evening, before the pie?"

"The ambulance arrived at 8:26." Charlotte held her hands to her head and closed her eyes. "Cracked Jack found Gracie's window open at 8:39. Officer Dayna Pelletier came at 8:54, and Officer Marcel Trudeau at 9:08."

"Thank you, Charlotte. What else can you tell us?" Good for Marcel for taking over. Reggie wouldn't have thought to say thank you.

"Molly called Amanda." Charlotte began pacing the length of the counter. "It was 8:52. Amanda hadn't heard from Gracie. Not a word." Charlotte darted a glance at the table and immediately looked away.

"How 'bout before that?" Marcel again.

"Molly went to the bathroom at 7:45. Walter had to go, too, but he waited until Molly disinfected the toilet. Relieved himself from 7:50 to 7:59."

Molly blushed. Gracie supposed she didn't like Marcel knowing she went to the bathroom.

Marcel was grinning now. "What happened next?"

"I went to the bathroom much later—at 8:36. Number two. Fifteen minutes total. The color was off, and it floated. Probably the lard Molly uses in her pie crust."

Gracie giggled. Marcel bit down on his lip. The fancy detective fidgeted as if he'd sat on an ant hill. The man needed to learn a thing or two about patience.

"Zoe Trudeau and Cracked Jack interrupted *Dancing with the Stars*. Molly woke Gracie at 8:31. Zoe yelled at Jack at 9:05. Gracie must have left between 8:31and 8:39. The gunshot was at 8:40. That was when I washed my hands. I used the anti-bacterial soap—"

"Gunshot?" Reggie leaned across the table.

Charlotte spoke into her collarbone. "Gunshot. Yes. At 8:40."

"I heard that, too," Gracie said. "Sounded like it came from Eric's field."

"You don't think a gunshot is unusual?" The detective nearly spit.

"No. Not unusual. Not here." Charlotte continued pacing. "Shouldn't shoot after sunset, but everyone does."

"People shoot a lot here," Gracie added.

The detective gave Marcel a withering look. "I thought you said Coyne Falls was quiet."

Marcel shrugged. "A lot of folks shoot, but most of the victims are beer cans."

"It was dark." Charlotte walked faster. "But they had lights."

"Lights?" This time Marcel and the detective both asked.

"Yes, lights." Charlotte shook her head in time with her pacing. "Headlights on the truck."

"What truck?"

"The truck!" Charlotte's voice rose. "The only truck there was! Arrived at 9:17 and left at 9:26." She paused a moment, head hanging. "That was unusual, too."

"Why?"

"No headlights when they left."

The detective stared at Marcel. "They turned the lights off."

"Something to hide?" Marcel wasn't smiling anymore.

"Unusual. Lights off. Big truck. Diesel. Sounded like a plane."

"And it drove out of our driveway?" Molly looked nervous.

"No. Next door. At 9:26." Charlotte held out her notebook. "See?"

Molly accepted the notebook and handed it to Marcel. He thumbed through the pages, stopped, and read aloud. "Truck drove from Thompson driveway 9:26. Diesel. No lights." Then he backed up several pages. He held his breath for a moment before asking, "Charlotte, can you tell me what happened at 8:25?"

"Neighbor, dropped off."

"I see that, but can you be more specific? Which neighbor? Dropped off where? By whom?

"Eric Thompson, end of his driveway." Charlotte fisted her hands. "Couldn't see who dropped him."

For a moment, no one said anything. Marcel's gaze didn't leave Charlotte. "You saw someone leave Eric at the end of his driveway?"

"At 8:25." Charlotte's voice rose. "Couldn't see the car. Only heard it." She bit her lip in concentration. "Powerful engine."

"Wait. This means Eric was next door when I was talking to Abe and Candy." Marcel walked over to Charlotte and ducked down to her level. His voice shifted to National-Public-Radio tranquility. "Did you get a look at anyone, or did you hear any voices you might recognize?"

Charlotte clasped her hands to her ears. "Soup!" she said. "Now."

Molly had already filled a fresh cup, and now hurried to Charlotte's side. "Here, or in your room?"

"Soup." Charlotte resumed pacing.

"Here, then." Molly relaxed a bit. "I'll get you the placemat you like, the one with the kittens."

Charlotte's pacing slowed. "Kittens?"

"Nice fuzzy ones." Molly lifted a plastic mat from a stack near the stove and brought it to the table along with the soup. Charlotte fell in at her side, touching the placemat and cooing.

Reggie looked more suspicious than impressed. "Well, Gracie, it looks as if you may have been right on top of Eric's murder, after all."

"That's what Eric said." She pulled her cup of soup to her chest. "But he also said I killed him, and I didn't." She sighed into her chest. "Not that I remember."

Molly planted herself between Gracie and the detective. "You do know Gracie couldn't have done it, right? She had no reason."

"None that we're aware of." The detective's attitude said he hadn't decided, not yet.

Killers had motives. Gracie hadn't considered that. Truthfully, she didn't much care for Eric. "He hit Candy, you know. That didn't set well with me."

"Gracie!" Molly bent down and shushed her. "You didn't do it. Stop confessing."

Marcel, though— he looked thoughtful. "We should get a bunch of volunteers to search that field."

"What for?" Molly's hair frizzed in the humidity, and her clothes looked as if she'd had a long, hard day. But Marcel still looked at her as if she was beautiful.

"If that's where Eric was shot, then there might be a shell casing. And if we can determine when and where he was killed, maybe we'll find more evidence."

"Worth a try." Reggie looked as if he was rolling an awful lot of things around in his head. "How 'bout you make it happen, Trudeau. Find us some volunteers, and coordinate a search with your Chief."

"Will do."

Gracie's heart kicked into high gear. She'd crossed that field moments before the gunshot, and Marcel had found the murder weapon right alongside her canned goods. And motive? She'd just given them one.

She didn't have the best of memories. Everyone knew that. If the gunshot that killed Eric was the same one she'd heard the night she ran away, she'd been within a hundred yards of Eric's murder, and Scout was her only witness. That meant she didn't have an alibi, after all.

CHAPTER THIRTY-THREE

Marcel and Chief Farrell chose the portion of field closest to the Thompson residence. They paced off an acre and divided it into quadrants with wooden stakes and twine. Dayna Pelletier and Todd Lyman further split the quarter-acre portions into lanes approximately two feet wide. Farrell assigned a lane to each of the newly deputized volunteers.

Falls residents, excited to be part of a murder investigation, turned out in numbers that put Election Day to shame. Candy and Abe, out on bail and probably hoping to see the charges dropped, sat on the sidelines with Scout. They'd offered to help, of course, but Farrell refused, citing conflict of interest.

Tastes like Chicken, a local band, set up in the bed of Doug Marley's pickup truck. Doug ran an extension cord from Candy's house and cranked up the volume until the feedback nearly drowned out their original music. The Girl Scouts had a bake sale, and the Conservation Commission set up an education booth featuring a vase of Japanese knotweed and a bottle of hemlock infected with woolly adelgid.

Reggie Clark hugged the shade and swatted black flies while Chief Farrell led the search. Marcel stayed as far from Dayna as he could, but she still managed to cross his path.

"Can you meet me later?" She didn't look at him, same as always, just walked past him toward her lane at the opposite end of the field.

He grumbled back at her, "I think I'll be busy." The words made him feel small. Molly was probably right. He had to sit down with her and listen to whatever it was she felt the need to say, even if all she did was lie to him.

With a sigh that felt as if it crawled all the way from his toes, he turned around and caught up to her. "How 'bout we get a cup of coffee once all this is wrapped up?"

"I'd like that." She still couldn't seem to meet his eye but, for the first time in a long time, he didn't see her as furtive. She looked sad and worried and not at all deceitful.

The thought barely came to rest when a shout of, "I found it!" sounded from lane three, a section of ground encompassing a maple at the edge of the field. A tall blonde waved something in her hand. "It's a casing, brass, like you said."

"And I think I said not to pick it up." Marcel ran toward the spot.

"Oops. Sorry." Amanda Gavin dropped the casing and backed away. "I got excited."

"Didn't Chief Farrell ask you to sit this out? Your daughter's been charged." He left out the part where she'd just contaminated evidence. Instead, he squatted near the maple's trunk and brushed fingers through the weeds. "Where'd you say you dropped it?"

"Right there." With Amanda's help, he spotted the glint of brass winking amid star moss. He picked it up with tweezers and held it to the light.

"Could be the one. Good job, Mrs. Gavin." He'd never be able to call her Amanda, not after growing up alongside Candy and being taught young-gentleman manners by his mom. "Can you show me exactly where it was before you picked it up?"

"Here." She pointed to another patch of moss, farther back and beneath the tree.

"Can we get a tape measure, please?" Marcel knew from the ballistics report that Eric had been shot in the chest at a distance of approximately twenty feet, assuming a factory round. The casing could easily have flown another ten. He handed the end of the tape measure to Todd Lyman, then walked out thirty feet. Marcel paced a wide arc, all the while watching the ground at his feet.

"This could be it." Just inside his circle was a patch of earth where marijuana plants had survived Gracie's mowing. "This must be the area Gracie missed the first time she mowed, and this patch didn't get cut the second time, because they were already squashed flat. Could be where Eric fell."

Chief Farrell walked up beside him while Marcel eyeballed a path to Candy's driveway. More plants, bent and twisted, formed a faint trail through the grass.

"Might be where someone dragged a body out of the field." Marcel pointed. "Maybe someone shot Eric right here, and then they used a truck to help move the body. That would match up with Charlotte's recollection."

"Huh." Reggie came up behind them. "Good eyes."

Marcel shrugged off the compliment. His eyes were probably average, same as the rest of him. "Now what?"

"I doubt there'll be much to find, what with all the rain and mowing. But I'll see if I can scare up a team to go over the scene." Reggie pointed to the patch of marijuana. "Let's get a sample of that weed. Maybe it'll match the plant material on the body."

"Will do." Marcel pulled an evidence bag from his pocket.

"Nice work on this, by the way." Reggie cuffed his shoulder. "Toughen up a little, and you might make a decent detective someday."

"He'd have to toughen up a hell of a lot," Farrell said. "And then he'd have to toughen up some more."

Marcel wasn't sure what to say, but he didn't stand there feeling uncomfortable for long. One of the volunteers hollered, "I think I found it!" from across the field.

He, Reggie, and the Chief jogged to the spot, arriving a moment after Dayna. Sure enough, another brass casing lay in Gracie's new grass.

Marcel's optimism nosedived. He turned in Candy's direction and cupped his hands around his mouth. "Did Eric do any target shooting out here?"

"'Course he did. Why?"

"Never mind." Marcel bagged the cartridge, took the tape measure from his pocket, and handed it to Reggie. "Care to do the honors?"

Whatever it was Reggie said, Marcel missed it. His attention was drawn by three more voices, all shouting, "We found some too! Lots of 'em!"

Reggie's laughter started small and took off fast. Old Lyman's snicker joined in. Dayna was the only one who kept a straight face.

"It was a good idea, Trudeau, but it backfired." Reggie looked out over the crowd of volunteers, his face half amused, half disappointed. "But we got a party out of the deal, so I guess it was worth it."

"I suppose." Marcel wished maybe the ground would open up and swallow him. But when he glanced toward his feet, something shiny winked at him from beneath the grass. He bent down to investigate.

It was brass—another casing. Beside it were more casings, spread out over an area about a dozen feet in diameter. He sighted across the field to a hillock that could easily provide a berm. Must be about fifty feet away.

"Wait! This must be where Eric shot targets. And over there—" He pointed to a group of people excitedly scooping more brass from the dirt. "That's gotta be about a hundred feet from the berm, so those were from target practice, too."

He looked back to where Amanda Gavin had found the first casing. "That's the only one that was all by itself, so it still could be where Eric was shot."

"You might be right," Reggie said. "I'll call it in, and we'll see if there's anything left for forensics to find." He glanced at his watch. "I'm heading into Lebanon. Goin' up in a chopper."

"With Dr. Wheeler?" Dayna's new boyfriend. Marcel glanced at her, but she was squatting in the grass, sorting casings from the dirt with gloved hands.

"Yup. We're planning to fly over Coyne Falls, see how tough this field is to spot."

"Maybe you'll spot another one." The moment he said it, Marcel wondered—would Eric hang all his hopes on one crop? A field right in his backyard and so easily spotted?

No point shooting his mouth off before he had something concrete. Instead, he jogged across the field to where Candy sat with her legs splayed on the grass, Scout snuggled against her hip. Dayna followed a few feet behind him. She probably figured they were done here, and she wanted to make sure he wasn't trying to wiggle out of having that talk.

"I'm glad to see they finally let you out," he said when he got close enough to Candy to be heard without shouting. "Where's Abe?"

"I dunno. Went off to plug somebody's leak, I expect." Candy shaded her eyes and grinned up at him. She didn't look angry or disappointed, despite all she'd been through.

"I hear the bail was steep." Higher than he'd thought reasonable.

"My mom paid it, for both of us." Candy stopped rubbing Scout's tummy long enough to motion toward the field. "Mom says she found a casing. Will it help?"

"I hope so." Marcel dropped to the grass and ran a hand over Scout's head. "I did get to wondering, though. If Eric had another crop, where would it be?"

"Another one?" Candy put on a thinking face, complete with lip biting and forehead scrunching. "He has the greenhouses, of course, but I expect you already looked there. Maybe that blueberry field he uses?" For a moment, she looked embarrassed, but she managed to square her shoulders. "Technically, that piece of land belongs to Victor LeBlanc, but no one's seen him in years, and it seemed a shame to let it go fallow. Eric kinda took it over without asking."

"Molly's uncle?" A little burst of excitement had Marcel's inner policeman at full attention. "Mind if I take a look?"

"Knock yerself out, Marcel—it's not mine. The berry bushes are right off Pole Hill across from the old Pinkham place."

"Thanks, Candy." Marcel looked behind him for Dayna. Maybe she could come along, and they could have that cup of coffee afterwards. But she was gone. He searched the crowd until he spotted her. She was already halfway to her car, and she had her phone pressed tight to her ear.

Marcel drove the mile to Pole Hill, parked on a grassy verge, and stepped out into chest-high goldenrod. The mouth of the trail was choked with a wall of black raspberries, the foliage lush green with tiny thorns that clutched and pulled like kittens' claws. He took a moment to tuck his pants legs into his socks to keep ticks from reaching his skin. Then he shut his eyes and pushed through the prickers until he broke free into the trail proper.

The walk to Uncle Victor's field was shorter than he'd expected. After an easy five-minute hike, he entered a wide meadow, maybe three acres total. It was filled with blueberry bushes, most of them taller than his forehead and all sheathed in bird netting. On closer inspection, he picked out marijuana, already several feet high, netted

alongside the bushes. Hidden by the blueberry bushes and bird netting, they'd be tough to spot with eyes alone.

He walked to the center of the expanse, turned in a circle, and
tried to get his bearings. The station was almost due east, and Blue
Horizons lay to the west, just beyond a tall ridge topped with a massive pine.

"Son of a bitch." Gracie's tree stand was halfway up that pine,
and Marcel remembered seeing the white netting from the platform.
Could be someone used the stand to watch over the crop. That would
explain Gracie's missing canned goods. Might even explain the gun.

For that matter, somebody could watching right now.

Eyes on Gracie's pine, Marcel reached for his mic—better let the
Chief know what he'd found. Before he could say anything, he heard
voices from somewhere behind him.

He ducked lower. From behind a thick screen of blueberries, he
watched two figures emerge from the trees about fifty yards away,
one tall, one short, both female. The mic might give him away, so he
clicked it off, took his cellphone from his pocket, and dialed dispatch.

There was no signal, not unusual in the Falls, so he pocketed the
phone and listened. The little one sounded like Dayna. The other was
about Shay's height and build.

Then he saw Shay's shoulder holster. The woman who claimed
never to have shot a gun in her life had some explaining to do.

He unsnapped his holster and ran his fingers over the pistol grip,
just to reassure himself it was there. All sorts of thoughts went through
his head. *What if they're involved in this? What if I have to draw my weapon?
What if—* "What the hell are you two doin' here?" He hadn't meant
to holler.

Shay spun around and glared in his direction. Dayna shaded her
eyes and shouted, "Marcel? Is that you?"

He started toward them, caught his toe on a wad of cat grass, and
slammed to the ground. There was a CRACK from Bald Hill. Next
to where his head had been, a twig broke and fell. About the time he
realized someone had shot at him, Dayna fell, too.

Everything that followed happened in slow motion. Shay fired
over his head as he ran toward them. A bullet sang past his shoulder
and slammed into the blueberry bushes in his path, but he didn't drop

and weave like he should have. He just ran in a straight line to Dayna, dove to the ground beside her, and touched a finger to her throat.

"I'm not dead, Marcel, but I'm hit." Her voice was fragile as cobwebs and, when he took her hand, his fingers touched something sticky.

That was the problem with living in Coyne Falls. Emergency vehicles were thirty minutes out with the nearest hospital an hour away. And no matter how hard he pressed on the hole in her belly, the damn blood kept on leaking between his fingers. Shay was on the ground beside them, talking into a microphone clipped to her collar. The words she said weren't anything he would have expected from the woman he'd found duct taped to a toilet.

"Taking fire. Officer down. Request backup and air transport." Shay took her eyes off the opposite end of the field long enough to glance at Dayna, and the look on her face matched the screaming in his head.

She spoke into the mic. "Make it fast."

CHAPTER THIRTY-FOUR

Marcel couldn't stop thinking of the dead raccoon he'd scraped from the pavement at the end of Earle Bronson's driveway. Dayna's eyes had the same glazed look, fixed, like the Halloween marbles at the variety store next to Elvira wigs and fake vomit. Beneath his fingers, her pulse was hard to find, but he'd never been good at that sort of thing. "Stay with me, Dayna." His voice came out wobbly, so he clamped down and made it sound more confident. "I'm here."

"Move over." Shay pulled a bandage from a pouch in her pants leg, tore off the wrapper, and pressed it into the wound. Then she grabbed his hand and pushed it in. "I need you to bear down like you mean it, Marcel. Do you want her to live, or don't you?"

"'Course I do." He pressed harder. The flow dropped to an ooze, and the panic eased off. He realized he'd been holding his breath and made a point of sucking in as much as his chest would allow. "What is that?"

"A clotting agent. Should help." Another bullet pinged against the pine behind them, and Shay swore. "Think you can hold onto that while I drag her a few feet? We can hunker down behind that dirt pile until help arrives."

Marcel's stomach rocked. "I'd feel a whole lot better if you were doin' the holdin' while I did the draggin'."

"What does she weigh, ninety pounds? I think I can handle it."

"That's not what I—"

"I know." Shay ducked low and moved to Dayna's feet. "But ya gotta suck it up, rookie. I'm gonna need my hands free."

She slapped on a pair of binoculars and focused on the tree line at the opposite end of the field. After playing with the lenses for a moment, she said, "No wonder we're still standing. Lyman's aiming wide."

"Who?" Marcel winced when Dayna squirmed beneath his hands. She wrapped her fingers around his wrist. For a moment, her eyes focused.

"Don't trust them, Marcel. None of them." The words were soft and garbled, and he wasn't sure he'd heard right. Blood surged past his hand. He pressed harder as her fingers went slack.

"He's reloading. It's now or never." Shay grabbed Dayna's feet. "I'd rather not move her, but we don't have a choice. So cradle her head with your left hand and do your damndest to keep pressure with the right. Ready?"

Marcel felt about as coordinated as a newborn calf, but he ground his teeth and nodded. Shay dragged Dayna through the weeds until they were half hidden behind a snowmobile ramp. He'd always thought jumping snowmobiles was stupid, but now he wanted to send a donation to their club.

"Is that really Todd Lyman shooting at us?"

His words were lost in the staccato throb of an approaching helicopter. It rose past the trees, then circled in a low sweep before hovering at the far end of the field. Shots were fired, but Marcel couldn't tell who was doing the shooting. Someone in a police uniform stumbled toward the same trail he'd used to get there, grabbing his hip and running in stiff-legged spurts.

"Is that Lyman?" He had to shout above the noise.

"Sure is," Shay hollered back. "He won't bother us, and I think the other one is on the run. We should be okay."

"How many are there?"

The chopper roared across the field and set down not thirty feet away, bird netting genuflecting all around it. Shay was on her feet running a moment before the landing skids came to rest. Dr. Wheeler jumped out and tossed her an orange duffel. Reggie Clark hit the ground behind him.

"Saline?" Shay called over her shoulder as she sprinted back to Dayna.

"In the bag. How bad is it?" Dr. Wheeler ran behind her dragging a flat stretcher.

"Bad enough." Shay ripped open a sealed kit and went to work. "She's drifting. Romeo here has a finger on her pulse."

Dr. Wheeler dropped to his knees and wound a blood pressure cuff around Dayna's arm. "What the hell!" He glared at Marcel. "What did you do?"

"I was just—"

"Officer Trudeau didn't do anything, Wheeler. It was just bad luck." Shay jerked her chin toward Reggie. "You winged Lyman. Did you get a look at the other one?"

"He was in that tree on the hill. Bastard knew how to use cover." Reggie turned away and waded into the brush, shouting back over his shoulder, "Farrell called in the cavalry. We're gonna meet up at the trailhead."

Marcel couldn't watch when Shay slipped a needle into the fold of Dayna's elbow. Blood didn't bother him, but needles, they were different. So he focused on Reggie as he wound his way back toward the trail. Then he glanced back as Shay hooked up an IV, held a bag of clear liquid up high, and squeezed it between her hands.

"Don't look if you think you might faint," she told him. "I need you to keep pressure on that wound."

Marcel watched Dayna's face and willed her to keep breathing. "You sure are prepared," he said, more to himself than to Shay or Dr. Wheeler.

"I always keep the chopper stocked." Wheeler had a stethoscope against Dayna's chest, his face pale. "You never know."

Marcel glanced up. "Who's we? Who the hell are you people?"

"I'm with the DEA." Shay draped the IV bag across Dayna's belly, then turned and dug through the duffel. "And Dr. Wheeler here is the guy who reported Eric's field." She glanced at the blood pressure gauge, and the gravity of her expression lifted, if only a little. "I'm a decent medic too," she said, "better than Wheeler, anyway. Shrinks are as good as useless in the field."

Marcel figured he ought to shut his mouth, but—"You're a what?"

"She's handy," Wheeler said. "Let's get outta here."

"Sounds good." Shay nudged Marcel. "Ready to keep pressure on that thing while we move her?"

Marcel swallowed, nodded, and focused on Dayna.

"There's no exit wound, so the bullet's still in there. Keep her straight, understand?"

Shay and Wheeler transferred Dayna to the stretcher and carried her to the helicopter's floor with Marcel holding on as best he could.

Once they were all on board, Shay slammed the door, and a moment later they were airborne. She pulled headphones over her ears, then fitted a set to Marcel.

"Don't take your eyes off that wound." Her voice was louder than he'd expected. "Holler the moment anything changes—"

"So, is anyone gonna tell me what's goin' on?"

Shay's mouth snapped shut. Dayna's eyes fluttered open. For a moment, she looked at him. He tried to give her an encouraging smile since there was no way in hell she could hear him.

"Who shot her?"

Shay's jaw tightened. "There were two of them, one in that tree stand and Officer Lyman on the ground. Reggie clipped Lyman."

"Todd Lyman? Are you sure?"

"Yup." She bent over Dayna, took a long look at the slow ooze.

"Why was Dayna here?" No one answered. Dayna shifted, and blood spurted past his fingers. "What the hell!"

Shay was at his side in an instant. "Change the angle, like so." She adjusted his hand and pressed it in. The bleeding slowed. "Don't move, Marcel. If I have to take over, I will. But if we can avoid switching off, she'll do better."

Marcel nodded once. His hand was cramping but, compared to Dayna, he had it easy. "I'm fine."

"In answer to your question, Dayna was on loan to the DEA, assisting with an ongoing investigation. Thanks to Wheeler here, we knew about the field, and I'd secured Eric's cooperation." Shay flinched when she said Eric's name. She looked tired and cross and maybe a little bit guilty. "Our goal was to get his buyers, shut down distribution. But then that crazy woman mowed the field. After that, it seems all hell broke loose."

"Why didn't Dayna tell me?" This was the wrong time to worry about why she'd shut him out, but still.

"She was under orders." Shay took hold of Dayna's hand, squeezed it, smiled when Dayna's fingers closed around hers. "You were a suspect, Marcel. She wasn't allowed to tell you."

"I was a what?"

"Long story. It all started with your mom."

"My what?"

"Your mom." Shay finally looked at him, quirked a smile. "You know, cranky woman. Chews with her mouth open."

"But—"

"Almost there," Wheeler interrupted. "I'm not supposed to land a private aircraft on the helipad, but . . . fuck 'em."

Marcel risked a glance out the side window. The big H centered in a red cross surrounded by a perfect circle had him blinking against tears.

"You made it this far," he whispered into Dayna's ear. "The rest will be a cake walk."

He knew she couldn't hear him, not with the helicopter beating like a thousand drums, but he swore she smiled. The chopper set down with a bump, hospital employees surged forward, and Dayna was wheeled straight to an exam room with Marcel quick-stepping alongside. A nurse ran a gloved hand past his, pressed in, and nodded. Someone touched his shoulder. He turned to see Kate smiling up at him. She was still cute as a bug and, per usual, she was standing too close.

"You did great, Marcel," she said with hero worship in her eyes. "But this is the part where you need to let go."

CHAPTER THIRTY-FIVE

"Now? Can we go now?" Gracie had one foot on the threshold, the other on the front stoop. She smoothed her best dress over her bosom while she took another look at her legs, shaved smooth with only two razor nicks. She'd been straddling the doorway for twenty minutes. Molly was taking too long.

"It's still an hour early," Molly told her. "I know you're excited, but we have plenty of time."

"But what if we get a flat?"

"I'll fix it."

"What if we get stopped for speeding?"

"I won't speed."

"What if we get lost?"

Molly pitched an armload of laundry down the chute and raised her eyes to the ceiling. "We're meeting her at the Denny's next to Home Depot. I know how to get there."

"What if—"

"Gracie." Molly put her arms around Gracie's shoulders, and her warmth helped to calm some of the jitters. "We have no way of knowing whether she's really your daughter or just someone jerking us around. She wouldn't even give me her name, so I didn't give her ours, either."

"But she has the same birthday."

"Thousands of people do." Molly looked more and more concerned. "Try not to worry so much. We have three more hits after this one."

"Three more hits. Wow." Gracie felt like a kid with her toes curled over the edge of a diving board, wanting to jump but afraid of belly-flopping. "It's hard to believe there are so many people separated."

"And so many reunited." Molly walked back to the kitchen and put a dirty plate into the sink. "If she's out there, we'll find her. Marcel got hold of your old medical records, so we have lots to go on. And the church in Keene is mailing me everything they have on you and your family."

"I have family?" They probably didn't want to meet her. Probably hoped she couldn't find them.

"The church secretary found your birth records. I don't know yet whether you have living relatives, but we'll have the information soon. It might even come in today's mail." Molly glanced at her watch. "I guess it wouldn't hurt to go early. Let me grab my purse."

"I'll be in the car!" Finally. Gracie was halfway down the ramp when the sound of Molly's cellphone stopped her. "Dang it, Molly."

"It's just a text message." She frowned at her phone. "It's a blocked number. Might be her."

Gracie shifted from one foot to the other and made a point of sighing out loud. But the look on Molly's face had her hopes dying. "What's wrong?"

"There was an emergency. She has to cancel."

"Oh, no!" Emergencies were never good. "Is she okay?"

"Looks like." Molly read out loud. "All it says is, 'Medical emergency. Can't make it.' It's probably a friend or maybe a family member."

"Oh, balls." Gracie pinched herself hard. "No more balls! I've been trying to quit saying it, but it keeps coming out."

"Why are you trying to stop?"

"Bad enough I'm a murderer. I don't want my daughter to think I have a potty mouth." Gracie latched onto her hair and yanked. "Guess it doesn't matter now. Balls, balls, balls, balls, balls."

"You're not a murderer. You're not even a suspect. We've been over this."

"That was before Dick Tracy figured out I was right next to that field when Eric got himself shot."

"But you had no reason to kill Eric."

"Sure I did. He was hitting Candy." And she'd said so. Right in front of the detective. Gracie tried not to stomp when she came inside and shut the door.

"That he was. I have to admit, I disliked Eric, too." Molly sounded irritated now. "But if that were all it took, I'd be a suspect."

"I thought you were."

"Gracie!"

Molly's fuse was shorter than usual. She sure had been grouchy, ever since Marcel admitted he hadn't talked to Dayna the night she'd ruined that first date.

Perhaps a change of subject would help. Gracie stared at her feet and hoped she looked apologetic. "I just don't want my daughter to be sorry she found me."

"She won't be." Molly's voice got a whole lot softer. "And don't worry about the woman who cancelled on us today. We have three others to check out. This one was probably a prank."

"It's not funny."

"I know." Molly fingered her purse. "Wanna go to Denny's anyway? We haven't had lunch out in a long time."

"Sure." Gracie pulled the door open just as the kitchen phone rang. "Now what?"

"I'll be quick." Molly jogged back to the kitchen and picked up the phone. The conversation was quiet and brief, and when Molly hung up, she looked as if she'd seen Hannah without her head on.

Gracie took a last look at the outdoors before closing the door with a much softer thud. "What's wrong now?"

"That was Amanda Gavin. Dayna Pelletier's been shot."

"The little poodle?"

Molly nodded.

"So Marcel is up for grabs!"

"Gracie!"

"Sorry. My editor doesn't work. You know that."

"Dayna's a friend," Molly said, "and friends stand by their friends."

"Does that mean Marcel is standing by Dayna?"

Molly looked as if she couldn't decide whether to cry or spit. "I need moral support, and you're already dressed up. Come with me."

"To Denny's?" Probably not, but she could hope.

"Nope." Molly snatched her keys from the basket by the door, paused a moment, and then grabbed a hair brush. "Amanda's calling everybody who cares about Dayna. Looks like we're going to the hospital."

—w—

There was no clock in the waiting room. Marcel had a watch, of course, but each time he looked at it, he realized less than a minute had passed.

On the flat-screen television, a soap-opera blonde was rushed to the hospital. Her hair was perfect. Her makeup was perfect. Following a frantic sprint down a white hallway, a doctor took one look at her and said, "She's gone." Dramatic music swelled as the screen faded to black. Then a commercial for feminine hygiene protection came on. Marcel averted his eyes, checked his watch. Forty seconds.

Shay was gone. She'd caught a ride back to Coyne Falls, and no doubt charged off to help track down the shooter. Officer Todd Lyman. That was a kick to the gut.

How could someone he knew and worked with do such a thing? Lyman was a cranky old coot, but Marcel had always assumed they were on the same side. And who was with him? Not the Chief; he was dead honest. Besides, Chief Farrell could put five out of seven in the X ring at fifty meters. He wouldn't have missed.

And if I hadn't done a face plant, I'd be the one with a bullet where it doesn't belong.

Sometimes it paid to be clumsy.

"Marcel? Is that you?" He looked up to see a petite woman in a tailored business suit. Julia Pelletier. Dayna's mom. She always made him think of dead leaves. Her perfect makeup and sprayed-down hair defied wind, rain or a comforting touch.

He got to his feet, feeling like he'd downed maybe six beers on an empty stomach. Woozy. He knew Julia wasn't the hugging sort, but he crossed the room and gathered her into his arms, anyway. She didn't pull away or complain about the smell of his cheap deodorant. And she didn't call him a townie, not that he'd ever considered that to be anything other than true.

"I'm so sorry, Marcel."

"For what?" He ought to be the one saying he was sorry. Sorry for distracting Shay and Dayna, sorry for not taking the bullet meant for him, sorry for being a Coyne Falls townie with smelly armpits, sorry for—"

"I heard what you did. Dayna might be dead if not for you." A ripple went through Julia's bony frame, followed by a series of little aftershocks. He hadn't realized the woman knew how to cry.

"It was Shay." He'd best give credit where credit was due. "I was messing it all up."

"Modest, too." Julia leaned her head against his chest. "I might have misjudged you all these years."

"I think you had it about right." He patted her back. She patted his. He realized back patting wasn't comforting and took his hand away. Julia stepped back and dabbed at her eyes with an embroidered hankie that appeared out of nowhere.

"Thanks for the hug, Marcel."

"Any time, Mrs. Pelletier."

"Call me Julia."

"Will do."

Behind Julia was Amanda Gavin. He still wasn't used to seeing her outside Blue Horizons, and he had to remind himself she was retired now. But when he looked at her, all he saw was the woman who'd watched all of them after school: himself and Zoe, Candy and Molly, Dayna . . . even Eric had spent weekday afternoons with skittish Walter and his Captain America shield, and old Charlotte who documented the most mundane of daily occurrences. And Gracie—the spitfire of the group. That woman had more chutzpah than anyone he knew.

Thanks to Amanda, they were family.

He wondered whether Molly had spent nights at Blue Horizons as a child. Probably. She would have been careful not to overburden any one household, wouldn't want to appear needy or overstay her welcome.

No wonder Molly had made Blue Horizons her home.

Amanda threw her arms around him and squeezed harder than her willowy frame should have allowed. He looked up to see his mother framed in the doorway. She blundered forward and hugged Dayna's mom.

"How is she?"

"Still in surgery," Julia said. "I'm gonna get Dr. Wheeler, see what he knows."

"I'll go with you." Amanda let go of Marcel and whispered, "Thank goodness you were there to help."

He didn't have an answer. The way he saw it, if he hadn't been there, maybe Dayna wouldn't have been shot. So he did his best to smile, right up until Julia and Amanda rushed away, leaving him alone with his mother.

What was it Shay had said? He was a suspect because of his mom?

She latched onto his elbow. "You doin' okay?"

"Been better."

"C'mere." Suzanne clamped him in a viselike hug and blubbered at him, "She's gonna be okay."

"I know, Ma."

"I mean it." Suzanne wrestled him into a chair and dropped down next to him. She held her breath for a moment, then let it out in a long "Haaaaaaaaaa." Her hand seemed to grasp his of its own accord and, per usual, she squeezed harder than was comfortable. She didn't look at him when she finally asked, "How much do you know?"

"Not nearly enough." His mom must be hurting, but he couldn't make himself care as much as he thought he should. "What was Dayna doin' there?"

"What did Shay tell you?" His mom looked as if she'd been through a long, slow sort of torture.

"Don't you mean Agent Cooper?" There it was, his whiney voice. Marcel held down the feelings of betrayal. It was time to man up, so he took his mom's hand and laced his fingers with hers. Not easy. They both suffered from too much sweat and not enough hand.

"Let me guess. You couldn't tell me I was a suspect in a narcotics investigation, so instead you told Dayna."

"She already knew." Suzanne let go of his hand and wiped hers on her pants. Then she spit into her palm and reached for his face with a wet finger.

Marcel ducked backwards. "You wanna give me a spit bath? Really?"

"Just sit still, Marcel. You got some blood on your face." She scrubbed at his upper lip—inappropriate, but then, she'd never been good at decorum. Maybe if he let her keep her hands busy, she'd be more forthcoming.

"Why was I a suspect?" Probably had something to do with the things Eric had said. It couldn't have been his mother's doing, no matter what Shay had implied.

"It started with me," Suzanne said between spits. She didn't seem apologetic, but neither did she look straight at him. "An inmate offered information in exchange for privileges. I had to tell Sheriff Plunket, and he had to follow up."

"What did this inmate say?"

His mother scrubbed harder. It hurt a little, but he didn't let on.

"She claimed there was a drug connection at the Falls PD, and she said if you needed anything, anything at all, Officer Trudeau was the one to ask." Suzanne's breath was quick, and a snot blob dangled from her left nostril. "I'm sorry, Marcel. I was worried you wouldn't get a fair shake. I'm the idiot who pushed Dayna to get involved."

Marcel took a fresh tissue from the box and handed it to her. "Ya might want to blow, Ma." He waited while she wiped her nose. Then he took the wet tissue and gave her a dry one. "Was Chief Farrell in on it?"

"Definitely not. The Falls PD was under suspicion, so you were all kept in the dark." She dabbed at his chin, sniffed. "Farrell was looking for a temporary officer to help with vacation traffic, same as he does every year. Dayna already knew her way around the Falls, so her superior told her to go ahead and apply. It was supposed to be a lightweight undercover assignment, her first. Low risk."

Low risk? It hadn't turned out that way. "Did Dayna think I was dealin'?"

"Of course not."

"Did you think I was dirty? Does Dad know?"

"You've never been anything but a Boy Scout your whole life." Suzanne snuffled. "But this inmate, she named you. And I think maybe Eric got wind of it, and he named you, too. And the DEA was already here watchin' Eric's field."

"You mean Shay Cooper?" The name set off a flood of indignation, not just for himself, but for Candy, too. "Is that why she was stayin' in the cabin behind Candy and Eric? So she could spy on them?"

"Sort of." Susanne went back to dabbing at his face. "Eric was cooperating, and Shay was usin' him to set up a sting. She wanted the people above him, and she thought that might include you."

"Great." The thought rankled, even though he supposed Shay had done the right thing, stayed objective and followed the evidence.

"If not for Gracie mowing that field, Shay's plan might have worked out." Suzanne blew her nose again. It sounded like a fart.

Marcel rubbed his temples, but he couldn't get rid of the spinning sensation, like a tilt-a-whirl out of control. Dayna had been undercover, spying on him. Shay was with the DEA. Even Eric had been involved, not just as a suspect, but as an informant and mole. His own mom had kept secrets. The only people who'd been straight with him were Gracie and Molly.

"And this is why you didn't want me asking Molly out."

Suzanne nodded. "I didn't know how any of it would work out. And then Dayna, she came to me a week back and said she still had feelings for you."

"She did what?" This was too much. "Isn't she going out with Gary Wheeler, M.D.?" Marcel sneered the name. Funny how it still burned, being replaced by someone more worthy.

"They only just met a couple weeks ago, and he's her informant, not her boyfriend."

"Oh." The irritation hadn't diminished, but now he felt guiltier for all the hollering he'd done. Even so, "If she still had feelings for me, why didn't she say so?"

Suzanne gave him a disappointed look, the one that said he was being a dope. "Dayna couldn't risk getting close to you. You know what an awful liar she is."

True. Even though she'd shut him out, he'd seen the dishonesty. And he'd assumed the worst, suspected her of being involved in drugs and murder, when all she'd done was try to find the truth. "I'm an idiot."

"You were lied to." Suzanne's voice came out tight. "Shay had been keeping close to Eric, right up until she dropped him at the end of his driveway on the night he died."

"That was Shay dropping him off?"

Suzanne let out a sigh. "Shay also observed Eric and Jack Broussard meeting behind the hospital, but we don't know Jack's involvement, if any." Suzanne's fingers dug into her thigh.

"Eric was involved with Cracked Jack?"

"Looks like. After Shay saw Jack and Eric together, she approached Dr. Wheeler. He'd already reported that field, and she hoped he might be willing to do a little bit more.

"And he cooperated?"

"Sure did." She grabbed a tissue, wiped her hands. "Wheeler started keeping an eye on Jack, documenting his activities while he was on hospital grounds, but——"

"Then Gracie happened, and we got Jack fired."

"Yup. Once Jack was caught abusing patients, Wheeler had to cut him loose."

Of course he did. Gracie had been turning up all over this case, unknowingly interfering with everything the DEA had tried to put in place. "Sounds like nobody could catch a break."

"You got that right. Every time we have a decent lead, something messes it up. Even Eric was playin' both sides against the middle, tellin' Shay he'd roll over while all the while he was hiding a whole 'nother crop under bird netting."

Marcel tried not to think about the blueberry field. All he could see was Dayna, her skin turning gray and shirt slick with blood. It was her day off. She hadn't been in uniform, didn't even have a vest.

He pinched the bridge of his nose between thumb and forefinger and tipped his head back. "Has anyone questioned Jack?"

She shook her head. "We're not supposed to touch him. Not yet."

"What if Jack was the one watching that field? What if he shot Dayna?" Marcel rarely had violent thoughts, but right now he could see himself following in Molly's footsteps, knocking that idiot to the ground. "Anything more?"

Suzanne twisted her hands in her lap. "Remember when Dayna tried to get you to suppress evidence?"

"The text messages from Eric's phone?" Had Dayna tried to trap him, or was she giving him a chance to prove he was on the right side? Either way, she'd played him. "What about them?"

"You refused to withhold evidence, even when it pointed to you." For the first time, Suzanne smiled. "That's when Dayna started pushing Shay to let you in. She said you'd proven yourself, and she thought maybe you could help out."

"She did that?"

"She did. And after you called Chief Farrell and let him know about Eric's accusations, Shay gave the go-ahead—"

"That's when Dayna showed up at my house." She must have thought he'd be thrilled to have her back, figured he'd overlook all the lies once he knew what they were about. "And I walked in with Molly."

His mother was silent, but she nodded before she got to her feet. "I didn't mean any of the things I said about Molly. I just hoped maybe I could slow you down, give Dayna a chance to tell you how she felt."

Damn. If he'd never taken Molly to Echo Lake . . . but he had, and that night had changed everything. He sighed into his shirt collar. "Ya didn't slow me down enough, Mom."

She patted his shoulder. "Let all this settle before you go making any big decisions. Dayna risked everything for you."

Even her life. He wasn't sure how he felt about that, but one thing was clear: even with Dayna lying in the hospital, all he could think of was Molly. And that told him everything he needed to know.

"That's the problem with takin' a risk, Mom." He swallowed twice. Then he swallowed again, harder. "Sometimes you lose."

"But Dayna loves you, and I think you might still love her. You're just in shock." She looked past him and froze. He followed her gaze. Molly stood in the doorway clutching Gracie's hand.

He had to ignore the way everything inside him tried to shut down, the way his brain skinned over and his throat lumped up. Maybe this wasn't the time to be making decisions, but he had to stand firm, say the things his heart had tried to tell him ever since Dayna moved out.

"You're right. I always will love Dayna." He got to his feet and walked to Molly on shaky legs. "I love her as a friend, and I'm grateful for all she tried to do. But it's past time for both of us to move on."

Gracie let out a whoop. His mom's face went ashen, even though she murmured, "I understand." Molly looked more shocked than elated. A doctor came through a swinging door behind them, and the room went silent.

The doctor's smile lifted some of the weight from Marcel's shoulders, and his words, "She's a tough little thing. If we can avoid complications, I think she'll be fine—" that was better than anything he could have asked for.

Gracie let out another yell, not quite as enthusiastic as the first. Marcel hugged Molly, and she hugged him back. His mom started blubbering again while Dayna's mother pushed her way into the room with Dr. Wheeler in tow.

"Can I see her?" Julia Pelletier propped herself against Dr. Wheeler's arm as if he were a quad cane. She looked about ready to faint with relief.

"Just you," the doctor said. "Everyone else can try back in a couple days." Julia didn't look at any of them, just followed the doctor through the door. It swung shut with a soft and final thud.

Someone placed a hand on his shoulder, and Marcel turned to find Amanda Gavin looking as if she had more questions than her brain could hold. "I know this isn't the time or place," she said, "but will this make a difference, do you think, to Candy?"

He'd forgotten all about Candy and Abe. "I hope so. It should."

It seemed Shay had lied about going shooting with Candy and Eric. Marcel didn't see how revealing that information might have compromised her cover, but she must have had her reasons. Maybe now she'd come clean, give Reggie Clark a plausible explanation for Candy's prints being on Eric's gun.

"'Course it will." His mom grabbed both of Amanda's hands and squashed them in her own.

Amanda looked at Marcel with murder in her eyes. "Was Shay staying in Candy's cabin, pretending it was a vacation, when all along she was investigating Eric?"

"I can't say." Gossip sure spread fast at the hospital. Seemed Amanda had found out Shay's involvement almost as soon as he had.

"That's not right." Amanda's eyes turned a whole lot darker. "That woman put my Candy at risk, got her arrested, damaged her reputation."

"You can file a complaint if you like." He had a lot of things to discuss with Chief Farrell. If Marcel was right about Shay's lies, then she'd willfully obstructed Reggie's investigation. And if that were true, she'd gone too far.

"Candy may not have good sense in love, but she's never been on the wrong side of the law, Marcel. Never."

"I know, Mrs. Gavin." In her shoes, he'd be pissed as hell. "Everything will get straightened out."

"It better." Amanda marched out the door, her footsteps sharp as gunfire. Molly stared after her. Even Gracie seemed at a loss for words.

Marcel gave them both a smile, hoping it might ease a little bit of the tension, but it didn't help. Suspicion was growing in his own gut. Shay Cooper had some explaining to do.

He fixed Suzanne with the best police face he could muster. "Wanna tell me how Shay's handbag ended up in Echo Lake?"

"Oh, that." Suzanne's gaze lingered on the doorway for a moment before she turned back to her son. "It wasn't intentional. Candy's beagle swiped it. Once Gracie found it and turned it in, Shay figured she might as well use all the confusion as a way to make contact with you."

"Scout? Again?"

"Seems that dog is up to his eyeballs in this case." Suzanne chuckled. "Sometimes I wonder if he hasn't already got it figured out."

CHAPTER THIRTY-SIX

Lunch was more than an hour late, and Molly brought Gracie to the hospital cafeteria instead of Denny's. Even though Gracie knew her daughter was unlikely to be at *this* hospital, she still scrutinized every person who came through the door.

"What are you looking at?" Molly bit into a slice of pizza with everything. Cheese hung in strings from her grin, and she pinched gooey strands between her fingers and stretched them higher and higher until they snapped.

"Maybe she's here."

"Who?"

"My daughter." Gracie twisted in her seat, trying to get a good look at a short woman hurrying past the hallway door. "She was going to the hospital, right? This is a hospital."

For a moment, Molly looked as if she were going to say something sensible. Instead, there was a playful twist to her lips, and she pointed to a woman at the salad bar. "How 'bout her?"

"Too tall." Gracie tsk'd her disapproval. "And she has dark hair. Mine was red before it turned gray."

"Like mine?"

"More orange than yours. A carrot-top." Gracie nibbled at her cheeseburger. The meat crumbled like wet cardboard, and the lettuce was tissue-paper thin. Molly's pizza looked much tastier and, damn, there were tamales at the buffet. How could she have missed them?

"Did you have freckles?"

"Still do. These aren't all age spots." Gracie set the burger down and reached for her straw, still in its wrapper. Head bowed, she thought of her daughter—not the infant she'd lost, but the pretty redhead who'd always lived in her dreams.

She tore the very tip of the straw wrapper and made a tiny fold. She'd never talked to anyone about her dream-daughter and, even though Molly was unlikely to make fun of her, Gracie kept her eyes on her hands and spoke in a rush. "My daughter is short, red-haired, and freckled. And she's smart." She lowered her voice to a mumble. "And maybe a little bit nuts."

Molly chuckled while Gracie continued to concentrate on the wrapper, making minute accordion folds, top to bottom.

"Are you gonna wet it?"

"Why else would I go to this much trouble?" Gracie slipped the wrapper free, dipped her fingers into her water glass, and then flicked a few drops. The straw wrapper snake unwound slowly and smoothly, writhing around her plate like a living thing. She forgot everything else and giggled. Molly laughed, too.

The reason for Molly's high spirits was obvious. "Little Dayna got herself shot, and Marcel still picked you."

Molly's smile vanished. "It wasn't a contest."

"No?"

"No."

"Could've fooled me."

Molly sighed, a sound less happy than Gracie had expected. "Give it a few weeks. Marcel was too worried about Dayna to think straight."

"That's why you can believe him." Gracie poked at the snake, already dead, belly-up against the edge of her water glass. "Men shouldn't think. They're better off when they *do*."

"Stop that."

"It's true." Gracie took another bite of her burger. The colder it got, the more it tasted like socks.

Molly's smile was sneaking back, a good thing. But behind it was a pensive sort of yearning. "I do hope you're right," came out in a sigh.

"So hurry up and sleep with him." Okay, maybe that wasn't the most appropriate thing to say, but Molly didn't have a mother to talk to. Suzanne Trudeau wouldn't be any help, not with her son on the receiving end. And Amanda Gavin was tied up with Candy's problems.

"That's none of your business."

"Don't wait too long." Gracie discarded her hamburger bun and went for the pickle. "He slept with the little poodle woman for years. You'd better let him know you can take care of that for him."

"That's enough."

"I'm just sayin'."

"Well, stop just sayin'." Molly's sigh was more exasperated than the last. "And stop calling Dayna a poodle."

"But she's teeny and fluffy, and she can't sit still."

"Sounds like somebody else I know."

Gracie realized her knees were bouncing. She pinned them to her chair. "I'm not fluffy."

"True." Molly chuckled. "You're more of a terrier."

Gracie had her mouth primed for a clever retort but, at that moment, Cracked Jack came through the door. She froze, throat stuck in mid-swallow.

He was dressed in a muscle shirt over camo pants with leather hiking boots laced up the front. His nose sported bright white tape, and the skin beneath his eyes was purple. When he spotted Gracie, the scowl on his face chased her lunch right up to the back of her throat.

"Incoming!" Gracie ducked behind the table. She vibrated as if she'd knocked back an entire pot of coffee. Molly gasped. Jack came to a stop right in front of her, just as Marcel and Zoe walked in. Marcel quick-stepped to Molly's side while Zoe headed for Jack.

"What are you doing here?" Zoe's voice was like something from a vampire movie, low and threatening. Jack scowled at Gracie. She ducked behind the table leg, for once wishing she were even smaller.

"Picking up my last paycheck. I may not work here, thanks to that woman's lies." Jack pointed to Gracie. "But this cafeteria is open to the public."

Irritation flickered in Gracie's belly. She hadn't lied. Confronting him would be foolish, though. Jack wasn't the sort to forget such disrespect.

Zoe, however, got way closer to Jack than she ought to. "It's not Gracie's fault you got caught, and it's not Molly's either."

Marcel left Molly's side and took his sister's hand, thank goodness. Someone ought to reel her in. "That's enough, Zo."

Zoe pulled away from her brother. "I'd already filed a complaint, so what you did to Gracie was just icing on the cake."

"You did what?" Jack's voice scorched the air. Zoe didn't flinch.

"You can always contest the termination," Marcel said, latching onto his sister's shoulder and pulling her toward Molly. "Tell your side of things."

"Like anyone would listen." Jack's boots were enormous. Gracie wiggled away from them and tucked herself against Molly's knees.

"Ever since Dr. Wheeler got here . . ." Jack worked his way from a growl to something approaching a roar. "He's a goddamn nutter hugger. Things were different with Dr. Usef running the ward."

"Who?" Marcel asked.

"Dr. Useless," Molly whispered.

Zoe pushed Marcel's hand away. The little toes of her sneakers lined up with Jack's boots. She must be right in his face. "I suggest you leave these folks alone, Jack. Molly decked you once. She can do it again."

"ZOE!" Marcel hardly ever shouted.

"And I'm sorry about that," Molly said. "I shouldn't have lost my temper."

"I can't take sorry to the bank, now, can I?" Jack was silent for a long moment, but Gracie swore his feet were fuming. Finally his boots moved away, and he sulked off in the direction of the food line. Gracie thanked the heavens he was mad at Zoe and not her, and she was doubly glad he'd finally gone away. She got to her feet, dusted off her dress, and eased past Marcel to reclaim her seat.

"Zoe. . . ." Marcel ended the word in a sigh.

"I know. I'm not much of a diplomat."

"Understatement." Marcel still looked ill at ease.

"It's just that he was such an ass to work with," Zoe said. "You have no idea the things that man has said to me."

"I have an idea." Marcel cuffed Zoe's shoulder. "You need to quit antagonizing him, though. Leave it alone."

"He's a bully," Zoe said. "Bullies are the first to cave when someone stands up to them."

Marcel looked past her to the buffet, and Gracie followed his gaze. Jack had his food in a to-go bag, and he was already checking out.

"You could be right," Marcel muttered. "I hope so."

"Of course I am." Zoe swatted her brother's arm, grinned when he flinched. "My shift starts in ten, and I can't wait. Know why?"

"Why?"

"Because I don't have to ride with Jack anymore." With a final grin, she headed for the hallway. Marcel watched her go, his face lost in the sort of tenderness he probably reserved for family.

When he spoke to Molly, the worry lines beside his eyes got a whole lot softer. "You okay?" He glanced at Gracie, seeming to include her in his concern. "I asked Shay Cooper to come and see me back at the station, but I can wait until you two are finished here."

"We'll be fine. Jack's leaving." Molly didn't sound convincing.

Gracie couldn't help shuddering when Marcel walked away. She only half heard Molly's "How 'bout her?" She was pointing to a red-head at the next table.

"Too big. Too scary. Like Jack."

Molly let out a sigh that only heightened Gracie's worry. "Let's get out of here," she said. "We'll need to stop for groceries on the way home. All I have for dinner is chicken soup."

"Works for me." Gracie wanted to bolt for the exit. Jack was gone, but there was nothing to stop him from coming back. He wasn't the sort to walk away, not when he hadn't won.

Marcel waited at the station for Shay to arrive. He'd kept her handbag locked in evidence ever since Eric had turned up dead. Now that he knew her true involvement in the case, he saw no reason to hold her property.

That's what he'd told her on the phone. Truth was, he wanted to be there when Dayna's shooter got the payback he deserved. Seemed as if Shay was the person most likely to make that happen.

Despite his concerns, Marcel decided it might be best to work with Shay rather than questioning her prior actions—that could wait until Todd Lyman and the other shooter were both in custody. With Dayna in the ICU and Officer Lyman in the wind, Shay might accept the help of someone who knew the local landscape.

Maybe she'd let him in.

Don't trust them. He couldn't shake Dayna's warning. Who was she talking about? Todd Lyman was a given, but what about Shay, even Reggie? Hell, he wasn't sure he should trust Candy or Abe, and he couldn't ask Dayna what she'd meant, not until tomorrow.

And how was Jack Broussard connected to it all?

Jack's treatment of Gracie pegged him as someone whose inner voice had never learned right from wrong. He was the sort of person who might enjoy sitting in a tree stand with a gun, picking off crows, and helping himself to Gracie's canned goods.

Marcel was still trying to make sense of the puzzle when Shay swept through the door. She wore stretch jeans beneath a crop top showcasing breasts made for drunken motor-boating. A navel ring glistened from a perfect innie that formed a little bull's-eye in her flat tummy. Dangling beneath it, catching the fluorescents, was a key.

"Handcuffs, Shay? Really?" Change in plan. If Shay was back to treating him like a dope, he'd have to call her on her games, let her know he wasn't as much of an idiot as she thought. "What's the connection between Eric Thompson and Jack Broussard?"

"I have no idea." She slipped behind the counter and pulled up a chair, shot him a dazzling smile, and let her hand come to rest in the space between her thighs. Her breath caught, just a little.

Her antics had him more annoyed than turned on, though he admitted to a little of both. "Did you know about the second field?"

"Am I being interrogated?" She pouted. "There are better things we could do."

"Drop the act, Shay." Wasn't it about time she quit playing him? "You're interfering with a murder investigation, so you can either answer my questions, or plan to be here a while." He nodded to the holding cells at the back of the building.

"You wouldn't dare."

How had he been stupid enough to fall for her games? She was pretty, yes, and she knew how to make a person uncomfortable. But he could see through her now. She'd put Dayna in danger, probably got Eric killed. Yet here she was, still intent on pretending to be somebody else. He stood and unclipped his cuffs from his duty belt. "Maybe you should turn around."

She eyeballed him. He glared back. He was good at staring contests. The only person who'd ever beaten him was Abe, and that was because he'd fallen asleep with his eyes open.

When she lunged for him, he was pretty sure he'd made a tactical error, standing with his arms folded and feet together like a goddamn tackle dummy. He barely managed a "You're assaulting a police officer!" before he hit the floor. Shay was halfway out the door by the time he'd scrambled to his feet.

"Stand down, Officer!" She bypassed the handicap ramp and hurdled the railing. "Don't make me hurt you."

Marcel headed for the door. "What the hell, Shay."

"What the hell what, Marcel?"

That was cold, mimicking Dayna when she was lying in the ICU. He broke to a jog. "What the hell else is going on, and why are you so damned determined to keep me in the dark?"

She stripped off the wig as she walked. Plain brown hair tumbled out, still flattened to the top of her head and hanging in a loose rope between her shoulder blades. "You're better off not knowing."

"Maybe I can help." He caught up to her and kept his hands to himself. "Did you think of that?"

"No." She spun to face him, feet shoulder-width apart, knees just a little bit bent, and her eyes had the soft look of someone who did a lot of meditating. "You don't have the training, Marcel, and I don't want to get another officer shot." Her all-business demeanor cracked a bit. She turned her back and opened the door of a Mercedes-Benz G-Class. "That sort of thing tends to upset me. It muddies up an otherwise perfect record."

"I'm the one who got Dayna shot." Saying the words aloud hurt worse than he'd expected and, on a scale of one to ten, he'd planned on a twelve.

"No, I get all the credit for that one." Shay gave him the briefest glance as she slipped behind the wheel. "I had a freakin' chopper in play, and I told Dr. Wheeler to take Reggie joyriding rather than asking him to scout that field. There's no way I should have allowed anyone to get the drop on us."

"But I told people at the cartridge-hunt where I was going." Marcel tried to swallow, but the lump in his throat just got bigger. "Todd Lyman probably followed me to that field."

"Officer Lyman?" Shay snorted. "Maybe he did, but he wasn't the one shooting at us."

"What?"

"I know what I said before, but every time I saw that man shoot, he was aiming wide. I think he was trying to hit that pine on the hill."

She hesitated a moment, face lost in concentration. "Lyman didn't shoot Dayna. It was the other guy."

"The one in the tree stand?"

"Looks like." Shay stared out at Meetinghouse Hill with her face frozen in irritation.

Marcel leaned in. "Do you know, for sure, who's on our side?"

She didn't look at him. "I thought I did. But now . . ."

Marcel pressed. "I may lack experience, but I know these people better than you. Let me help."

She gave him a hard look, eyes focused like a barred owl on a chipmunk. "You have no idea what you're walking into, rookie. You could end up dead. So could I."

"Well . . ." He tried to catch her eye. "Right now, I got nothin' I need to do, and it seems you're short on people you can trust."

She started the engine, let it idle. Her cellphone chirped. She glanced at it, swore under her breath, and then flipped it face-down on the dash. "You on duty?"

"Not officially, but we're just about out of personnel."

She unlocked the passenger door and motioned him inside. He tried to ignore the apology in her tone when she said, "Don't say I didn't warn you."

CHAPTER THIRTY-SEVEN

Gracie was fading by the time they reached Blue Horizons, her energy spent and feet heavy as wet sod. She and Molly had stopped at the grocery store, then Wally's World, even went to the place where everything cost a dollar. Struggling beneath grocery bags and mail, Molly managed to hold the door while Gracie ducked inside.

The moment Gracie kicked off her sneakers and allowed her socks to touch cold ceramic, the hair on the backs of her arms rose. A vague sense of unease drew her gaze to the edge of the living room, just visible through the doorway. Hannah was back. She stood against the opposite wall, finger to lips in a soft *Shhhh*.

Walter sat in the overstuffed chair at the dead girl's side. He hated that chair. It wasn't covered in plastic and couldn't be disinfected, which probably explained why he was rocking forward and back, forward and back, all the while muttering so softly that Gracie couldn't make out his words. When she took a step into the foyer, she spotted Jillian and Charlotte side-by-side on the fold-out couch with their backs to her. They never sat together.

The dead girl drew an invisible knife across her throat.

"Molly, we need to go." Gracie stepped back into her sneakers so quickly, she lumped the heel of her sock. Molly was already in the kitchen. Gracie heard the bag of groceries plop onto the table.

"Who's hungry?" Molly's voice blended with the groan of the refrigerator door. "I have homemade chicken soup and butter rolls to tide us over till dinner. Any takers?"

No one answered. Gracie tried to get Molly's attention with throat clearing and a cautious wave, but Molly was busy pulling an enormous stock pot from the fridge and setting it on the stove. While Molly lit the biggest burner, Gracie crept back to the front door and tried to yank the lump out of her sock. It didn't budge, so she gave up, grabbed the door handle, and turned it.

Molly walked past her to the living room and gasped to a stop. A man's voice had Gracie's heart beating a whole lot faster.

"Have a seat, Molly, and ask Gracie to join us, please."

Gracie hesitated. Molly turned and met her gaze.

"RUN!"

Gracie was out the door and hot-footing it to Candy's before the echo of Molly's shriek died away. That's when she heard the CRACK!

She ducked, but she didn't slow down. The sock lump was more painful than she'd expected, and she bolted through Candy's gate at a high-speed hobble. The garage was open. She squeezed past Eric's accumulated junk to the door that led to the kitchen.

Gracie hitched up the steps, through the door, shoved past the plastic table, and only just managed not to trip over a lawn chair. Clutching at a stitch in her side, she grabbed the phone off the wall and dialed 9-1-1.

Her feet went out from under her before she felt his hands. The phone clattered against the wall, and she shouted, "Help!" even though she doubted there'd been time for the call to go through. Fingers dug into her throat and lifted her up and backwards. A moment later something smacked her head.

She didn't notice the pain so much as a feeling of euphoria, like one of Jack's sedatives, what with the white noise and a murky tinkle that reminded her of a child's xylophone. Hard tile struck her knees. Dazed, she stared at the splotched earth tones of camo pants above oversized hiking boots.

Panic welled up and tried to scream its way right past her throat. But a show of fear would only encourage Jack. Instead, she thought about what it would be like to pass out.

She let herself crumple, allowed her forehead to bounce against the floor, and very deliberately closed her eyes.

"Where are we going?" Marcel resisted the urge to grab the panic strap. Shay blasted down Devil's Elbow at a speed that would have earned her a hefty fine had he been in pursuit rather than seat belted at her mercy.

"I need to make an arrest, and you're gonna back me up."

"An arrest?" Maybe she had a handle on the shooter. "Who? Did you find Lyman?"

She shook her head and, for a moment, her tone shifted to something that sounded a lot like regret. "It's David."

Crap. He sucked in a breath and did his best not to let her see how shocked he was. "David Cooper? Your husband?"

She was silent for a moment, as if she regretted her words. Then she swallowed, cleared her throat. "As it happens, David was working with Eric."

Damn. Marcel couldn't imagine having to arrest someone he loved, but that wasn't all. What if David had been involved in Eric's death? And Dayna's shooting—that possibility had his hackles up. "What exactly was he doing?"

"Distribution." The word came out heavy as lead. "I had my suspicions when I first caught this case, but I didn't know for certain until the night Eric died."

Shay let out a sigh then, a blast of emotion that she'd probably kept in check far too long. "The day before Eric got himself dead, I went shooting with Candy and Eric." Her face scrunched in apology, no doubt because she'd lied. "Anyway, Eric mentioned that his trucker was on the road. Said he'd be back Thursday. David was on the road, too, due back the same day."

"That's not much." Eric could have been talking about anybody. Maybe Shay had jumped to the wrong conclusion.

He sure hoped so.

But she was already shaking her head. "You know the look, when a suspect lets something slip, and they wish to God they could reach up and snatch the words right out of the air."

Marcel nodded. He'd seen the expression, usually plastered all over the faces of drunk drivers.

"When Eric mentioned this trucker, he was mortified. You would have thought he'd just taken a shit at his high school graduation." She spun the vehicle around the turn to Depot Road and gunned the engine past the fire station. Too fast, but she had other things on her mind. "He clammed up then, wouldn't say another word. Two days later, there he was, dead and headless."

She whispered, "David does kinda get off, you know . . . cutting off heads. But he wouldn't do that to a person. Just game. You know. Deer and bear and shit."

Marcel tightened his seatbelt, tried to ignore the voice in his head that said David Cooper had just been added to the long list of murder suspects. "So, did you confront David?"

"Not exactly. When Candy's dog ran off with my handbag and phone, I figured it must be fate, ya know? I knew David would have a hissy if I didn't check in like I always do, and I thought he might get his ass to Coyne Falls."

"Why did you want him here?" Marcel managed to stay calm despite the roller coaster ride. Shay was more than a little bit unglued, not that he blamed her.

"I wanted to put him and Eric together, get a sense of whether there was something going on between them."

"And Eric died before you could do that?"

"Yup."

David could have been the killer, no matter Shay didn't think him capable. Marcel decided to push, just a little bit. "You believe Eric died before David got here."

"Damn right." Now she looked defensive, the way her face closed in on itself. "David might be involved in transporting a little pot to Florida. But don't you dare suggest he's a killer." She shot Marcel a sideways glance. "He was as surprised as anyone when Eric's body dropped."

"Are you sure?" Under the right circumstances, anyone might kill. Even Candy, though he hated to admit that. And how many people took pleasure in cutting off heads? "People can surprise you, no matter how well you think you know them."

"Not David." There was a tenderness on her face that hadn't been there a moment ago. "He was so relieved when I showed up at his hotel—told me everything—the marijuana, his involvement. He came clean, and he begged me to give him a couple days before I turned him in."

"And you did." He waited for her to say more, but when she remained silent, he had to ask. "Did you let the DEA know about David?" Shay would have a handler—a person in the DEA who kept tabs on her undercover activities. She should have passed the information along. Immediately.

But then she would have been removed from the case. Conflict of interest.

"I didn't tell anybody. Not even my handler." She kept her eyes straight ahead, but he swore she was watching his face. "David said he'd give me somebody higher up the ladder if I looked the other way. So I gave him a chance to get himself out of the mess he was in."

That shouldn't have been Shay's call. The decision ought to have been made by someone who wasn't so emotionally involved. "Did David give you a name?"

"Sure did." Her laugh sounded more hysterical than amused. "He gave me the same name I already had. Yours."

Not a surprise, but the revelation burned anyway. "That's why you showed up in David's room that day at the Coyne Cot. You were setting a trap."

"Affirmative. Dayna called me when you headed to the Cot to question David. Everything that happened next was staged for your benefit." She let out a long and forceful sigh. "Especially the part where I asked you for drugs."

"And I looked the other way." He'd been all kinds of stupid. Shay had tried to bust him. If he'd called her on her game, maybe things would have been different.

"Yup." She stared at the empty road, looking more heartsore than contrite. Her words were soft and filled with longing. "Why couldn't you be dirty, Marcel? That would have solved everything."

He didn't answer. There wasn't much he could say to a woman whose husband had so thoroughly disappointed her. David had probably used their relationship to gain information, betrayed her in the worst way.

And now she had to bring him in. Better late than never, and he understood her need to take charge and maintain control of the situation. Might be best, though, if she did the right thing and handed this particular arrest to somebody else.

The set of her jaw told him she'd not take kindly to such a suggestion. Telling Marcel the truth and allowing him to come with her was probably the best she could do. "Where are we heading?"

"David's been using Candy's cabin. It was a meeting place for him and Eric, probably Jack. Lyman, too."

No wonder Scout had been so weird about the place. That and— "That's why Lyman was hanging around there the day you went missing. And that's why I saw a light there one night last week." He should have stopped and investigated. Instead, "I convinced myself it was nothing but the moon."

Shay glanced sideways, all smirk and no smile. "And?"

"I'm an idiot."

"No argument here." She took a left on County Road, maneuvered past a sink hole. She seemed to have regained her composure, no longer taking out her emotion on the accelerator. "Was that the night Dayna tried to talk to you?"

"You know it was."

"Can't say she didn't try." Shay snorted. "Even though I wanted to pin this whole pot operation on you, even though I was dead sure you were in it up to your nose hairs, Dayna managed to convince me you were clean."

He didn't say anything. Not much point.

"Dayna said you have an overabundance of integrity, and I guess she was right. She also said you've always been bull-headed, even when you were kids playing good guy, bad guy."

Odd, the way Shay switched gears. One moment she'd played the part of a betrayed cop struggling to do the right thing. Now she was making fun of him, teasing him as if they were old friends.

Dayna's words rose up in his mind. *Don't trust them, Marcel. None of them.*

Shay had said they could both end up dead. Now she acted as if David's arrest would be no big deal. Marcel ignored the warnings in his head and let out an embarrassed groan. "Dayna told you about that?"

"Sure did. She said you always wanted to be the good guy pretending to be a bad guy, and you never would suck it up and play the villain. She even told me your secret code word." Now she smiled. "*Pussy*. Good God, Marcel."

"I was nine. I didn't know what it meant." His face must be red now. His ears were burning. "Girls sure do like to talk."

"Isn't that how you get to know whether you can trust a person?"

She must be trying to make a point, but he couldn't tell whether she was playing a part or being honest. Might be best to focus on the job. "So how do you want to handle this?"

"Just walk in and cuff him." She didn't look the least bit worried, but her foot landed harder on the gas. Marcel gave up his pretense of calm and latched onto the door handle when they fishtailed through the intersection of Sandpit Road.

"Can you pull over a minute?

"Why?" She drove to the side of the road and shut off the engine less than a hundred feet from Blue Horizons's driveway.

"We still don't know who shot Dayna, and she told me not to trust anybody. Do we really want to walk into Candy's backyard without backup?"

"David doesn't own a gun." She shrugged, not believably. "And I'd rather not have too many people in the mix. We've got a week-old murder and a cop shooter on the loose. Everybody's on edge, and someone might get trigger happy."

Obviously she thought there was a risk of getting David shot. "We could call my mom." Now he felt like a mama's boy. "Not because she's my mother. She's smart and level-headed. She'd never shoot if she didn't have to."

Shay cocked an eyebrow. "Might not be a bad idea, but I'm just paranoid enough to want to avoid dispatch." She pulled out her cell phone. "What's your mom's number? I'll shoot her a text."

CHAPTER THIRTY-EIGHT

Gracie kept her eyes shut, lids squashed together while they strained like a Jack-in-the-box wound tight and ready to pop. Her head throbbed where she'd been hit, but her skull was probably hardened by age and a hundred other bumps, therefore unlikely to have suffered permanent damage. And even if it had, who would notice?

Jack was carrying her now. She couldn't escape his antiperspirant, a menthol-scented pong that added to the acrid scent of sweat and heat. The stench made her want to curl into a ball and throw her hands over her head, not because it was horrible, but because it was tied to memories of things that were.

Why did it have to be Jack?

His shoulder ground into her ribs, but she let herself dangle anyway, like a shot deer slung over an ATV, limbs waving goodbye with every rise and fall of the trail. The thought made her feel like an old woman, as impotent as Walter's Captain America shield.

Had Marcel been as careless when he'd lugged her out of the woods? Doubtful. He would have cradled her, all the while regretting the necessity of placing her face close to his armpit, embarrassed.

A door creaked open, and her attacker bumped down three stairs. In the sudden brightness she could see the dull red insides of her eyelids. Humid air breathed across the exposed skin of the small of her back. She resisted the urge to tug her shirt back to where it belonged, but she did peek, just for a moment, when a pickup truck rolled into the yard.

"What the fuck, Jack?" The other man stopped two feet away, giving Gracie a clear view of L.L. Bean socks and black Hush Puppies. "Isn't that the old bat with the mower?"

Jack shifted Gracie to the opposite shoulder. "She got away. And Lyman's next door with hostages."

"I know all about Lyman, and I know you shot that little blond cop, you idiot." The man sounded as if his teeth hurt. "Thanks to you, I had to let Shay all the way in."

"Shay? I thought you didn't trust her."

"No choice." A pause. Then, "She did mislead the Staties when I asked her to—lied about going shooting with Candy. Now she's on her way here to take care of Lyman, and I have to clean this mess up."

The thought of Officer Lyman waiting in the living room, armed and bleeding, made Gracie's stomach pitch. Molly must be scared half to death, and the boarders—they'd be too terrified to be much help.

She risked another peek, past the man who carried her, to a sky filled with upside-down clouds. A rhythmic thud . . . thud . . . thud . . . sounded from somewhere, like a boot against metal. Jack must have heard it, too, because he burst into laughter. Gracie tried to figure out where the sound was coming from, but instead her attention caught on a flash of light at the side of the road.

A windshield?

The flicker vanished as quickly as it had come, and she wondered if the bump to her head might be making her see things. She closed her eyes and hoped it was real—maybe someone was there and knew what was happening. Then she hoped even harder that Jack hadn't seen it, too.

"What the hell, Shay?"

"Shut up, Marcel."

But she saw them, too. Marcel could tell by the way her breath caught.

"Is that Gracie?" Shay was all-business. She'd probably never openly admit to being startled or scared. Even so, there was a queasy timbre beneath her calculated tone.

"I think it must be." His own voice skipped right past tenor and landed square in the soprano range. "Isn't that David?" She must realize now that David wasn't as innocent as she'd believed.

Shay went silent, but Marcel could feel anger rolling off of her. Finally she whispered, "I'm a fucking idiot."

Marcel swallowed. "Never disagree with a lady."

A growl worked its way past her throat, and her jaw looked tight enough to bite clean through her husband's dick. She kept herself together, though, stayed on task. "Looks like Molly's home. I see her car."

"Uh-huh." He would have said more if the words hadn't queued up on the back of his tongue and pushed each other into a meaningless jumble. His breath seemed to congeal, lungs burning with the effort of sucking it all the way to his chest.

"This isn't good." Understatement. Shay clicked her tongue against the roof of her mouth. The sound made Marcel wince, and the last of his patience came out loud.

"Ya think?"

Jack carried Gracie up the handicap ramp and vanished into Blue Horizons. David followed. Marcel reached for the door handle.

"Don't even think about it." Shay's fingers dug into his elbow. She seemed to know just where to press to hit the crazy-bone. But then, she would.

He managed not to yelp. "We can't just sit here."

"Sure we can. Help is fifteen minutes out, and there's no point heading in there without adequate preparation. It's not been my best day, and I'm not about to get anyone dead." She twisted around and opened a compartment behind the passenger seat—pulled out tactical gear.

"I want you to swap your vest out. This'll be a little tight on you," she added, "but fortunately its owner has a lot of muscle where you have other things, so it ought to even out."

"Thanks, I guess." Marcel sucked his stomach in. He put the vest on, taking note of the added neck and groin protection and fingering the ceramic plate—a higher level of protection than his own. Shay leaned across him and yanked the side straps tight enough to make his eyes water.

"Jeezus, Shay. Was that necessary?"

"Sure was. Don't want any gaps." She rolled up her pants leg to reveal an ankle holster. Then she pulled a spare Glock from the glove box. He watched while she chambered a round, topped off and replaced the magazine, and then clipped the gun in place. "Your mom's taking her sweet time getting here. I don't dare wait any longer to assess the situation, so you need to do exactly as I say. If you go all hero on me, I'll shoot you myself." She glanced at his vest and added, "In the head. I mean it."

"Fine." Marcel took an experimental breath. The vest was heavy and hot as hell, but not as tight as he'd feared. "What about you?" Shay was still dressed in jeans and a crop top.

"I have an idea. This outfit will work better." Shay did look as if something brainy had occurred to her, but she didn't elaborate. Instead, she opened the door and jumped to the ground, reaching back for the cellphone she'd left on the dash. She pounded out a text message before heading to the hill that separated them from Blue Horizons. Marcel eased his way out the side door and followed.

She turned back for just a moment, long enough for him to catch up. "You ready?"

He wondered if he'd imagined the regret in her tone. "Guess so."

She cuffed his shoulder like his sister would have, turned her back, and started up the hill.

"You lost one." Jack's voice burned in Gracie's ears as she sprawled on the floor in a jumble of limbs.

"What did you do to her?" Molly spoke above the more subtle sounds of Jillian trying not to cry, Charlotte's piercing recitation of the day's events, and Walter chanting in whispers so soft that Gracie could only hear the consonants.

"What the hell, David? What's *Jack* doing here?" Gracie recognized Officer Lyman's voice, reed thin, as if some of the life had bled out of it. "You said no one would get hurt."

"Things change. Try to keep up." David stepped over Gracie. His shoe scraped her hip.

Molly persisted. "Let me go to her. She's not moving."

"Good. She's trouble." David brushed past Molly, his attention on Lyman. "Jack says he heard a gunshot. Who'd you shoot?"

"I didn't shoot anyone, you idiot. I fired one round in order to signal Jack."

Gracie tried to make out what was happening, but Walter, still caught up in a whispered chant and rocking like a bobble-head, blocked her view. She could barely see Molly, just to Walter's right and duct taped to a plastic-wrapped chair. Only her mouth was free.

"The new neighbor," Charlotte squeaked, "David Cooper arrived at 2:57 with Jack Broussard, carrying Gracie." She pointed at the man on the couch. "Officer Todd Lyman arrived at 2:14. Interrupted sandwich time. Upset Walter."

"What did I tell you?" Jack advanced on Charlotte. He'd gone very soft, but there was a rhythm to his words that made Gracie shudder.

"Cut it out, Jack. As long as we don't let her write anything down, who cares what she says?" David pointed to an empty chair, the one with its back to Molly's picture window. "Sit. Now."

Jack didn't look happy, but he complied. "You do realize I was in the middle of something."

"The girl? She'll keep." David stopped next to the window and moved the curtain aside.

"She won't last long, not in this heat." Jack grinned. "She was still kicking when we walked by, banging away with her little feet."

"Officer Lyman needs to go to the hospital." Molly's voice again, soft and wobbly. "He's lost a lot of blood."

"Oozing, not spurting," Charlotte said. "Messy. Not critical."

"He'll be fine." David glanced back. "If I'm not mistaken, help is right outside."

"Shay's here?" Officer Lyman sounded hopeful. "Are ya gonna invite her in? I could use a few stitches, and she needs to look at Gracie."

"She'll let herself in." David's phone chirped. Once he'd read the text message, he sounded a whole lot happier. "It's Shay. She brought the package I asked for."

"What package?" Lyman rocked far enough forward that Gracie caught sight of his face. He looked older than she remembered, grizzled and pale.

"The package who's going to let you and me walk out of here." David put a hand on Lyman's shoulder. "I know this isn't how things were supposed to go, and I know you don't approve. But this can't be helped." He moved the curtain aside again. Something beyond the glass had his complete attention.

"Thanks to Eric, everyone thinks Officer Trudeau is dirty," David said. "Seems the poor guy finally lost it, shot a bunch of crazy people, and then turned his gun on himself."

Lyman tried to stand, but he crumpled back against the couch. He looked stunned, mouth gaping like a trout. "You're talking murder, David."

"What did you expect?" David sounded resigned, now. He peeled his gaze from the window and headed for the back door. When Molly sobbed, he paused and said, "How the hell did you think this was gonna end?"

CHAPTER THIRTY-NINE

Marcel dropped into Shay's slipstream and let her pull him along. She moved like an athlete, not just fit, but graceful. Behind her, snapping twigs and scuffling through deadfall, he felt like a market hog, made soft and tender by level ground and plenty of corn.

Follow my lead, she'd said. *We need to assess the situation*. But near as he could tell, they were heading for Blue Horizons's front door. And if he wasn't seeing things, someone had just looked straight at them through Molly's bay window.

"We've been spotted." He was puffing to keep up, probably nerves, since they'd only traveled maybe a hundred yards. "Did you hear me?"

"I did." Shay didn't miss a step. "I'm making this up on the fly, rookie. You're gonna have to trust me."

"I'm not sure I do."

Shay slid to a stop, jaw clenched so hard he thought she might split her teeth. But she didn't lose control. Maybe she didn't know how. When she spoke, she used the precise inflection he'd come to recognize as her own, rather than one of the parts he'd seen her play.

"I get that, but you'd better make up your mind to try."

Her eyes had a burnt look. Marcel reminded himself he wasn't the only one with someone he loved on the other side of that door. Shay had been betrayed, probably wasn't sure what to believe. Yet here she was, ready to do what had to be done.

He nodded once. "Will do."

"Good." She must be working out how to bring David in, thinking through options, forming a plan. In her position, having to arrest someone she loved, knowing she may have to use—he hoped not—deadly force, he'd be a mess. Shay, though, finally seemed calm.

"Did I ever tell you about killin' roosters?"

"What?" He wiped sweat from his forehead, knocked his glasses askew.

"Roosters." She had a funny look on her face, as if she'd only now made a decision, one that didn't make her happy. "I grew up on a farm over in Hillsborough. We kept chickens for eggs, but every year we'd have a bunch of chicks, and we always ended up with too damn many roosters."

"And?"

"It was always my job to kill one for dinner." She turned away and headed straight up the hill. "I didn't want to have to choose which one I killed, because that seemed too much like playing God. So I left a cage on the lawn with the door open—roosters are curious, you know—and I told myself, whichever one went in first, he'd be dinner."

"Why are you tellin' me this?" Marcel slipped on dead leaves, righted himself. "What's it got to do with anything?"

Shay vaulted over a stone wall and continued through mountain laurel. Her feet barely made a sound. "When I came for my handbag, I considered leaving without you, even though your presence was requested. But you wouldn't let me go. You just had to put yourself in the cage." She reached the lawn and broke to a jog. Marcel hustled behind her.

"Are ya just gonna walk in?"

"Why not?" She bounded up to the front door and knocked twice, then once more. "He already knows we're here, and he knows I brought what he asked for."

"What did he ask for?"

The sound of a slide racking gave him his answer.

Shay looked like a kitten with a cricket when David took purchase of Marcel's only weapon. She cooed, "That was easy," pushed past Marcel, and wrapped herself around her husband. "What next, sweetie? Wanna tie him up, and then maybe tie me up, too? I have duct tape in the car."

"Don't tempt me." David's smile had his damn dimples popping, and Shay looked about ready to wet herself.

"Cuff him." She walked past David into Blue Horizons's front hallway. Marcel watched as her gaze traveled from one end of the living room to the other in a quick assessment. When she said, "No, wait," the accompanying laughter sounded a little too real. "Don't cuff him—that'll leave a mark. Follow me."

David looked more curious than anything when he said, "You heard her." Shay bounced down the ramp and turned toward the backyard. David shoved Marcel right back into her wake.

She stopped at the edge of the property where the ground dipped sharply, then rose in a natural berm. After popping the magazine from Marcel's Smith & Wesson, she sited through the chamber, then handed him the gun.

He tried to catch her eye. Maybe this was the moment where they'd work together to bring David down.

David kept his weapon pressed against Marcel's neck while Shay rattled off instructions.

"There's one round in the chamber, Marcel. Would you please do me the favor of firing into that hillside?"

David's laughter crackled like soft wood on a slow fire. "That's just plain cruel, Shay. I knew there was a good reason I married you."

"More than one reason, I expect."

The dizziness caught Marcel by surprise. It shouldn't have. He'd never been good in crisis situations, and this was one. They'd given him his own weapon, and now they wanted residue on his hands. Chances were he'd be dead as soon as he did as they asked.

He shook his head. "I'd prefer not."

"I could shoot you first," David said, "and fire that gun with your dead hand."

"Please." Shay looked as if she were pretending to care.

The muzzle of David's gun dug a little deeper into the base of Marcel's skull. His hands shook more than he thought they ought to, even knowing he was a wuss, but he raised his gun and placed his feet shoulder-width apart.

As he wrapped his index finger around the trigger, he felt a little less vulnerable, almost high. The sense of being invincible traveled from his hand to his brain, and his body acted on its own. His legs collapsed, and he fell in slow motion, rolling free, sweeping the gun around to aim at David's scrambling form. He ignored Shay's "Oh God, no!" and fired.

—◊—

He wasn't sure how he'd made it to Blue Horizons's entryway. There were snatches of memories: David and Jack half dragging, half carrying him across the lawn, kicking him the one time he'd dropped to his knees. He only vaguely remembered being hit on the head, knew he'd been dazed and wobbly, clumsy, but conscious.

The first thing he saw clearly was blood spattering his hands and smearing Molly's white ceramic.

The second thing he saw was Jack, dangling a Walther P99 from his fingertips and laughing at a crimson trickle making its way past a shallow furrow on David's arm. Then he saw Shay, her face blotched with fury. Must have misread her intentions, but if that was the case, Marcel didn't care.

His head throbbed, probably no worse than Gracie's. She was unconscious—please not dead—lying in a heap on the floor. Molly was imprisoned by duct tape, and the other boarders were incapacitated by fear.

Shay hovered over someone in a Falls PD uniform, propped up with pillows on Molly's couch, shirt unbuttoned and trousers lowered to expose a thick white bandage, seeping red. Todd Lyman. That answered one question. Marcel looked straight at Shay and said, "I knew I couldn't trust you."

"And yet, here you are." She backed away from her patient and rested both hands on her hips, a femme fatale, all boobs and booty with a face lost to the wrong sort of conviction. "You've got instincts, rookie," she said in a tone that wasn't quite her own. "Shame you can't seem to trust 'em."

"That's enough." It was David. He'd walked to the center of the room and now faced Marcel. His lips barely moved when he said, "Get up."

Jack laughed harder.

Marcel got to his feet, swayed a bit, wondered what was coming next, and hoped backup might already be outside. He glanced toward the window.

Shay followed his gaze. "The cavalry's maybe five minutes out. We'd better get a move on."

The dizziness came back along with a dose of nausea. Marcel tried to breathe the way Shay did, as if she were having her hair done, bored. Then he wondered who'd hit him. David or Shay. He guessed it didn't matter, since they were working together, probably planning to use the gun he'd fired to kill everyone there.

That made his knees weak, but he didn't have time to dwell. In one smooth movement, David raised his gun, aimed straight for Marcel's chest, and fired.

Marcel fell against the wall, the pain that ripped through him a whole lot worse than he'd imagined. His face skidded into Molly's carpet before he realized he'd hit the floor.

Molly screamed. Lyman hollered as if he'd lost a loved one. Jack's laughter turned into the drawn-out gasping howls of someone who couldn't catch his breath.

"What the fuck, David! This needs to look self-inflicted." That must be Shay. He could barely hear her past the ringing in his ears.

"He's got a vest—a good one."

"He'll still bruise like a banana, and you better not have cracked his ribs. Now we have to kill him quick, lay him face-down, and hope the damage might be mistaken for lividity."

Marcel felt the thud of Shay's boots as she strode toward him, heard Molly calling from far away, "Marcel, Marcel, don't be dead, Marcel," and he managed to open his eyes. Shay's expression told him there was something she had to do, and she wasn't about to back down. She squatted next to him and shoved a gun in his face.

"Here's what's gonna happen. You're gonna sit up, and I'm gonna take that vest off. Then I'm gonna put the barrel of this gun in your mouth. You already have residue on your hands, so I'm not gonna make you fire it yourself."

Molly was crying, a slew of hiccups strung together. Walter chanted, and Charlotte called out, "Shot Officer Trudeau at 3:07! Not dead, not yet, but soon," while Jack laughed and Lyman muttered like a man caught up in delirium. Gracie was still out cold. For that, at least, Marcel was grateful. He hadn't been able to stop what was coming, but at least she wouldn't be awake for the screaming.

"I think you know you're not gonna walk outta here," Shay continued, the rhythm of her words metronome steady, "so quit bein' such a pussy. Sit up for me and do this right."

Marcel's thoughts were whirling out of control, but he latched onto one word and held on. "Did you just call me a *pussy?*" His question came out in a grunt, which made him feel even more like a pig-to-slaughter.

"I sure did." She hitched up her pants leg a quarter inch, and he could just make out the edge of her ankle holster. A quick survey of the surroundings told him Shay's body blocked his movements from everyone else's view.

If only he could think, but his heart pounded, and his ears were filled with noise. One question came to mind. What did he have to lose?

He slipped his hand up Shay's calf, unclipped her Glock, and drew it out, not daring to breathe. He wanted to shut his eyes and hold his ears. Shay might do anything, might shoot him where he lay, could easily pass it off as self-defense. *He admitted to all of it: the drugs, Eric's murder, everything. I tried to subdue him, and he went for my gun.*

But she'd said *pussy,* his childhood code word that meant she was a good guy pretending to be a bad guy. That couldn't be coincidence. While he found his way to the trigger, she moved the barrel of her gun to one side and looked him straight in the eye.

"Sit up, Marcel. Now. I need the blood spatter to match the story we're gonna tell." She settled into a low, wide stance.

"Okay." The word burned through his chest. He pulled himself up, tilted, propped his back against the wall. Shay shifted marginally to one side and reached for his vest, giving him a clear shot at David if he sighted right between her thighs.

The words he'd learned back at Academy flashed through his mind. *Aim for the center of mass. Stop the threat.*

He ignored Shay's little cry and the way her face twisted like a girl at a horror movie when he took aim and drew back the trigger. She would have done the same thing herself—God, he'd better be right—if it had been anyone other than David.

Scared though she was, Gracie couldn't help but appreciate the smell of Molly's chicken soup, thick with garlic and parsley and Basmati rice. It must be boiling by now, and soon it would be ruined. A shame. Stomach rumbling in protest, she peeked through half-closed lids. Marcel had Shay's gun. His finger rested on the trigger and drew back.

David did the same. He was desperate, and he had Shay in his sights.

If Shay had meant to kill Marcel, wouldn't she have done it by now? Her delaying tactics had transformed David's resolve into something a lot angrier, and now she was gonna end up dead. Chances were the rest of them would follow.

Someone had to do something.

Gracie rolled to her knees, clambered to her feet, and ran. Screaming like a banshee in a B movie, she hurled herself at David, shouting her best cuss words as he spun to meet her. The CRACK of gunshots slammed into her ears. David's face went slack a moment before blood sprayed her. The heat of it was a surprise, and the smell.

The dead girl flashed into her mind, but she wasn't singing or making demands or talking in riddles. Her body lay twisted in stalks of corn, her head yards away, puddled in red.

The smell. Gracie scrubbed at the blood covering her arms, her hands, her shirt. Hannah looked up, for a moment seeming to connect with Gracie's gaze. The ghost's mouth worked as if she wanted to say something, but no words came out.

The next thing Gracie knew, the front door burst open, and Suzanne Trudeau was there, gun drawn. Sounds seemed to come from a distance, even though Suzanne was only a couple feet away and appeared to be shouting. "Drop your weapons! All of you."

Shay's pistol landed at Marcel's feet. She bolted to David's side and plunged her hands into the ruins of his chest, crying, "He's gonna bleed out. I can't stop it." She turned back to Marcel. "Call an ambulance."

His words were softer than a heartbeat. "I expect they're on their way." But he reached for his mic and said something about needing medical assistance, even though it looked as if David was a gurgle short of the other side.

Todd Lyman had his gun in his fingertips, halfway to the floor, and he wheezed, "I shot Jack. I shot Jack." Only then did Gracie realize the big man's mouth was gaping, and Molly's picture window was splattered with blood.

Shay didn't cry, but her gaze haunted the room. "Lyman's on our side," she murmured. "Has been for a full fifteen minutes." Then she looked down at David, brushed the hair from his face, and bent to kiss his forehead. She said, "He's gone," but her words were murmured, almost lost in the aftereffects of gunfire.

Charlotte's proclamation rose above Molly's anguished cries and the panicked scramble of Walter bolting from the room. "Time of death, 3:11:58."

The room went church quiet. Then a soprano voice so pure it made Gracie's throat ache soared above the silence. *Amazing Grace.* It was Jillian, and she was beautiful.

Marcel squeezed Gracie's shoulder as he passed her and made his way to Molly's side. He unwound the tape from her wrists while she strained toward him, laughing and crying and gulping like a little girl on a candy high. Gracie shivered as the last of the hymn swelled the air and died to a whisper . . . faded . . . gone.

She stood in silence while pandemonium played around her. People in uniforms swirled past, an assemblage of parts with no idea how to become a whole. The confusion didn't matter, because the crisis was over and they'd survived.

Maybe, just maybe, this was the moment Hanna had predicted.

But that was silly. Gracie's own daughter hadn't been found, and wasn't that supposed to happen first? Besides, there was only one person in the room who looked anything like Hannah, only one young woman with fiery red hair. The longer Gracie stared at her caretaker, the more she wondered: Molly? Was she Hannah's great-granddaughter?

If so, she'd been saved, and that meant Hannah would go back to where ghosts belonged. Life should return to normal.

Normal sounded good.

CHAPTER FORTY

Gracie snatched Molly's mail from the kitchen counter, skittered past David's body, and found an empty place on the living room carpet. With her back pressed against a plastic-wrapped chair, she groaned deep in her throat and pressed the heels of her hands against her eyes.

The vision of the ghost girl's severed head still swam before her, clinging like lint on wool no matter how hard she tried to blink it away. It seemed real, like something she could reach out and touch. But Hannah was already dead, so she couldn't bleed, couldn't suffer, and certainly couldn't die all over again.

It must be the smell of blood that set off the memory, or hallucination, or whatever it was supposed to be. The vision was all in her head and wouldn't last.

Two deputies, armed with Molly's clean towels, stood over Cracked Jack—must be trying to stop the bleeding. Jack made the sort of sounds that suggested he'd join David long before an ambulance could arrive.

On the couch beside Gracie, just visible out the side of her eye, Todd Lyman sat cuffed and waiting. He looked old, weak, and tired, even though he must be about her age, or maybe a couple years younger. She supposed a bullet would do that to someone with a pacemaker bulging just above his unbuttoned shirt, and blood likely thinned with Coumadin.

Blue Horizons was bedlam. Walter had locked himself in his room. Furniture gouged across the floor and slammed against his door while Deputy Suzanne Trudeau called to him in a surprisingly gentle voice, "It's all over now, Walter. You're safe."

Charlotte and Jillian fought to tell their stories at the same time while Chief Farrell herded them away from the immediate crime scene. Gracie was pleased to see Charlotte so willing to speak to strangers. Could be surviving the ordeal had given her courage.

Sheriff Plunket arrived along with two more deputies. This had
to be the largest group of law enforcement personnel ever to congre-
gate within Coyne Falls's borders, except maybe for the time Earle
Oakham had set his barn and one and a half tons of pot ablaze.
Everyone came to watch the flames. They were spectacular. Attendance had nothing to do with the secondhand smoke, no matter what
the *Falls Facts* had implied.

Marcel looked like a wax statue of himself, sitting stiff and pasty
with Molly clutching and pulling at him, as if wrestling him away
from death. His shoulders were drawn up, and his hands seemed to
hover; probably he was afraid to let the full weight of his arms rest
on hers.

Molly ought to do something to reassure him, not just suck up
all the comfort he had to give. He'd killed a man, and that had to
be chewing at him, necessary though it was. And he'd been hit hard,
probably more than once, likely had a headache to rival her own.

Gracie reached for the back of her head, felt the knot growing
at the base of her skull, and remembered what a nurse had said the
first time someone hit her. "Swelling outward is a good sign. Swelling
inward is bad. So a big lump is what we want to see." Then she'd held
out a cup of pills and said, "Stop annoying people."

Shay sat at the kitchen table, head bowed. She shivered, even
though the temperature must be near ninety. Reggie Clark sat beside
her, and he didn't have a charitable look on his face.

Gracie hadn't known which side that woman was on until she'd
burst through the door and ordered Jack to help David with Marcel.
Then she'd made a show of checking Gracie's pulse, all the while
whispering, "I'd prefer you stay alive, so keep playing possum."

Shay's next stop had been Todd Lyman. Their conversation was
too soft to overhear, but apparently Shay had talked Lyman into
switching sides.

Someone had turned off the stove, thank goodness, but the smell
of burnt chicken soup filled the room. Ruined. Like the carpet and
the couch and the afternoon that had started out filled with so much
promise.

Gracie plucked a letter from the pile, one with a return address
belonging to a church in Keene. She wadded it in her fist and told

herself no good would come from knowing more about her past. Even so, her thumb seemed bent on sliding beneath the seal.

Officer Lyman was staring at her, but when she twisted her head and shot him the most ferocious glare she could manage, he immediately looked away. Interesting. He wasn't the least bit threatening now. She pulled the letter from its envelope and tried not to think about him, but she had questions that needed asking. He owed her answers.

"Did you put that gun in my tree?"

Once the shock left his face, he shook his head. "That was Jack. He was supposed to get rid of it, but kept it for himself."

That made sense. Jack was sneaky, and he rarely did what he was supposed to do. Gracie pouched her lower lip, wondered whether to quit before she started trouble. Officer Lyman was in no condition to hurt anyone, though, so she glared and said, "Why did you come here? You nearly got us all killed."

Lyman seemed to shrink, like a dead rat with its belly eaten by maggots. But he worked his jaw as if he had something to say, if only the words weren't all caught up in his dentures.

"Jack and I were supposed to meet David next door, but I had to talk to you first." He folded his hands, unfolded them, folded them again. "You weren't here. I was bleeding, and . . . I wasn't thinking straight. Everyone panicked, and things got out of hand."

"You wanted to talk to me?" That made no sense. "Why?" She didn't much care for the man. He seemed bitter, as if everything he wanted had been taken from him. She knew what that was like, but there was no use crying over it.

"I thought I might die." He winced, then spoke again in a soft rasp. "I needed to tell you who your daughter is."

The words slapped her to an alertness so bright, her brain stung. "What?"

"I should have told you a long time ago." He paused while his breathing caught up to his talking. "But I'll be damned if I wasn't afraid." He'd stopped looking at her, couldn't do her the courtesy.

"I don't have a daughter. She's dead."

"She's alive. She's right here."

Gracie itched to be somewhere else. She scooted away, sliding on her bottom until she'd backed herself into the recess beside the bay window. Lyman seemed oblivious to her distress and kept talking, as if he'd opened a verbal artery, and the flood was beyond his control.

"Her name is Suzanne, and she's standing right over there."

His index finger slowly uncurled, but Gracie didn't look where he pointed. There was only one Suzanne in the room, and that wasn't possible. She was tall and dark-haired, chubby, with a husky voice and . . . "She chews with her mouth open."

"So do you."

Gracie shut her mouth. Suzanne couldn't be hers. Her daughter would be more like little Dayna than the stout deputy.

She distracted herself by picking at the dried blood on her finger-nails. *Suzanne Trudeau.* She was nice enough in a coarse sort of way, even helped out at Blue Horizons from time to time. "Suzanne used to make lunch for us when Amanda was running this place. Never washed the vegetables. Said it was healthy to eat a little dirt now and again."

"And?"

"Could be, but I don't like the grit between my teeth." Gracie looked down at her hands, her sleeves, her shirt front, all splattered with a man's blood. Some things needed washing. "Does she know about me?"

"No." Lyman's voice was unexpectedly tender. "I'm not sure she knows she's adopted. But I moved here right after the Campbells took her in, made sure I drew detail for her graduation, worked traffic at her wedding, took the call when she went into labor—"

"Why?" The moment she asked, Gracie's throat closed up. There wasn't enough space in the room to get as far from Todd Lyman as she wanted to, not enough air to escape the stink of his breath.

"She's my daughter, too." The man's voice was hoarse, and he looked about ready to break down. Crying was stupid, even though a fat tear had already splashed over the back of her own hand and wetted bits of caked blood. Gracie rubbed at it, made a spot of rust-colored mud.

"Marcel. He's—"

"Your grandson. Mine, too."

Couldn't be. Gracie stared at her own slim legs, even now vibrat-ing in protest at having sat for so long. They wanted to hike the trails, swim, climb Pole Hill, and visit the old cemetery there. "But Marcel can hardly walk a mile."

"Carried you farther than that."

"So I'm told." She looked hard at Marcel. He'd finally let his hands fall. His arms wound tight around Molly, and his face pressed into her hair. "He's a nice boy."

"The best."

Gracie couldn't stop staring at Marcel. He had to be the kindest, most honest man she'd had the pleasure of knowing. And he wasn't all that chubby, probably just big-boned. And brave, too. He'd been scared, but he'd kept his head, waited for his opportunity, done what he had to do.

"Zoe."

"Your granddaughter. Tough little bit of a thing like you."

Gracie's grin nearly jumped off her face. "She's not even afraid of Jack."

"She should be. That man's not right." His face fell. "Sorry. I didn't mean—"

"It's okay. I'm not quite right, either." She scanned the room. Zoe wasn't there, but she'd show up when the ambulance did. "I'm not dangerous, though. I've had lots of tests."

"I know." Lyman's face seemed to thaw a bit, the sharp edges melting smooth.

"Do they know about you?"

Lyman shook his head. "No, and I'd rather keep it that way."

"Why?"

"Because of how Suzanne came to be."

Gracie nodded, even though her fists wanted to do something far less passive. "You mean an assault on a mental patient."

Now Lyman was snuffling, which didn't do a damn thing for his breathing. His face got blotched in purple, and his voice sort of lost its air. "I didn't realize. I thought—"

"Thought what?" It was hard not to taunt the man. *I couldn't find anyone in a coma, and I figured mental patients were fair game. I knew you wanted it. You never complained. Hell, you never moved.*

"You have to realize, I was only seventeen and none too bright. Working at that hospital was my first job where I wasn't bent over in a field picking something." He gulped for air, wheezed it back out. "You walked right over and kissed me. I thought it was real."

"You thought—"

"I thought you liked me." Lyman snorted, the sound obviously meant to convey the absurdity of anyone being attracted to him. "You talked like a normal person, and you knew where all the corners were, every bit of privacy that could be had in that hell hole. We planned on getting you out of there, having a life together."

"I don't remember any of that."

"I know." Lyman wiped his nose on his sleeve. "I got you a court date, but your medication got changed, and you were too out of it to speak with the judge. You just sat there talking all kinds of nonsense, didn't even remember who I was."

Damn. Lyman's explanation was a whole lot easier to swallow than the one she'd concocted. "So I wasn't assaulted, not really." Funny how the thought lifted a weight she hadn't known she'd been carrying.

"I didn't think so at the time," Lyman said. "But, yes, I guess you were. I just . . . I didn't know a crazy person could look so normal."

"I guess the joke was on you." But she didn't feel like laughing.

"I got you out of there as soon as I had enough money, and I made sure you had a chance to know your daughter." He paused a moment, caught his breath. "When Peter Gavin passed away, I asked Amanda if she'd be willing to take you in. I gave her money."

"Drug money?"

"Not then, but later on . . . how else could I afford it?" He looked embarrassed, maybe ashamed. "I dropped off a cash donation every month. I never kept any of it."

"But you and Amanda grew pot? For twenty-five years?"

He nodded slowly. "We did. And you were all the better for it."

"Huh."

A moment of silence. Then, "Is that all you have to say? *Huh?*"

"What else is there?" Gracie turned her attention to the letter in her hand and read the first sentence. *Grace Hannah Ouellette was born on May 19th in her parents' home here in Keene.*

"You could ask why I let them take your baby away, why I didn't say a word when they put her up for adoption."

"That's easy. I was crazy, and you were an idiot. That's what they did then."

"But it was wrong."

"Maybe yes, maybe no." Gracie looked up when Suzanne crossed the room and planted a kiss on her son's forehead. "Seems she was raised right, probably better than I could have done."

Molly's arms wound tight around Marcel, and Gracie couldn't help smiling. "Hannah's gone. I'm hoping Molly is the great-grand-daughter she was worried about. She's got red hair and everything."

"Who's Hannah?"

"My ghost." Gracie read another sentence. *Her daddy was overseas, so Gracie's mom had to bring her with her when she worked in the fields. Grace was a handful, always into everything, never could sit still . . .*

Gracie looked at Lyman's ashen face and sighed. "You already knew I was nuts, so my ghost shouldn't be a big deal." She leaned against the wall and let her feet disappear beneath Jack's chair. The deputies were switching off with CPR, for all the good it would do.

"You still hallucinate?"

Gracie ignored the question long enough to read another line. *She was only four when it happened. They said Gracie pushed her, but Hannah might have just tripped. . . .* "Depends who you ask."

"What do you want to do about Suzanne?"

The question came sooner than Gracie had expected—shouldn't she think about it? But she wasn't all that good at thinking. She was better at doing.

"Nothing, I guess."

"Nothing?" Lyman's jaw hung slack. "But you've been looking for her. Why?"

"The ghost made me."

Lyman sucked in a breath. Gracie stared down at her hands. There were other reasons, and maybe Lyman deserved to know them.

She whispered the rest. "To know who she is. To make sure she's okay." Gracie glanced back to Marcel, let herself grin. "I did that."

She returned her gaze to the page in her hand, skimmed the part she'd already read, and picked up at the next line. *They were walking ahead, making sure the dogs stayed out of the way of the new harvester. When Hannah fell, the blades took her head clean off.*

"Oh balls."

"What?" Lyman looked as if he'd seen a ghost. Either that, or he'd heard the sirens. The ambulance must be almost there.

She re-read the line, the one where Hannah's head was taken off. A whole lot of things fell into place, no matter they didn't seem real.

Her father abandoned her, but not before he convinced everyone she was dangerous and had to be locked up. Poor kid ended up institutionalized.

"The dead redhead must be my mother."

"What dead redhead?" Lyman's frustration was obvious, maybe stronger than the pain. "Wait. Is this the head that turned out to be a handbag?"

"Yeah." Gracie's heart stepped up its pace. "It says here I killed her."

"You did what?"

"Not on purpose." The sirens were deafening now, probably right outside. Gracie's brain worked overtime to fit the pieces together. "If the ghost is my mother, then Molly isn't her great-granddaughter. Zoe is."

She got to her feet and scanned the room for the dead girl. Two EMTs came through the door, and Gracie searched for Zoe's green ball cap over unruly brown hair.

She wasn't with them, and Zoe was definitely working today— wasn't that what she'd said at the hospital?

A second ambulance pulled in behind the first. Gracie pressed her nose to the glass, watched two new figures head for the front door. Both tall. Both male.

Marcel's little sister was nowhere to be seen.

CHAPTER FORTY-ONE

"Marcel!" Gracie tried to shout, but her breath was shallow, her tongue thick. What was it Jack had said? He'd been interrupted by Lyman's gunshot, and whatever it was he'd been doing, it involved a girl.

Jack hated Zoe.

She pushed away from the wall and lurched across the floor, trying to reach Marcel. He seemed oblivious to her. The room revolved like a carousel spinning out of control, but there weren't any horses, and the music was gone.

One of the EMTs appeared and guided her toward Walter's favorite chair. The man's gloved hands made her arms tingle like cold feet in January.

"Zoe Trudeau." Gracie tried to keep her voice calm, rational, believable. "Have you seen her?"

"She didn't show up for her shift." If the man was worried, he hid it well. Any concerns he might have were tucked behind the talking-to-a-mental-patient mask. "I'm sure she's fine."

"No you're not." If Zoe were anything like her brother, she wouldn't miss work, not without calling in. "She had a fight with Jack Broussard, and now she's missing, and it looks as if he's dead."

The man shined a light in her eyes. "Can you tell me what day it is?"

"It's the day Zoe Trudeau went missing," Gracie spluttered. "Isn't that more important than the date?"

"Marcel!" It was Candy, and she was loud enough to cut across the Verizon Wireless Arena. She stood in the doorway, Abe a step behind her. "Marcel! Suzanne! Have either of you seen Zoe?"

"She's missing!" Gracie shouted past the blue uniform of the man winding a blood pressure cuff around her arm. "She's missing, and Cracked Jack did something to her."

Candy's gaze locked with hers, and Gracie knew she had an ally. Candy looked as if she'd seen something a whole lot worse than a headless redhead.

"Everyone shut the hell up!" Candy hollered into the room. "I need a police officer right this minute." She pushed through the crush and lunged for Marcel, grabbed his arm, and yanked him away from Molly. "Abe, you keep Molly company. Marcel, you need to see this, you and your mom both."

The EMT moved on to Jillian, and Gracie took the opportunity to hightail it out the door. Scout met her on the ramp, looking more anxious than if he'd dropped his favorite bone in Candy's goldfish pond.

"Where is she?" Gracie pleaded with the little dog. "Hannah always says to follow the beagle, so you'd darn well better know what to do."

Marcel burst through the doorway. He and his mom rushed past Gracie with Candy leading the way. Candy broke to a run, her words tumbling over themselves in a voice sharp with panic.

"I came by to check on the house, and . . . there are pictures. One was taken right in my living room. There's blood on the chair by the window, the good chair, not the plastic one, so it's harder to see. But it's blood. I'm sure of it."

Gracie followed the trio across the yard, through the garage, and into Candy's house. Candy headed straight to the living room and pointed to an old printer. It sat on an overturned bushel basket next to a desktop PC, swathed in cat hair and dust bunnies. "Look at the pictures, and then look over here."

Gracie peeked past Suzanne's broad back to the pictures laid out like tiles on the plywood floor. They were all of Zoe, some outside the hospital, others on a sidewalk in front of what must be her apartment. Then there was one taken through a window, her hair wet, a towel slipping from her shoulders.

The last one showed a wash cloth crammed into her mouth, wrists bound and duct taped against her throat. One eye was red and swollen, and blood dribbled from her nose.

Marcel stumbled when he turned and pointed to the overstuffed chair next to an open casement window. "That one was taken right here, and it can't have been long ago. I just saw Zoe at lunchtime."

"That's where the blood is." Candy's voice had gone soft as a minor chord.

Panic rolled off Marcel in waves. Gracie could feel it, tangible as the St. Fillan's to-go bag he plucked from the floor and crushed in his hands. "Jack's unconscious. How do we find her?"

"Call her cell." Suzanne already had her phone out.

Suzanne dialed, her fingers clumsy on the keypad. Marcel's eyes were half closed, and he still seemed unsteady. He probably ought to be in an ambulance.

"It's ringin'."

Everyone breathed in at the same time. No one breathed out.

There was nothing, not here, anyway. Gracie scooted out the doorway, through the garage, and turned her ear toward the bushes, the trees, and the junk cars lining the verge.

She heard music. The theme to *Spongebob Squarepants*.

"Over here!" She broke to a jog. Marcel burst past her and yanked open the door to a white Chevy Malibu. He popped the trunk. It was empty except for a cellphone still blasting Spongebob.

Marcel grabbed the phone and held it to his chest. Gracie had never seen him cry before, even when he thought he might die. But now tears poured down his face.

Gracie moved closer, but Suzanne was already there, blubbering against his shirt, and Molly was running toward them from Blue Horizons, closing the distance fast. Gracie backed from the driveway to the lawn and tried to piece together her memories. She'd been upside-down, swaying from Jack's shoulder. He'd said the girl was kicking, said he could hear her when they walked past. She focused on the sound—a rhythmic thud, thud, thud. She'd heard it, too.

She cupped her hands around her mouth and shouted. "Jack said we walked past her, so she's between the garage and the gate to Blue Horizons."

Everyone looked at her. The hope in Marcel's eyes was hard to bear.

"I think I heard her, too, but I don't remember exactly where. It would have been before Jack carried me onto the path, so . . . ." She closed her eyes and made a mental picture, easier than she'd expected. "She has to be somewhere to the right of the driveway, in this area."

She pointed toward a herd of junk cars surrounding the barn, hoping she was right, scared of what they'd find. The temperature was over ninety degrees in the sun, and Gracie couldn't get Jack's words out of her head. *She won't last long, not in this heat.*

All of a sudden, everyone was in motion, running from car to car, jerking doors open and popping trunks while Candy wailed, "Eric must have a dozen junkers. Watch out for hornets." People flooded the driveway and poured past the barn until Marcel shouted for quiet.

"Everyone stop talking and listen. Maybe she's still kickin'."

Nothing. Even the birds were silent.

Someone sneezed, once, twice, three times, followed by a whimpered burst that quickly escalated to a ghostly keening. Scout's voice was so desperate that Gracie thought it might chafe her raw. The beagle's nose stuck into the empty socket of a missing tail light in a faded blue Camaro, the car swaddled in bittersweet, half sunk into the landscape just beyond the barn.

Marcel ran past Gracie faster than she thought possible. He landed a fist on the trunk, hollered, "Zoe? You in there?" and then rushed to the driver's door and hauled on the handle. A dozen hornets boiled through a crack in the window.

"Damn it!" Marcel shouted. "Is there a key for this thing?"

"I don't know, Marcel. Maybe a rock?"

Rocks were plentiful in the Granite State. Marcel hefted the nearest boulder, slammed it through the window, leaned into the hornets, and pulled the trunk release. A deputy arrived with a can of insect spray and coated him in stink while he ran to the rear of the car, flung the trunk open, and clutched at a still form in EMT green.

"Zoe? Damn it, Zoe, you'd better be all right."

Suzanne pushed past him and pressed two fingers against Zoe's throat. "She's alive, but she's burning up. We need to cool her down."

Gracie pushed forward. "What about Candy's goldfish pond?"

They all looked at each other for about a second before they carried Zoe to the shallow pond and lowered her in. Goldfish scattered when Marcel climbed in with her and cradled her to his chest, whispering against her ear and slopping water over her neck.

That pond was sun warmed, probably more hot than cool. Gracie ran for the house, skidded to a stop in front of the refrigerator, and grabbed all the ice cube trays along with frozen peas and corn. It seemed to take a long time to hobble back to the yard and, when she got there, another ambulance was pulling in. Zoe was already breathing more normally, her color less red. The EMT's didn't look all that panicked when they loaded her up and drove away with the sirens screaming hallelujah.

If life were fair, Gracie told herself later, that would have been the end of it. Instead there was a commotion behind her. When she turned to see what was going on, Marcel crumpled to the ground. Molly dropped beside him, screaming.

"He's not breathing!"

Gracie's heart thrashed like a catfish hooked through the gills. She'd never been the mushy sort, never had anyone in her life close enough to miss once they were gone. Not until now.

Why would the universe give her grandkids, just so it could snatch them away?

CHAPTER FORTY-TWO

Marcel parked outside the Falls Library, walked around to the side of the building, and headed up the steps to the Town Hall. He stopped on the porch and looked out over a star-moss lawn dotted with Indian paintbrushes. It was the sort of lawn that wouldn't fly in places like Dover or Hollis, but it belonged in Coyne Falls, same as he did.

Waking up at St. Fillan's had been a surprise. Molly was there, squashing his hand in hers and so swollen with tears, he wasn't sure her face would ever shrink back to normal. Zoe had looked even worse, but he sure had grinned at the sight of her.

With two more weeks of paid leave, he figured he'd best catch up on all the things he'd let slide. Working stuff out with Dayna had been his first concern, but that was while they were both stuck at St. Fillan's. Nights on the hospital's third floor were longer than a Clydesdale's dick, and there wasn't much else to do but sneak into each other's rooms, play *Go Fish*, and talk about all the things they'd almost died without saying.

He understood that Dayna's actions had been sort of heroic, and he was grateful to her for making sure he'd got a fair shake. But the taste of deceit was hard to spit out. Maybe in time he'd find a way to let go of those feelings and forgive her for the lies. He sure hoped so.

At least he understood why she'd left him, and why he couldn't take her back, even if things with Molly ended before they began. Dayna had always wanted more than Coyne Falls had to offer, and he was a part of those offerings. He knew she loved him, and he loved her back, but none of that mattered. Someday she'd wake up and realize he wasn't up to her standards. Then she'd probably turn into her mother.

Dayna deserved better than that.

He wiped his feet at the door, tromped over to the cubbyhole with the Town Clerk sign, and called to Jane Edmunds over the bottom half of the Dutch door. She looked up from her desk, and Marcel could feel her eyes land on the shaved part of his head—the side with the crescent-shaped scar. He'd been meaning to take clippers to the other side, even things up.

"I heard something came for me."

"From the registry of deeds?

Marcel nodded.

"I left it next door. Back in a jiffy."

Normally, he'd have been the one running and fetching, but everyone was doing stuff for him these days. Probably because he'd been injured in the line of duty and a surgeon had sawed right through his skull. He'd expected the attention to fade along with the bruises, but a sort of glamour still surrounded him. It felt phony, like redhead on Shay.

He thanked Jane for the deed, and for the coffee and homemade lemon cake that followed, pulled up a chair to the round maple table, and focused on Candy's plot plan. Peter Gavin's grave was recorded, all right, but it was at the opposite end of the property from where they'd buried Eric. If Amanda's signature was to be believed, Candy's dad was resting in peace about twenty paces from the third cow. Eric's grave was labeled meticulously, right where it belonged, alongside Candy's signature with little hearts in place of the vowels.

"I'll be damned."

"Something I can help you with?" Jane rushed in with more cake.

"Can I get a copy of this?" He handed the paper over, part of him wishing he hadn't bothered to look. But there was also a need to tie up loose ends, to make sense of all that had happened.

Chief Farrell would be on patrol for at least another hour, so Marcel stopped at the Falls PD, left the photocopy on Farrell's keyboard, and headed for Blue Horizons.

His heart started pounding the moment he made the turn onto Sandpit Road, so he parked a hundred yards from the mailbox, same as he did every day, and waited out the fear.

He could still see Jack lugging Gracie through the brush, hear the sound of the slide racking, and feel cold metal against his skull.

Shay sure had played him.

She'd claimed she only did what was needed. Marcel wasn't an actor, she said, and his fear and confusion had to be real enough to fool someone who was. All she'd wanted was to get David out alive. But she'd ignored procedure and put a lot of people in danger. Damn near got everyone killed.

Marcel wondered if there'd been a moment when Shay might have considered switching sides. She wouldn't be the first person to lose her way. Having a husband who was both coercive and cruel might have sealed the deal.

Didn't matter. She was in big trouble either way. No matter her intentions, she sure had messed up.

The sweat started right on schedule when he drove up the hill to Blue Horizons, rolled to a stop by the handicap ramp, and sat gripping the wheel long after he'd shut off the engine. His heart flailed a bit, and he reminded himself he had to be strong. None of them had come through entirely whole, except maybe for those who'd started out in pieces.

"Marcel!" Gracie met him at the door. She'd been treating him special ever since . . . he guessed she felt closer to him now that they'd both almost died.

He took hold of her hand, only because she'd taken to grabbing his and comparing it to her own. Funny old gal.

"How's Molly today?"

"Better." Gracie squished her face up. "I think."

"And you?"

This time she grinned. "I'm good."

"Glad to hear it."

They exchanged a look, one that said they understood something no one else did. Not the therapists they'd all talked to, not the newspaper reporters or the self-appointed hot meals folks. Not anyone, except them.

He heard Amanda Gavin in the kitchen, cooking from scratch the same way Molly did. She'd moved in the day after the shooting, looking after the boarders so Molly could spend more time at the hospital crushing Marcel's hand. Candy had pitched in, too. They both seemed happy to be involved in the home where they'd spent so much of their lives.

"You're just in time," Amanda sang from the breakfast nook. "I've got meatloaf and three-bean salad. Monkey bread, too." She poked her head into the hallway. "So get that gal of yours to come and eat something. She's nothin' but bones."

Marcel winced. Food hadn't appealed to him, either. A benefit, he supposed. "Will do."

Molly was in front of the new sofa spraying room deodorizer. She'd worn her hands lobster red what with all the bleach, insisting she could still smell it.

He knew what she meant. It wasn't the stink of all the things that happened when a person died. That was gone. It was all the normal scents that wrapped themselves up with the ones they tried so hard to forget. The odor of new couches and just-laid carpet wasn't enough to hide it. Even the smell of chicken soup and butter rolls made it hard to breathe.

"Hey." He wrapped his arms around Molly's shoulders, and she did what she'd done ever since he'd come out of the coma; shuddered into his shirt. "It's gonna get better," he said to her hair. "The doctor says so."

"I know." She wiped her eyes and grabbed for the bleach. "But there's a spot over here, Marcel. I gotta get it before it spreads."

"Or you could take a break. Have lunch?" He guided her hands back to his waist, flinched when his thumb caught on a blister. "The room looks great, Mols."

"No it doesn't. It'll never be okay again."

"Then come to the kitchen." He tugged her along with him, trying not to let her stare at the center of the room. He knew she could see the body, the same one he saw. "You could stay at my place, or with my mom. Amanda's happy to help for as long as you need."

"Sure am." Amanda set a platter on the table, reached up and ruffled what was left of Marcel's hair. "Retirement wasn't as much fun as I'd hoped. It's good to have a purpose."

Walter was already seated on the bench by the window, still insisting on wearing his Tyvec suit, even in bed. Charlotte sat at the far end of the table, lips moving, mechanical pencil hovering above her notebook.

"I'm fine," Molly insisted. "Look. I'm eating." She picked up a kidney bean and tossed it into her mouth. Marcel resisted the urge to check and see if she'd cheeked it.

"I just have to adjust. We all do."

"I still think you should take Marcel up on his offer, Molly." Amanda set out cups and napkins, and then brought over a pitcher of iced apple cider. "I got this. You two need to get away, head for the White Mountains, take a real vacation."

"I need to be here with my family." Molly sat down hard, claiming her place.

"Whatever you want." Amanda winked at Marcel just as Gracie came in and winked back. Jillian shuffled behind her, spotted Marcel, and smiled so wide he could see the gap between her teeth.

"I've never been one to run from my problems," Molly said. "Not startin' now." As if to prove the point, she ate a chunk of monkey bread. This time she swallowed.

"The thing that scares me most is, we don't know for certain who killed Eric. Jack and David are dead, and we can't ask them." She turned to Marcel with a haunted look. "What if we still have a killer out there? What if he thinks we know something?"

"I don't know anything." Walter pulled his Tyvec suit tight, repositioned his shield.

"Don't be talkin' silly." Amanda slid a slice of meatloaf onto Molly's plate. "You're scaring Walter."

"She does have a point," Gracie said, chewing with her mouth open. "Everyone just assumes."

"Well, we know Jack shot Dayna. The slug from her belly came from his gun." Marcel reached for the meatloaf. It smelled good. "And those prints on the gold and on the murder weapon turned out to be Jack's. We figure he's the one who delivered payment to Eric. And according to old Lyman, Jack put the gun in the tree stand."

"After he shot Eric," Molly said.

"Couldn't have." Marcel had thought the same thing until he'd put together a timeline. "Jack was working with Zoe that night. We all saw him at Blue Horizons."

"I didn't think of that." Molly took a bite of meatloaf. Good for her. "I assumed he and David killed Eric together."

"Nope." That left David, Marcel supposed, since Lyman denied involvement in anything beyond growing pot. "The Staties did find traces of Eric's blood in the back of David's pick-up, so David must have moved the body. He got the key to the rail trail from Officer Lyman. And Eric's phone was in the glove box, so David must have sent those text messages to Abe and Candy."

"Why?" Gracie this time.

"To make my daughter look guilty," Amanda said. "Once they had her and Abe in custody, there was no point in looking for anybody else."

"David had a hunting knife, too, long and sharp enough to cut off a head." Marcel still cringed at the thought. "It had traces, too."

Jillian giggled. "So it was David who dumped Eric's body in Echo Lake, and he must have cut off the head." She seemed to enjoy discussing things that messed with the appetites of normal folks.

Marcel started in on the monkey bread. He'd learned something from Gracie—always eat the best part first. "Abe's fedora disappeared from his van that night—I saw him put it there, and he says it was gone when he left Candy's. David could have taken it and dropped it into the lake in order to cast suspicion on Abe and Candy."

"Then David must have killed Eric," Amanda said. "I mean, he chopped the heads off my daughter's doll collection, and Eric was beheaded. How many people do that?"

"But why?" Jillian dusted her meatloaf with salt, went for the pepper.

"Solar flares," Walter replied. "Shouldn't mix with fruit."

"He was supposed to keep that field safe." Amanda tipped her head toward Gracie. "And she mowed it."

"Gracie mowed a decoy field," Marcel said, only now voicing the doubts that had niggled at him since he woke up at St. Fillan's. "They'd already lost that crop to the DEA. Why would David care if it got mowed?"

"Because he was nuts?" Amanda looked about ready to start shouting. "He had four deer heads and a moose head in his living room, even a black bear, poor thing."

"I know." Marcel never had been able to understand why anyone would want to decorate their house with dead animals. "I suppose he put Eric's head on display at Coyote Rock because taking it home wasn't an option."

"Exactly." Amanda looked as if she'd just solved one of the great mysteries of the universe. "David had a compulsion to keep heads as trophies, and he liked to hang them up where folks could see them. So after he killed Eric—"

"David didn't kill Eric." Charlotte shook her head like a spaniel shaking off pond water. "Not possible. Not at all."

Amanda was at her side in an instant. "Don't upset yourself, Char. Lemme go get that stuffed kitten you like."

But Marcel was frozen in place, couldn't take his eyes off Charlotte. "Why isn't it possible?"

"Kitten?" Charlotte looked toward her room. "Here? At the table?" She scrawled in her notebook, whispering, "Kitten allowed at dinner table, 12:51."

"Everyone's been through the ringer," Amanda said in a soothing voice. "We can break the rules just this one time. I'll go get your kitten."

"I'll get you a brand new stuffed kitten if you tell me why David couldn't have killed Eric." Marcel knew he shouldn't be stirring up the boarders, not so soon after—

"Marcel!" Molly spit out a bean. "You're on leave. So leave it."

But Charlotte was already writing and chattering. "New kitten promised, 12:52." She looked up at Marcel. The trust in her eyes made him squirm. "When?"

"Tomorrow? I'll shop for it today."

"Tomorrow." Her face shone. "Deal."

"Charlotte already told us what happened that night," Gracie said. She'd started with monkey bread, finished her meatloaf, was halfway through the beans. "She won't change her story. She never does."

"Detective Clark asked for things that were *unusual*." Charlotte's tone gave the word added importance. "And I told them about the truck."

"Truck?" Molly gulped the word.

"The one with its lights off." Charlotte seemed calmer now, not vibrating and darn near self-assured. "David's truck."

"David's?" Marcel said. "Why didn't you tell us it was David's truck?"

"I didn't know. Not then." Charlotte's gaze met his. She whispered, "Kitten?"

"A nice fuzzy one, if I have to go all the way to Boston."

"Marcel . . ." But Molly was curious, too. He could see the spark in her eye, burning against the pain.

"The truck with its lights off. It was the same truck David drove the day Officer Lyman held us hostage, the day Officer Trudeau almost died." Charlotte looked up in response to Molly's whimper. "But he didn't die. Thought he would, but I was wrong."

"Well, there ya go," Amanda said. "Charlotte places David next door when Eric died."

"Gunshot first. David later." Charlotte held out her notebook. "David wasn't here yet."

Marcel took the notebook and scanned the notations and times. Charlotte was right. The gunshot happened at 8:40, and the truck arrived well after 9:00. If the truck really was David's, then someone else must have killed Eric, and David came to clean up.

"Who else could have done it?" He set down the notebook, managed to catch Charlotte's gaze. Maybe she knew more than she was saying. He just had to ask the right questions. "Can you tell me who *was* next door when Eric was shot?"

Amanda put her arm on Charlotte's shoulder. "You can pick this up another time, Marcel. Let's let her get some rest."

But Charlotte wasn't tired. She seemed excited. "Candy Thompson was there, in her house with Abe Rafferty." She shifted beneath Amanda's hand. "And Amanda, of course, just like always."

"That's crazy talk." Amanda looked nervous now, the way she dug her fingers into Charlotte's shoulders.

Marcel got to his feet, realized he'd set them down shoulder-width apart. "Let Charlotte say her piece," he said. "Quit leanin' on her."

Amanda looked at him as if he'd gone mad. "Oh, come on, Marcel. Charlotte's changing her story. What in the world would I be doing here that night?"

"It was Thursday," Charlotte squeaked. "Amanda meets Eric in the cabin every Thursday at 8:30. Not unusual. No need to tell."

The room went silent except for the sound of Walter's breath shuddering in and out. He ducked behind his shield. "Make her go away."

"Mrs. Gavin . . ." Marcel let his eyes go soft, steadied his breath. "I'm gonna have to place you under . . . take you in for questioning."

"Marcel!" Molly's gaze shifted from Marcel to Amanda, then over to Charlotte. She must be working hard to process what Charlotte had said. He could see her brain somersault with the effort. "Marcel, she can't have done it. She just can't."

But Amanda already had her arms around Molly's shoulders, shushing her as if she were a little girl. "Hush now, Molly. Sometimes love will make you do things."

Molly threw Amanda's arms away and pushed her chair back. "No. You didn't." Amanda tried to hug her, but Molly fled the room, shouting, "No, no, no! She didn't!"

"I'll go with her." Gracie got up and followed Molly. Marcel reached for his mic, then remembered he wasn't in uniform. No mic and no cuffs, and he wouldn't make the same mistake he'd made with Candy. Instead, he pulled out his cellphone and dialed Chief Farrell's private line.

"But you know what Eric was like, Marcel. He about lost it when he saw Abe's van in the driveway."

"Mrs. Gavin . . ." He didn't know what to say.

"I made him give me his gun, but he was still so angry, out of his mind. He said he was gonna teach Candy a lesson she wouldn't forget."

Eric probably would have messed Candy up bad. In Amanda's position, he might have—

"I only meant to scare him," Amanda said. "I told him I'd shoot him if he didn't leave. But he didn't go, and I think he must have done something to the trigger, made it so light, I barely touched it when it went off." She clutched at Marcel's arm. "I didn't mean to shoot him. It's not as if I'm a killer."

"Killed Victor," Charlotte said in a matter-of-fact tone.

"What?" Marcel listened to the ring tone . . . two . . . three.

"He's buried by the trees," Charlotte said, "under Eric."

The Chief answered, but Marcel couldn't stop staring at Charlotte. "That's Molly's Uncle Vic in that grave?"

Charlotte nodded. "No more bruises on Molly. Not after that."

"Please, Marcel." Amanda looked terrified. "Someone had to stop them. You know what they did."

He blocked out Amanda's pleading and focused on Charlotte. "If you knew about Victor's murder all this time, why didn't you tell anyone?" Chief Farrell was saying something, but Marcel couldn't answer, not yet.

"No one asked." Charlotte cut into her meatloaf. She smiled, shy as a child, and said, "Kitten?"

"Tomorrow," he said. "I won't let you down."

Then he spoke to the Chief, said what he had to say, and waited until Farrell arrived to place Amanda under arrest. Funny how solving Eric's murder didn't make him feel good. In fact, he was colder than when he'd arrived.

CHAPTER FORTY-THREE

Gracie never could understand why people turned their air conditioning up so high. The temperature outside was eighty-nine degrees, and she'd dressed appropriately in lightweight shorts and a cotton blouse. Now, here she was in Dr. Wheeler's office, sitting in a draft that had nothing to do with her dead mother.

"Next month, I'll bring a coat." She shoved her hands into her armpits. "How is anyone supposed to relax in here."

Dr. Wheeler looked over the top of his reading glasses. "You aren't shy, are you?"

"I have an extra sweater in the car," Molly said. "Want I should get it?"

"Nuh-uh. You're my witness." Gracie scooted her chair a few inches closer to Molly's. Changing doctors never went well. Wheeler looked nice enough, but new doctors always wanted to *modify* things, experiment, take risks with other people's lives.

"Molly is your proxy. That's better than a witness." Dr. Wheeler reached into a cubby behind his desk and pulled out a blanket. "And your proxy is going to take an active role in the next phase of your treatment."

"Next phase? I don't have to stay here, do I?" Gracie shot a worried glance at the dead girl, her *mother*. Hannah leaned over Wheeler's shoulder, scanning the computer monitor on his desk.

"Absolutely not." Dr. Wheeler handed the blanket to Molly. She draped it over Gracie's shoulders, warm, but rough as burlap. "Molly will keep an eye on you and make sure you aren't experiencing symptoms of withdrawal."

"Withdrawal?" That didn't sound good.

"I'd like to wean you off your antidepressant." He leaned back in a relaxed manner that looked as if it might not be entirely faked. "I think your ghost might be a side effect of your medication."

"A what?" Gracie shifted her hand to Molly's armrest. "I thought the pills were supposed to get rid of the ghosts."

"They are, but not everyone responds the same way."

Hannah straightened up. "I suppose he could be right. Looks as if I showed up right after Dr. Usef changed your medication."

"No, he can't be right." Gracie moved her hands to her lap and pressed thumbs into her belly. Sitting still was hard, especially on the fourth floor.

"Are you talking to Hannah?" Molly, of course, was one step ahead of the doctor.

"Might be."

Dr. Wheeler continued as if he hadn't heard. "Officer Trudeau was able to locate decades of records. I've gone over them and, from what I've been able to piece together, your ghosts appear when you're given an antidepressant."

"Maybe that's because I'm not depressed." The presumption was irritating. "Never have been."

"There are other reasons for prescribing antidepressants."

"Then why don't you change the name?" The words came out louder than Gracie had intended. Molly touched her elbow. Gracie lowered her voice. "It seems a silly name for something that gives you the toots."

"Toots?" Wheeler again.

"Farts," Molly said. "Humdingers. Good thing we have Scout to blame it on."

"Who's Scout?" Dr. Wheeler was slow as a cherry frappe through a skinny straw.

Gracie looked at the ceiling. "Scout is our beagle. Try to keep up."

Molly nudged her, probably for being rude. "A gift from a friend."

"That's great," Dr. Wheeler said. "Pets can be therapeutic." He pulled out a prescription pad and scribbled something that might have passed as a signature, had he been six years old.

Molly picked it up. "What have you changed?"

"Same drug, lower dosage, the first step in weaning her off. You'll need to watch for changes in mood or behavior, nightmares, brain zaps, nausea—"

"Who are you talking about?" Gracie looked back and forth between them.

"You," Dr. Wheeler and Molly said in unison.

"Then talk to me. I'm right here." She folded her arms. "It's not as if I'm invisible."

"He could be right about the ghost," Molly said. "Dr. Usef changed your meds a few weeks ago, and Hannah appeared within days."

"That's what Hannah said." Gracie couldn't help sputtering. "But she came for a reason. She warned us about David and Jack, maybe even Amanda. And she knew Zoe was in danger." She turned to Hannah—her mother. "Right?"

"What do you think?" Hannah's habit of answering questions with questions hadn't changed. Irritating.

"What's Hannah saying now?" Dr. Wheeler seemed interested, but he might be pretending.

Gracie snorted. "She says 'Don't trust the new doctor.'"

"I did not!" Hannah kicked Dr. Wheeler's desk, but there was no accompanying bang or shudder. Patience wasn't Hannah's forte, probably because she was only twenty-three.

Dr. Wheeler seemed to be saying something important, so Gracie focused on the mole next to his left eye and made an effort to listen. He was confusing, same as Dr. Useless. Better looking, though. Little Dayna looked good on him and, according to Molly, they were officially dating. What was he saying?"

"It has a short half-life, so we should know soon if this approach will rid you of Hannah."

"Whu?" Gracie shook her head, focused. "But I like Hannah."

"She's not real." Dr. Wheeler seemed to think that should end the discussion.

"Says you." Maybe he was an idiot, same as all the other doctors. "Jack was real. I would have gladly popped a pill to get rid of *him*."

Dr. Wheeler smiled, a good sign. He turned the computer monitor toward the wall and finally looked straight at her. "It's your choice. I'm not opposed to leaving things as they are."

"My choice?"

"All yours."

"My choice. That's a new one." She wished her tongue weren't so sticky. Made it hard to ask questions. "Which one am I supposed to choose?"

Molly got to her feet, probably in a hurry to go home so she could get ready for her date. "You don't have to decide today," she said. "You still have a month's worth of the higher dosage, so you can think about it, take your time. Okay?"

Wheeler nodded. "Works for me. Just call and let me know." His next question was softer. "How are you doing, Molly? Feeling better?"

"She has a date," Gracie announced. "She's gonna get naked with Marcel. He borrowed my foam mattress and everything."

"Stop it!" Molly grabbed Gracie's elbow and towed her toward the door. "I'm doin' better all the time, Dr. Wheeler. Thank you for asking."

Gracie twisted free of Molly's grip and scrambled into the hallway. "What's wrong?"

"My personal life is none of your business." Molly let the door thump behind them. "And it's not Dr. Wheeler's business, either."

"But he's dating the little poodle." Gracie shoved her ear against Wheeler's door. "He wants to make sure Marcel is all set in the bedroom so he won't be sniffing around Dayna. And right now," she said, squishing her ear to the door, "he's laughing his balls off."

The tree stand hadn't changed much. The pine railings were bare now, wind-stripped of modesty and twined like lovers. An assortment of canned goods offered themselves up, but Marcel had something better.

"Extra anchovies." He held out a slice.

Molly took it with the barest stirring of her usual grin. When she bit into the pizza, her groan of contentment was sexier than she probably meant it to be. Pizza and Molly would always remind him of that night at Echo Lake, the best parts, no matter that Dayna had nearly stomped out the flames.

"Sweetened condensed milk?" He offered a can.

Molly wrinkled her nose, and the smile flickered again, brighter. "Beer, please. Unless you want me to hurl."

"That's hot." It wasn't, but she laughed anyway. He wiped the grin off his face and handed her a Sam Adams. Drove all the way to Lebanon to get it. She tipped her head back, and he watched her swallow, wondered if she was thinking sexy thoughts, too.

"Amanda," she said on a slow exhale, wiping her chin with the back of her hand. "I still have trouble believing it."

Nope. Not sexy. He eased away from her and settled against the tree's massive trunk. "We don't need to talk about it, Mols. It's over and done."

"I know." She brought pizza to her mouth, gathered mozzarella strings on her tongue.

"Just let it go."

"But I should have known." She laid the pizza on her napkin. Sauce smudged her thigh, and she traced the drips, scooped them onto a finger. "Uncle Vic had slugged me around the night before, no worse than any other time. But Amanda must have noticed when I showed up at Blue Horizons with long sleeves and jeans, even though it was a scorcher. I didn't think she——"

"You were just a kid." Marcel rested his hand between her shoulder blades. "Looks like Amanda tried to protect you, same as she protected Candy." Chances were Amanda had made the salad that poisoned David, too. Candy and Shay's apartment was in Amanda's name, and she doubtless had a key.

Should have thought of that sooner.

Molly scooted closer, licked sauce off her fingers. "Gracie told me to take her off that adoption site. She says she's decided not to find her daughter." She brought the last of her pizza to her lips, sucked off the cheese, then folded the crust and crunched into it.

"Could be she got scared." Probably. "Maybe she realized she could end up with someone like Jack for a grandson."

"Or Amanda Gavin for a daughter. Can't believe she was taking drug money." Molly tucked the last bite of crust deep in her mouth before she nestled against him.

"Yup." Thing was, Marcel sort of admired Amanda for looking after her girls, even though he wished she'd found a better way.

"Amanda says she and Lyman kept the operation small for two decades, grew just enough pot to fund Blue Horizons. But then Eric found out and wanted in, and he hooked them up with David." Marcel slid his hand to Molly's waist, smaller than he remembered. "That's when Amanda retired from Blue Horizons and tried to distance herself."

"And let me walk right into the middle of it."

"Guess so." All of a sudden, Amanda Gavin seemed less principled.

Molly laid her head on his shoulder and breathed against his neck. "Why in the world was Lyman funding Blue Horizons? He doesn't seem the altruistic type."

"I didn't think so, either." He kissed her cheek, felt for her hand. "But he gave his share of the money to Amanda. Every penny. He's the one who's been leaving those cash donations all these years."

"It doesn't make sense." She slipped her hand beneath his shirt. He darn near gasped out loud while she looked calm, contemplative, and sexy as hell.

Marcel's underwear began to bind. He tried to adjust himself without looking like he was adjusting himself. "Amanda says Blue Horizons was all Lyman's idea. He paid her to get Gracie out of the State Hospital and give her a home."

Molly straightened up. "So it was because of Gracie? Blue Horizons? The drugs? Everything?"

"Looks like." And that was the real mystery. "Lyman said he did everything so he could save Gracie from a life in the State Hospital, but he refused to explain why." Marcel pulled Molly onto his lap. She dropped her hand between his thighs and let it lie there as if it were an accident.

"I don't get it. What's Gracie to him?"

"No idea."

Molly sank her fingers into his thigh, inched them upward. "You're gonna figure it out though. Right?"

"That's what I told Lyman." His skin tingled everywhere she touched.

"What did he say?" She kissed his ear, his cheek.

"Who?" Lord, he was getting lightheaded.

"Lyman."

"He said—" Marcel let out a groan when she moved against him, slow and delicious.

"Said what?" Molly's breath tumbled past a cotton candy grin. She sure did like teasing him.

"He said he hopes I do."

"Me too." She swatted at a deer fly and burst into laughter. "You'd think maybe the bugs could leave us alone for just this one time."

"Wanna go to my place?" The moment he said it, he wished he hadn't. No good would come from reminding Molly of the way their first date had ended.

"No way, Marcel. I'll take my chances with the bugs." She went back to kissing him, whispered, "Gracie says we're gonna get naked."

"She said what?" He tried to remember exactly what he might have said to Gracie. It couldn't have been that.

"Don't worry about it, Marcel. It's not as if we haven't been thinkin' about it." She kissed his cheeks, his mouth, sent shivers to places that were already getting ahead of themselves.

"Let's go slow," he whispered, even though slow was the last thing he wanted. Molly was hot as all get-out and probably the best friend he'd ever had. What if he messed things up with her the way he had with Dayna?

She cocked her head to one side. "Slow sounds good, just as long as we can have sex in the meanwhile." She unfastened her top button, then the next. "I can get creative if you want, Marcel, but this would be a whole lot more fun if you'd lose the jeans."

"Crap, Molly." This wasn't the shy little girl he'd known his whole life, and he wasn't sure what to say. "Where have you been hiding all these years?"

"Right under your nose." She swatted his shoulder, followed up with a whisper against his ear. "Aren't you glad you finally looked?"

Gracie let her legs dangle against the dust ruffle, toes brushing the top of Scout's square head. In her hand were two pill bottles. Molly had filled the new prescription on her way home. She'd hidden it, of course, but not very well.

The new pills might send Hannah back to wherever spirits were supposed to go. The old pills would keep things as they were. People seemed to think losing contact with her dead mother was the sane choice, but Gracie wondered if so-called mental health was worth the price.

Hannah sat on the pink comforter wearing the same powder blue swim dress she'd worn the night of the thunderstorm. "Choose whatever works best for you," was all she'd say. She kinked a lock of Raggedy Ann hair between her fingers, but otherwise appeared calm as a puddle. "I have other things to do, and it's not as if you're all alone. You have family now." Hannah looked solid and warm, as real as anyone, even though everybody said she was nothing more than a hallucination. How was a person supposed to tell the difference?

"They're real, aren't they?"

"Who?" A sunbeam burst through the window and shimmered across Hannah's face. She shaded her eyes.

"Everyone. Molly, Charlotte, Marcel, Zoe, Jillian, Walter, Suzanne, even Dr. Knows-Everything." Gracie tightened her grip on the bottles. "I can't tell, not for sure."

"They're real enough." Hannah's laughter tinkled like wind chimes. "None of them will disappear if you stop taking those pills. And the doctor's name is Wheeler. He's the one who fired Cracked Jack."

"So he might be a pretty good doctor. Better than the last one."

"Could be. Seems he's a decent person, at least."

"So maybe I should try things his way." Gracie dropped the old bottle into the trash and set the other on her nightstand.

"Just like that?"

"Just like that."

"Well, I guess I'll be off then." Hannah might be disappointed, but she didn't let on. "No point waiting until I start to fade."

Gracie's throat ached, but this was the right choice, wasn't it? No more talking to ghosts, just flesh and blood—the real world, the same world everybody else lived in. But . . . "It was nice."

"What?"

"Getting to know you." She couldn't bring herself to look higher than Hannah's knees. "And I'm sorry about the harvester."

"I know." Hannah scooted closer, and Gracie could swear the bed creaked beneath her weight. "You were so little. I hated that you grew up thinking it was your fault, hated that your father convinced people you were better off institutionalized." She bent down to Gracie's eye level and whispered, "I tripped, is all. You were too small to knock me down."

"Really?" The ache lessened, just a little.

"Yes, really."

"That's good to know." Gracie scrubbed at her eyes and, for a moment, wondered if she might choose the old pills instead. But when she looked up, the ghost was gone.

"Balls."

In the space of a breath, Gracie pulled the bottle from the trash and stuffed it beneath her pillow. The beagle whined up at her, and there was no mistaking the worry in his eyes.

Gracie lowered herself to the floor and ran a hand over Scout's head. "I might need her again someday," she told him when he snuggled onto her lap and licked her chin. "Besides, there's something I've figured out, and it's about me."

She hadn't said the words aloud, not to anyone, even though she'd thought them many times over the preceding days. Saying them would make them true and might bring about changes to the life she'd never thought to question. No one had expected much from her in the past. But now . . .

She lifted the dog's floppy ear and whispered close, stunned by the way her heart lifted at the words.

"I'm not as crazy as everyone thinks I am."

ACKNOWLEDGEMENTS

Writing a novel is a lengthy undertaking. From initial concept to finished product, many people, in addition to the author, have vital roles to play.

It takes a village.

I want to thank J.E. Nissley, who always challenges me to do better, and Tammy McCracken, who sat in my kitchen and listened while I read every page. To Annelie Wendeberg, thank you for your encouragement and support, and for generously sharing your marketing expertise.

Thank you, Norma Traffie, for answering my dumb law enforcement questions. Thank you to my many beta readers: Andrea Pawliczek, Sandi Nason, Mary McHugh, Robin Hebert, Lisa Cook, Sara Fowles, Rachel Benoit, Shayna Appel, and Connie Lee, to name but a few.

Thank you to my fellow Sisters in Crime, authors Sylvie Kurtz and Lorrie Thomson, for taking the time to read the manuscript and for insisting it was good enough to publish.

A special thank you to Thonie Hevron, who patiently checked my law enforcement procedures and made sure I didn't mess up too, too badly.

Thank you to Mosaic Bookworks, who designed the book's cover and interior, making those words on the page appear to be more than they probably are.

Thank you to photographer Vladimir Morozov for making it possible for me to use the stunning cover image, and thank you to model Megan O'Malley who will someday be a star.

Finally, thank you to Phyl Manning, who gave me more credit than I deserved and told me I'm better than I think I am. Love you and miss you always.

ABOUT THE AUTHOR

The author, pictured here with Scout,
the beagle who inspired the character.

Nancy DeMarco considers herself lucky to have spent her life in rural New England. In the small New Hampshire town where she makes her home, police sirens are rarely heard, and most shootings involve paper targets and empty soda cans.

In her writing, DeMarco seeks to convey a sense of small-town community, where pot luck suppers abound, politicians campaign at the landfill (because everyone has to go there sometime), and good friends become closer than family.